"The Secret in"
and
"The Giggling Ghosts"

TWO CLASSIC ADVENTURES OF

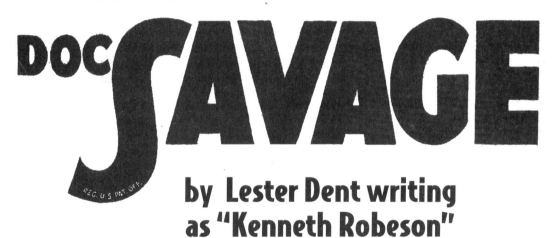

DOC SAVAGE

by Lester Dent writing as "Kenneth Robeson"

with new historical essays by Will Murray

Published by Sanctum Productions for
NOSTALGIA VENTURES, INC.
P.O. Box 231183; Encinitas, CA 92023-1183

This Nostalgia Ventures edition is an unabridged republication of the text and
illustrations of two stories from *Doc Savage Magazine,* as originally published
by Street & Smith Publications, Inc., N.Y.: *The Secret in the Sky* from the May
1935 issue, and *The Giggling Ghosts* from the July 1938 issue. Typographical
errors have been tacitly corrected in this edition. These two novels are works
of their time. Consequently, the text is reprinted intact in its original historical
form, including occasional out-of-date ethnic and cultural stereotyping.

ISBN 1-932806-93-8   13 DIGIT 978-1-932806-93-9

First printing: April 2008

Series editor: Anthony Tollin
P.O. Box 761474
San Antonio, TX 78245-1474
sanctumotr@earthlink.net

Contributing editor: Will Murray

Copy editor: Joseph Wrzos

Proofreader: Carl Gafford

Cover restoration: Michael Piper

The editor gratefully acknowledges the contributions of Gene Curtis, John
Worley and Rachele Vaughan of the Tulsa *World,* John Wooley, Joel Frieman,
Jack Juka, John Gunnison and Tom Stephens.

Nostalgia Ventures, Inc.
P.O. Box 231183; Encinitas, CA 92023-1183

Visit Doc Savage at www.shadowsanctum.com and www.nostalgiatown.com.

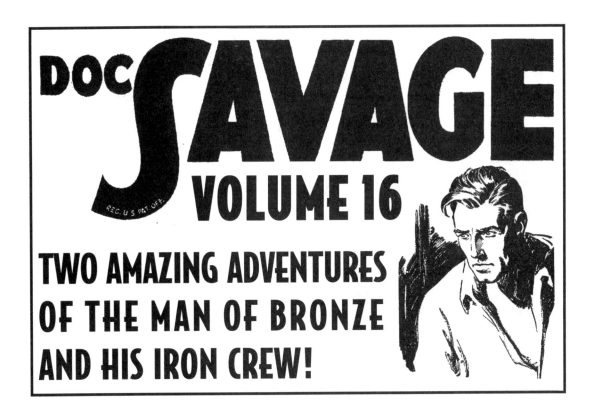

DOC SAVAGE

VOLUME 16

TWO AMAZING ADVENTURES OF THE MAN OF BRONZE AND HIS IRON CREW!

REG. U.S PAT. OFF.

Thrilling Tales and Features

THE SECRET IN THE SKY by Lester Dent (writing as "Kenneth Robeson") 4

INTERMISSION by Will Murray 63

THE GIGGLING GHOSTS by Lester Dent (writing as "Kenneth Robeson") 68

THE MAN BEHIND DOC SAVAGE 125

DOC'S AIDES 126

Cover art by Emery Clarke and Walter Baumhofer
Interior illustrations by Paul Orban

Dead at noon in California — and three hours later the body is found on the streets of New York City! Even Doc Savage is mystified as he sweeps the heavens for

The Secret in the Sky

A Complete Book-length Novel

By KENNETH ROBESON

Chapter I
THE FRIEND WHO DIED

THE matter of Willard Spanner was almost unbelievable. It was too preposterous. The newspapers publishing the story were certain a mistake had been made somewhere. True, this was the Twentieth Century, the age of marvels. But—then—

At exactly noon, the telephone buzzer whirred in Doc Savage's New York skyscraper headquarters. Noon, straight up, Eastern Standard Time.

The buzzer whirred three times, with lengthy pauses between *whirs*, which allowed time for anyone present to have answered. Then an automatic answering device, an ingenious arrangement of dictaphone voice recorder and phonographic speaker—a creation of Doc Savage's scientific skill—was cut in automatically. The phonograph record turned under the needle and sent words over the telephone wire.

"This is a mechanical robot speaking from Doc Savage's headquarters and advising you that Doc Savage is not present, but that any message you care to speak will be recorded on a dictaphone and will come to Doc Savage's attention later," spoke the mechanical contrivance. "You may proceed with whatever you wish to say, if anything."

"Doc!" gasped a voice, which had that strange quality lent by long-distance telephonic amplifiers. "This is Willard Spanner! I am in San Francisco. I have just learned something too horrible for me to believe!"

Several violent grunts came over the wire. There were thumps. Glass seemed to break at the San Francisco end. Then came silence, followed by a *click* as the receiver was placed on the hook at the San Francisco terminus of the wire.

The mechanical device in Doc Savage's New York office ran on for some moments, and a stamp clock automatically recorded the exact time of the message on a paper roll; then the apparatus stopped and set itself for another call, should one come.

The time recorded was two minutes past twelve, noon.

Thirty minutes later, approximately, the newspaper press association wires hummed with the story of the mysterious seizure of Willard Kipring Parker Spanner in San Francisco. Willard Kipring Parker Spanner was a nabob, a somebody, a big shot. Anything unusual that happened to him was big news.

The newspapers did not know the half of it. The biggest was yet to come.

Financially, Willard Kipring Parker Spanner did not amount to much. A post-mortem examination of his assets showed less than five thousand dollars, an insignificant sum for a man who was known over most of the world.

Willard Kipring Parker Spanner called himself simply, "a guy who likes to fiddle around with microscopes." It was said that he knew as much about disease germs, and methods of combating them, as any living man. He had won one Nobel prize. He was less than thirty years old. Scientists and physicians who knew him considered him a genius.

When Willard Spanner was found dead, many a scientist and physician actually shed tears, realizing what the world had lost.

When Willard Spanner was found dead, the newspapers began to have fits. And with good reason.

For Willard Spanner's body was found on a New York street—less than three hours after he had been seized in San Francisco! Seized in Frisco at noon; Eastern Standard Time. Dead in New York at ten minutes to three, Eastern Standard Time.

A NEWSBOY with a freckled face was first to convey the news to Doc Savage. The newsboy was also cross-eyed. Neither the newsboy, nor his freckles, nor his crossed eyes had other connection with the affair, except that the lad's reaction when he sighted Doc Savage was typical of the effect which the bronze man had on people.

The boy's mouth went roundly open with a kind of amazement when he first saw the bronze giant; then, as he sold the paper, his demeanor was awed and very near worshipful.

"I know you, mister," he said in a small voice. "You're Doc Savage! I've seen your picture in the newspapers!"

Doc Savage studied the boy as he paid for the paper. He seemed particularly interested in the crossed eyes.

"Wear glasses?" He asked. He had a remarkable voice; it seemed filled with a great, controlled power.

"Sure," said the newsboy, "They give me headaches."

Doc Savage produced a small business card. The card was not white, but bronze, and the printing—his name only was on it—was in a slightly darker bronze.

"If I asked you to do something," he queried, "would you do it?"

"Betcha boots!" replied the newsboy.

Doc Savage wrote a name and address on the card and said, "Go see that man," then walked on, leaving the boy puzzled.

The name and address the bronze man had written was that of an eye specialist whose particular forte was afflictions such as the boy had.

More than one gaze followed Doc Savage along the street, for he was a giant of bronze with a face that was remarkable in its regularity of feature and a body that was a thing of incredible muscular development. His eyes attracted no little attention, too. They were like pools of flake-gold, stirred into continuous motion by some invisible force.

He read the newspaper headlines, the galleys of type beneath, but there was nothing on his features to show that he was perusing anything of importance.

The skyscraper which housed his headquarters was, in size and architecture, probably the most impressive in New York City. A private high-speed elevator lifted him to the eighty-sixth floor. He passed through a door that was plain, except for a name in small bronze letters:

CLARK SAVAGE Jr.

The reception room inside had large windows, deep leather chairs, a strange and rich inlaid table of great size, and an impressive safe.

An automatic pistol lay on the floor. A pig, a shoat with long legs and ears like boat sails, walked around and around the gun; grunting in a displeased way.

A man sat in a chair. He was a very short man and the chair was huge and high and faced away from the door, so that only red bristles which stuck up straight on top of the man's head could be seen.

The man in the chair said in a small, childlike voice, "Shoot off that gun, Habeas, or I'll tie knots in all your legs."

With an uncanny intelligence, the pig sat down, inserted a hoof inside the trigger guard, and the gun went off with an ear-splitting report.

"Swell!" said the man in the chair, "Only you better stand, Habeas. Next time, the gun might be pointed at your posterior and there might not be a blank in it."

Doc Savage said, "Monk."

"Uh-huh," said the man in the chair. "Sure, Doc, what is it?"

"Willard Spanner was a friend of mine."

"MONK"—Lieutenant Colonel Andrew Blodgett Mayfair—lifted out of the chair. He was not much over five feet tall. He was only slightly less broad than that, and he had a pair of arms which gave the grotesque impression of being nearly as long as he was tall. Red hairs, which looked coarse as match sticks, furred his leathery hide. His was the build of a gorilla.

"I read about it in them blasted newspapers," he said, and his small voice was doubly ridiculous, contrasted with his physique. "Willard Spanner was seized in Frisco at noon. He was found dead here in New York at ten minutes to three. Screw loose somewhere."

Monk wrinkled a fabulously homely face to show puzzlement. He looked amiable, stupid, when, in truth, he was one of the most clever industrial chemists alive.

"Maybe the newspapers got balled up on the difference in time between San Francisco and New York," he added.

"All times given are New York time," Doc Savage said.

"Then the guy seized in San Francisco wasn't Willard Spanner, or the one dead here in New York isn't Spanner," Monk declared. "The bird didn't go from Frisco to New York in a little over two hours. It just isn't being done yet."

Doc Savage asked, "Any messages?"

"Ham phoned, and said he was coming up," replied the homely chemist. "I haven't been here long. Dunno what was recorded before I got here."

The bronze man went into the next room, which was a scientific library, one of the most complete in existence, and crossed that to the vast, white-enameled room which held his laboratory of chemical, electrical and other devices. He lifted the cover on the telephone recorder, switched a loudspeaker and amplifier into circuit with the playback pickup, and started the mechanism.

Monk came in and listened, slackjawed, as the device reproduced the call from San Francisco, complete to its violent termination. The pig—Habeas Corpus was the shoat's full appendage—trailed at the homely chemist's heels.

Doc Savage examined the time stamped on the recording roll.

"Two minutes past twelve," he said.

"Was that Willard Spanner's voice, or would you know it?" Monk demanded.

"I would know his voice," Doc replied. "And that was, unquestionably, Willard Spanner."

"Speaking from San Francisco?" Monk grunted incredulously.

"We will see." Doc Savage made a call, checking with the telephone people, then hung up and advised, "The call came from San Francisco, all right. Willard Spanner appears to have been seized while he was in the booth making the call."

Monk picked the pig, Habeas, up by one oversize ear—a treatment the shoat seemed not to mind.

"Then the dead man here in New York is not Willard Spanner," declared the simian chemist. "Nobody goes from Frisco to New York in not much more than two hours."

"We will see about that," Doc told him.

"How?"

"By visiting the New York morgue where the dead man was taken."

Monk nodded. "How about Ham?"

"We will leave him a note," Doc said.

APPARENTLY, it had not occurred to anyone in authority on the New York civic scene that the surroundings of the dead were of aesthetic value, for the morgue building was a structure which nearly attained the ultimate in shoddiness.

Its brick walls gave the appearance of having not been washed in generations, being almost black with soot and city grime. The steps were grooved deep by treading feet, and the stone paving of the entry into which the dead wagons ran was rutted by tires. Rusting iron bars, very heavy, were over the windows; for just what reason, no one probably could have told.

"This joint gives me the creeps—and I don't creep easy," Monk imparted, as they got out of Doc Savage's roadster before the morgue.

The roadster was deceptively long. Its color

was somber. The fact that its body was of armor plate, its windows—specially built in the roadster doors—of bulletproof glass, was not readily apparent.

Monk carried Habeas Corpus by an ear and grumbled, "I wonder why anybody should kill Willard Spanner? Or grab him, either? Spanner was an all-right guy. He didn't have any enemies."

Doc listened at the entrance. There was silence, and no attendant was behind the reception desk where one should have been. They stepped inside.

"Hello, somebody!" Monk called.

Silence answered.

There was an odor in the air, a rather peculiar tang. Monk sniffed.

"Say, I knew they used formaldehyde around these places," he muttered. "But there's something besides—"

Doc Savage moved with such suddenness that he seemed to explode. But it was a silent explosion, and he was little more than a noiseless bronze blur as he crossed to the nearest door. He did not try to pass through the door, but flattened beside it.

Monk, bewildered, began, "Say, what the blazes? First I smell—"

A man came through the door, holding a big single-action six-gun. He said, "Start your settin' up exercises, boys!" Then his eyes bulged, for he had apparently expected to see two men— and Doc Savage, beside the door, escaped his notice.

The man with the six-shooter was bony and looked as if he had been under bright suns much of his life. He wore a new suit, but his shirt was a coarse blue work garment, faded from washing. The tie was blue and looked as if it had been put on and taken off many times, without untying the knot. The knot was a very long one.

Doc Savage struck silently and with blinding speed. The gun wielder saw him, but could not move in time, and the bronze man's fist took him on the temple. The six-gun evidently had a hair trigger. It went off. The bullet made a hole, round and neat, in the wall behind Monk.

Monk began howling and charged for the door. "Now ain't this somethin'!" he bellowed.

DOC SAVAGE had gone on with a continuation of the dive which he had made at the six-gun wielder, and was already through the door. The room beyond was an office with four desks and four swivel chairs.

Five persons were arrayed on the floor. The morgue attendants, obviously. They were neither bound nor gagged, but they lay very still. The odor of chloroform was heavy in the air.

Two men were on their feet. One was tall, the other short, and the short one wore overall pants and his legs were bowed. Both were weather-beaten.

The tall one held in one hand a blue revolver and in the other a bandanna handkerchief, which gave off chloroform stench. The short man had an automatic rifle from which barrel and stock had been bobbed off short.

A bundle of clothing lay in the middle of the floor.

The automatic rifle smacked loudly as Doc came through the door. But the marksman did not lead his target quite enough. He shot again. The cartridge stuck in the ejector.

"Damn it!" the rifleman bawled.

"Throw it away!" gritted the tall man. "I told you that gun wouldn't work if you bobtailed it!"

The tall man danced back as he spoke, seeming in no hurry to shoot. He waved his blue revolver, that Doc Savage might be sure to see it.

"Don't be a sucker!" the man suggested. "Behave yourself."

Doc Savage held his hands out even with his shoulders and came to a stop, but not until momentum had carried him to the center of the room.

Monk lumbered through the door. He stopped, looked closely at the blue gun as if it were some strange animal, then put up his stub-fingered hands.

"That's bein' sensible," said the tall man. "I can bust poker chips in the air with this here hogleg. Stunted, there, is a good shot, too, only he thought he knew more about that auto rifle than the gent who made her."

"Stunted," the short man, was peering into the innards of his doctored rise.

"Aw-w," he mumbled. "I took too much tension off the spring."

Monk grunted, "What's the idea, you guys?"

"We like to look at dead people," the tall man said dryly. "We're strange that way."

Doc Savage was standing with his toes almost against the bundle of clothing. The bundle was snug, being strapped around tightly with a belt.

Doc hooked a toe under the bundle and kicked with great force.

THE human nervous system is capable of registering impressions only so fast. The tall man undoubtedly knew the missile was coming, but could do nothing. When it hit him, he recoiled instinctively.

The next instant, he was flat on his face, held there by one foot which Doc Savage jammed down on his neck.

MONK

HAM

DOC

JOHNNY

LONG TOM

RENNY

Monk whooped loudly, rushed Stunted. Monk's fights were always noisy.

Stunted clung like a zealot to his bobtailed auto rifle, trying to get it in operation. He failed. He tried to club with the gun. Monk jerked it out of his hands as if he were taking a lollypop from a child, then dropped it.

Monk picked the short man up bodily, turned him over and dropped him on his head. He accomplished the motion with such speed that the short man was helpless. Stunted did not move after he fell on his head.

Monk blinked small eyes at his victim.

"Gosh," he said. "I wonder if that hurt him?"

The tall man on the floor snarled, "What in blue blazes kind of a circus is this, anyhow?"

Monk felt of Stunted's head, found it intact, then twisted one of the short man's rather oversize ears, but got no response. The homely chemist turned on the tall man.

"So it's a circus, huh?" he grunted. "I wondered."

"Aw, hell!" gritted the other.

Monk came over and sat on the lean prisoner. Doc Savage removed his foot from the man's neck. Monk grabbed the fellow's ears and pulled them. He seemed fascinated by the rubbery manner in which they stretched out from the man's head.

"They'd make swell souvenirs," Monk grunted.

"Cut it out!" the tall men howled. "What're you gonna do with me?"

"I'm gonna ask you questions," Monk told him. "And I'm gonna be awful mad if you don't answer 'em."

"Nuts!" said the captive.

"Has this raid, or whatever it was, got anything to do with Willard Spanner?" Monk asked.

"What do you think?" the other snapped.

Monk pulled the ears. Tears came to the man's eyes. He cursed, and his voice was a shrill whine of agony.

"I'll kill you for that!" he promised. "Damn me, if I don't!"

Monk shuddered elaborately, grinned and said, "If I had on boots, I'd shake in 'em. What did you come here for?"

A new voice said, "You gentlemen seem to be humorists."

MONK started violently and twisted his head toward the door. He gulped, "Blazes!" and got hastily to his feet.

The man in the door was solid, athletic-looking, and he held a revolver with familiar ease. He was in his socks. That probably explained how he had come in from the outside so silently; that, and the faint mumble of city traffic, which was always present.

"Get up!" he told the tall man. "Wipe your eyes. Then grab that bunch of clothes. This is sure something to write home about!"

"I'll kill this ape!" bawled the tall man.

"Some other time," the rescuer suggested. "Get the clothes. Say, just who is this big bronze guy and the monkey, anyhow?"

"How would I know?" snarled the man whom Monk had been badgering. He picked up the bundle of clothing and started for the door.

"You wouldn't leave Stunted, would you?" asked the first.

Without a word, the tall man picked up the short fellow and made his way, not without difficulty, out through the door.

The gun wielder looked on benignly. He had one stark peculiarity. His eyes were blue. And something was wrong with them. They crossed at intervals, pupils turning in toward the nose. Then they straightened out. The owner seemed to do the straightening with visible effort.

Monk demanded, "Who did them clothes belong to?"

The man said, "They'll answer a lot of questions where you're going."

Monk did not get a clear impression of what happened next. Things moved too fast. Doc Savage must have read the intention of the man with the queer eyes. Doc lunged.

The gun went off. But the man with the eyes had tried to shift from Monk to Doc for a target and had not quite made it. His bullet pocked the wall. Then Doc had a grip on the revolver.

The man let go of the revolver. He bounced back, fast on his feet, reached the door and slipped through. He was yelling now. His yells caused noise of other feet in the next room. There were evidently more men.

Doc grasped Monk and propelled him backward. They got into a rear room and slammed the door. Doc shot the bolt.

Revolver bullets chopped around the lock. Wood splintered. The lock held. A man kicked the door. Monk roared a threat.

There was no more kicking, no more shooting. Silence fell, except for the traffic noises.

Monk looked at Doc.

"That guy with the performing eyes was gonna kill us both," he mumbled.

Doc Savage did not comment. He listened, then unlocked the door. The room beyond was empty. He advanced. In the next room, one of the chloroformed morgue attendants was sitting up and acting sick.

The street outside held no sign of the violent raiders. There was no trace of the bundle of clothing.

The reviving morgue attendant began to mumble.

"They wanted clothes off a corpse," he muttered. "Whatcha know about that?"

"Off what corpse?" Doc asked him.

"Off Willard Spanner," said the attendant.

Chapter II
THE HIGH-PRESSURE GHOULS

DOC SAVAGE exited to the street and made inquiries, finding that the men had gone away in two cars. Persons questioned named four different makes of cars, in each instance insisting that their information was correct.

"They're all wrong, probably," Monk grumbled.

Pursuit was patently hopeless, although Monk cast a number of expectant glances in Doc Savage's direction. The bronze man had a way of pulling rabbits out of hats in affairs such as this. But Doc only reentered the morgue. None of those who had been chloroformed were in immediate danger.

"We came here to see the body of Willard Spanner," Doc told the attendant who had revived.

"Sort of a coincidence," said the attendant, and managed a sickly grin which typified a peculiarity of human behavior—the fact that persons who work regularly in close proximity to death are inclined to arm themselves with a wise-cracking veneer.

The bodies were stored in bins not unlike huge filing boxes. The marble slabs on which they lay slid into the bins on rollers. The attendant was still too groggy to bring the Willard Spanner slide out after he had found the identifying card, and Monk helped him.

Doc Savage looked at the body for a long time.

"This is Willard Spanner," he said finally.

They went out.

Monk scratched his head, then said, "But the man seized in San Francisco—that couldn't have been Willard Spanner."

"The voice on the phone recorder," Doc reminded.

"You said it was Willard Spanner's voice." Monk found his pig, Habeas, and picked him up by an ear. "Could you have been mistaken about that voice?"

"I think not," Doc Savage said slowly.

They examined those who were still senseless from the chloroform, gave a description of the morgue raiders to police officers who had arrived, then walked out to the roadster.

Monk seemed to be thinking deeply. He snapped his fingers.

"That bundle of Willard Spanner's clothing!" he grumbled. "Now what in the dickens did they want with that? The police had searched the pockets and had found nothing."

"It must have been something important," Doc told him. "They wanted the garments badly enough to make quite a disturbance in getting them."

A policeman came to the morgue door and called, "You are wanted on the phone."

Doc and Monk went back, and Doc picked up the receiver and said, "Yes?" inquiringly.

A clipped, melodious voice spoke rapidly. It was the voice of an orator, and it carried the accent which is commonly associated with Harvard.

"I got to the morgue in time to observe that something was badly wrong," advised the speaker. "I followed the chaps outside when they left in such a hurry. They are now at Albemarle Avenue and Frame Street. I will meet you at the corner."

Doc Savage said, "In ten minutes," and hung up.

Monk, making for the street in a series of ungainly bounds, demanded, "Who was it?"

"Ham," Doc replied.

"The shyster!" Monk growled, and there was infinite contempt in his tone.

ALBEMARLE AVENUE was a twin groove through marsh mud on the outskirts of New York City. Frame Street seemed to be a sign, scabby and ancient, which stuck out of the salt grass. If there ever had been a Frame Street, it had long ago given up to the swamp.

Darkness was coming on when Doc Savage and Monk arrived in the roadster.

"There's Ham," Monk said.

"Ham" was Brigadier General Theodore Marley Brooks, Park Avenue fashion plate, and a lawyer, the pride of Harvard Law School. He was a slender man with the manner of a wasp and a tongue as sharp as the fine Damascus sword blade concealed in the innocent-looking black cane which he carried.

He came out of the marsh grass, stepping gingerly to avoid soiling his natty afternoon garb, the sword cane tucked under an arm.

"Hy-ah, you fashion plate," Monk growled.

"Hello, stupid," Ham retorted insultingly.

The two glared at each other. A stranger would have thought fisticuffs imminent. As a matter of fact, each of these two had time and again risked his life to save the other, although no one had ever heard one of them address a civil word to the other.

Ham opened the roadster door on Doc Savage's side, and said, "I got the note you left at headquarters, telling me you had gone to the morgue. I went to the morgue. As I said over the phone— those chaps were clowning around, so I followed them."

"Where are they?" Doc asked.

Ham pointed across the swamp. "An oyster plant over there."

"Oyster plant?" Monk grunted.

"They probably use it as a blind for whatever they are doing," Ham observed. "And, incidentally, just what is behind this?"

"It's all screwy so far," Monk snorted. "Willard Spanner is reported grabbed in Frisco at noon, and is found dead in New York before three o'clock. Then a gang of birds raid the morgue and steal his clothing. That's all we know."

Ham said, "I'll show you where they went. They had that bundle of clothing, too."

There were a few comparatively firm spots in the marsh. The rest of the terrain was covered with water which ranged in depth from an inch to two feet, with spots which were deeper, as Monk promptly proved by going in above the waist.

A cloud bank in the west shortened the period of twilight. They were soon in complete darkness. Using flashlights would have given away their position. Making any speed through the coarse grass, without noise, was almost impossible.

"You fellows take it easy," Doc directed. "Do not try to get too close."

Monk began, "But what're you—" and did not finish. The bronze man had vanished in the darkness.

Monk listened, then shook his head. It was difficult to conceive of anyone moving with such silence.

It was no casual trait, this ability of Doc Savage's to stalk quietly. He had practiced a great deal, had studied the masters of the art: the carnivorous beasts of the jungle.

The bronze man had covered not more than a hundred yards when something happened—something that was, later, to take on great significance and a terrible importance.

He heard a peculiar crashing sound. That described it more accurately than anything else. It was not a series of crashes, but one long, brittle report. It started faintly and attained, in the span of two seconds or so, a surprising loudness.

Doc glanced up. Hanging in the sky was what appeared to be a taut rope of liquid fire. This faded in a moment.

It was an uncanny phenomena.

DOC SAVAGE crouched for some time, listening, flake-gold eyes on the sky. But there was nothing more. He went on toward the oyster plant.

The odor of the place was evident long before the low, rambling processing building showed up. It was built on the beach, with a wharf shoving out porch fashion to one side. A channel had evidently been dredged for the oyster boats. The plant was used for the sorting and opening of oysters.

Mounds of oyster shells were pyramided here and there, and were thick on the ground. They made walking difficult. Wash of waves on the nearby beach covered up lesser sounds.

Several times Doc Savage stooped and brushed away oyster shells, that he might step on the bare ground. The brittle shells would break with loud reports. The side of the building which he approached was dark. He worked around. Lighted windows appeared.

Smell of oysters was strong. Two small schooners were tied up at a wharf. The cabin portholes of one of these were lighted. An instant later, the light went out, and three men came up the companion. They stepped to the wharf. One used a flashlight, and this illuminated them.

One was Stunted. His companions were the tall man and the one with the peculiar crossing and uncrossing eyes. One carried a bundle which resembled clothing.

Stunted said, "Danged if I don't still maintain that an automatic rifle can be bobbed and still—"

"Aw, hell!" The tall man spat disgustedly. "Here we really got things to worry about, and you go on and on about that gun. Man, don't the fact that that bronze guy was Doc Savage impress you none a-tall?"

Stunted stopped suddenly.

"Look, you gents," he said. "You been cackling around like two old hens since you learned that bird was Doc Savage. Now I want you to tell me something."

"Yeah?" said the tall man.

"Ain't it a fact that with what we got, we don't need to be afraid of anybody?" demanded Stunted.

"You mean—"

"You know what I mean. You saw that streak in the sky and heard that crack of a noise a while ago, didn't you? Now answer my question."

"Aw-w-w!" The tall man spat again. "We ain't exactly afraid of him. Only it might've been more convenient if he hadn't turned up on the spot. That Savage is nobody's cinch, and don't forget that."

"I ain't forgettin' it," said Stunted. "And quit squawkin', you hombres. We're settin' pretty. Doc Savage ain't got a line on us. And didn't we get Willard Spanner's clothing. And ain't the rest gonna be taken care of?"

The tall man burst into sudden laughter.

"Now what?" Stunted growled.

"Just thinkin'," the other chuckled. "People are

gonna wonder how Willard Spanner was in Frisco at noon and dead here in New York at three o'clock the same afternoon."

DOC SAVAGE was close to them. He could have reached out and tripped any one of the trio as they filed past.

The silent man of the three, the one with the unnaturally roving eyes, brought up the rear. Doc Savage had been crouching. He stood erect. His fist made a sound like a loud finger snap on the man's jaw. The man fell. The bundle of clothing flew to one side.

A number of surprising things happened. The surrounding darkness erupted human beings. At least a dozen men appeared with magical effect. Each had a flashlight, a gun.

"Take 'im alive?" one shouted questioningly.

"Not much!" squawked another, evidently the chief.

Doc started for the clothing bundle. A man was leaping over it, coming toward him, gun spouting flame and thunder. Doc slipped aside. He twisted. Lead slammed past.

Doc hit the ground and rolled. Tall marsh grass took him in. He burrowed a dozen feet, veered left. Slugs tore through the grass. They made hoarse snarls.

A pile of oyster shells jutted out of the darkness in front of him. The bronze man got behind it. He ran a score of paces, went down in a hollow where there was soft mud, but no water, and waited, listening.

Stunted was yelling, "He's behind that shell pile! If I had an auto rifle, it would put a pill right through that stuff!"

"Suppose you use your legs more and your mouth less!" someone suggested.

The men scattered, hunting. They were in pairs, a neat precaution. The couples did not walk close enough together that both could be surprised at once, yet nothing could happen to one without the other knowing it.

Stunted shouted, "You jaspers knew he was around here! How in thunder did you know that?"

"You wouldn't understand," a voice told him.

Stunted swore at the speaker. "C'mon, feller, how'd you know it?"

"There's a bank of alarm wires strung around here," said the voice.

"Nuts!" Stunted told him. "I haven't seen any wires."

"They're underground," the other snapped. "Just barely covered. Anyone walking over them changes the capacity of a high-frequency electric field enough to show on a recording device inside."

"Well, sink me!" Stunted snorted.

Doc Savage, listening, made a mental note that someone of considerable scientific ability was involved with the gang. Such an alarm system as had been described was feasible, but required high technical knowledge to construct.

The bronze man crawled away through the tall grass.

DOC did not go far, however. A score of yards, and he stopped. He spent a moment or two tensing his throat muscles, striving for a certain effect.

"Hands up, you fellows!" he said loudly, using his own natural voice.

A split of a second later, he shouted again. This time, his tone was a splendid imitation of a man greatly frightened.

"It's Doc Savage!" he shrilled. "Give us a hand over here, somebody!"

Results were instant and noisy. Men howled irately and made a great clatter in the marsh grass, charging for the spot. They were completely deceived.

Doc Savage moved swiftly, not in flight but circling back toward the oyster shell mound near which he had made his attack. He wanted the bundle of clothes.

He reached the shell pile, paused, listened. Men were making angry sounds, but not close by. Someone had dropped a flashlight in the excitement. Its beam did not play directly on the spot where the garments lay, but the backglow disclosed the parcel. It was hardly more than thirty feet away. It lay in the open.

Doc continued listening. His ears were remarkable, for he had trained them from childhood with a sonic device calculated to develop the utmost in sensitivity. He evidently caught some small sound, for he produced from inside his clothing a coil of thin silken cord to which was affixed a folding grapple hook.

That he had practiced a great deal with the grapple was shown by the accuracy with which he tossed the hook. It snared the bundle of clothing. He hauled it toward him, remaining sheltered behind the shell pile.

Stunted and other men bounded up from where they had been lying and watching the bundle.

"He slicked us!" Stunted bawled.

Doc Savage gave the silk cord a brisk yank, stooped, and caught the garments, and was off like a sprinter. Guns made whooping thunder behind him. He pitched right, then left, zigzagging. Then he doubled over and changed course.

The last was a wise move. Some type of light machine gun blared out behind him. Its lead stream sickled off the marsh grass across the spot where he had vacated. The gunman did not fan his fire, but concentrated it, and the ammo drum went empty. Violent cursing followed.

Doc was some distance away now. He heard noises of men sloughing about in mud, and enraged grunts and growls.

"Monk!" he called softly. "Ham!"

The pair were waist-deep in mud. Doc extricated them. They joined him in flight.

"Monk, the baboon, led us into that bog!" Ham complained.

Monk found his pet pig before he shouted, "That's a lie! I was followin' that overdressed shyster!"

Sounds of pursuit dropped rapidly behind, and it became evident that they were going to get clear.

"We oughta do something about them rambunctious jaspers," Monk announced.

"The police will do something about it," Doc told him.

DOC SAVAGE, Monk, and Ham were in the skyscraper headquarters when the police telephoned the results of their raid, staged on the strength of the bronze man's information.

The oyster factory, they advised, had been found deserted. The "birds" had flown.

"They must have a bally tight organization to move that fast," Ham opined. "They knew their hangout was no longer a secret, so they cleared out."

Monk lifted his pig, Habeas, by one oversize ear and swayed the porker slowly back and forth, a procedure the shoat seemed to enjoy.

"What gets me," muttered the homely chemist, "is what that streak of a thing in the sky could have been. Did you see it, Doc?"

The bronze man nodded.

Monk persisted, "Hear the funny long crack of a noise it, or something like it, made?"

Doc nodded again, then said, "The men at the oyster factory mentioned the streak in the sky and the sound as having some mysterious connection with their own project."

Monk let Habeas fall. "Say, what's behind all of this, anyway?"

The telephone rang.

"This is the central police station," a voice stated. "You seemed to be interested in that Willard Spanner killing, so I thought we'd better let you know his body has been stolen from the morgue."

"You mean Willard Spanner's clothing was stolen?" Doc queried.

"I mean his body," said the officer. "They got his clothing first. They came back about fifteen minutes ago for his body."

"Same crowd?"

"Sure.

"They got away?"

"They did. Or they have, so far."

Doc had switched an audio amplifier-and-loudspeaker into circuit with the telephone, a procedure he commonly followed on calls in which his aides might be interested. Monk and Ham heard.

"Jove!" Ham exploded. "They made no move to take the body the first time."

"At the oyster factory, I heard them speaking of 'taking care of the rest,'" Doc said slowly. "This matter of the body must have been the 'rest.'"

Ham lifted the bundle of clothing which Doc Savage had taken at the oyster factory.

"We still have Willard Spanner's garments here," he declared. "Since those men wanted them so badly, they may possibly furnish us with a clue."

Monk got up, grunting, "Maybe the duds had papers or something sewed in them, like they have in story books. Let's have a gander at 'em, as we lowbrows say."

The garments were tied together with tarred twine of the type which seagoing men call marlin. Ham took hold of it, after trying the knot, intending to break it; but finding it much stronger than he had expected, gave it up, grimacing, snapping his strained fingers.

Doc examined the knots.

"No sailor tied those," he decided.

"They didn't talk like sailors, either," Monk offered. "What part of the country d'you figure they came from, Doc?"

"The West, or the Southwest," the bronze man said, and, with no perceptible difficulty, broke the cord which had baffled Ham. He sorted through the pieces of clothing.

"They outfoxed us," he said. "Fixed this up as a decoy by that shell pile merely to draw me back, hoping to get a shot at me."

Monk squinted. "Meaning?"

"These are not Willard Spanner's clothes," Doc said. "They are for a much larger and fatter man."

Monk groaned, "We're sunk!"

"We have," Doc corrected him, "one chance."

Chapter III
THE MAN FROM OKLAHOMA

THE bronze man lifted the telephone receiver and dialed a number.

"Police headquarters?" he asked. "Homicide bureau, please." There was a brief wait. "Homicide? This is Doc Savage speaking. I believe it is your custom to secure pictures of murder scenes, and also photographs of the body of the victim.

I wonder if you would send me copies of the pictures taken of Willard Spanner."

"You can have them," advised the voice at the homicide bureau.

"By messenger, immediately," Doc requested.

That he had been promised the photographs so readily was not remarkable, since the bronze man held a high commission, no whit less effective because it was honorary, on the New York police force. The commission was a gesture of appreciation for past aid.

Doc Savage's life work was helping others out of trouble—those who deserved aid. It was a strange career, one with few financial rewards. But the bronze man did not need money, for he had access to a fabulous treasure trove. He followed his career for the return it gave in excitement and adventure. And he had five aides who followed it for the same reason.

Monk and Ham were two of the five. The other three were, at the moment, in upper New York State, where Doc Savage maintained a remarkable institution for making honest men out of such criminals as he caught, a treatment which entailed brain operations and which wiped out past memories. A course of vocational training followed the surgery.

Monk frowned, demanding, "How in the heck are those pictures gonna help us?"

Doc Savage did not answer, seemed not to hear. Monk showed no resentment at not getting an answer. It happened frequently. The homely chemist went out and came back with late editions of the leading newspapers.

"Lookit!" He pointed at headlines.

UNPREDICTED RAIN OF COMETS
SCIENCE CANNOT EXPLAIN

Those residents of New York City, particularly those residing near the marsh section of Long Island, were treated to the sight of a comet tonight. Many reported a loud crack of a sound and a streak of fire in the sky.

Inquiry develops that such phenomena have been reported within the last few days, from various sections of the United States.

Monk said, "And they kindly neglected to state just where the other comets were seen."

"Telephone the newspapers," Doc requested.

Monk went to the instrument, made several calls, and hung up, wearing a puzzled expression.

"The comets have appeared within the last two weeks," he reported. "Several were seen around San Francisco. That kinda hooks in with this Willard Spanner killing. But most of the comets were seen in Oklahoma, around Tulsa."

Doc Savage was examining the bundle of clothing.

"Come here," he said, and pointed at the label inside the coat.

THE OIL MAN'S TAILOR
TULSA, OKLAHOMA.

Monk grunted, "That'll bear looking into."

Doc Savage put in a long-distance telephone call, and because it was late, some time was required in obtaining the information which he desired. In the interim, a messenger arrived from police headquarters with a parcel of pictures. Finally, the bronze man secured from the Tulsa tailor the name of the man for whom a suit answering the description of the one in the bundle had been made. It was a suit distinctive enough to be remembered, being rather loud in color.

"The garment was tailored for Calvert R. Moore, who is more commonly known as 'Leases' Moore," came the report from Tulsa.

"Just what do you know about this man Moore?" Doc asked.

"He is very wealthy." The Tulsa tailor hesitated. "He is also considered a bit sharp as a business man. Nothing crooked, you understand. Merely, well—a man who misses few bargains."

"What else?"

"He has disappeared?"

"He has what?"

"Disappeared."

"A kidnaping?" Doc demanded.

"There has been no indication of that. Leases Moore merely dropped out of sight two weeks ago, on the same day that Quince Randweil vanished."

"Quince Randweil?" Doc asked sharply. "Who is he?"

"The owner and operator of a local dog-racing track," explained the tailor.

"There is no indication of what became of these men?" Doc persisted.

"None."

"Have either of these men been considered crooked?" Doc asked.

"Oh, they ain't neither one been in jail, that anybody knows of," said the tailor, who seemed to be a frank and talkative individual.

MONK squinted at Doc when the conversation ended. "More angles?"

"Two men named Leases Moore and Quince Randweil vanished mysteriously in Tulsa, two weeks ago," Doc told him. "Leases Moore's clothing turned up in that bundle."

The bronze man now scrutinized the pictures of Willard Spanner's body. Spanner had been shot to death. Two bullets had hit him in the chest.

But it was another wound, a wrist cut, upon which the bronze man concentrated attention.

"This was not a new cut," he pointed out. "You

will notice marks made by adhesive tape, indicating it was bandaged. The manner of the tape application indicates the work of a physician. The man would hardly have applied the tape himself in this manner. I observed this fact at the morgue, but unfortunately, not close enough to be sure."

Monk looked surprised. It was not often that the bronze man had to go back over ground he had already covered for information.

"But where's this getting us?" asked the homely chemist.

"Our problem is to ascertain whether the man seized in San Francisco was the one found dead in New York," Doc told him. "On the face of it, that seems an impossibility—for less than three hours elapsed."

Doc resorted to the long-distance telephone again. He first called the San Francisco police. They gave him the name of the hotel at which Willard Spanner had been staying. Incidental was the information that Spanner had arrived in San Francisco only the previous day.

The call to the hotel was fruitful. Willard Spanner had slipped in the hotel bathroom, struck his arm against a glass shelf over the washstand, and the shelf had broken, cutting his wrist. The hotel physician had dressed the wound, which was undoubtedly the one the pictures showed.

"*Whew!*" Monk exploded. "Willard Spanner *was* seized in San Francisco a little over a couple o' hours before he was found dead in New York!"

Ham flourished his sword cane. "But it could not happen!"

Monk stood up. "The telephoning has taken time. There oughta be fresh newspapers out. I'll go get some."

He was back in a few moments. He looked excited.

"Lamp this!" he barked, and exhibited extra editions.

The headlines were large, black.

SEEK SPANNER RANSOM IN
FRISCO—$50,000 DEMANDED

A San Francisca newspaper editor late today received a note stating that Willard Spanner, reported slain in New York this afternoon, was alive, and would be released upon the payment of fifty thousand dollars.

There was more of it, but the opening paragraph told the substance of the story.

Monk eyed Doc. "Hadn't we better look into this? Ham or me can go."

"We will all three go," Doc told him. "We will leave a note advising the other three members of our outfit to do what investigating they can, when they return from upstate. They can handle the New York end."

"What about the Tulsa, Oklahoma, angle?" Ham queried.

"We will stop off there," Doc advised.

TULSA likes to call itself the capital of the oil industry. Oil men do much flying. The Tulsa municipal airport is a source of local pride. Facilities and appointments are excellent.

Floodlights fanned brilliance as Doc Savage dropped his big speed plane in for a landing. The night force of mechanics stood about and stared. Someone ran to a nearby flying school, and shortly afterward there was a stampede to the tarmac of aeronautical students in all states of partial dress. It was not often that a plane such as the bronze man was flying was seen.

The speed ship was tri-motored, and all three motors were streamlined into the wings until their presence was hardly apparent to the eye. The hull breasted down so that the plane could be landed on water, and the landing gear was retractable. The cabin was as bulletproof as was feasible, and inside were innumerable mechanical devices.

One individual did not seem interested in the bronze man's remarkable craft. He was a pilot in greasy coveralls who tinkered with the motor of a shabby-looking cabin monoplane over near the edge of the field.

He had dropped into the airport two hours before, and had been tinkering with his plane since. He had given short answers to the field mechanics, and thereafter had been left severely alone. It was now not long before dawn.

Doc Savage taxied over near the covered pit which held the gasoline hoses and cut all three motors. He stepped out of the plane and glanced into the east, as if seeking the sunrise.

"I've heard a lot about that bird," a flying student said, unconscious that his whisper carried. "They say he designed that sky wagon himself and that it's the fastest thing of its size in the world."

Over at the edge of the field, the motor of the shabby cabin monoplane came to life. It roared loudly.

A small crowd surged around Doc's speed ship. They were flying men, greatly interested in a sample of the most advanced aerial conveyance. Most of them were interested in the layout of navigating instruments, in the robot pilot.

"I've heard this bus can take off and fly herself, and can be controlled by radio from a distance," a man said. "Is that a fact?"

One man was interested in the tail structure of the plane. He found himself alone back there. He flashed a long knife out of his clothing, ripped and gouged, and got open one of the inspection ports through which the control connections could be examined.

The man was thin; his movements had the speed of an animal. He whipped a series of three packages out of his clothing. They were connected by wires, and none were extraordinarily large. He thrust all three inside the inspection port, then closed the flap. Then he backed away into the darkness.

He blinked a small flashlight four times rapidly.

Motor a-howl, the cabin monoplane scudded away from the edge of the field. It headed straight for Doc's ship.

THE bronze man had to all appearances been occupied entirely in answering questions. But now he flashed into life, and seemed to know exactly what he was doing.

"Run!" he rapped at those standing about. "Get away from here! Quick!"

His great voice was a crash. It was compelling. Three men turned and fled without knowing why. The others retreated more slowly. They saw the oncoming cabin plane.

"Runaway ship!" someone howled.

Monk and Ham had stepped out of Doc's speed craft. They whirled to clamber back inside. But Doc Savage was ahead of them. He banged the cabin door in their faces, then lunged to the controls. The big motors whooped out at the first touch of the starters, and because they were hot, instantly hauled the speed craft into motion.

There was a tense second or two. Then it became evident that Doc's plane was going to get clear. The men scattered from the path of the oncoming cabin monoplane. It went bawling past, doing no harm, except to give an aviator student a bad fright.

All who looked could see by the floodlight glare that the cabin was empty.

"Where's the pilot of that trap?" yelled the night field manager. "Such damned carelessness—"

He swallowed the rest. An unexpected thing was happening. A weird thing.

The old cabin ship had gone on, but instead of crashing into the fence at the edge of the field, as everyone expected, it was turning—swinging as if a hand of uncanny skill were at the controls. It arched completely around and cannoned after the speed plane of Doc Savage.

The onlookers gasped, unable to believe what they were witnessing. They saw the pig, Habeas Corpus, come hurtling from the cabin of Doc's speed ship. Then they saw the bronze man appear in the cabin door.

He seemed to be trying to reach the tail of his plane, for he dropped off and sought to seize it as it went past. But the streamlined metal surface offered no grip. He was knocked aside and the ship went on.

Doc scrambled to all fours, seized the pig, Habeas, and fell flat with him. He lay there.

The shabby cabin ship charged in pursuit of the speed plane. The two ships approached at an angle. They met. The whole world seemed to go in blinding white.

The tarmac jumped, quaked. Windows fell out of the operations office, hangars, the flying school buildings across the paved road. The side of one huge hangar buckled inward, and the roof came down as if a giant had stepped upon it.

The noise of the blast thumped and rolled and finally went into the distance like a heavy salvo of thunder.

Out where the two planes had met, there was a hole in the earth which would require two days to fill.

Chapter IV
OKLAHOMA ACTION

DOC SAVAGE heaved up from where he had lain after failing to reach the tail of his plane. He ran—not toward the blast scene, but toward his men. Monk and Ham veered out to meet him, Ham unconsciously knocking dust off his natty raiment.

"Why'd you quit the plane?" Monk gulped. "Why didn't you take it into the air?"

"We were low on gas," Doc clipped. "That other ship probably had full tanks. It would have caught me. Come on!"

"But there wasn't nobody in it!" Monk exploded as he ran.

"Radio control," Doc told him, racing toward the edge of the flying field. "The ship was loaded with explosive!"

Monk and Ham pounded in his wake. The pig, Habeas, trailed.

Monk puffed, "But no radio control would—"

"This was a device which would send the plane toward a sending set operating on a designated frequency," Doc advised over his shoulder. "It is merely an adaptation of the robot pilot which keeps planes in the path of a beam radio."

Monk yelled, "But there wasn't no sending set in our bus!" He ran with the waddling gait of a scared bull ape.

"On the contrary, there was," Doc rapped. "A fellow stuck a tiny portable set inside the empennage shortly before the excitement started. I saw him. There wasn't time to grab him."

"Where'd he go?" Monk roared, and put on more speed.

"This way," Doc said, and vaulted the metal fence which surrounded the field.

Ham tried to use too much care in mounting the fence, with the result that he slipped, caught his immaculate afternoon coat on the barbed top strand and left the entire back of it behind.

HAM

"Where'd the pilot of the plane go?" he gritted.

"This way," Doc said. "He and the fellow who planted the decoy radio transmitter probably intended to meet."

They covered a hundred yards. Weeds about them were tall. The rotating beacon at the airport flashed white light at regular intervals. The airport floodlights were still on, making a great glow.

Doc Savage stopped, breathed a "Listen!"

Monk and Ham both strained their ears. They heard crickets, sounds of distant automobiles and voice murmur back at the flying held, but nothing else.

"The two are heading a bit to the right," Doc decided.

Monk and Ham showed no surprise, being aware of the bronze man's almost superhuman ability to hear. Countless times, they had seen him employ the sonic device with which he had developed his aural organs over a period of years.

Weeds became more profuse, then ended suddenly at the edge of an evidently little-used road. There was a fence which they managed to keep from squeaking while climbing it. Clouds were making the night darker than before. They crawled up an embankment, evidently some kind of dike. Hulks like gigantic pill boxes loomed ahead. The night air acquired a definite odor.

"Oil tank farm," Ham decided in a whisper.

"Not being used," Doc added.

Ham asked in a surprised tone, "How can you tell?"

"The odor," Doc told him. "The smell of fresh crude oil is lacking."

Off to the side, a smaller, squarer hulk appeared. A light came on suddenly and whitened soiled windows. Inside was the gleam of dull gray machinery and brasswork which needed cleaning.

"The pump station," Monk grunted. "They must be using it for a headquarters."

Ham offered abruptly, "Doc, what say the missing link and myself circle and watch the rear, while you are reconnoitering?"

"Do not get too close," Doc requested.

Ham eased away in the darkness, Monk on his heels. The pig, Habeas, trailed them. They made half a circle and were behind the pump station. There was a pile of pipe there. They eased behind that.

Two men arose from the darkness and put guns against their backs.

"What the—" Monk began.

"I know it's a shame," said one of the men. "You two boys must have thought we were pretty dumb."

MONK and Ham turned around. There was not much light, but they did not need light to observe that the guns were genuine, and of large caliber. The hammer of each weapon was also rocked back.

Habeas, the shoat, faded away into the night with the soundlessness of a shadow.

Monk jutted his small head forward to peer more closely at the two who had sprung the surprise.

"You'll get eyestrain," one of the men admonished. "We're the two yahoos you followed here from the airport, if that's what's worryin' you."

The speech had been in whispers, unconsciously. Now Ham decided to speak aloud, hoping to advise Doc of their predicament.

"You two—*ugh!*"

He doubled over painfully. His mouth flew wide, and breath came past his teeth with such force that it carried a fine spray with it.

The man who had jammed a gun into Ham's middle with great force hissed, "We know the bronze guy is around in front. You try to tip him again and you'll spring a leak just about the third button of that trick vest!"

The other man said, "We hate to part you two from that big bronze shadow, but we fear we must. Shake a leg."

They backed away from the pump station, came to a path, and went down it. Monk and Ham were searched expertly as they walked, and relieved of the only weapons they carried—the small supermachine pistols which were Doc Savage's own invention.

"What's the idea?" Monk demanded.

"A gentleman wants to see you," one of the two replied.

"Who?"

"A man whom I'm more than half convinced is one of the cleverest gents in the world," said the other. "And mind you, partner, I know all about the rep of this Doc Savage."

"The guy who thought up that bright idea of fixing the plane bomb so it would chase a radio transmitter, and who also rigged up that burglar alarm at the oyster plant in New York?" Monk hazarded.

"Sure," said the man. "He's thought of some other things that would surprise you, too."

"Shut up!" advised the man's companion. "Someday you'll talk yourself inside a wooden jacket, and they'll sprinkle some nice clean dirt on you."

They went on in silence. There was roadway underfoot now—a dirt road, hard packed by heavy traffic.

"What about Doc?" Ham demanded.

"We ain't ambitious," said one of the captors. "We'll dispose of *you* first. He'll get his later."

They rounded a bend hinged by scrub oak and came suddenly upon a truck waiting. The truck was large and had a flat bed, the type of machine employed in hauling pipe and oil-field supplies.

A stubby man came forward, also a tall, thin one and a man who had, when flashlights were turned on, eyes which turned inward at intervals. It was Stunted and the rest of the coterie from New York.

"It's a regular reunion," Stunted chuckled.

"You got that sawed-off auto rifle to working?" Monk asked him.

"You bet," Stunted retorted. "I worked on it all the way from New York."

"You made a quick trip," Monk suggested.

"Sure," said Stunted. "We came in a—"

The man with the uneasy eyes whipped forward and slapped Stunted in the face. The force of the blow sent Stunted reeling back.

"What in blue blazes was the idea?" he snarled.

"You got a head like a toad," the man with the weird eyes snapped. "You was gettin' set to tell this monkey how we came back!"

"Huh!" Stunted fell silent, his mien sheepish.

TWO pairs of greasy overalls and two equally soiled jumpers were produced. Menace of gun muzzles persuaded Monk and Ham to don these. They were compelled to sit on the flat bed of the truck, legs dangling over, and the machine got into motion.

Some of the captors stood erect on the bed plat-form. All wore work clothing. They might have been some pipeline crew, bound into the fields.

"Let out a bleat and we'll certainly weight you down with lead," Monk and Ham were advised.

"Deuced boorish treatment," Ham said primly.

Someone laughed. The truck had a rear end gear grind and the sound went on and on, like something in pain. There was little traffic on the road, passenger cars for the most part. Once two policemen on motorcycles went past with a violent popping, but did not even glance at the truck.

Later, a ramshackle delivery car ran around the truck with a great clatter, cut in sharply and went on.

"Durn nut!" growled the truck driver.

Hardly more than ten minutes later, there was a loud report from a front wheel. The truck began to pound along in a manner which indicated a flat tire. The driver pulled over to the edge of the road. He began to swear, making no effort to get out and start repairs.

"You waiting for it to thunder, or something?" Stunted demanded.

"No spare tire along," said the driver. He alighted and used a flashlight until he found a large-headed roofing nail embedded in the tire. He kicked the nail and swore some more.

Down the road, a light flashed.

"Who's that?" a man demanded.

One of the men advanced down the road, keeping in the darker shadows beside the ditch. He returned soon.

"Delivery truck with a puncture," he reported. "It's that nut who passed us. He must've picked up another of them nails."

"He got a spare tire?" Stunted demanded.

"Seems to have," said the other.

Stunted chuckled. "Old Nick takes care of his own, eh, boys?"

Two guns were kept jammed against Monk and Ham. Three men went forward. There was a wait, during which pounding noises came from the delivery truck, then a sharp exchange of commands. One of the men called back, "Come on, you birds."

The guns urged Monk and Ham forward. They came to the truck.

The driver was an unusual-looking fellow, having a tremendous girth and a right leg which twisted out in grotesque fashion. His face was puffy. He had a swarthy skin and dark hair.

"This Mexican has kindly consented to give us a lift," chuckled Stunted, and flourished his sawed-off auto rifle at the swarthy driver.

The driver wailed, "Señors, my poor car—"

"Shut up!" advised Stunted. "You just drive us carefullike. We'll tell you where to go."

... a weird streak of luminance appeared in the reddening sky.

AN hour later, they were traveling where there seemed to be no road at all. The sun was rising, but not yet in view.

"Turn right," Stunted advised, and they pulled down a precipitous bank and took to the gravel bed of a dry stream.

The swarthy driver complained, "Señors, my poor car will never run back over thees road. Tell me, how shall I return?"

"You'll find out all about that," Stunted told him.

"Hey!" one of the men barked. "Lookit!"

They craned necks. After a moment of that, they all heard a long, tending crack of a sound, and a weird streak of luminance appeared in the reddening sky. It seemed to stretch in an arch away into the infinite reaches of the heavens.

"Now, what?" Stunted grumbled. "Could that mean that—"

"Shut up, stupid!" the man with the peculiar eyes snapped.

The streak in the sky died away quickly, vanishing completely.

The rickety truck went on. In spite of the deserted appearance of the region, it was undoubtedly a road of sorts which they traveled. Twice, when they crossed sandy stretches, the men alighted and, with leafy boughs, carefully brushed out their tracks.

"Don't want 'em to look too recent," Stunted grinned.

The driver showed alarm. "What ees thees mean, señores?"

"In about three minutes, you'll know," Stunted leered.

The driver reacted in a fashion which was the more surprising, since he had previously shown a surprisingly small degree of backbone. He lashed out a fist toward Stunted.

It was a terrific blow. After it, Stunted's face would never look quite the same. Stunted fell out of the seat.

The driver emitted a blood-curdling yell and took to the opposite direction. He had chosen his spot well. A narrow rip of a draw entered the creek bed at that point. The dark man dived into that. His game leg seemed, if anything, to add to his speed. He disappeared.

The truck unloaded in roaring confusion. Wild shots were discharged. The men rushed into the gully. Some climbed the steep sides. After the first excitement, they used flashlights and searched more thoroughly. They found no trace of the fugitive.

"One of that guy's ancestors must have been a rabbit," Stunted grumbled.

They consulted for a time. There seemed to be little they could do about it.

"That Mex won't know what it's all about, anyhow," someone decided.

They got in the truck, and it had rolled hardly less than half a mile before it pulled out on a flat and stopped before what seemed to be literally a mansion.

It was a great brick building, two stories in height, with flanking wings and a garage capable of housing four cars. Situated on the outskirts of a city such as Tulsa, the mansion would have aroused no more than admiration, but located here in a wilderness of scrub oak and hills, with no roads worthy of the name nearby, it was a startling sight.

The headlights played on the place at closer range, and it became evident in the early morning light that many of the windows were broken out, that the woodwork needed painting, that the lawn had not been trimmed in years. Yet the place could not, from the style of architecture, have been more than ten years old.

Monk asked, "How did this dump come to be here?"

"Osage Indian," Stunted leered through his smashed face. "Heap oil, catchum many dollars. Build um brick tepee. Then Osage, him turn around and croak. Tepee, him go pot."

"You're quite a smart guy, ain'tcha?" Monk growled.

They unloaded beside the mansion. A lean, brown man stepped out to meet them, squinting in the headlights. He had a rifle.

"We got two visitors for the chief," said Stunted. "The chief just left," said the man with the rifle.

"Oh," said Stunted. "So it was him in—"

The man with the queer eyes screamed, "Damn you! All the time about to let things slip where these guys can hear!" He slugged Stunted heavily with his right fist.

Stunted's face was already sore from the blow landed by the swarthy delivery truck driver. The new pain maddened him. He went down, but retained his grip on his rifle, rolled over and lifted the weapon.

Men shouted, and sprang forward to prevent bloodshed.

Ham kicked Monk on the shins. Monk bellowed in pain and knocked down the handiest of his captors.

"The house!" Ham yelled. "They'd shoot us down before we could get across the clearing."

The house entrance was not more than a dozen feet away. They dived for it. A rifle slug tore an ample fistful of splinters off the edge of the door as they went through.

Chapter V
FLAME THREAD

THE door was of some rich dark wood. Paint had peeled off, but the panel still retained its strength. Monk tossed out one long, hairy arm and slammed it. Echoes of the slam echoed through the house, which seemed virtually devoid of furniture.

Monk snarled, "You didn't need to kick me!"

"It was a pleasure," Ham told him. "I mean— I had to get you in action."

"Yeah!" Monk hit a door at the end of the reception hall where they stood. It was not locked. Momentum sent him across the chamber beyond on hands and knees.

There was a table at this side of the room. It had been thrown hastily together from rough wood. But there was nothing crude about the apparatus on it. Black insulating panels, knobs, and switches glistened.

Monk veered for the apparatus.

Ham yelled. "That won't help us!"

"Heck it won't!" Monk began fumbling with the dials. "This is a bang-up radio transmitter-and-receiver."

"I know it." Ham was making for another door.

"What good will the bally thing do us?"

"Bring help." Monk made a fierce face. "Trouble is, I gotta figure out what knob does what."

Glass crashed out of a window, a rifle smashed, and the high-powered slug clouted completely through the walls, missing Monk by something less than a yard.

"Take your time," Ham told Monk dryly. "You only have to get that thing working and call until you raise a station. Five or ten minutes should be all you need."

Two more rifle bullets came in, showering Monk with plaster dust.

Monk made another fierce grimace and gave up working with the radio mechanism. He followed Ham into another room—which held numerous boxes, all of them of stout wood, none of them bearing markings which might have hinted at their past contents.

Monk upset a box, found it empty, and began heaving the containers against the door to block it. Rifle lead went through the boxes with splintering ease.

"Them high-powered guns kinda complicate things," Monk grunted.

They retreated, finding an empty chamber, then one with cheap canvas camp cots on the floor. Blankets were piled carelessly on the cots. Odds and ends of clothing lay about. Cigarette stubs spotted the floor.

Monk scooped up an armload of the clothing.

"Maybe there's something in the pockets that'll tell us things," he said.

He carried the clothing as he lumbered in the wake of Ham. The latter peered through a window, rubbed dust off the pane, looked again, and began knocking glass out with quick blows.

"Sure, we can just walk away," Monk told him sourly. "They'll stand by and sing us a bedtime story, or something."

"Look, you accident of nature!" Ham pointed an arm. "There is a car behind the house, which we failed to sight before."

MONK looked and saw that the car was large and powerful; it was inclosed. He helped smash the rest of the glass out, let Ham jump down to the ground, then followed, retaining the clothes and grunting loudly as he landed.

They reached the car together and crowded each other getting inside. Monk threw his right hand for the switch, then made a fist of the hand and struck the instrument panel.

"Blast it!" he grated. "They *would* take the key out!"

He flopped down on the floorboards, tore a fistful of wiring bodily from under the instrument panel, took one rather long second in sorting them over, then joined the ends of two and the motor whooped into life.

"Handy to know how these cars are wired," Monk grinned.

The machine moaned and pitched in second gear, making an ample circle around the house. Ham drove recklessly, shoving his head up at intervals to ascertain their course. Brush switched the underside of the car. A loud clanking sound came from one of the windows, and Monk squinted at a spidery outline of cracks which had appeared magically in the glass.

"Glory be!" he snorted. "This chariot has bulletproof glass! There sure is a Santa Claus!"

Ham sat up, drove more carefully, and they pitched into the obscure roadway by which they had arrived. Ham was overanxious. He put on too much speed and the car skidded, went into a ditch and stopped. He looked outside.

"We can back out," he said.

Then he sat very still, for he had felt a small spot of metallic coldness come against the back of his neck. He had felt gun muzzles on his bare skin on other occasions.

"We should have looked in the back seat," he told Monk.

THE homely chemist reared up and peered around. The gun was removed from Ham's neck and shoved almost against Monk's flattened nose. It was a single-action six-shooter of tremendous size.

A young woman held the gun with one hand.

She was a lean, tanned young woman with a few freckles, not at all hard to look at. Her eyes were a rather enchanting blue, and she showed teeth which would have graced the advertising of any dentifrice. It was not a smile which showed her teeth. Rather, it was a grimace intended to convey fierceness.

"These are hollow-point bullets," she advised. "They would just about remove your head."

Monk swallowed. "Now, listen—"

"Shut up!" she requested. "I never saw you before, and don't know you. Maybe you don't know me. But you've heard of me. I'm Lanca Jaxon."

"Oh," said Monk.

"You've heard enough to know I'd as soon shoot you as not, or sooner," said the girl.

"Two-gun Lanca Jaxon," murmured Monk, who had never before heard of any young woman with such a name.

"A wise-cracker, like the rest of them," the girl said, frostily. "I never dreamed there could be so many alleged humorists in one gang of crooks."

Monk said, "Young lady—"

"Quiet!" she snapped. "One of these bullets won't be funny. You two sit still. I'll get out and then you get out. I'll tell you what to do next."

She got out.

Three men came from the adjacent brush. Their arrival was so sudden that it was evident that they were men who had scattered to the edges of the clearing surrounding the house when the action had started, that they might be in a position to shoot down anyone attempting to cross the open space. Each of the three held a gun.

"We'll take it over now, Lanca," one said.

The young woman looked at them very hard. She seemed to be trying to make up her mind about something of great importance. The gun was perfectly steady in her hand. She shrugged at last, and one of the men came over and got the gun she had wielded.

"You helped us a lot," he chuckled.

The girl said nothing.

Puffing and growling at each other, the remaining members of the gang arrived shortly. They surrounded Monk and Ham. Discussion followed. Three of them favored shooting Monk and Ham immediately. Others held saner convictions.

"Let the big boss decide," suggested the man with the peculiar-behaving eyes.

They walked Monk and Ham back toward the house.

The man with the queer eyes linked an arm with the girl, and said, "My dear Lanca, would you explain just how you happened to be in that car? And with a gun, too? It was Stunted's old six-shooter, wasn't it?"

The girl managed to say nothing in a very vehement manner. The man's eyes seemed to shift more queerly than usual. He conducted the girl into another part of the house.

Monk and Ham found themselves in the room with the radio apparatus. One of the captors went out, came back with a lariat of the cowboy variety, and they were bound with expert thoroughness.

"What'll we do with 'em?" Stunted asked, nursing his bruised features.

"I'll find out," said one of the men, and went to the radio apparatus. He switched the mechanism on. It was apparently of all-wave construction, because an ordinary broadcast program began coming from the receiver. It was a newscast. The commentator had a pleasant voice, rapid enunciation.

"—weird phenomena reported from various sections of the nation," said the voice from the radio.

The man at the apparatus started to turn knobs.

"Wait!" Stunted barked. "Get that!"

THE man reset the dial to the broadcast station.

"Some of the reports state that long ribbons of flame were seen in the heavens, accompanied by a weird crashing noise," said the radio newscaster. "Others insist they saw balls of flame. Astronomers, for the most part, insist that the phenomena witnessed are not meteors, as was at first believed. In no case has it been reported that a fallen meteor has been found."

One of the men laughed harshly, said, "It's got 'em worried."

"It'll have 'em a lot more worried before it's over," Stunted muttered.

"The last streak of flame in the heavens was reported over north-central Oklahoma and over Kansas," said the broadcaster. "This was hardly more than an hour ago—" The voice stopped coming from the radio. During the pause which ensued, crackle of papers in the distant radio station could be heard.

"Flash!" said the broadcaster, an undercurrent of excitement in his voice. "Here is an important item which just arrived."

"Aw, turn it off!" growled one of the men in the room. "Somebody has shot somebody else in Siberia or somewhere, probably."

Stunted snapped, "Nix! Get the news before we contact the chief."

They fell silent. The broadcaster was still rattling papers. He began speaking:

"It has just been announced that the explosion heard in downtown Kansas City, and which broke studio windows in this station, was a blast which thieves set off to enter the vaults of the city's largest bank," said the newscaster. "The raid was on a gigantic scale, and daringly executed. At least ten men participated. Bank officials have not been able to make a check, but estimate that the thieves could have escaped with nearly three million dollars."

Stunted seemed to forget all about his facial injuries. He grinned from ear to ear and slapped a palm resoundingly against a thigh.

"Boy, oh boy!" he chortled. "Get that! Get that!"

"Shut up!" someone told him.

They were all intent on the radio now.

"A few minutes after the robbery, one of the strange streaks of fire in the sky, which have so mystified the nation, was sighted," said the radio announcer. "Police are investigating a theory that this might be connected with the robbery of the bank."

Stunted said, "They begin to smell a rat."

"This concludes our news broadcast," said the loudspeaker voice. "We will be on the air later with more details of the sensational robbery."

One of the men shifted the radio control knob,

clicked a switch and got down on shortwave bands. All of the men looked suddenly and extraordinarily cheerful.

The man at the controls made adjustments, switching on the transmitter. Then he picked up a microphone and a small notebook, evidently a code book of some kind.

"Calling CQ, calling CQ," he said into the microphone. "Station W9EXF calling CQ."

Monk blinked as he heard that. It was the accepted manner in which amateur radio stations took the air and sought to establish connection with other amateurs. The "CQ" was merely the radio "ham" manner of stating that the station wanted to talk with anybody who would answer.

Out of the radio loudspeaker came an answer.

"Station W9SAV calling station W9EXF," the voice said.

The man at the apparatus grinned, winked. He consulted the code book.

"I have two headaches today," he said, obviously using the code. "How are you feeling?"

"The two headaches you were looking for?" asked the distant voice, which was somewhat distorted.

"That's the two," advised the man in the room.

"Have you tried diagnosing them?" asked the voice from the loudspeaker.

The man at the apparatus consulted the code book.

"Sure, I diagnosed them," he stated. "But they ain't the kind of headaches that tell you things."

MONK scowled darkly as he listened. There were thousands of amateur radio stations on the air all over the country, and a conversation such as this would not arouse suspicion. The code was simple, so simple that anyone knowing it was code could guess what many of the statements meant. But a casual listener would not catch the hidden significance.

The radio conversation continued.

"You talked about a big headache that you felt coming on, the last time we hooked up," said the distant voice. "Any sign of that one?"

"Nope," said the man in the room. "But I may get it yet."

Monk decided they were referring to Doc Savage.

"Otherwise, you are all well?" asked the loudspeaker voice.

"Nothing to complain about." The man at the transmitter hastily thumbed the code book. "How is your case of ptomaine—the one you got out of a can?"

"All cleared up," chuckled the radio voice.

Another look at the code book. "What do you suggest doing for my two headaches?"

"I'll see what the manual says," replied the faraway speaker

The man at the transmitter laughed; then there was silence, during which Monk concluded that the "manual" referred to must be a cipher word designating the mysterious chief of the gang.

"The manual says to use two pills," growled the radio voice.

Grim expressions on the features of the men in the room as the radio conversation terminated showed Monk that they all knew, without referring to the code book, what a "pill" meant.

Stunted stood up, scowling.

"I don't like that," he said sourly.

"What's eating you?" the man with the queer eyes snapped.

"I ain't exactly a puritan," Stunted grunted. "But croakin' these two guys in cold blood don't come in my bailiwick. If they've got a chance—

MONK

sure! But just to plug 'em, feed 'em one of them pills a piece, which we all know darn well is the boss's word for a bullet—not me!"

"Turned champion of defenseless manhood?" the uneasy-eyed man grated.

"Nuts!" Stunted glared at him. "I ain't forgot that pop in the kisser you give me, you cock-eyed gazoo!"

"Cut it out, you two!" a man barked.

Stunted continued to glare. The eyes of the other man crossed, uncrossed; then he shrugged.

"Aw, the delivery-truck driver getting away had me fussed up," he said. "I guess I shouldn't have smacked you."

Stunted said, "We'll let it go at that, then."

The man with the unusual eyes drew a revolver.

"I'll take care of the pill doses," he said. "I'm not as finicky as some."

He shoved Monk and Ham, propelling them before him through the door. They staggered about, helpless to do more than voice threats, which had absolutely no effect. The lariat bindings on their arms were painfully tight, securely tied.

One of the men left behind in the room called, "Say, what about that delivery-truck driver?"

"We'll look for him after I take care of this," said the self-appointed executioner.

They passed outside. The man with uneasy eyes did not close the door. Evidently he was calloused enough to want the others to hear the shot.

"Walk!" the fellow snarled. "You guys make one move and I'll let you have it here, instead of outdoors."

Monk and Ham walked. They could hear the

tread of the man behind them. It was heavy, regular, betraying no nervousness, and there was in it the quality of doom.

Then the tread stopped. Monk thought afterward that there was also a faint gasp about the same time that the tread ceased. But he was never quite sure.

It was a long moment before Monk, apprehensive lest their captor shoot, turned. The homely chemist's little eyes flew round. His mouth came open.

The delivery-truck driver stood spread-legged in the passage. He had the uneasy-eyed man gripped by the neck with both hands. He held the fellow off the floor with an obvious ease, and the victim was making no outcry, hardly twitching.

Monk ogled the delivery-truck driver. The latter had changed appearance vastly, although he still wore the same garments and his skin and hair were swarthy. But the limp was gone, and the stature and fabulous strength identified the man.

"Doc Savage!" Monk gulped.

Chapter VI
TWO GENTLEMEN OF TULSA

DOC SAVAGE was not choking his prisoner, but rather working on the back of the man's neck with corded bronze fingertips, seeking out certain sensitive nerve centers on which pressure, properly applied, would induce a state of paralysis lasting some time.

When the man was completely limp, with only his eyes and breathing showing that he still lived, Doc lowered him to the floor.

Monk and Ham stood immobile while the lariat was untied. Doc's finger strength managed the knots with ease.

"You hear anything that was said in that room?" Monk whispered.

"Practically all of it," Doc told him. "After using the ruse of the delivery truck I—"

"You sprinkled nails in the road?" Ham interjected.

"Exactly," Doc answered. "I hired the truck from a fellow who chanced to pass, and his clothing as well. He was carrying some roofing material, and the nails came in handy. The make-up material I always carry on my person. It was largely dye and wax for the cheeks."

Monk and Ham shook off the ropes.

"Where's my hog?" Monk demanded.

"Back at that old tank farm," Doc said. "I had to leave him behind."

Monk waved an arm. "What do you make of this mess, Doc?"

"Their chief obviously robbed that Kansas City bank," the bronze man pointed out.

"Sure. But what about those streaks of fire in the sky? They've got a connection with the gang. And why'd they kill Willard Spanner? And who is that girl and what's she doing here?"

"Always thinking about women," Ham told Monk sourly.

"She acted queer," Monk said. "This whole thing makes me dizzy."

Doc picked up the gun which had been carried by the man with the roving eyes. He fired it twice. The reports were ear-splitting.

"To make them think you have been executed," the bronze man breathed. "That should give us a moment or so respite."

They eased back through the house until they encountered a door which seemed to be locked. Ordinarily, a lock offered Doc Savage few difficulties. But this was a padlock and hasp—on the other side of the door.

"We will try it through the basement," the bronze man whispered.

The basement stairs were behind an adjacent door and squeaked a little, but not too much, as they went down.

The room below had once been a recreation chamber and held a huge billiard table, the green covering mildewed and rotted. The table must have been too ponderous to move away. Adjacent was the furnace room. Grimy windows afforded faint illumination.

Monk stopped the instant he was inside the room.

"Lookit!" he gulped.

Two men were handcuffed to the pipes which comprised the heating system.

ONE man was long and lean, and his body looked as if it were made of leather and sticks. He grinned at them, and his grin was hideous because he must have had false teeth and was not wearing them now. His clothing was fastidious. When he tried to beckon at them, it was evident that the thumb was missing from his right hand, making that grotesque, too.

"I dunno who you are, but you look like angels to me," he said thickly. "You don't belong to this crowd. Turn us loose, brother."

The second man was a sleek, round butterball, entirely bald. Not only was his body round, but his head, hands, and his arms were like jointed, elongated balls. He wore a ring which had once held an enormous setting, but the stone was missing now and the bent prongs of the ring showed it had been pried from place, possibly without removing the ring from his fat rounded fingers.

"Yuss," he said, and his words were a mushy hissing. "Turn us loose." His "loose" sounded like "lush."

Monk lumbered forward, asking, small-voiced, "Who are you birds?"

"Leases Moore," said the leathery man with the missing teeth and thumb.

"Quince Randweil," said the man with the rounded anatomy.

"Oh!" Monk squinted. "The two missing men from Tulsa?"

Ham snapped, "It was Leases Moore's clothing that we got hold of in New York!"

Leases Moore made a leathery grimace. "How do I know what they did with my duds? They took 'em when they grabbed me and Quince, here, out of my car."

"A bulletproof sedan?" Monk demanded, thinking of the machine in which they had tried flight.

"Sure," said Leases Moore. "Are you gonna turn us loose, or not?"

Doc went to the handcuffs, examined the links, and found them of no more than average strength. The pipes formed an excellent anchorage. He grasped the links, set himself, threw his enormous sinews into play and the thin metal parted with brittle snappings.

"I'm a son of a gun!" Quince Randweil made it "gunsh." "That tells me who you are."

Doc said nothing. He finished breaking the cuffs.

"I heard them talking about you," said Randweil. "You are Doc Savage." The way he said it, the name sounded like "Savvash."

"We had better get out of here," Doc said. "We will try that bulletproof car again."

. They moved for the grimy window.

"Why were you being held?" Monk asked Leases Moore.

"That," Leases Moore said promptly, "is the blackest mystery a man ever went up against. They wouldn't tell us."

"Ransom?"

"They never mentioned it."

"Know their names?"

"Only that runt Stunted," said Leases Moore. "I never saw any of them before. Neither has Quince, here."

The rounded man bobbed all of his layers of fat in agreement.

"What is their game?" Monk asked.

"Search us," replied Leases Moore. "That's another mystery."

Doc Savage was working on the window, and now it came open with only minor squeaks of complaint.

"Out," said the bronze man, and boosted lean, leathery Leases Moore out through the aperture, after first taking a look around.

Quince Randweil was helped out next. He and Moore ran for the car, which had been wheeled back into the clearing and stood not many yards from the house. They ran boldly, with more haste than caution.

"The dopes," Monk growled. "They oughta be careful until we get out."

Then his jaw fell, for Leases Moore and Quince Randweil had started the car and were racing wildly away, the engine making a great deal of noise.

"Why, the double-crossers!" Monk gritted.

THE homely chemist had one pronounced failing. When he got mad he was inclined to go into action without forethought of the consequences. Now he gave every indication of intending to climb out of the window and pursue the two fleeing men.

Doc dropped a hand on Monk's shoulder and settled him back on the basement floor.

"Wait," said the bronze man.

Upstairs, there was excited shouting. They had heard the car's departure. Guns began going off.

"They may not see who is in the car, and think we have escaped," Doc said. "That will give us a chance to prowl about this place, and possibly overhear something that will give us a better line on what is going on."

There was a staccato series of deafening reports, undoubtedly the voice of Stunted's cherished automatic rifle from which the barrel had been bobbed. Six-guns made noises more nearly resembling firecrackers, and a shotgun boomed deeply.

There was a general charge of men from the house. They had obviously found in the hallway the senseless man with the queer eyes. Their wild rage might have been ludicrous under other circumstances.

Doc had gotten the soiled cellar window shut. They watched the excitement from behind its semiopaque screen.

Monk grinned. "Wonder how many of 'em was around?"

"I was unable to ascertain," Doc told him.

"Looks like more'n a dozen pulling out after that car," Monk offered. "Bet they're all leaving."

Doc Savage nodded, admitting, "Now is as good a time as any to look around."

They left the basement. The stair squeaking as they went up seemed louder than before, for the house was very silent.

"I didn't see that girl leave," Monk whispered. "Maybe we can find her and ask questions."

"And probably get shot," Ham said pessimistically.

They listened. Outdoors, in the morning sunlight, birds were making sound. Wind fluttered scrub-oak leaves.

Then they heard a voice. It was a steady, well-modulated voice, and it came in spells. There was also an answering voice, this one metallic and difficult to distinguish.

Monk breathed, "The radio! Somebody is using it!"

They made for the room which held the radio transmitting-and-receiving apparatus. The door was open. One of the gang crouched over the mechanism, code book in one hand.

"So you think the weather should be warmer out in San Francisco," he was saying. "Yes, old man, that's probably true, and if, as you say, the manual says Frisco is a good place to be, we'll go—"

Behind Doc Savage and his companions, Stunted yelled, "Get them lunch hooks up, you three guys!"

Stunted, for all of his villainy, seemed to have some of the spirit attributed to old-time Western bad men. He disliked shooting down his victims in cold blood.

Had he, having come back unheard, or possibly never having left the house, started shooting without warning, Doc Savage or one of the pair with him, possibly all of them, would have died then. As it was, they reacted unconsciously to the command. They pitched forward into the radio room.

THE man at the radio apparatus cried out in excitement and went for a gun. He was infinitely slow.

Doc Savage, lunging across the room, sent out a fist and the man bounced from it to the apparatus table. His weight ruptured wiring, and sparks sizzled and blue smoke arose.

The fellow had succeeded in freeing his gun from a pocket, and it bounced across the floor. Monk got it.

Out in the corridor, Stunted bawled, "You guys ain't got no sense a-tall! Come outa there! This cannon of mine'll throw lead right through them walls!"

Monk lifted his captured revolver, then lowered it, grimacing to his companions. "Maybe he won't shoot if he thinks we're unarmed."

Stunted lifted his voice, yelling for assistance. He did not enter the radio room. His bellow was ample to carry to his associates.

The man on the radio table fell to the floor, but did not move afterward. A spot on his coat was smoking where it had been ignited by an electric arc.

Ham went over and rubbed the smolder out with a foot.

Doc threw up the window, making ample noise for Stunted to hear. Then he listened. Stunted had fallen silent. Doc picked up a chair and dropped it out of the window. Hitting the ground outside, it sounded not unlike a man dropping from the window.

Stunted swore, and they could hear him rushing for the door which led outside.

Doc led his two men out of the radio room—not through the window, but back into the corridor which Stunted had just vacated. They found a window on the opposite side of the house. It was open, and they dropped through.

Some distance away, men were calling excitedly. They had heard Stunted's yell. The latter answered them, advising what had happened. Doc and his men began to run.

It was the bronze man's sharp ears which ascertained that Stunted was running around the house and would soon glimpse them. Doc breathed a command. They all three slammed flat in the coarse grass.

Stunted came puffing around the corner of the house, and stopped. His breathing was distinct, loud. He muttered in a baffled way.

Doc and his men were perfectly motionless. It seemed incredible that they had escaped discovery so far. But Stunted was certain to sight them. Monk held his revolver expectantly.

Then a clear feminine voice called, "Stunted! They went around the other way!"

Doc and his two aides eyed the house. The girl who had said her name was Lanca Jaxon was leaning from a second story window, looking down at Stunted and waving an arm around the building.

"They got out of a window on this side," she cried excitedly. "They ran around when they heard you coming. Hurry up! They may be getting away!"

Stunted hesitated, growling. Then he spun and sprinted around the house, deceived by the girl.

THE young woman looked at Doc Savage and his two men. She could see them plainly, looking down from above as she was. Her arm waved sharply, gesturing that they should take advantage of the moment to escape.

They did so.

Scrub brush hid them just as a flood of men poured into the clearing which held the strange mansion. Monk had underestimated the numbers of the gang, for there was nearer two dozen than one, and all were heavily armed.

"What say we stick around and bushwhack with 'em?" Monk queried.

It was an idea which Doc Savage seemed to favor, but which proved unfeasible, for the gang found their trail and followed it with a rapidity which indicated that a skilled tracker was numbered among the enemy. Doc and his men were forced to retreat, closely followed.

A small stream, rocky of bottom, gave them respite. They waded along it—first going up and making a false trail on the bank, then reëntering the water and wading downstream. They turned back toward the house, confident the pursuers would waste much time untangling the tracks.

"That girl," Monk breathed wonderingly. "She helped us! But before, she stopped our getting away."

"You know," Ham said slowly, "It strikes me that when she held us up the first time, it might have been an accident. She might have thought we were with the gang."

"But what was she doing in the car?" Monk countered.

Ham shrugged. "I don't know. Possibly trying to get away herself."

Monk looked at Doc. "What about this girl?"

The bronze man said, "That is why we are going back."

Their flight had taken them almost two miles before they encountered the stream, and now, going back, they were cautious. They spread, separating from each other by the space of a hundred feet or so, in order that if one were discovered, the other might be clear to render assistance.

IT was Ham who, some ten minutes later, stopped in a clearing and squinted intently. He could see a building, a large shack of a structure, through a rent in the scrub-oak thickets. The obvious newness of the building intrigued him. He veered over to find Doc.

He was surprised, and a little chagrined, to discover the bronze man had already sighted the structure and had climbed a small tree in order to view it more closely.

"Think it has any connection with this gang?" Ham asked.

"They have been around the building," Doc said. "All of them just went inside. They had that girl along."

Ham exploded, "But I thought they were tailing us!"

"They gave that up some minutes ago," Doc advised him.

The bronze man whistled a perfect imitation of a bird common to Oklahoma, giving the call twice. It was the signal which they had agreed upon to summon each other, and Monk ambled up shortly, his small eyes curious.

"That shed of a building," Doc told him. "All of our friends seem to have gone inside it."

Monk swung up a small tree with an ease that could not have been bettered by one of the apes which he so closely resembled. He peered for a moment.

"That thing don't look like an ordinary shed," he said. "It's kinda round, for one thing."

"We are going to investigate," Doc told him.

The scrub oaks were thick, and down in a small valley which they found it necessary to cross, briars and small thorny bushes interlaced to form a barrier that they penetrated but slowly. On either side of the defile trees grew high, so that view of the shed was cut off completely.

They were still in the arroyo when they heard a long, brittle crack of a noise. It was very loud, with an utterly distinct quality. They had heard that noise before—in New York City, and in Oklahoma. It was a noise such as had been heard, according to newspaper and radio reports, by many persons in various parts of the United States. Always, it had been accompanied by threads of flame in the sky.

Doc and his two aides looked upward. There was no trace of a fiery ribbon in the heavens.

"Come on!" Doc rapped. "Let's get to that shed."

They raced forward. A moment later, Monk emitted an excited howl.

"That shed!" he bawled. "It's afire!"

THE shed must have been soaked with some inflammable compound, some substance which burned even more readily than gasoline, for it was a crackling pyre of flame when they reached it.

Trees, ignited by the terrific heat, were bursting into flame as far as a score of yards from the structure.

Doc and his men circled the spot. They saw nothing, heard no screams which would indicate human beings inside the burning structure. They would have been dead by now, anyway. There was nothing for the bronze man and his aides to do but to stand by and extinguish such of the flames as threatened to spread and become a forest fire.

Eventually, they went back to the house where they had been first attacked. Their attackers had flown thoroughly. The radio transmitting-and-receiving apparatus had been smashed. The odds and ends of clothing were gone.

Doc Savage had no fingerprinting outfit with him, but managed to improvise one by employing a mixture of ordinary pulverized pencil lead and burned cork on white surfaces in the kitchen regions.

He examined these, using the bottom which he broke from a milk bottle for a magnifier. He looked intently for some time at the prints thus brought out.

Monk and Ham watched him. Both were fully aware of the facility with which the bronze man retained a mental image. They were willing to bet he could run through a fingerprint classification days later and pick out any prints which matched those he was viewing now.

They searched for some time, but the house offered nothing more to solve the mystery of what was behind the murder of Willard Spanner, and the robbery of some millions of dollars from a Kansas City bank. Neither was there a clue to the meaning of the streaks in the sky and the accompanying cracking noises.

They went back to the shed, which had burned itself down. Poking through the hot embers was a procedure more fruitless than the search of the house. The incredibly hot fire had consumed everything inflammable, had melted together such metal work as there had been inside, making it unrecognizable, except for what apparently had been two large and excellent metal-working lathes.

"We're drawing blanks fast," Monk said.

Ham was sober. "I wonder what happened to that gang and the girl? Were they burned to death?"

Doc Savage said nothing.

They found the pig, Habeas Corpus, on their way back to Tulsa.

Chapter VII
PERIL IN FRISCO

THEY spent four hours investigating in Tulsa. Interesting things came to light.

The revolver which Monk had secured from the man knocked out in the radio room of the strange house in the brush had been sold to Leases Moore a year previously. Further inquiry brought to light the fact that Leases Moore had purchased a number of firearms, revolvers, shotguns, and automatic rifles, during the past six months.

"Which makes me think of Stunted's bobtailed automatic rifle," Monk growled.

The house in the hills had been built by an Osage made wealthy by oil, who had later died. This fact, corroborating what the gang had told Monk, Doc Savage secured from a rather remarkable "morgue" of personal sketches maintained by a feature writer on the *Graphic*, a Tulsa morning newspaper.

The feature writer was a dresser whose sartorial perfection rivaled that of Ham, and he was a mine of information. It seemed that he kept in his morgue bits of information about all persons of importance in and about Tulsa.

Doc Savage was enabled, through the morgue, to make an interesting scrutiny of the careers of Leases Moore and Quince Randweil.

Leases Moore was a broker of oilfield leases; in popular parlance, a "lease robber." He had never been in the penitentiary. That was about all that could be said for his business tactics. He was sharp, squeezing and scheming, qualities, it seemed, which had made him a millionaire.

Quince Randweil had started life as a small-time gambler, had trafficked in liquor during Prohibition, and had later taken over the local dog-racing track, a profitable affair indeed. He was also reported to be the undercover gambling czar locally, and not above turning a dishonest penny now and then.

But, like Leases Moore, he had never been convicted of a crime more serious than overtime parking, speeding, parking without lights and even jay-walking.

Of these trivial offenses, there was an incredible array of convictions. Doc Savage asked about that.

"The police tried to ride him out of town by picking him up on every conceivable charge," advised the sartorially perfect *Graphic* feature writer. "That was two years ago. It didn't work."

The really important development of the investigation came from the local airport. Monk turned it up when he perused the list of passengers taking planes that morning. He was excited when he got Doc Savage on the telephone at the *Graphic*.

"The Frisco angle is getting hot, Doc!" he declared.

The bronze man queried, "Yes?"

"Leases Moore and Quince Randweil caught the morning plane for San Francisco," Monk advised.

DOC SAVAGE did not hire a fast plane for the trip to San Francisco, as might ordinarily have been his course. There was a regular airliner due shortly, and it was faster than anything available for a quick charter. When the liner pulled out, he and his two aides were aboard it.

The plane had a radio. Doc communicated with New York, consulting his three aides who were there—"Johnny," "Long Tom," and "Renny." They had turned up nothing of importance in connection with the death of Willard Spanner.

At the first stop, Doc bought newspapers. There was much news concerning the flame streaks in the sky. Police were beginning to connect the phenomena with criminal activities, for in three distinct cases, in addition to the bank robbery in Kansas City, profitable crimes had been committed shortly before the weird streaks appeared in the heavens.

Doc and his two companions read the headlines while the plane was being fueled, and punctuated their reading with munches at sandwiches secured at the airport restaurant. Perhaps that was why they failed to notice a lean, neatly dressed man watching them.

The lean man was careful to keep his scrutiny furtive. He had boarded the plane in Tulsa, along with three other passengers in addition to Doc's party. He had two suitcases—one of medium size, one very large. He had seated himself well forward in the plane and had not once looked in Doc Savage's direction with anything bordering more than usual interest. He was doing his watching now from outside the airport restaurant window.

After the fueling, the man was first to enter the plane. He stooped over quickly, opened his small suitcase and took out an object which at first might have been mistaken for a bundle of tightly wound steel wire. He walked back and tucked this in one of the baggage racks where it would not be observed.

He left the plane, went hurriedly to the restaurant, and put in a long-distance call to an Arizona city. The promptness with which the call was completed indicated the other party had been awaiting it. The man consulted a code book.

"The weather is perfect," he said.

"Swell," said the voice over the wire. "We will pick you up, understand?"

"I understand," said the man.

He hung up, returned to the plane, and resumed his seat just before the giant craft took the air, motors making high-pitched sound outside the sound-proofed cabin. The air was rough, and the ship pitched slightly.

Below was an expanse of terrain not especially inviting to the eye, being composed mostly of sand and sagebrush, with here and there a butte, hardly impressive from the air, to break the monotony. The plane flew for two hours. The afternoon was well along.

The lean man stooped over and opened his large suitcase. It held a parachute. He had some difficulty wriggling into the harness, bending over as he was in order to avoid notice. When he had the harness almost in place, he lifted his head to see if he had attracted attention.

He had. Doc Savage was already in the aisle, and coming forward.

The lean man dived for the door. He had difficulty getting it open against the force of the propeller slipstream, but finally succeeded and lunged through. The face was triumphant. But the expression changed quickly. A hand—it felt like the clamp of some metal-compressing machine—had grasped his ankle.

The man cursed shrilly. He hung down from the plane, smashed about by the terrific rush of air, only the grip on his ankle preventing him from

falling clear. His body battered the hard plane fuselage. Then he was slowly hauled upward toward the plane door.

Desperate, the man whipped out a gun. He was not unlike a rag held in a stiff breeze, and his first shot went wild. Then, grasping the edge of the cabin door, he took deliberate aim.

Doc Savage let him fall. It was the only move that would preserve the bronze man's life.

THE lean man fell away behind, turning over and over in the air. That he had made parachute jumps before was evident from the way in which he kicked his legs to stop his gyrations in the air. Then he plucked the ripcord and the silk parachute blossomed out whitely.

The plane was in an uproar. Passengers yelled excitedly and crowded to the windows on the side of the door, upsetting the equilibrium of the plane and causing the pilot to do some howling of his own.

Doc Savage lunged to the side of the pilot.

"Follow that man down!" he rapped.

Such was the quality of compelling obedience in the bronze man's remarkable voice that the pilot obeyed without stopping to reason out why he should.

Monk charged forward, reached Doc and demanded, "Why'd that guy jump?"

Doc Savage sent one glance fanning the horizon and saw nothing to cause alarm. There was no signal visible below.

"Search the plane!" he said crisply.

Passengers objected strenuously to having their baggage rifled, and there was no time for explanations. Ham lost his temper and knocked out a young salesman who tried to defend a stout black case which, when Ham opened it, proved to contain a small fortune in gem samples.

Monk lost numerous of the red bristles which served him as hair to a fat woman who had no idea of seeing her fitted case opened by the simian chemist.

The pilot still fought the controls. The associate pilot and the hostess trying to do their bit toward restoring calm, only added to the bedlam.

It was Doc Savage who found the bomb that the lean man had hidden. He smashed a window and heaved it overboard. Whether the missile exploded when it hit the hard earth below, or slightly before, was difficult to decide, but a sizable cloud of smoke and debris arose—enough of a cloud to prove that the plane would have been blown into fragments.

THE pilot had followed the man with the parachute only until the balance of his plane had been affected by the shifting passengers, and in the ensuing excitement, he had forgotten the bronze man's orders. The ship was now some distance from the parachute.

The white silk lobe was only a spot on the desert floor. It had settled into a canyon, they saw.

Doc advanced again and spoke grimly to the pilot, and that worthy, suddenly apprised of the bronze man's identity and shown a small card, hastened to send the plane toward the parachute.

The card Doc displayed was one directing all employees of the air line to put themselves at his service upon request, and had been issued partially because Doc Savage, a man of more wealth than anyone dreamed, owned a goodly portion of the airline stock.

It was impossible to land in the canyon. The nearest terrain for a safe descent was fully a mile distant. The pilot put his ship down there.

"Armed?" Doc asked the pilot.

The flier nodded.

Doc, Monk, and Ham raced for the canyon. It was rough going. Mesquite prongs raked their clothing and cactus prodded painfully. Once a rattlesnake *whirred*, and shortly after that Monk made a loud gulping noise and stopped. He said something.

Whatever he said was lost in a loud, rending crack of a noise which seemed to come from the direction of the canyon.

"There's that thing again!" Monk growled, and searched the sky in vain for some trace of a flame thread.

They ran on.

Then they heard the crack of a noise again, and once more listened and searched with their eyes. Again, they saw nothing in the sky.

The perusal of the heavens might have been an omen—they found no trace of their quarry when they reached the canyon. They did locate the parachute where it had been abandoned. Tracks in the sand showed where the would-be killer had fled. They followed these.

The tracks terminated in inexplicable fashion in the midst of an expanse of sand which bore every imprint with amazing distinctness. But where the tracks vanished there was a queer disturbance, as if a small and terrific whirlwind had sucked up the sand, then let it sift back.

Monk, frowning, insisted that some of the sand already floated in the air.

They hunted for an hour before they resigned themselves to conviction that, in some manner as yet unexplained, the one they sought had managed to vanish.

"This thing has had a lot of dizzy angles so far," Monk grumbled. "But this one takes the cookies."

Chapter VIII
THE DEAD MAN'S BROTHER

IT was foggy in San Francisco. The air was full of moisture. The newspapers which Monk brought into Doc Savage's hotel room were soft with wetness. Monk seemed baffled, and he waved the papers.

"It's all over 'em!" he complained. "Here we've been in Frisco less than two hours and it's all over the newspapers. Now what I want to know is who told 'em we were here?"

Doc Savage said, "I did."

Monk shook his head. "But we generally keep out of the papers all we can."

"We have few clues to go on," Doc said. "None, in fact."

"Don't I know it!"

"So if these men come to us, even with the intention of getting us out of the way, it will put us in contact with them, at least," Doc said.

Monk grinned doubtfully. "Well, that's one way of doing it."

Doc Savage took one of the newspapers, but gave only brief attention to the story concerning his arrival in San Francisco. The item indicated, among other things, that the bronze man was on the West coast to investigate the murder of his friend, Willard Spanner. Or had there been a murder?

There was another story concerning the Willard Spanner affair. The newspaper publisher who had received the first letter demanding a money payment for Spanner's release had received a second missive, insisting that Spanner was still alive and demanding money for his safety.

"This may be a newspaper publicity stunt," Monk suggested. "I've known some of the wilder papers to stoop to things like that."

Doc Savage lifted the telephone and got in communication with the publisher who had received the missives. Doc made his identity known.

"I would like to see those notes," he said.

The publisher tried to bargain.

"In return for them, you'll have to let us write up your movements exclusively in our paper," he said.

"We will do nothing of the sort," Doc said promptly.

"Then you can whistle for the notes," he was told.

The bronze man showed no emotion.

"Suit yourself," he said.

The publisher sounded less certain when he asked, "What are you going to do about it?"

"Tell the other newspapers what you are doing," Doc advised. "The fact that you are going so far as to block efforts to find Spanner, if alive, for the sake of a story, should make interesting reading. I also have a Federal agent's commission. The Federal authorities will be interested in your refusal of information and cooperation to an agent. I may think of other measures. For instance, the majority stock in your sheet is owned by a chain of which I am a director."

"You win," said the newspaperman. "I'll send the notes over."

Doc had hardly hung up when the telephone rang. It was the clerk downstairs.

"A Mr. Nock Spanner to see Doc Savage," he said. "Mr. Spanner says he is a brother of Willard Spanner."

"Send him up," Doc said, and replaced the receiver.

THE bronze man advised Monk and Ham that a visitor was coming up, and told them his name.

"Willard Spanner's brother!" Monk exploded. "I didn't know he had a brother!"

"He has," Doc said.

"Ever met him?" Monk asked.

"No," Doc said. "The brother is a military expert, and has been in China for a number of years."

There was a knock at the door, and Doc arose and admitted the visitor.

Nock Spanner was a hard-bodied man of more than average height. Although his hair was slightly gray at the temples, his age was probably not much past thirty. On his left hand he wore a rather large wrist watch, the band of which was composed of Chinese coins, linked together.

"I read in the newspapers that you were in San Francisco, investigating the mystery about my brother," he said in a crisp voice which held a hint of the accent sometimes acquired by Americans spending a period of years in a foreign land. "I just arrived this morning."

"Have you any idea why your brother was in San Francisco?" Doc queried.

Nock Spanner turned the wrist band of Chinese coins, which seemed to fit a bit too tight for comfort.

"To meet me, of course," he said. "We had not seen each other for seven years. I had finished my work in China and was coming back to the States to live."

"You have any ideas about this?"

Nock Spanner straightened the wrist band. "I have made enemies in China. I did not think, however, that they would strike at me through my brother."

"You think that possible?"

Nock Spanner shrugged. "I am at a loss to think of anything else. Of course, I knew little about my brother's connections in the States. He might have made enemies of his own. Or someone may merely want money. If so, I am willing to pay. Fifty thousand was the sum demanded, so the newspapers say."

"You have it?"

Nock Spanner nodded. He took a large automatic with a thin barrel from a pocket. Then he brought out a roll of bills, tapped them and returned them to the pocket.

"I can pay," he said. "But I want to know if my brother is alive. I want the writers of those notes asked a question. If they answer it correctly, I will know my brother is alive."

"Is it a sure-fire question?" Doc asked.

"It is. I'll ask him my middle name, which I haven't used since childhood, and which I'll guarantee no one but my brother knows."

"All right," Doc told him. "The notes will be here shortly."

A MESSENGER brought the notes. They were printed on rough brown paper, the hardest kind of material to identify, and there were no fingerprints on them. They were simple and intelligently worded, stating that Willard Spanner was alive and would be released upon the payment of fifty thousand dollars in small bills. The last line gave the method of communication:

WILL TELEPHONE YOU WHEN
WE JUDGE TIME PROPER

"They're taking a chance when they use the telephone," Monk offered.

"They can call from some remote spot and depart quickly," Doc replied.

The telephone rang.

"Yes," Doc said into the mouthpiece.

"That newspaper guy said to call you," stated a voice which held a deliberate, artificial shrillness.

"About what?" Doc asked.

"About Willard Spanner," said the voice. "I'm one of the guys who's got him."

Using the hand with which he was not holding the telephone, Doc Savage made small, rapid posturing motions. Monk watched these, reading them—for the gestures were those of the accepted one-hand deaf-and-dumb sign language, and the homely chemist was being directed to trace the call.

Monk departed hastily.

"We have to know for certain that Willard Spanner is alive," Doc said. "It is reported that his body was found in New York somewhat less than three hours after he was seized in San Francisco."

"How we gonna do that?" the shrill voice asked.

"Ask Willard Spanner for his brother Nock's

middle name," Doc advised. "The answer will tell us if he is alive."

"Sure." The other hung up.

It was some five minutes before Monk entered the room, wearing a downcast expression.

"Too fast," he said. "The connection was down before we could trace it."

"Instantaneous tracing of telephone calls is successful in fiction," Doc told him. "In actual practice, there are slips."

Nock Spanner had stood by, fingering the tight band of Chinese coins about his wrist during the last few minutes. Now he stepped forward.

"Just so there won't be any doubt," he said, and got a sheet of paper and an envelope from the room desk. He wrote briefly on the paper, standing so that none could see what he was imprinting, then inserted the sheet in the envelope, sealed it and gave it to Doc Savage.

"The name is written inside," he advised. "Unless they come back at us with that name, they haven't got Willard."

The telephone rang. It was the voice with the disguising artificial shrillness.

"The brother's middle name is Morency," the voice stated.

Instantly afterward, the other receiver clicked up. There had been no chance to trace the call.

Doc Savage opened the envelope handed him by Nock Spanner. There was one name printed on the stationery inside:

MORENCY

"Willard is alive," said Nock Spanner. "This proves it to me!"

JUDGING that there would be future calls from the men who claimed to he holding Willard Spanner—if, incredibly enough, he was still alive, as it seemed now—Doc Savage made preparations.

He got in touch with the telephone company and, after some discussion, succeeded in having the entire testboard crew set to work watching such calls as might come to his hotel. They were to trace each call instantly. With luck, they might succeed.

It was fully an hour later when the call came. The same disguised voice made it.

"You will take the money, get in an automobile and drive out of San Francisco on the main Los Angeles road," the voice directed. "Watch the fences on your right. When you see a piece of green cloth on a fence, throw the money overboard. We'll turn Spanner loose."

There was a momentary pause while the other took a deep breath.

"And listen, Doc Savage," he continued. "You're supposed to be a tough guy, but if you cross me, it'll be tough for you and Willard Spanner both!"

The other receiver clicked.

Doc Savage kept his own receiver to his ear, and not more than twenty seconds passed before a briskly business-like feminine telephone operator came in on the wire and said:

"That last call was made from 6932 Fantan Road."

Doc's arrangement for the immediate tracing of incoming calls with the telephone company had worked.

Nock Spanner waved his arms wildly when the bronze man started for the door.

"But aren't you going to do what they demanded?" he barked.

"No," Doc informed him. "The voice on the telephone was not sufficiently anxious about the money."

Spanner blinked. "What do you mean?"

"I mean simply that the thing smells like an ingenious scheme to draw us to this 6932 Fantan Road."

Monk and Ham were following the bronze man.

"A trap?" Nock Spanner exploded.

"Possibly," Doc agreed.

"What are you going to do?"

"Oblige the gentleman on the telephone, to some extent," Doc replied.

Nock Spanner trailed along behind them, looking very uneasy.

FANTAN ROAD started auspiciously with fine mansions and new asphalt, but that was down in the five and ten-hundred-number blocks, and when Doc Savage had followed the thoroughfare out to the sixties, it had dwindled to the remnant of some high-pressure subdivision realtor's bad dream.

Finally, there was no pavement at all, and not much road, only two ruts in sand and weeds. Even the telephone line draped slackly from poles which were not all of the same length. It had been a long time since they had seen a house with a number on it, and just why there should be numbers on a dwelling out this far, without a rural designation attached, was a mystery.

Doc Savage made no effort to pull their rented car off the road, but stopped it and cut the engine.

Nock Spanner stood up in the seat—the car was an open phaeton—and peered about. The radiator made boiling noises.

"Darned if I see a house," he said.

"It should be less than half a mile ahead," Doc told him.

They left the car with its hot, sobbing radiator and advanced, walking through sand that repeatedly filled their low shoes, a circumstance which moved Monk to take off his footgear and pad along barefooted.

"The jungle ape in you coming out," Ham commented.

Monk only grinned and kicked sand back against the overlong snout of the pig, Habeas, who had paused to harass a large, black, frightened beetle. On either side there was woodland, the trees thick and large, sprouting from a mat of brush.

Doc Savage watched the road closely and discerned the prints of tires. They were not many. At one point, he noted in which direction spinning wheels had tossed sand. Before long, he had concluded three cars had traversed the road recently—two rather, for one had come and returned, and the other, its tires of a different tread and state of wear, had gone only one way. All of the tracks had been made that day. Night dew has a way of altering the appearance of a trail.

Doc Savage left the other three abruptly without explanation, and went ahead.

"What's his idea?" Nock Spanner demanded suspiciously.

"He does that regular," Monk explained. "He's gonna look things over. We'd better take it easy."

Doc Savage did not follow the two ruts along the sand that was the road, but turned into the undergrowth and moved there. It was uncanny, the silence with which he traveled. There was no sign of a house as yet. But the telephone people had said there was a dwelling here, so there must be one.

The bronze man was traveling downwind from the road, and was scenting the air from time to time. Years of training had not quite given him the olfactory organs of a wild animal, but his senses were developed far beyond those of ordinary ability.

He caught the odor of tobacco smoke. He trailed it upwind, and if his caution had been remarkable before, it was miraculous now. He made no sound in coming upon two figures crouched beside the road.

They were men. They were arguing.

"I tell you I heard a car," one said. "It stopped down the road. That's suspicious!"

"You're always hearing things," said the other, sourly.

Possibly the hearing of both was a trifle deficient, for it was hardly reasonable that neither should know of Doc Savage's presence until the giant of bronze hurled down upon them; but such was what happened.

Doc had calculated his leap carefully and nothing went amiss. He landed with a hand on the back of each man's neck, and the shock of that drove them down, burying their faces in the gritty earth. They struggled. One man managed to bleat out a cry. He sounded like a caught rabbit.

Terrific pressure, skillfully administered, began to tell, so that the pair groveled with less violence, finally becoming limp and all but unconscious. Doc turned them over.

They were Leases Moore and Quince Randweil.

Chapter IX
MURDER SPREE

THE piping bleat—Quince Randweil had emitted it—had been loud enough to carry to Monk, Ham, and Nock Spanner, and they came up, running on their toes for greater silence.

"Ah, the two gentlemen of mystery," Ham said dryly.

"They were watching the road," Doc told him.

Doc Savage had not induced the remarkable paralytic state which he could administer by pressure upon certain spinal nerve centers, so Quince Randweil and Leases Moore soon revived enough to speak. They behaved in a manner somewhat unexpected.

"Boy, I'm glad to see you!" said Leases Moore, who had put false teeth in his mouth and now did not look unhandsome.

"You said it!" echoed Quince Randweil, making it sound like "shedd."

"Oh," Monk leered fearsomely, "so now you're glad to see us! Yes, you are!"

"Truly we are," lisped Quince Randweil.

"And why in blue blazes shouldn't we be?" Leases Moore demanded sourly. "We made a bad move and we know it now."

"I see." Monk made his leer more impressive. "An explanation for everything, I bet."

"Nuts!" said Leases Moore, and began to look mad.

"Now, now!" Quince Randweil lisped excitedly and made admonishing gestures. "It will not do good to get all bothered. Of course you gentlemen are aggravated with us!"

"That's a mild word for it," Monk told him.

Randweil lisped on as if he had not heard, saying, "It was our rugged individualism which made us act as we did. Yes, our rugged individualism."

Individualism was a strange sound the way he said it. He made it, "inniwissilissim."

He continued, "You see, we were mad. *Very* mad. We had heard that our enemies were coming to San Francisco, to this house at 6932 Fantan Road. We overheard that. So, being very mad and wanting to get even, we came out here. But we have not been having such good luck."

Monk said, "It's a good thing lightning don't strike liars."

"You don't believe it?" Randweil sounded hurt.

"Sure I do," Monk replied, as sarcastically as possible.

Randweil looked at Doc Savage. "Do you believe me?"

Doc Savage asked, "By now, have you any idea of what is behind all of this—the murder of Willard Spanner, the queer streaks in the sky, and the rest?"

"Not an idea," declared Randweil.

"And that's the truth," echoed Leases Moore, rubbing the knob which was his missing thumb.

"Of course," Monk agreed, more sarcastically than before.

Leases Moore yelled, "It is, and all of you can go chase yourselves! I'm not a guy you can horse around!"

Monk looked at Doc hopefully. "Shall I do some of my exercises on this guy?"

Doc replied nothing.

Monk registered cheerfulness, told Leases Moore, "There'll be more than your thumb and teeth missing when I get through with you."

"Hold it," Doc said, "while I look around a bit."

THE bronze man employed his usual caution in advancing through the brush, and when he had traversed a hundred feet, paused and listened at great length, in order to ascertain if anyone were approaching, drawn by the noise made when Moore and Randweil were seized.

He heard nothing suspicious.

Birds had fallen silent, quieted by the sounds of the brief scuffle, but now they became noisy. So furtive was the bronze man's progress that not often were the feathered songsters disturbed.

The timber became thicker, with less brush and higher, more sturdy trees. Underfoot, the brush gave way to moss and dead leaves. Ahead, Doc Savage caught sight of a building of some kind.

The crack of a noise came then.

Its note was the same as on other occasions—sudden, strange, a noise unlike anything else Doc Savage ever had heard.

There was a strange thing in the sky....

The bronze man whipped for the handiest tree. His climbing was amazing. He had picked a tree of somewhat thin foliage. A moment later, he was high up in it. His eyes roved overhead—and riveted there.

There was a strange thing in the sky. No ribbon of weird fire. It looked like a ball of some dull, glassy substance. In diameter, the thing approached a score of feet, and its surface was not all of the same obsidian nature, but freckled with lighter and darker spots in an even pattern.

The fantastic ball was hanging back where Monk and the others had been left. It appeared to be little more than a hundred feet up. Nor was it perfectly stationary, but bounced up and down slowly, as if it had just landed on an invisible rubber mat.

The thing was surrounded by a faint haze which resembled steam—and *was* steam, Doc surmised an instant later: water particles in the mist being vaporized against the ball, which had been made hot by its terrific rate of passage through the air.

The ball was an aerial conveyance obviously, a thing of new and amazing design, a vehicle along lines utterly at variance with those on which aeronautical engineers commonly worked.

Most surprising, of course, was the lack of streamlining to be expected in a device capable of such unearthly speed. It bore no resemblance to the fish-bodied conformation sought after by designers. It was a perfect globe.

There was an explanation, somewhat startling in its possibility. The planets in space, the stars, moon, sun, were round or nearly so, and this, some scientists maintained, was a result of the application of the mysterious gravitational forces.

Was some machination with gravity responsible for the amazing powers of this ball?

There was another explanation for the lack of streamlining, a bit more sensible. The ball seemed

It looked like a ball of some dull, glassy substance.

capable of moving in any direction without turning. Was not a spherical shape the most perfect attainable streamlining for a body which must move in any direction?

Doc drove a hand inside his clothing, where he carried a small, powerful telescope. But before he could focus the lenses, the amazing ball dropped with eye-defying abruptness, and was lost back of the trees. Judging by the swiftness of its descent, there should have been a loud jar as it struck, but there was no such sound.

Doc Savage released his grip on the limb to which he had been clinging. He dropped halfway to the ground before he grasped another bough, held to it long enough to break his fall, then plunged on to the ground. He sprinted through the growth.

At first, he was cautious. Then something happened which led him to surrender silence to speed. He heard a loud, agonized bawl; unmistakably Monk's voice. Someone cursed. Doc ran faster. He heard brush crashings ahead.

Then came the cracking sound. It was something different this time, starting with a whistle of something going with terrific speed—and the crack followed, long and mounting frightfully, then dying away, as if betaking itself into the distance.

At the first note, Doc halted, stared. His scrutiny was on the sky. He thought he saw something. He was not sure. If anything, what he glimpsed was a blurred streak which arched upward until it was entirely lost. It was no fiery ribbon, however. The bronze man went on, seeking the party he had left shortly before.

He found Monk, Ham, and Nock Spanner, but not Leases Moore and Quince Randweil. The first three were stretched out motionless in the brush.

THERE had been a terrific fight, judging from the violence done and the state of the victims. Monk had two ugly cuts on the head, Ham one. Spanner had evidently been slugged in the face, for his lips were stringing scarlet over the green leaves of a bush which he had mashed down in falling.

Doc Savage listened. There was a leafy shuffling, and the pig, Habeas, came out of the brush, looked at Doc with small eyes, then turned and went back into the undergrowth. There was no other sound. Even the birds had fallen silent.

Doc Savage bent over the victims. Ham was already mumbling incoherently and endeavoring to sit up. Doc gave attention to Monk, and was working over him when Ham's head cleared.

The dapper lawyer stared at the prostrate, apish chemist. A horrified expression overspread his features as he saw the gore about Monk's head wounds.

"Monk!" he rasped. "Is he dead?"

Doc Savage said nothing.

Ham staggered up and wailed, "Monk—is he all right? He's the best friend I've got!"

Without opening his small eyes, Monk mumbled, "Who's my friend? I ain't got a friend, except Habeas."

Ham switched his anxiety for a black scowl and came over and kicked Monk, far from gently, in the side.

"I was not talking about you," he snapped.

The pig, Habeas Corpus, came out of the brush again, looked at them queerly, then turned around exactly as he had done before and entered the brush.

Monk sat up and began administering to himself, and Doc gave attention to Nock Spanner, chafing his wrists, pinching him to induce arousing pain, until finally Spanner rolled over and put both hands to his bruised mouth.

The instant Spanner was cognizant of his surroundings, he whipped his hand from his mouth to the pocket in which he carried his money.

"Robbed!" he screamed. "Fifty thousand dollars! Gone!"

He began to swear loudly, his profane remarks growing more and more shrill and violent until they were almost the utterings of a madman.

"That won't help." Monk put his hands over his ears. "Besides, I ain't used to such words."

"My life savings!" Spanner shrieked. "And you crack wise! It's no joke!"

"With this head of mine, nothing is a joke," Monk growled. "Only, bellowing won't get it back."

Habeas Corpus came out of the brush and went back again.

Doc Savage said, "The pig is trying to show us something."

Monk swayed erect, weaved a small circle and fell down; groaning, he got up again. Nock Spanner stared realizing that the homely chemist had been badly knocked out. For the next few moments Spanner was silent, as if ashamed of his own hysterical outburst.

They went through the brush slowly, for the three who had been attacked were in no shape for brisk traveling.

"What happened?" Doc Savage asked them.

"IT was that thing in the sky," Monk said hoarsely. "We heard a crack of noise, and looked over here"—he pointed ahead—"and there it was. It looked like some kind of hard, funny glass—"

"A new and unique terrestrial space ship," Doc interposed.

"Yeah?" Monk frowned.

"Globe shaped," Doc elaborated. "It can move in any direction. Its actual propelling machinery I do not yet understand, except that it is almost soundless."

"Soundless!" Monk exploded. "That crack of a noise—"

"Did you ever have a bullet pass very close to your ear?" Doc asked.

"Have I?" grunted Monk.

"What did it sound like?" Doc persisted. "Was it a whine?"

"Heck, no," said Monk. "It was—" He stopped, mouth open, understanding coming over him.

"Exactly," Doc told him. "A body moving through the air at terrific speed pushes the air aside and leaves a vacuum behind, and the air closing into this vacuum makes a distinct report. That accounts for the noise these terrestrial ball ships make."

Monk sighed mightily.

"Well, if a devil with two spikes on his tail had jumped up, we couldn't have been more surprised when we saw this ball thing, ship or whatever it is," he mumbled. "I was goggling at the thing when the lights went out for me."

"Leases Moore picked up a stick and hit you," Ham told him. "About the same time that Randweil struck me, knocking me senseless."

Nock Spanner chimed in, "And they both piled onto me. Randweil held me and Moore used his fist. That was the last I remember."

Monk said soberly, "Funny thing."

Ham snapped peevishly, "Everything seems funny to you the last few days!"

Monk shook his damaged head as if he did not want to squabble.

"When I was struck down, I didn't go out immediately," he said, speaking slowly, as if the information he were giving was painful. "I was in kind of a coma, or something. And just before I passed out, I'll swear that I saw the girl."

Ham demanded, "What girl?"

"The one in Oklahoma," Monk elaborated. "Lanca Jaxon."

"Hallucination," Ham said, skeptically.

"Maybe," Monk nursed his head. "But she was coming through the brush with that runt Stunted. Then she turned around and went back toward where that ball of a thing had been hanging in the sky."

Doc Savage stopped. "It was no hallucination."

"I didn't think it was," Monk told him. "But how do you know?"

Doc pointed at the sandy ground underfoot. It retained the impression of a foot—narrow, high of heel, unmistakably feminine.

"I wish we could talk to that young lady for a while," Ham said grimly. "She could deuced well explain a number of things."

They caught sight of the pig, Habeas. The shoat's enormous ears were thrown back in order that they might not be scratched by the thorny undergrowth, and if actions were any indication, he had been waiting to see if they were following him.

Nock Spanner said, "That is the most remarkable hog I ever saw."

"He's been trained for years," Monk grunted. "Say, that ball of a jigger was hanging over here somewhere."

They stepped forward more briskly and came out in what amounted to a clearing, although the place was furred over with short brush and tall grass. This growth was mashed down over a spot a dozen feet across, as if something heavy had come to rest upon it.

At the edge of the area where the brush was crushed, there lay three dead men.

Chapter X
DEATH ZONE

DEAD bodies have a certain distinctive grotesqueness which indicated their condition, and these three were certainly dead. Bullets had finished one of them, knives the other two.

The knife victims were not dressed as expensively as the one slain by lead, their clothing being cheaply made, nor did they seem as intelligent a type.

Doc Savage and his aides had seen the two knife victims before.

"Members of the gang!" Monk exploded.

"Worthies who were with the crew in Tulsa, and in New York," Ham said more precisely.

Doc glanced at Nock Spanner. "Ever see them before?"

Spanner shook his head. "Strangers to me."

Doc Savage bent over the victims, searching, but with little expectation of finding anything, for he had already seen that the pockets were turned inside out, indicating the unfortunates had been previously gone over.

The garments of the bullet victim held no label. These had been cut out carefully.

There were labels in the clothing of the other two, and these indicated, not surprisingly, that the suits had been purchased from a department store in Tulsa, Oklahoma.

Doc returned his attention to the man who had been shot.

"Been dead at least ten hours," he said.

Monk and Ham showed no surprise at that until Monk, watching the knife victims morbidly, suddenly perceived that scarlet still oozed from their wounds.

"Hey!" he exploded. "These other two—"

"Were killed only a few moments ago," Doc told him. "Probably while that mysterious ball of a thing was resting here."

Doc Savage gave more attention to the body of the victim who had been dead the longer period. He unscrewed lenses from his telescope, and these served as excellent magnifiers; in proper combination, they afforded magnification which could be surpassed only by the more expensive of microscopes.

"Finding anything?" Ham asked.

Doc did not reply, and Ham showed no sign of being offended, for he was accustomed to the bronze man's manner of lapsing into unexplained spells of apparent deafness, usually when questioned upon points about which he had formed no opinion definite enough to voice, or when asked about something which he wished to keep for himself, possibly to spring later as a complete surprise.

Monk nursed his gashed head and complained, "So far, I don't make heads or tails of this. It's the dizziest dang thing I've run up against!"

Nock Spanner waved his arms and growled. "What about my brother? What about that house we came out here to investigate? We haven't done anything about that yet."

Doc Savage reassembled the parts of his telescope and pocketed it.

"We will have a look at the house," he said.

"If any," Spanner muttered.

"There is one," Doc told him. "I saw it through the trees just before this—interruption."

THE house was about what might be expected. It was old. Once, when this had been a more remote region, and before some over-enthusiastic real estate promoter had gotten hold of the region, it had been a fruit ranch. It looked as if it had not been lived in for a year or two.

They came upon a path that lay about a hundred and fifty yards from the structure, and Doc Savage at once moved ahead, voicing no word of explanation. The others were too concerned with their own hurts to be overly inquisitive.

The path turned. For a brief time, Doc Savage was concealed from the others, and during that interval he went through some rapid motions. A bottle came out of his clothing. It held a liquid which resembled rather thick, colorless syrup, and he sprinkled this over the path.

The bottle was out of sight when the others came in view. They walked through the sticky substance on the path without noting its presence. Doc said nothing. They went on.

Behind weeds that grew thickly along the fence of what had once been a corral, they waited and used their ears. Monk and the other two heard nothing, but aware of the bronze man's super-trained hearing, they glanced inquiringly at him.

"Apparently no one around," Doc said.

They eased toward the house. Its decrepit nature became more pronounced. Portions of the roof had no shingles at all. Most of the windows were gone.

Monk suggested, "Wonder if we hadn't better scatter out, in case something happens. If it's a trap, we don't want 'em to nab us all in one bunch."

"Good idea," Nock Spanner agreed, and when Doc Savage did not veto the proposal, they separated, flattening out in the weedy cover.

"I will go in," Doc said.

He left the others, worked ahead on all fours, and gained the door. Only the top hinge supported the panel. No sound came from within. Doc entered.

Plaster had fallen off walls and ceiling and was in lumpy profusion underfoot. Powdered spots indicated where the stuff had been stepped on recently. Doc made a closer examination. Men had been in the house very recently. He went on to another room, equally as cluttered up, and stood listening.

There was sound now, rather strange sound—a faint, high-pitched singing noise. It did not undulate, but came steadily, proof that no cricket was making it, although the note did sound vaguely like that insect.

Doc whipped for the source of the noise—an adjacent room. The instant he was through the door, he saw what was making it.

A portable radio transmitter stood on the floor. It was in operation. Nearby was another, slightly larger box of apparatus, and from that ran wires which progressed through cracks in the floor.

Doc hurriedly examined the second box. The workings of the thing were intricate, but not so complex that the bronze man's scientific skill failed to perceive their nature.

The box was a delicate electrical capacity balance, an instrument constructed to register, by having its capacity balance upset, when any new object came near it. It was merely a development of the old regenerative radio receivers which howled when a hand was brought near them—only this, instead of howling, actuated a sensitive relay which in turn set the radio transmitter to sending a steady oscillating signal.

Exactly such a device as this must have been employed back at the oyster plant in New York to detect the approach of Doc Savage. Here, it had served the same purpose, except that it started the radio transmitter in lieu of actuating some other signal.

Doc spun about, raced out of the room. There was furious haste in his movements. The instant he was outdoors his powerful voice crashed a warning.

"Get away from here!" he rapped. "It's a trap!"

Monk heaved up instantly from among the weeds. Ham appeared a short distance to his right.

They waited.

"Spanner!" Doc called.

Nock Spanner did not show himself. Doc called again. Only silence answered.

"Blazes!" Monk snapped. "That's blasted strange!"

"WHERE was Nock Spanner when you last saw him?" Doc Savage questioned.

Monk pointed. "Over there."

They went to the spot. There was a trail where the leaves had been mashed down, the weeds crushed. But it only led for a short distance before it became difficult to follow.

"He was heading back toward the brush," Ham said dryly. "Now I wonder what his idea was?"

"Might have seen someone," Monk said, in a tone which indicated he doubted the prediction.

Doc Savage dug a small flat flask out of his clothing. It was filled with greenish pellets hardly larger than common rice. He began shaking these out on the ground, and the moment they were exposed to the air they began turning into a rather bilious-looking vapor. This was swept away quickly by the wind.

But the strange vaporized pellets did one remarkable thing to the surrounding growth and the ground: they brought out tracks—tracks that showed with a distinct, sinister yellowish tint.

Monk gulped, "Well, for—" He looked down and saw that he himself was leaving the yellowish footprints wherever he moved. Ham's tracks likewise showed. Only Doc Savage left no trail.

"A sticky chemical I let you walk through," Doc explained. "This vapor causes a chemical reaction which makes your tracks visible."

Ham clipped, "Then you suspected that—"

"Just a precaution," Doc told him. "Hurry! We've got to find Nock Spanner and get away from here."

They began following the remarkable trail which Spanner had unknowingly left.

"Any sign of Nock Spanner's brother, Willard?" Ham asked.

"No," Doc replied.

They were in the woods now, away from the corrals, the rickety sheds. The tracks became farther apart, as if Nock Spanner had started running here.

"Darn his soul!" Monk ejaculated. "I can't understand what got into him."

"Listen!" Doc ripped suddenly.

He said only the one short word, but it was hardly out of his mouth before their eardrums all but collapsed under a terrific, rending crack of a report. Instinct made them look up. Surprise put expressions of blankness on their faces.

A fantastic, glistening ball of a thing was suspended above them. It was not the same ball they had seen before. This one was smaller, its color slightly different. And stretching from it and away into the sky was a trail that might have been left by a fast-moving skyrocket.

The ball was hot. They could feel its heat against their faces—heat which undoubtedly came from the friction of the air against its shiny hull at tremendous speed. As gusts of particularly damp mist struck it, the gleaming skin threw off faint wisps of steam.

"Under cover!" Doc shouted.

They lunged under the trees, and a fractional moment later, the ball dropped, hitting with a pronounced jar where they had stood.

"Blazes!" Monk gulped. "It's a stout thing!"

The ball seemed to be cooling off rapidly—more rapidly than was quite natural.

"Probably has an inner and outer shell, heavily insulated against heat," Doc said grimly. "Otherwise, it would get too hot inside for human life, and that in only a short period of traveling. And from the way it's cooling off, I judge that much of the heat is absorbed by refrigeration from within."

The ball lifted slowly and hung suspended in the air, unpleasantly like a fantastic bird of prey.

MONK, scrambling through the undergrowth, rasped, "The darn thing is trying to mash us!"

The ball floated back and forth and, peering closely, Doc and his men discovered what might possibly be periscopic windows, showing outwardly as little more than big lenses, at various points on the skin of the thing. They were not in one spot, but were located on top, bottom, sides.

"Got eyes all over, like the head of a fly," Monk complained.

The terrestrial ship leaped to a spot above them. As it moved, it left a distinct trail of what resembled glowing red sparks.

"That explains the fire streaks in the sky!" Monk barked.

Doc Savage nodded. "The luminous particles are exhaust from whatever mechanism propels the thing."

"But some of the balls don't leave a trail!" Monk pointed out.

"Possibly more perfected specimens," Doc told him grimly. "They may have equipped some of the ships with digesters which eliminate the luminous exhaust!"

That was a rank guess on the bronze man's part, a guess which, later developments showed, was accurate.

Doc and his men began to run, seeking to keep under cover. It was difficult, almost impossible, for the woodland here was open, and the fabulous bulb sank itself in the trees and turned slowly, as if it were a fantastic organism, with eyes, brain, and perceptive senses all in its round, gleaming torso.

Then it lifted a little and drifted over Doc and his men where they had been spied out.

There was a clicking noise and a small metal blob dropped earthward. It thudded into the dead leaves and popped itself open not unlike a large and very rotten egg. Exactly the same thing happened a bit to the other side of Doc's party.

"Gas!" Ham shouted, then coughed violently, stood up very straight, grasped his throat with both hands and pulled at it as if trying to free something lodged there. He was still pulling at his throat when he fell over.

Monk tumbled over beside him.

Whether it was due to his superior physical resistance, or to the fact that he held his breath, Doc Savage was able to run some distance and probably would have gotten away, except that the gas seemed to be assimilated through the pores of the skin almost as effectively as through the lungs.

Doc fell down a full hundred yards from the others.

WHEN Doc Savage awakened, the voice of the short man known as Stunted was saying, "I didn't figure I'd live to see this day. I sure didn't!"

When the bronze man opened his eyes, it was to see Stunted standing over him, a sawed-off automatic rifle tucked under an arm.

"No, sir, I didn't think we'd ever get you," Stunted told the bronze man.

Doc moved his arms over an area of a few inches. They were limited to that motion by handcuffs, huge and strong, one pair with oversize bands located above his elbows, three more pairs above his wrists.

He shifted his ankles. There were three more pairs of manacles there, and his knees were roped together and the knots wired.

"We're getting cautious," Stunted told him.

Doc moved his head. Monk and Ham lay nearby, both handcuffed, Monk with nearly as many pair of manacles as secured the bronze man. Neither Monk nor Ham were conscious.

"They'll come out of it," Stunted said. "That gas wasn't the kind that kills, according to what the chief told us."

The man with the queerly behaving eyes came over scowling, shoved Stunted away and said, "Still working that mouth overtime!"

Stunted glared at him. "My rope's got an end, fella."

The lanky man with the queer eyes ignored that, and frowned at Doc Savage.

"Where did Leases Moore and Quince Randweil go?" he demanded.

"That," Doc told him slowly, "is something I also should like to know."

The other blackened his frown. "So they were around, huh?"

"They were."

The man swore, and the nature of his profanity indicated he had lived some of his past on a cow ranch.

"The two locoed jugheads!" he finished. "We found two of our boys dead out in the brush, where one of the balls had landed. Leases Moore and Quince Randweil killed them and took charge of the ball, didn't they?"

"The thought has occurred to me," Doc admitted.

"Just the thing we've been trying to prevent!" the man snarled, and his eyes crossed horribly.

Doc asked, "Who was the third dead man? The one who had been dead some time?"

The other man opened his mouth as if, in his absentmindedness, he was about to make a correct answer, then his eyes suddenly straightened.

"Never mind that," he snapped.

"Where is the girl?" Doc queried.

Stunted said dryly, "Them two skunks, Moore and Randweil, must've kept her alive. They would. Gonna use her the same way he was."

The man with the roving eyes yelled, "Looks as if only a bullet will cork that trap of yours!"

Stunted advised, "Any time you feel lucky, you can try to put the cork in."

Instead of taking up the challenge, the other wheeled and stalked away.

THE man with the uneasy eyes was back some five minutes later. He looked rather happy.

"You must have had a drink," Stunted suggested.

"Nuts!" The other grinned evilly. "I been in touch with the boss. We all get an extra cut for nailing our big brass friend here."

"When you bear such tidings, all is forgiven," Stunted told him.

"The boss is gonna handle the rest," the thin man said.

"What rest?" Stunted questioned.

"Doc Savage has three more men in New York," said the other. "Guys called Long Tom, Johnny and Renny. They've got to be taken care of."

Chapter XI
THE FARMER GAG

RENNY had big fists. A medical authority had once claimed they were the biggest fists ever known on a man, including those of the Cardiff Giant. Renny was not a boasting man—except on one point, and that was the claim that there was not a wooden door made the panel of which he could not batter out with his fists.

Renny, as Colonel John Renwick, was an engineer with a reputation that extended over much of the world. He did not work at that profession much these days. He loved excitement, and to get it, he was a soldier of trouble in Doc Savage's little group.

Renny sat in Doc Savage's skyscraper headquarters in New York City. There was a newspaper on his lap. Under the newspaper and hidden by it was one of the bronze man's supermachine pistols capable of discharging many hundreds of shots a minute.

There came another knock on the door.

"Come in," Renny invited.

The man who entered was a tower of bones. He blinked at the newspaper, then fingered a monocle which dangled by a ribbon from his lapel.

"Your demeanor instigates apprehensions," he said in a scholastic voice.

"Didn't know it was you, Johnny," Renny rumbled, in a voice that had the volume of an angry bear in a cave. He pocketed the machine pistol.

The newcomer was William Harper Johnny Littlejohn, a gentleman with two loves—excitement, and big words. That he was considered one of the most learned experts on archaeology and geology was incidental.

"Has Long Tom communicated with you in the preterlapsed hour or so?" Johnny asked.

Renny blinked. "That one got me."

"Long Tom called me," advised Johnny in smaller words. "He indicated he possessed information of equiparable import."

"I see," Renny said vaguely. "No, he didn't call me."

Johnny stalked into the library, appearing thinner than any man could possibly be and still live, and came back with a book only slightly smaller than a suitcase. He opened it and began to pore over the pages of fine print.

It was a book on the life habits of the prehistoric Pterodactyl, which Johnny himself had written.

"Brushing up?" Renny asked.

"I left something out," Johnny

explained. "A matter of ponderable consequence, too, concerning the lapidification, or progressive lapidescence, of the oval—"

"Spare me," Renny requested. "I've already got a headache. Any word from Doc?"

"No," Johnny said shortly.

The door burst open, admitting a pallid wan man who looked unhealthy enough to be in a hospital. He was hardly of average height, and his complexion had all of the ruddiness of a mushroom.

"Something important!" he yelled, and waved a paper.

He was Major Thomas J. "Long Tom" Roberts, electrical wizard extraordinary, and he had never been ill a day in his life.

THE paper bore typewritten words:

> I know you're a right guy and know you're interested in this Willard Spanner killing. Go to 60 Carl Street and you may learn something. Be careful, though. I'll look you up later and if you want to do something for me for tipping you off, that's all right, too.
>
> Buzz.

"Who's Buzz?" Renny rumbled.

"Search me," said Long Tom. "But this is worth looking into, simply because the public don't know we're interested in the affair. This man knew it, so he must have gotten a line on something worthwhile."

"It's eminently plausible," Johnny agreed.

Renny, after making remarkably hard-looking blocks out of his great fists, grunted, "Wonder what kind of a place this Carl Street is?"

It was a swanky residential thoroughfare. They found that out when a taxicab carried them along Carl Street half an hour later. The street was lined with apartment buildings, and it was necessary to look nearly straight up to see the sky. The buildings looked new.

No. 60, when they passed it, was one of the most imposing buildings, its apartments having large windows, and there were two uniformed doormen under the canvas canopy, instead of the customary one.

"What shall we do?" Long Tom pondered aloud. "That's a large place. Must be three hundred apartments. And we don't know what we're looking for."

"Charge in and start asking questions," Renny suggested.

"Aboriginal reasoning," said Johnny

"Sure," Long Tom agreed. "We wouldn't get to first base, and maybe scare off our birds."

JOHNNY

"It won't hurt to take a look," argued Renny. "I'll turn up my coat collar and go in."

"Where'll you put them fists?" Long Tom snorted. "I'll do the gumshoeing."

They directed their taxi around the corner and got out. Long Tom stood on the curb, scratching his head.

"It's just as well not to walk in too boldly," he declared. "These birds may know us by sight."

A bright idea apparently seized him then, for he left the other two, dodged traffic across the street, and entered a telegraph office.

Renny and Johnny waited. Five minutes passed, and the waiting pair became impatient. They were on the point of investigating when a messenger came out of the telegraph office. He was directly before them before they recognized Long Tom.

"Gave a kid two bucks to loan his uniform to me," the electrical wizard grinned.

HE went into the apartment building carrying a telegraph company envelope which was empty, and when one of the doormen tried to stop him, he glared and said, "Nix! You guys don't gyp me out of the tip for delivering this!"

Long Tom walked on in, and over to the directory board which displayed a list of the tenants, office-building fashion. This last was an unusual custom for an apartment house, and a break for Long Tom.

Long Tom took one look; then he wheeled, walked out. Excitement was on his pale face when he joined the others.

"Guess what!" he exploded.

"Blazes!" grunted Renny. "That's some way to start out. What's eating you?"

"Willard Spanner had a laboratory and room down on Staten Island," Long Tom said. "The police searched it, but found nothing to indicate why he was murdered. Am I right?"

"Right," Renny boomed.

"Yet Willard Spanner is listed in that apartment house as having an apartment there," Long Tom advised.

Renny lumbered forward. "There may be something to this angle after all. What number is this apartment?"

"Apartment 2712." said Long Tom.

FIFTEEN minutes later, Renny and Johnny appeared at the service entrance of the apartment building carrying a large wooden box which bore

the designation, "Apartment 2712" on its sides in black crayon. Their scheme did not go far without hitting a snag. It seemed that the apartment house had a service department which delivered packages.

"We were to install this thing," Renny rumbled, and tapped the box. "Don't bother ringing the apartment. We got the keys."

A service elevator took them up, and, grunting a little, they carried their big box down the corridor. They stopped at the door and listened, heard nothing, exchanged glances, then rang the bell. There was no reply.

From a pocket, Renny removed a sizable array of skeleton keys. These he had brought from Doc's headquarters. He tried almost twenty of them, and his long, sober face was registering some anxiety, before one of the keys threw the tumblers.

Inside was a modernistic reception room done in black and shining chromium. Renny eyed it appreciatively. He was a connoisseur in modernistic apartments himself, possessing one of the most extremely decorated apartments in the city. He and Johnny skidded their box inside with little regard for the polished floor. They closed the door.

"Hello!" Renny called tentatively.

Only echoes answered.

They passed through the first door. If the reception hall had been modernistic, this chamber was an extreme in the opposite direction, being fitted up in early Twelfth Century style. There were great broadswords over the fireplace, the table was massive and handhewn, and two suits of armor stood at opposite ends of the room. Mounted boar heads set off the scheme of decoration.

"Not bad," Renny said.

They advanced.

The two suits of armor moved simultaneously. Each turned a steel gauntlet over, revealing a small automatic pistol which had been hidden from view.

"You walked right into it," said a voice back of a slitted helmet.

Renny broke into a grin. It was a peculiar characteristic of Renny that when the going got tough, he seemed to become more cheerful. By the same token, when he looked most sad, he was probably happiest.

"You took a chance," he rumbled.

"Oh, we figured you wouldn't ring in the police," said the man in the armor. "Doc Savage's men don't work that way."

Four other men now came out of the rear

RENNY

regions of the apartment. They carried guns. Two of them searched Johnny and Renny thoroughly.

"Lock the door," one suggested.

A man went to the corridor door and turned the key, then came back juggling it in his palm.

"Get us out of these tin pants," suggested one of the pair in the armor.

This was done.

JOHNNY and Renny said nothing, but studied their captors, and the appraisal was not particularly cheering, for the six were not nervous, and their manner was hard, confident, while the clipped unconcern of their speech indicated that they were no strangers to situations involving mental stress. They were the kind of men who could be thoroughly bad; none of them looked soft.

"Well!" snapped one. "How do you like us?"

"You'd look better with a black hood over your head," Renny said dryly. "That's the way they fix you up before they put you in the electric chair!"

"Aha!" The man waved an arm. "He threatens us!"

Another said dryly, "We got Doc Savage in California, and now we collar these three. Strikes me we've about cleaned up our opposition."

"The boss worked a sweat up for nothing," said the first. "This Doc Savage wasn't such hot competition."

"It was that damn Willard Spanner," grumbled the first man. "He was tipped off about the thing, and asked to get in touch with Doc Savage. We had to smear him."

"It wasn't so much the smearing," the second man corrected. "It was the way we had to grab him in Frisco at noon, then croak him here in New York a couple of hours later, when he tried to get away."

The first speaker nodded. "But he had mailed all of the dope to his New York apartment, and we had to bring him here and make him get the letter for us."

Renny did not ordinarily show surprise. But now his eyes were all but hanging out.

"You came from San Francisco to New York in less than two hours?" he exploded.

"Sure," sneered the other. "Ain't it wonderful?"

"I don't believe it!" Renny rumbled.

Johnny put a question which had been bothering him. "Was this ever Willard Spanner's apartment?"

"Heck, no," the other chuckled. "We just fixed that up as a kind of sugar coating on the bait."

Then the man snapped a finger loudly. "Blast it! There's one of these guys loose yet! The one who looks like he's about ready to die. Long Tom, they call him."

The man who seemed to be in charge consulted his watch.

"We'll take care of him later," he decided. "They start unloading the *Seabreeze* in just about an hour. We'll have to move fast."

The men now began handcuffing, binding and gagging Johnny and Renny, working with swift ease, a hard tranquility in their manner, as if they were perfectly sure of their ground and expected no interruption.

They were more than mildly astounded when Long Tom said, from the modernistic reception room door, "Everybody stand very still."

Behind Long Tom was the box in which Renny and Johnny had carried him upstairs—against just such an emergency as this.

THE six sinister men in the apartment had been calm before, and their composure did not desert them now, for they merely turned around, saw the supermachine pistol in Long Tom's pale hand, were duly impressed, and made no exciting gestures.

They slowly held their hands out from their sides, let their guns fall on the carpet, and raised their hands over their head.

"Hold that position," Long Tom advised.

He went forward and freed Renny and Johnny, who in turn searched their prisoners thoroughly, disarming them. The search was not as productive as they had hoped, the pockets of their captives holding nothing but money; the labels inside their clothing had been cut out carefully.

"Tie them up," Long Tom suggested.

This was done, curtain cords, wire off floor lamps, serving as binding.

Long Tom frowned at them, asked, "What was that I heard about *Seabreeze*? What's *Seabreeze*?"

"A race horse," said one of the men promptly.

Long Tom shook his head. "You said something about unloading—"

"Sure!" The other shrugged. "The horse just came in from the South on a train. We gotta unload him."

Renny boomed, "That's a lie!"

The man looked hurt. Long Tom lifted his brows inquiringly.

"The *Seabreeze* is a new ocean liner," Renny said. "I read about it in the newspapers. It comes in today, and there's a lot of gold bullion aboard. The stuff is being shipped over from Europe."

"So!" Long Tom glared at their prisoners. "What's going to happen to the *Seabreeze*?"

No one said anything.

"It's just a coincidence!" growled one of the gang. "*Seabreeze* is a race horse."

"We'll see about that." Long Tom waved at the door. "We're going down to the pier where this ocean liner is docking."

"Somebody's gotta watch these birds," Renny boomed.

"You can have the job," Long Tom told him. "You thought of it."

They argued briefly and it ended by them matching coins, in which procedure Renny lost; so, grumbling and looking very solemn, he took over the job of guarding the captives while Johnny and Long Tom went to the pier where the liner *Seabreeze* was docking, to see if it had any connection with the present affair.

Long Tom and Johnny were jaunty indeed as they rode down in an elevator and hailed a taxi in front of the apartment building.

They would not have been as cheerful had they chanced to note the actions of a man at that moment in the act of parking his car down the street a score of yards.

THE man in the car bent over hastily, so that his face was concealed, and when he bobbed up to watch Long Tom and Johnny out of sight, he held a newspaper before his features in a manner which was casual, but effectively shielding.

When the man got out of his car, he had a top-coat collar turned up and his hat brim snapped

The Masked man shook one of them violently. "What happened?" he snapped.

down very low. He walked rapidly and entered the apartment house, managing to keep his face averted from the doormen.

In his free hand, the man was carrying a small case which might have contained a physician's tool kit.

An elevator let him out on the twenty-seventh floor. He waited until the cage departed, then glided to the door of the apartment to which Long Tom, Johnny, and Renny had been decoyed.

The man opened his little case. First, he took out a rubber mask which fitted his face tightly. The thing was literally a false face, padded so that it now appeared that the man had bulging cheeks, a crooked nose and more than one chin.

The case also disgorged a tin can with a screw top, and a funnel, the lower end or spout of which was flattened out. The man inserted the flattened portion of the funnel under the door. He poured the contents of the can into the funnel, and the stuff, a liquid, ran into the apartment.

The man stepped back hurriedly, and it became apparent that he was holding his breath. He went to a window at the end of the corridor, opened it and stood squarely in the stiff breeze which now blew in. He breathed deeply.

He stood there fully five minutes, consulting his watch. Then he turned and went to the apartment door, drawing a key from his pocket. Fortunately, the other key had not been left in the apartment door when it was locked from the other side, so the man with the rubber mask admitted himself readily.

The stuff on the floor had evaporated. The man held his breath until he had opened the windows, then went outside and waited for the apartment to clear of the gas which he had poured under the door.

Renny and the rest of the men in the apartment were now unconscious.

Chapter XII
MAN IN THE RUBBER MASK

THE man in the rubber mask seemed to know a great deal about the effect of his gas, and how to revive its victims, for he went to work on the late prisoners, first unbinding them, and transferring a number of the ropes to the person of Renny.

It was not long before inhalation of certain bottled compounds caused the men to blink and moan themselves awake. The masked man shook one of them violently.

"What happened?" he snapped.

The sound of the voice—it was not a particularly unusual voice, yet distinctive enough to be readily recognized—snapped the man who heard it into wide wakefulness.

"The big chief," he exploded. "But what're you wearin' that mask for? You look like a goblin!"

The man in the mask ripped out, "I asked you what happened here! I didn't ask for any wise-guy stuff!"

The story of the raid by Doc Savage's three men came out—the narrators doing their best to gloss over the parts unfavorable to themselves, but, judging from the angry snorts of their leader, not succeeding very well.

"Fools!" the man yelled. "You do things just like a herd of donkeys! Where did Johnny and Long Tom go?"

The one telling the bad news looked as if he had found a worm in his apple. He hesitated. He had neglected to tell about the *Seabreeze* slip.

"It's bad," he groaned, and told the rest of it.

The masked leader proceeded to have something approaching a tantrum. He swore, and kicked those who were just regaining consciousness, so that they awakened more hurriedly and scrambled erect to get the more sensitive portions of their anatomy out of foot reach.

"You bunch of nitwits!" the man choked. "You should have told me that first! It may be too late now."

He charged into another room, grabbed a telephone, and could be heard snapping the dialing device around madly. When he got his number his voice dropped. Those in the other room did not hear a word he said, except for a final sentence which showed the man had been speaking in the strange private code which the gang employed.

"The cake should be baked half an hour earlier," was his last sentence.

He came back into the room looking somewhat less mad than before, and said, "Maybe I managed to get the bacon out of the fire."

"How?" he was asked.

"I contacted the boys and told them to go through with it half an hour earlier than planned." He consulted his watch. "That means right away. They may get it done before Johnny and Long Tom arrive on the scene."

The man eyed his watch again. "Half an hour should see the job done."

AT about the same moment, Long Tom was examining a thin wafer of a watch which had cost the electrical society which had presented it to him a small fortune. "We won't make that pier much before the half hour," he said to Johnny.

However, they had secured a driver who was willing to take chances, and by stopping a traffic policeman and exhibiting their police commissions—they, too, held them, as well as did Doc

Savage—they persuaded the officer to ride the running board.

The results were remarkable. Traffic split for them. Their horn blasted steadily. They chopped fifteen minutes from Long Tom's time estimate.

"There's the pier," Long Tom advised.

Johnny craned his long neck.

"The situation has certain aspects of a premonstration," he said.

Long Tom looked puzzled. "A what, did you—"

From ahead came a sound as if a snare drum had been beaten hard for a short interval. The driver stopped the cab so suddenly that the wheels skidded. He heaved out of the seat, took a good look.

There was a crowd ahead, an excited crowd. At the snare-drum sound, the crowd showed an abrupt tendency to leave the vicinity. Many policemen were running about. Police-car sirens made an unholy music.

"This is as far as I go," the taxi driver advised. "There's a young war ahead!"

Johnny and Long Tom were already getting out of the machine. They forgot to pay the driver, and he in turn did not think of collecting. They ran forward. Men and women passed them. Two men led a woman who was having hysterics.

"They killed fifty men or more!" the woman screamed. "The bodies were everywhere!"

Johnny registered incredulity, and gasped, "A Brobdingnagian exaggeration, let us hope."

The snare-drum sound—surely a machine gun—rattled out again. Smaller firearms cracked. Shotguns went off. Gas bombs made rotten-egg noises.

A burly policeman loomed up and yelled, "Hey, this ain't no show! Get back where it's safe!"

Long Tom and Johnny showed their police-commission cards.

"What's going on?" the feeble-looking electrical wizard asked.

"Pirates!" said the officer. "They're cleaning out the *Seabreeze!*"

Going on, Long Tom and Johnny rounded the corner and came upon a surprising sight.

THREE very large trucks were backed up to the pier at which the bright, new liner *Seabreeze* was tied. The van body of the outer truck had been shot away over a small area, and it was evident that the interior was lined with thick steel. The truck tires were ragged where bullets had struck, but had not gone flat, indicating they were of solid rubber.

The engine hoods and radiators also seemed to be armored, although the engines were of a type which sat inside the cabs, and thus were difficult to shoot into.

A man—probably a news photographer—was getting pictures on top of a nearby building. A machine gun snarled from behind one of the trucks, and he dashed for cover. A fresh burst of firing started.

Possibly fifty policemen were in sight. Others were arriving. They had set up a regulation Lewis gun, and its drumming uproar burst out.

Johnny got his bony length down behind a row of parked cars. Windows were shot from some of the cars. Trailed closely by Long Tom, he worked to the side of a police sergeant. He asked questions.

"The *Seabreeze* is carrying gold bullion," the officer explained. "They're looting her. Must be thirty or more of them."

The sergeant drew the pin of a gas bomb, drew back and hurled it.

"Won't do any good," he added. "Them birds are wearing masks."

"Using regular army tactics," Long Tom growled.

"We'll get 'em," said the cop. "We got men taking their pictures with telephoto lenses. We're blocking every street leading away from here."

It became evident that the ship raiders had thrown up a barricade of sand bags, probably unloaded from the trucks, behind which they could crawl to load the trucks. Only rarely did one of them show himself above the barrier. Each lapse of this kind drew a fusillade of bullets.

Long Tom unlimbered his machine pistol, as did Johnny. They joined the police besiegers. There was little else they could do.

"Consummately unbelievable," said Johnny, referring to the whole affair.

"It does seem to be about as big a thing as was ever pulled in New York," Long Tom agreed. "Hey! Something's gonna happen!"

The truck engines had been turning over steadily. Now they roared. The huge vehicles began to move.

This was the signal for the police. Everywhere, officers leaped up, emptying their guns. Crash and roar of firearms was terrific. Bits of siding fell off the trucks.

The giant vehicles did not turn up or down the street, as expected. They continued straight across the wide waterfront thoroughfare. They were aiming for a large wooden door in a building. The first truck hit the door. It was of very thin wood, and caved in. The truck vanished inside. The others followed.

AN instant later, it was evident that a stout steel door had been put up from the inside of the building in place of the wooden one. A great roar of gunfire came from the building as bricks fell out of the walls here and there, exposing loopholes obviously prepared aforehand.

The police retreated. Occasionally, one fell, wounded.

The officers began to yell for ladder wagons from the fire department, in order that they might scale the roofs of the buildings.

"There's a court behind that building," a blue-coat shouted. "Try to get into that!"

"They're trying," he was informed. "The gang has the walls covered."

Some fifteen minutes passed. The vicinity began to take on the aspect of a battlefield. Out in the bay a tugboat maneuvered, a light field gun, secured from the fort in the bay, on its after deck. Police in number had grown to several hundred. White-clad ambulance attendants were thick.

Then something happened that knocked everyone speechless. There was a rending crack—it really started with a whistle that might have been made by somebody going at terrific speed. The throng gazed, stupefied, at the sky, scarcely believing what they saw.

"A big ball!" a cop gasped. "It come up out of the court behind that building and went away so fast you danged near couldn't see it!"

WHILE they still goggled at the heavens, there was another echoing report, and a second ball sailed upward, visible at first, but rapidly gathering speed until it could hardly be followed with the eye.

No more balls arose. Shooting from the building had stopped. Policemen stormed the place.

"They'll find exactly nothing, is my guess," Long Tom prophesied.

He was right. The officers found the trucks, badly riddled. They found one bar of gold which had somehow been overlooked in the excitement. Considering the magnitude of the theft, and the roaring manner in which it had been executed, it was remarkable that only one gold bar had been overlooked.

Six million dollars had been taken. The *Seabreeze* purser gave out that information. Not quite a dozen men had been killed, although one excited tabloid newspaper placed the estimate at two hundred. Altogether, it was the most spectacular bit of news which New Yorkers had experienced in a long period.

Most stunning of all, perhaps, was the manner in which the thieves had vanished. When last seen, they were fast-traveling specks in the sky. Nor was another trace of them discovered.

Of course, everyone now connected the streaks in the sky—at first thought to be peculiar comets—with the mysterious balls. There was one point which caused confusion. At first, the balls had made streaks in the sky. Now they made none.

Long Tom and Johnny discussed that as they rode uptown, baffled and a little sheepish because they had been of practically no assistance in preventing the robbery.

"I don't understand it," Long Tom said. "Maybe the streaks weren't made by balls, after all. And what kind of things are these balls, anyway? How do they work?"

They got out of their cab in front of the apartment building where they had left Renny guarding the prisoners. Paying the fare took a few moments. They turned to go in.

"Look!" Long Tom exploded.

Renny sat in a car across the street; his head and shoulders showed plainly, so that there was no doubt about it being Renny.

"What the heck's he doing down here?" Long Tom quipped.

The next instant, one of Renny's huge hands lifted and beckoned to them, indicating that they should come over.

They ran across the street, unsuspecting, hands far from the armpit holsters which held their supermachine pistols.

Two men came from behind a parked car on the right. They flourished revolvers. Three came from the left, also with guns. They were members of the gang who had been in the apartment.

They said nothing. They did not need to, for their manner was fully explanatory of their intentions. Long Tom and Johnny put their hands up.

A small man got up from the floor of the car beside Renny. Crouched down there, out of sight, he had grasped Renny's arm and waved one of the engineer's big hands, thus giving the summons which had deceived Long Tom and Johnny.

Renny, it became apparent, was unconscious.

THE gang was using three cars, all large sedans of somber color. In not more than twenty seconds after the first man with a gun had appeared, the cars were in motion—Long Tom in one, Johnny in the other.

A woman had been hanging with her head out of a nearby window. Now she began to scream. Her shrieks were so piercing that a baby in a perambulator up the street burst into loud crying.

One of the men stuck a gun out of a car window. The weapon sent thunder along the street. The woman's head disappeared.

Another man in the car snarled, "We ain't killing women, you louse!"

"Who's killing women?" the other snorted. "I shot out a window twenty feet from where she had her head!"

The cars did not travel swiftly enough to attract attention. After a dozen blocks, they stopped in an alley. No one was in sight. A shift was made to three other cars of entirely different color and model. These separated.

Long Tom squirmed about as they began to bind his arms securely with bits of cotton rope. There was little he could do.

"What are you going to do with us?" he demanded.

"Plenty," a man informed him.

Long Tom managed to grab a wrist and twist it, causing the victim to cry out in pain, and, as he flounced about, his gun was dislodged from his waistband, where he had stuffed it.

Long Tom had been contriving at that. He tried mightily to get the gun. They beat him down and kicked him soundly for the trouble he was causing.

A long time later, the car stopped in a woodland. Long Tom peered out and discovered that the other two machines had also arrived by other routes. Far away, through the trees, the electrical wizard caught sight of a gleaming object.

"What next?" asked one of the men.

"The chief says to get Doc Savage and all of his men together," replied the man in charge.

"Risky, ain't it?"

The other shrugged. "We're going to do some tall question asking. Chief wants to know just how much Doc Savage has learned about us, and whether he has left a written record of what he has dug up."

Squinting at the gleaming thing through the trees, Long Tom suddenly decided it was a ball— a large globe of some obsidian material.

One of the men came over, took a bottle and a handkerchief from his pocket, poured some of the contents of the bottle on the handkerchief and suddenly pounced upon Long Tom, clamping the saturated cloth to the electrical expert's nostrils.

Long Tom held his breath as long as possible, but they punched him in the stomach until he had to take air.

The first whiff brought the odor of chloroform. He coughed, flounced. He managed to get a lungful of fresh air. Endeavoring to make them think he had succumbed, he tried to fake oncoming unconsciousness while holding his breath again.

"Full of tricks, ain't you?" snarled the man, and hit him just above the belt.

Long Tom inhaled the anaesthetic in gobbling haste, and, before long, felt it take hold. His last impression was that of Johnny and Renny fighting against handkerchiefs being pressed against their nostrils.

Chapter XIII
SINISTER ORGANIZATION

THE room was dark, so very dark that it seemed filled with something solid. At one point only did a trace of light show, a small faint glow which, on closer examination, would have been ascertained to be the luminous dial of a wrist watch.

After a while, there was noise of a door opening, and a flashlight lunged out whitely, picking up a prone figure. The beam collapsed. The motion of the watch-dial light patch indicated the man was being lifted and borne into another room, equally dark, but into which the jangling sound of a radio speaker penetrated. He was dropped heavily, and those who had borne him stalked out.

Doc Savage's trained voice asked, "Who is it?"

The man who had just been carried in said, "Nock Spanner."

From elsewhere in the room, Monk's small voice spoke up, "How did they get you? And why'd you run off from us at that old ranch?"

"Oh, that?" Nock Spanner made a disgusted noise. "I saw somebody and followed them. At first, I wasn't sure it was someone. You see, I just saw a movement. Then, when I did make sure it was someone skulking, it was too late to turn back and get you. I wish I had. They grabbed me a little later."

Ham said from close by, "I am getting very tired of this."

Nock Spanner asked, "You all tied up?"

"Like mummies," Monk growled. "And handcuffs galore."

The radio ground out music steadily.

"What do you think they'll do with us?" Nock Spanner asked.

"No idea," said Monk.

"Have you—learned if my brother is still alive?" Spanner questioned.

Monk hesitated, then admitted, "No."

The radio stopped jangling music; there was a station announcement, then a news broadcaster with a staccato manner of speaking took over the microphone.

"Our affair of the flaming comets seems to be taking on the complexion of one of the most gigantic criminal rings of all time," he said, the radio loudspeaker reproducing each word distinctly. "At least half a dozen crimes of importance can be attributed to the Comet Gang so far today, the largest being the fantastic robbery of bullion from a ship at a New York City pier, only a short time ago. In addition to this, a jewelry concern was rifled in Chicago, and banks robbed in various other cities. In each case, it is certain that the robbers were members of what is now being called the Comet Gang, and escaped in the fantastic ball vehicles, which scientists admit to be some new type of terrestrial ship capable of traveling at terrific speed, and of handling with remarkable facility."

The radio commentator went on, and his broadcast became dryer and dryer as he ran out of concrete information and began generalizing.

"He's been on the air steady, pretty near," Monk grumbled. "Boy, am I getting tired of that voice!"

Nock Spanner said, "It is evident that we are entangled with a gigantic criminal ring which has perfected this terrestrial ship, or whatever you would call it, and are using it as a getaway vehicle in the commission of huge crimes."

The radio in the other room suddenly went silent.

"They cut the speaker into their private transmitter-and-receiver hookup when they communicate with each other," Monk said in a stage whisper. "Listen to what they say. They've sure got an organization!"

SHORTLY afterward, the radio in the next room went into operation. Evidently a call had been picked up on a supplementary receiver, and the large speaker cut in for convenience in operation.

"This is W20LA coming back at my friend in California," said the faint speaker voice. "This is W20LA in Corona, Long Island, New York City, coming back to California. I just got all of the tubes in the box, old man. Your system for doing it worked splendidly. All three tubes are thoroughly boxed. Yes, sir. I am going to deliver them now. So long—and seventy-threes, old man."

That was all from the radio.

Monk muttered in the darkness. "I'm getting able to pick out the general meaning of their code," he grumbled. "Take that confab just now. It meant they've got something done in New York, something involving three—"

He left the words hanging. Silence was thick. The ticking of the watch with the luminous dial was audible.

"Go ahead—say it," Ham suggested. "That radio talk might have referred to Renny, Long Tom and Johnny."

"Yeah," said Monk, "that's what I was thinking."

Nock Spanner snarled, "Ain't there any way of getting out of this?"

"I wouldn't worry too much," Monk told him.

Spanner swore joyfully. "Then you have a plan?"

"No," Monk told him. "But Doc, here, is something of a magician."

Spanner muttered, "If the police only knew where to look for us. Why in Sam Hill didn't we leave a note or something, telling what we had learned, or what we intended to do?"

Monk advised, "Like lots of good ideas, that one comes too late."

Time passed. It could not have been much more than an hour and a half. They heard a cracking noise characteristic to the arrival, departure, or passage of one of the mysterious aerial globes. Then there came a voice.

There was something familiar about the voice. It took them a moment to place it. Then Ham gasped incredulously.

"That voice—the same one was on the radio from New York not over two hours ago!" he said sharply.

No one said anything for a while; then they heard the voice of the newcomer again, and within a few moments, other voices and the tramp of feet. These approached. Scuffling quality indicated men carrying heavy burdens. They came inside.

They bore Johnny, Long Tom, and Renny, all of whom were unconscious. The trio were deposited in the darkness.

"You birds enjoy yourselves," a voice said. "We're going to hold a party later."

The men departed.

DOC SAVAGE heaved up and strained mightily against the handcuffs which held his wrists. There was no hope of breaking them. It was doubtful if, even with his incalculable strength, he could have broken one of them, for they were very heavy.

And three manacles held his arms. In addition, there were many turns of rope. It was against this that he struggled, and he was loosening it, getting a little play into his arms.

A stirring indicated that either Johnny, Long Tom, or Renny was reviving. It was Johnny's voice which first broke the silence.

"I'll be superamalgamated!" he mumbled.

The word was a favorite of Johnny's. He used it to express disgust, despair, surprise, or any other violent emotion.

"Feel all right?" Doc asked.

The ropes on the bronze man's arms had loosened somewhat, enabling him, by squirming mightily, to reach the row of buttons on the front of his coat. He tore one of these off, got it between his fingers, slipped it down between his manacled ankles, and began to work with it.

Johnny mumbled gloomily, "I feel like a valetudinarian."

"A man who can think of a word like that can't be so bad," Monk told him.

Doc Savage had managed to unscrew one half

of the button from the other half; a threaded joint permitted this, although so skillfully done that no casual examination would have disclosed it. He carefully tilted the button and let the stuff in the hollow interior trickle on the handcuff links. He did this most painstakingly.

Nock Spanner growled hopelessly, "Isn't there some chance for us?"

Long Tom and Renny had both regained their senses now. Voices anxious, they made sure Doc and the others were unharmed. They noted the luminous dial of Nock Spanner's watch and asked the time. He told them.

"Holy cow!" Renny boomed. "We were brought from New York out here to California in not much more than two hours!"

Nock Spanner demanded desperately, "Didn't you fellows leave some sort of a trail by which the police may find us?"

"No," Renny said.

Doc Savage had taken four more buttons off his coat, carefully unscrewed them, and emptied the contents on the cuff links. Try as he would, he could not reach the others. He waited. The radio in the next room had not been switched on. Silence was deep.

Once Monk pondered aloud, "I wonder what happened to that girl?"

"And Leases Moore and Quince Randweil," Ham echoed.

IT must have been more than an hour later when voices became audible in one of the adjacent rooms.

"There's nothing more to hold us up," a voice said. "The balls are perfected to the point where they don't leave luminous trails at night, as did the first ones. We can go and come, and no one on earth can stop us."

Monk, in the intense darkness of the inner room, muttered, "So that's why there were streaks in the sky at first, but none anymore."

"What about the prisoners?" a voice from outside queried.

"We'll get rid of them now."

Stunted's voice spoke up, saying, "I tell you jaspers, I don't like the idea of shootin' down anybody in cold blood."

"Aw, don't be a sissy!" he was advised.

The door had been locked. Now the fastenings rattled, and the panel opened. Men came in cautiously, spraying light from flashes. They cast the beams about.

"Look!" one of the men howled suddenly. He raced the white funnel of his flashlight. Stunned profanity came from those with him.

Doc Savage was missing from among the prisoners. The bronze man was not in the room.

Stunted ran over and howled at Monk, "How long has he been gone?"

"I dunno," Monk said, truthfully.

The man with the queer eyes dashed inside, heard what had happened, and snapped out a revolver. Stunted shoved against him heavily.

"Use your head!" Stunted snapped. "With those birds alive, Doc Savage will come fooling around, trying to get 'em loose. That way, we'll have a chance at him."

"You have got a brain, after all," growled the cross-eyed man, and pocketed his weapon.

The man went over to the spot where Doc Savage had been lying. He stooped, picked up a bit of metal, and examined it. The thing was a portion of a handcuff link.

The man touched a finger to it, then cried out in sudden pain and wiped the finger frantically on a handkerchief. He threw the handkerchief away.

"What is it?" Stunted demanded.

"Some powerful chemical of an acid nature," the man growled. "That infernal bronze fellow must have had it hidden somewhere on him, and put it on the handcuff chains. It weakened them until he could break them."

Stunted mumbled, "That's a new one on me."

DOC SAVAGE could hear the voices—rather, hear the murmur of them, for he was not close enough to distinguish the words. He was in the gloom just outside the old ranch house. He had been free something like ten minutes, but had not left the vicinity for more than one reason. It was essential that he free the others. And he wanted a look at one of the fantastic ball conveyances.

There was one of the mysterious vehicles off to the right; its rounded hulk was vaguely distinguishable. Fog was making the night very dark. Doc eased toward the thing.

The size of the ball became more impressive as he drew close. He touched its smooth surface. It felt like glass. He moved around it, noting the polished nature of the covering, probably made thus to reduce friction. Even then, the heat generated must be tremendous.

He came finally to a door, barely large enough for him to wedge through. The door operated like a plug. The walls were thick—almost four feet, he judged.

Inside the thing, a small electric bulb glowed, furnishing illumination enough to get an idea of how the shell of the vehicle was constructed.

The outer surface, some compound resistant to friction and heat, no doubt, was only a skin, and under that was layer after layer of asbestos, interlaced with cooling pipes and wires and tubes and mysterious channels having to do with the operation of the contrivance.

The interior chamber was roughly circular, literally a bit of open space completely surrounded by machinery. There were devices on the walls, even the ceiling. Remarkable indeed was the fact that the control room seemed to have neither top nor bottom, as far as arrangement of the mechanism went. There were polished pipes, crisscrossing, their purpose hard to explain.

Doc examined the machinery. The first device he came to was an electrical mechanism for producing tremendous degrees of cold, a contrivance utilizing liquid air as its cooling element, in place of the more common ammonia.

This, then, was what kept the ball cool when in motion.

The liquid air-cooling device was a commercial product in part. Trademarks of the manufacturer were distinguishable. Doc read the plate.

REFRIGERATING, INC.
New York

The bronze man passed that up as not being of chief interest. How was this device propelled? What gave it the fantastic power to rip through space without benefit of propellers, or, as far as could be seen, rocketlike discharges.

Certain it was that the luminous exhaust which some of the balls exuded when in motion was not discharge of a rocket nature, as some had at first thought.

DOC SAVAGE began going over the largest and most intricate mass of apparatus. He had already gathered an infinite respect for the brain which had conceived all this. That respect became infinitely greater as he surveyed a set of huge motors which utilized a compressed gas as fuel. The things were of fabulous horsepower for their size. There were, as far as Doc knew, no others like them in existence.

The exhaust of the motors explained the streams of sparks which some of the balls left. The burned gas came out of the exhaust in the form of flame. In this ball, the exhaust led through a digester which cooled it. Without the digester, the ball would leave a trail of the still-burning vapor.

The motors operated compact generators which undoubtedly delivered great voltage. Wires from the generators led into a metal-covered receptacle which undoubtedly held the secret of the whole incredible propulsion method. This was locked. Doc went to work on the locks.

He had operated only a moment when he heard voices outside. Men were approaching.

"We'll clear out of here before Doc Savage can come back with help," Stunted's voice said.

Doc's flake-gold eyes whipped about. Interior arrangement of the ball was fabulously compact. Only a locker device to the left seemed to offer concealment. Doc lunged for it, got the metal door open.

The place had evidently been intended as a storage place for loot. It was empty, now, but yellowish marks on the rough metal showed where heavy gold bars had reposed—no doubt loot from the liner robbery in New York.

Doc closed the door. There were slits for ventilation, and through these he could look, if he were not discovered. He waited.

Men clambered up the narrow channel that led through the thick hull. The door was evidently heavy, for they closed it mechanically, then spent some moments with wrenches, connecting the pipes from the door to the cooling machine. Stunted was among them.

Under an arm, Stunted carried Monk's pet pig, Habeas Corpus. He had muzzled the porker to discourage biting tendencies.

"Let's go," Stunted said.

PROFUSE and strange experiences had come Doc Savage's way in the past, including many that bordered on the incredible, the fantastic. But this was one which was to stand out always in his memory.

His great metallic frame seemed to grow suddenly and mysteriously light. He lifted an arm instinctively, and the effort was incredibly easy. And once the arm was up, it did not drop back to his side. It seemed to possess no weight. The effort made him start a little, so that he lifted from the floor. He hung there, in mid-air. It was necessary to push himself back to the floor.

Out in the control room, things were happening which would have driven a superstitious person into a frenzy. Men were walking on the walls, the ceiling, adjusting the controls, and throwing switches.

The crisscrossing tubes, which had seemed so useless before, now advertised their use. They were handrails, employed in going from one place to another. A man ran up one, spider fashion, body seeming to float in the air, then released his grip and floated where he was.

Doc Savage moistened his lips. He rarely showed excitement, but he was animated now.

Here before his eyes he was seeing demonstrated the product of a fantastic scientific discovery, a discovery so advanced that even the bronze man, for all of his learning, was somewhat dazed.

If he correctly interpreted what he was seeing, the creator of this aerial device had discovered how to nullify that type of force generally designated as momentum, as well as various forms of attraction, gravitational and otherwise.

No unschooled person could hardly have been more amazed than the bronze man. Here was inertia, gravitational attraction in all or most of its forms completely stifled. Some incredibly keen brain had penetrated one of the scientific fields probably least known to man. Modern science in general was not even quite sure what gravity was. Here was one who had mastered the subject.

The ball must be in motion. The machinery was making a great uproar. Shouted orders could not be heard. The men were communicating by gestures. One man in particular watched a bank of electric thermometers which registered the outer temperature of the shell and warned of increasing friction heat generated by their passage through the air. This man made a sudden gesture when the needles crept too high, and the speed of the ball was evidently slowed.

Other men glued eyes to periscope devices which evidently permitted them to look outside. Two more worked frantically with radio direction finders, evidently keeping track of their position by spotting well-known broadcasting stations on the earth below.

It was superscientific travel in its superlative degree, and Doc Savage could only stare and marvel. He was getting a vague idea of how the ball was made to move. No doubt gravitational force was nullified on top, on one side, creating in effect a vacuum in the lines of force which sucked the ball along.

It was a vague theory, capable of many refutations according to known scientific data, but it was the best solution the bronze man could assemble until such time as he had an opportunity to inspect the power plant itself.

The ball seemed to be arriving at its destination. Men made gestures. Others jerked levers, opened switches, and turned valves.

So completely was momentum nullified that even their stop, abrupt though it must have been, was not apparent. The noise of the mechanism ceased.

Doc Savage was conscious of an abrupt return of the normal heaviness of his limbs. He was conscious of something else, too—a terrific force which hauled him against the locker door, so that the door, unfastened as it was, fell open, and he came crashing out into the control room.

Too late, he understood what had occurred. The ball had stopped in a different position, so that the locker was now on what had become the ceiling. With the mechanism turned off, he had simply fallen out.

Chapter XIV
OSAGE RENDEZVOUS

STUNTED saw the bronze man first. Stunted, knowing what would happen when the ball stopped, was holding to one of the crisscrossing bars. He let out a howl, dropped from his perch, and lunged for his sawed-off automatic rifle, which he had tied to a stanchion with a bit of stout cord.

"The devil himself!" Stunted bawled.

Two other men had gotten the hatch open and were making it fast. The opening was now on the side. They swung around, but were in a bad position to fight.

Doc lunged at Stunted. The latter was having trouble with the cord that held his rifle. He had used a cord too strong for him to break. He gave it up, retreated, and threw a wrench at Doc.

The bronze man dodged it, leaped upward and caught the crisscrossing bars. He made for the men at the hatch.

Doc was a master at this method of fighting. Where the others had to move slowly, supporting themselves, the bronze man whipped about with infinite agility. One man at the hatch dropped away. The other held his ground, maintaining a grip with one hand, trying to fend Doc off with the other.

That was a mistake. An instant later, he slammed heavily down on the metal plates beneath. A bronze, clublike fist had knocked him senseless.

From his vantage point under the hatch, Doc saw that he had a moment's respite before any of them would be in a position to use a gun. The bronze man was curious about where the ball had landed. He decided to look, and bobbed his head up.

What he saw changed his whole plan. He had intended to fight, overpower the men, take the ball, fathom its secrets. But he could never do that because, outside, there was a high concrete fence, and inside that, four other balls and something near two score of men. If the bronze man escaped, it would be a miracle.

A bullet smacked the rim of the hatch as he vaulted out. Stunted had gotten his rifle loose and fired it. The pig, Habeas, squealed shrilly.

Doc poised on the hatch edge, hanging by his fingers. There were men below, many of them. It was too dark for them to make out details, however.

Doc Savage exerted all of his powers of voice imitation and sent out a sharp, excited shout.

"Something's gone wrong!" he yelled. "This thing may blow up! Get away! Run!"

It was Stunted's voice which he imitated, and

the shout held an edge of terror and warning which sent those below surging back.

Doc dropped down. The ruse would give him not more than a second or two. Less than that, it developed, for Stunted's real voice swore out from inside the ball, advising his fellows of the deception.

Doc ran for the wall. It was high, too high for him to leap. But it had been poured in a rough plank form, the planks stepped in toward the top for a narrowing effect. It could be climbed.

The bronze man leaped, caught hold, climbed, slipped, then gained the top just as a spotlight caught him and guns began crashing. He went over safely.

The other side, he discovered, was camouflaged with brush and transplanted vines. He carried some of the stuff with him as he went down. Then he ran. It was infinitely dark. He kept hands out before his face, in case he should run into something. Behind, they were organizing a pursuit party.

Then, to the left, a feminine voice called, "Over here, whoever you are!"

It was the girl, Lanca Jaxon.

DOC SAVAGE found her a moment later. "We had better leave here," he told her.

"Oh, it's their big bronze trouble!" She sounded relieved. "You are supposed to be dead!"

"According to whom?" Doc asked.

"Leases Moore and Quince Randweil," she replied. "Listen to that uproar! We're going to have some trouble."

The shooting from inside the concrete compound had lost its confused note. A great many hand searchlights had appeared. Men were assembling outside the enclosure.

Doc found the girl's arm, and they began to work through the undergrowth. Timber here was thick, many of the trees large. Fallen logs made travel difficult.

"Three of the balls just arrived," said the girl. "I guess you were in one of them. Where are your men?"

"Prisoners," Doc said. "I suspect they are in the other balls."

"How did you get away?" she asked.

Doc told her, very briefly, making it sound rather simple, and finishing his recital with a question, "What are you doing here?"

"Leases Moore and Quince Randweil let me out of their ball," she replied. "They were afraid I would make trouble at the wrong time."

"Where do they hook into this?"

The girl laughed harshly, without humor. "They were slated for suckers."

Doc was ahead now, his superior agility and keener senses making for faster progress. Even at their best, they could hardly hope to distance those behind.

"The man who invented the balls got Leases Moore and Quince Randweil to finance him," said the girl, resuming. "Their idea was to do what they are doing: organize a gang and use the speedy balls for getaway vehicles in the commission of big robberies. But Leases Moore and Randweil were greedy. They demanded too big a cut. The gang grabbed them and held them. They were prisoners when you found them."

"And you?" Doc prompted.

Brush through which they traveled made *swishing* noises. There seemed to be no night birds. Evidently these had been frightened away by the arrival of the balls.

"They've been holding me out here for six months," the girl snapped. "I own the land around here. They're using it. And they've ordered all of the materials with which to build those balls in my name, the idea being that I was the goat in case the law found out where the construction work had been done."

She gasped as a bough whipped her.

"It's too bad I didn't know who your two men, Monk and Ham, were when I tried to escape in that car yesterday," she said. "We might have gotten away. As it was, I ruined their break."

A bullet whistled through the branches, making sharp, ugly sounds, and the shot noise itself followed, thumping and echoing from the surrounding hills.

"This is the most deserted place in Oklahoma," the girl murmured. "Nobody will hear that shooting."

THE girl was breathing heavily now. She had fallen before, but she was falling more often now, and more heavily. She was slower getting up.

"I haven't slept for days," she said. "I guess I'm tuckered out."

Doc Savage picked her up, found what felt like a large tree, and moved out until, by jumping, he located a branch. With the grip of only one hand, and still carrying the girl, he swung up. He mounted with surprising speed.

"Take it easy," Lanca Jaxon said, uneasily. "This stuff might do on a circus trapeze, but I don't care for it here."

"We will wait here," Doc told her quietly. "If they miss us—excellent! If not, we'll try something else."

The bronze man waited, listening. With his free hand, he tested the dryness of the bark on the tree. Then he sniffed the air. It seemed that there had been a rain recently. That meant they had left footprints.

The rapidity and sureness with which their pursuers approached indicated they were following a trail.

"They'll come right to this tree," the girl breathed.

"Let me have your shoes," Doc requested.

She began, "Now, what—"

Doc whipped the shoes off her feet without more argument. Carrying them, he dropped downward and expended some moments locating the exact limb which he had seized from the ground in starting his climb. From there, he went on.

He used the girl's shoes, one in each hand, to make tracks beside his own footprints. Light and time for a finished job was lacking. He did the best haste permitted.

Men with searchlights and guns came up rapidly. They drew near the tree which held the girl. Just before they reached it, Doc grasped a dry limb and deliberately broke it. The cracking noise rattled through the timber.

"They're ahead!" Stunted roared, and the gang charged past the tree which held Lanca Jaxon, without dreaming of her close presence.

Doc found another tree and climbed it. He took a chance on the spreading boughs interlacing with other trees. They did. He went on. Reflected glow from the pursuing lights occasionally dashed palely among the treetops. Using that illumination, Doc picked the spreading limb of another tree, and with a tremendous swing through space, reached it. A professional gymnast would have been proud of that feat.

Shortly, the gang came upon the spot where Doc had gone aloft. They wasted much time probing the treetops, then spread out slowly, searching fruitlessly. But, by now, Doc was safely away.

The pursuers were persistent. It required fifteen minutes of hunting to disgust them, and then all did not favor giving up.

"Aw, we'll wait for daylight," advised the voice of the man with the uneasy eyes.

They turned back.

Aware that they might have left spies behind, Doc Savage was more than ordinarily cautious in returning to Lanca Jaxon. So silent was he that she gasped out sharply when he dropped to the limb beside her.

"They've given up!" she breathed. "When they passed under me, I thought sure—"

"I did not get to ask you the most important question of all," Doc told her. "Who is the individual behind all of this—the inventor of the balls?"

"I don't know for sure," she said.

"You have an idea?"

"That man with the shifting eyes," she said. "I have overheard things. If he is the big chief, not all of the gang know it."

"What did you overhear that led you to that idea?" Doc asked.

"The man with the crossing eyes was arranging with some of the others about murdering the one they call Stunted," she said. "He's to be killed whenever they have a chance to make it look like you did it."

"So they're going to kill Stunted," Doc murmured.

A moment later, the bronze man was gone into the darkness.

DOC SAVAGE traveled swiftly, overtaking the party which was returning slowly toward the camouflaged compound which held the four weird ball craft, and the workshops where they had been manufactured.

The men were traveling without haste. All of them seemed to be tired. They walked around logs rather than over them, and their conversation was gloomy.

"This is sure a swell kettle of fish," Stunted said gloomily. "Right when we're set for a clean-up."

"Quit grousing!" snapped the man with the queer eyes.

Stunted stopped. He put out his jaw. His sawed-off automatic rifle shifted slightly under his arm.

"So you're still tryin' to push me around!" he gritted.

The other snapped, "Pipe down, you sawed-off runt!"

Stunted had ordinarily seemed a cheerful soul, inclined to keep control of his emotions even when aggravated to the point of desiring to shoot someone. But now he seemed changed. He glared. The gun moved under his arm; his hand dropped back to the trigger.

The other men saw the signs. They sprang forward, growling angrily, and got between Stunted and the man with the uneasy eyes.

"Cut it out, you two!" one ordered. "You're going to ride each other until one of you winds up picking lead out of himself!"

Stunted, glaring, said nothing. Shortly afterward, he permitted himself to be urged on ahead. Some of the group accompanied him. Others remained behind with the shifty-eyed man. These dropped well to the rear, and there was something deliberate about their behavior.

"We got a chance to talk now," one muttered.

"Them guys ahead won't hear us. What're you gonna do about this bird Stunted?"

"I'll get him!" gritted the man with the roving eyes. "But I gotta be careful."

"Did you talk to the chief about disposing of Stunted?" a man asked.

"I did!" The other's eyes crossed and uncrossed evilly in the flashlight glare. "And what do you think?"

"What?"

"The chief said that if anything queer happened to Stunted, he'd croak me," gritted the conspirator.

"That's one for the book!"

"Uh-huh." The cross-eyed man turned his flash off. "It's kinda queer. Stunted seems plumb worthless to me. Him and his sawed-off rifles! Blah!"

THEY were silent a while, listening, evidently to make sure no one was near, then they dropped their voices a little and began to discuss something which was obviously of greater importance.

"You found out for sure who the big chief is?" a man asked.

The one with the restless eyes cursed.

"No. He wears that mask all of the time. You know—that rubber hood of a business."

There was a meaningful pause.

"Our plan still goes, eh?" one growled.

"Sure." The uneasy-eyed man swore again. "We croak this head guy. We do it in a quiet way, see? Then we just tell the boys that I'm really the guy who invented the balls, and they won't know the difference. I'll get the chief's cut. You gents get yours."

"Swell!" said one. "When?"

"Soon as we can."

They went on, walking rapidly now, as if their tiredness was gone, overtaking the others.

Doc Savage clung to them like their own shadows. He had been close during the conference, and what he had heard was interesting, refuting as it did the girl's conviction that the man with the peculiar eyes was the actual mastermind.

They drew near the compound. A shrill, anxious challenge ripped out.

"Who is it?"

"Us," said the man with the uneasy eyes. "Retune that capacity alarm to compensate for our arrival."

Doc Savage heard that and moved even closer to the others in the darkness. One of the delicate capacity-balance alarms was in operation here, it seemed, and by adding or subtracting capacity at the controls, the operator managed to maintain a balance which would show the arrival of even a single man in the vicinity.

Doc's plan was to get close enough to the others that his own presence would be allowed for. He seemed to succeed.

The men filed through an opening in the high compound wall.

Doc did not follow them. That was too risky. The bronze man tackled the high wall, and covered by the noise of the others' arrival, managed to surmount it.

He lowered himself slowly down the other side, utilizing the indentations left in the concrete by the original plank forms.

Chapter XV
PLANS SINISTER

THERE was some faint light inside the compound. Men who had been working had moved over to the entrance—a gatelike affair flanked on one side by a building and on the other by a round tank. Evidently they were interested in how the search had come out, and being informed on that point, they scattered and busied themselves making the balls secure.

Doc Savage glided back through the shadows, reached one of the balls, and got under it, undiscovered. He was interested in getting inside, in examining the mechanism.

A stepladder evidently led up to the hatch. He climbed it, being careful that the ladder did not squeak. At the top, he explored with his fingers, but felt only the smooth, rounded, obsidian chillness of the hull. The hatch was there, its outlines barely traceable. But it was fastened, and there seemed to be no lock visible.

Feet scuffed the hard earth. Doc dropped from the ladder, scrambled behind the ball and crouched there. Men were approaching.

Stunted led them. The short man's chest was out and he looked pleased with himself. He came to the ball and climbed the ladder. Flashlights were turned on him.

From a pocket Stunted took what was unmistakably ordinary copper wires, a telegraph key and a battery, hooked in series. He touched the wires to two portions of the ball hull, where there were evidently contacts, held them there; then, covering the key with his coat so no one could see just what combination he tapped out, he manipulated the key.

The hatch was evidently operated by some electrical combination, for it opened. Stunted clambered inside, replacing his unique battery "key" inside his clothing.

He came out a moment later with a box larger than a suitcase. He handled this with great care. He passed it to those below.

"Watch it!" he snapped. "This is the heart of

the invention. Take that away and there ain't nobody can figure out how these balls work."

He descended the ladder, closed the hatch—which locked itself—then visited the other balls, and from each removed a similar case of mechanism.

"What's the idea of taking these out?" he was asked.

"Don't we always do it?" Stunted demanded. "Supposin' that Doc Savage would get inside one of them balls? That'd be a swell howdy-do! We'll put these pieces of apparatus where we can watch 'em every minute."

Very gently, they carried the boxes to the large building beside the gate. All lights in the compound were now extinguished by way of precaution against being sighted by some nocturnal plane. They seemed surprisingly careless in the matter of a guard, too, evidently placing full dependence in the capacity alarm.

Doc Savage was not foolhardy enough to try to get into the building by the door. He moved to the right, felt along the rough concrete wall and found an open window.

An instant later, he was inside.

IN the murk, a generator made a shrill hum. Over to the left, something hot glowed. Doc studied it, and decided it was a forge with a banked fire.

Directly ahead, ranging along the side of the interior, was a partition perforated with doors, and some of these apertures were lighted. The men were toward the front.

Doc approached them. There was enough machinery to hide him—big drill presses, lathe beds, and other metalworking devices. Little expense had been spared in equipping the shop for the manufacture of the ball conveyances.

Stunted was saying loudly, "Everybody stay here and everybody stay awake. You can sleep later."

"What's up?" someone asked him.

"The chief is coming," Stunted said. "He told me to tell all of you that he wanted you on hand when he got here. He's gonna outline our next job, and it's to be bigger than anything we've pulled before."

"Since when did you become the chief's mouthpiece?" demanded the man with the shifting eyes.

Stunted grinned.

"Does it hurt?" he asked.

He was sworn at. Someone, evidently an admirer of Stunted, laughed. The man with the uncontrollable eyes got off by himself and mumbled.

Doc Savage eased closer. He was seeking his five aides and Spanner. A moment later, he saw them—all except Nock Spanner. Monk and Ham were tied together, probably because one of the gang had overheard them squabbling, and had mistaken their vocal hate as genuine.

Renny was by himself, trying to work his big fists through handcuff links. Long Tom and Johnny were barely discernible.

All five prisoners were in the room with the gang. Possibly twenty of the latter were present, every one armed. If Doc Savage had any impulse to charge in and attempt a rescue, he suppressed it carefully. He took chances, but never suicidal ones.

He moved back from the door as the lean man with the restless eyes came out of the lighted room, accompanied by two others. They lighted cigarettes, then strolled off.

"Stick around," Stunted called.

"We'll be in the radio room," one of the trio growled.

Doc Savage noted the direction they were taking—toward the monotonous hum of the generator. He put on speed himself, cutting in ahead of them, reaching the door of the room where the generator ran. He sought the corner by the door, and got down behind what was evidently a spare motor-generator unit.

The man with peculiar eyes came in. He cast a flash beam about.

"They're all with Stunted," one of the pair with him grunted.

"Watch the doors." The cross-eyed man went to the radio apparatus and turned on a light with a green shade. The radio was very modern. The man seemed to know a great deal about it, for he adjusted knobs and watched meters intently, then picked up a microphone.

The other two were at the door.

"No one coming," they advised.

Their leader's eyes crossed and uncrossed, and he spoke into the microphone, saying, "Hello—hello—hello," three times very rapidly, with pauses between, as if it were a signal.

Out of the loudspeaker came a lisping, hissing voice.

"How are things coming?" The voice made "things" sound like "thingsh."

"Slow," said the man with the roving eyes. "But we'll get the big shot tonight. He's due here before long, Stunted just said."

The lisping voice came over the radio again. Doc knew it; he could not be mistaken. The speaker was Quince Randweil, who must be cruising the skies somewhere nearby in the stolen ball.

"Leases and me just loaded a few hundred quarts of nitro," said Quince Randweil.

"What's the idea?" demanded the man at the radio.

"If it comes to that, we can blow that dump down there off the map," imparted Randweil. "Here's what we'll do if everything else fails: you and the guys working with you clear out and leave the others. Before you go, turn this radio transmitter on, and leave it turned on."

"I don't get this," said the man with the roving orbs.

"We'll use a direction finder on the radio," said Randweil. "That'll guide us to you. Then we'll use this nitro. That'll clean up the gang and wipe out their chief."

"But it'll mess up the balls," the other objected.

"We've got one," said Randweil, shortly. "That's enough. We can duplicate it if we have to."

"O. K.," agreed the man at the radio.

He laid down the microphone, switched off the apparatus, laughed once and walked out, followed by his two companions.

DOC SAVAGE gave them time to join the others. He had plenty to think about to keep him from being impatient. These men were not conspiring alone, as it had at first seemed, but were associated with Leases Moore and Quince Randweil. Moore and Randweil, in turn, were proving more canny than hitherto.

Doc Savage left the radio room. He did not go too near the door beyond which the gang awaited—the room which held the prisoners. The bronze man stationed himself to the side of the gate, against the tank.

The tank was large, and smelled as if it held gasoline, possibly fuel for engines that ran the machine tools. The night had quieted down remarkably, and the cries of nocturnal birds had resumed.

There came a faint scraping from the gate.

A voice—it was the man with the peculiar eyes—demanded, "Who is it?"

"Me," said another voice shortly. "The chief."

There was a short scuffling sound, a blow, ugly but not loud, followed by a cry, a wispy, hideous thing that never really got started.

Doc Savage whipped from his cover, took half a dozen steps, then halted. Sane reason had told him he was late.

By the gate, a man laughed. The sound was strained. Someone lighted a cigarette.

A man put his head out of the workshop door and yelled, "Was that the chief?"

"Hell, no," said a man at the gate.

"Cut out the smoking," said the workshop voice. "Might be seen from the air."

"Sure, sure!"

The head withdrew into the workshop.

A moment later, Doc Savage heard three men coming from the gate toward the tank. They were infinitely furtive and walked as if burdened. Doc retreated slowly before them, and as they came around behind the tank, one displayed a flash beam cautiously.

It was the cross-eyed man and his two conspirators, and they carried the limp form of a fourth. The latter wore a long topcoat and a dark suit.

Seen in the flashlight glow, the limp individual's face was covered by a grotesque mask of flexible rubber; it could be seen plainly that the mask was padded so as to alter the apparent contour of the wearer's features.

"It's the big shot—the brains," the flashlight wielder grunted. "Let's have a look at that kisser of his."

They yanked off the rubber mask. Then they stared. They looked as if they were about to fall over. One dropped the flashlight.

The uncovered face was that of the girl, Lanca Jaxon.

Chapter XVI
DEATH RODE THE SKY

THE cross-eyed man didn't hear Doc Savage coming, didn't dream of his near presence, probably never did know exactly what happened. His two companions knew. It helped them little, for there was not time to do anything about it.

They heard a jarring *thump,* and awakened from their surprise to see their chief collapsing under a tower of bronze. Then went for their guns. They carried the weapons in the open, in low-slung holsters, and old-time Western badmen could not have gone for them in more accepted style. One gun barely left its holster; the other stayed in the leather.

The two struggled a bit, madly. Their tongues ran out, and their faces purpled, even if they were not being choked. Nothing they did loosened the clutch on the backs of their necks, a grip of awful fingers which kneaded about as if searching for something down close to the spinal cords. After a while, the pair went limp.

Doc dropped them. He yanked the topcoat off the girl. The topcoat was big, loosely made, and Doc was just able to get into it. He picked up the mask. The rubber was of good quality, and it stretched. He got it down over his metallic features. He had some difficulty with the eyeholes.

The girl was limp when he picked her up. But there was life in her. She had been struck over the head, probably.

A man came out of the tool house. He was not excited.

"I heard something else," he said. "Was it the chief this time?"

Doc Savage stumbled toward him with the girl.

"Quick!" yelled the bronze man. "Doc Savage is in here!"

The other jumped as if a firecracker had gone off under his feet. He hit the ground with a gun in either hand, running. The fellow had nerve.

"Where'd he go?" he bawled.

Doc Savage was not using his normal voice, but a shrill, nondescript tone which might easily be mistaken for the unknown leader. He did not risk speaking now, but wheeled and leveled an arm toward the gate.

More men came out of the workshop, their wild exodus somehow remindful of the comic movies wherein a lion is discovered in a filled room. They saw Doc Savage, and since the bronze man was crouching to shorten his apparent stature, they mistook him for the mysterious leader whom they were awaiting. Doc's leveled arm sent them toward the gate.

"Where'd you get the girl?" one man yelled.

"She *was* with Savage," Doc said. And that was no lie.

Doc Savage looked into the room which held the prisoners. There were two men on guard, both pressing close to the one window, watching the pursuit conducted by their fellows.

The two were lax at the moment, whereas, a bit later, they would have been alert. But the moment was sufficient. Doc put the girl down, rushed them. They saw him just as he descended upon them. It was too late.

During the brief struggle, as the bronze man accomplished the by no means easy feat of holding a man with each hand and making them senseless simultaneously, Monk began to thrash about on the floor, and the pig, Habeas Corpus, came out of a corner, where he had been secreted.

Monk and his pet had recognized Doc.

WHEN the two men were unconscious, Doc lowered them. He leaped to the prisoners and began working on their bindings. He loosened their legs first. Wrists would have to wait, for they might need to move fast.

Monk got the gag out of his mouth. He was only handcuffed at the wrists, and hence could move his fingers.

"What happened?" he gulped.

"Help me loosen the others," Doc rapped.

Renny, ankles loosened, heaved erect.

"What do you think?" he boomed. "What do you think about that Nock Spanner?"

Monk growled. "Aw, you can't hardly blame Spanner."

"They promised Spanner that if he'd tell them what all we had learned about them, they'd turn him loose," Renny growled. "So he told them we hadn't learned much of anything, and they did turn him loose, back there in California, before they brought us here in them infernal balls."

"Spanner wanted to save his neck," Monk defended. "You can't blame him. That runt, Stunted, made the deal with Spanner. I think Stunted didn't want any more killing than was necessary. I think he got Spanner turned loose."

Ham got up and wrenched his gag out, then snapped, "I've been wondering if that Nock Spanner couldn't really be the chief of the ring?"

Doc Savage made no comment on that, a circumstance which caused Monk to look suddenly suspicious.

"Where did they put the apparatus that is the heart of those balls?" Doc asked.

"They've got a big iron safe in the next room," Monk explained. "Locked 'em up in there."

Doc Savage left the prisoners to free each other and lunged into the adjoining room. He found the safe. It was big, modern, and the lock was evidently similar to the electrical devices on the balls, for there was no knob visible.

The bronze man began to work at the door, seeking a method of opening it.

It was a baffling problem. He had no special tools. The vault was as burglarproof as science could devise.

Doc backed away and went into the workshop, searching for a cutting torch. There was almost certain to be one around. Eventually, he did locate one, but the tanks were disconnected and he had to assemble them, and the torch he had selected did not function properly.

He was working madly when two shots ripped out noisily and a man shouted. Doc lunged to the door. Three men had returned through the gate and discovered that something was wrong.

An instant later, Renny's big hand appeared in a window. It held a gun, evidently one taken from the guards. The gun went off four times so swiftly that it required a sharp ear to distinguish the reports.

One man fell down, then dragged himself out of sight, shot through the legs. The other two bounded back through the gate.

There was shouting from the woods. It did not come from very far away. The searchers were coming back. Against such a force—almost forty men—Doc and his group had little chance. The bronze man ran out into the open.

"We'll have to get out!" he shouted.

Renny bounded into view, still carrying the revolver. Long Tom, Johnny and Ham followed, supporting between them the girl, Lanca Jaxon, who seemed to be regaining consciousness. Monk did not appear.

"Monk!" Doc called.

There was a pause and no answer.

"Monk!" Doc made it louder.

The homely chemist popped through the door. He had his pig.

He gulped, "If I only had a minute or two more—"

"Come on!" Doc clipped.

THEY did not run for the gate. The men outside would make exit by that route difficult. They moved back to the rear, and climbed the wall. Doc assisted in getting the girl up and over. She was able to help herself a little. Five revolver bullets made the final stages of their climb exciting.

Going down the other side, they carried much of the camouflaging along. Renny produced a flashlight.

"Found it on the floor!" he boomed. "It's sure gonna help!"

"It will," Doc agreed. "It may save our lives."

They used the flashlight as little as possible at first, not wishing to draw more bullets.

The girl dropped alongside of Doc Savage. She fell down frequently. Her voice was hoarse.

"I made a bad move," she said. "I got tired of waiting in that tree. I was worried about you."

Doc advised, "You should have stayed there."

"I know it." She took a header, got up at once. "I climbed out of the tree and went toward the compound, and pretty soon I heard someone. He used a flashlight and I saw it was their chief, wearing his rubber mask. So I got a stick and clubbed him."

"Kill him?" Doc asked.

She gasped out, "No! He was still alive! I felt of his pulse."

Doc queried, "Then what?"

"I put on his regalia," she said swiftly. "I thought maybe I could get in and help you, or free some of the other prisoners before they got wise. I can make my voice hoarse. Listen."

She made her voice hoarse, and it sounded almost masculine as she continued, "I got as far as the gate, and was coming in when some one must have struck me down."

"I saw that part," Doc told her.

She sobbed once.

"I've made an awful mess," she wailed. "I've got men killed and everything."

"Got men killed?"

"Two of them," she elaborated. "The first was one of the gang, whom I bribed to send a message to Willard Spanner. You see, I knew Willard

Spanner, and knew that he was a friend of yours, and I wanted you on this affair, and thought I'd get you through Spanner."

"So that's how it was." Doc helped her. Pursuit was overtaking them.

"They must have spied on the man who took the message, made him tell about it, then killed him," she said. "Then they killed Spanner, first seizing him in San Francisco, then taking him to New York and making him get a letter telling the whole story, which he had mailed to his New York address, in case anything happened to him. He marked the envelope so it would be turned over to the police if he did not appear to claim it. I heard them talking about it."

Monk howled, "We're gonna have to travel faster than this."

Doc Savage stopped very suddenly. "Listen!"

They halted.

"I heard it, too," Monk muttered.

Chapter XVII
HOLOCAUST

"IT" was a faint moan of a noise, and seemed to come out of the sky far above, persisting only a moment before it died away.

Doc Savage, listening, made a faint, exotic trilling noise, a sound which he made under profound emotion, surprise, sometimes puzzlement. It was an indistinct tone, eerie in quality, and covering a large range. Then, with a snapping leap, he was at Monk's side.

"What's wrong?" Monk gulped.

"What were you doing back there when we called you?" Doc rapped.

"Why—uh—I was in their radio room." The imperative tone of Doc's demand had taken the homely chemist's breath.

"Why?" Doc barked.

Monk let his pet pig fall. Something was up.

"Uh—I thought I'd send out an SOS," he explained. "Somebody might have picked it up and notified the cops. We need all of the help we can get. I intended to tell you about it."

"Did you leave the transmitter on?" Doc queried with a studied calm.

"Sure. Why?"

It was a long moment before the bronze man answered, and during that interim, it was noticeable that sounds of pursuit had ceased, indicating those behind had also heard the moaning sound in the night sky and correctly interpreted its meaning.

"Leases Moore and Quince Ranweil had an arrangement with their friends in the gang to drop nitroglycerine on that enclosure if the radio was turned on and left on," Doc said.

Monk said cheerfully, "Well, that oughta wipe the place off the map. Good riddance, I'd call it!"

But Doc Savage seemed to have other ideas. He listened. Shouting of their pursuers was faintly audible.

"Leases Moore and Quince Randweil are above us in their ball!" a man yelled. "We'd better get back to the pen."

"Sure!" barked another. "We'll rig our own balls! It'll be daylight soon. Then we'll chase this Doc Savage in the balls and use gas on him. We may be able to spot Moore and Randweil, too."

Doc Savage left his own group suddenly, and went toward the pursuers. He moved swiftly. Sounds told him they were going back.

"You fellows!" he called sharply.

They stopped. Silence held them. Then one shouted suspiciously.

"Whatcha want?"

"This is Doc Savage," Doc told them.

"We know that voice," one barked. "Whatcha want?"

Doc hesitated. He had faced this problem before—whether to guarantee his own safety and the safety of his friends by permitting others to die. But it was against his policy, a policy to which he adhered rigidly, to see human life taken needlessly if there was any possible method of avoidance. He reached the decision he had known he would reach.

"Do not go back to that compound," he shouted. "Leases Moore and Quince Randweil may drop nitroglycerine on it!"

Stunned silence fell over the darkened timberland.

THE quiet held for some moments, and toward the end of the interval, Doc was not looking at the spot where the foes stood in the darkness, but at the sky above the compound.

The compound was lighted brilliantly now, illumination having been switched on during the excitement. The lights were very bright. They threw a glow upward some distance.

A gleaming object was outlined above the compound. It poised there, bobbing up and down a little, its presence marked only by the vague rays from below. The ball vehicle of Leases Moore and Quince Randweil!

"It's a trick!" a man shrilled. "The bronze guy is trying to keep us away from the pen!"

They ran back, and although Doc Savage called out again, it had no effect. Doc fell silent, and stood there, unpleasant expectancy gripping him.

Renny came up, splashing a flashlight beam.

"Didn't do much good," he said dryly.

Doc made no reply; the others of his party

gathered nearer. The ball was still above the compound, swaying up and down, as if the control device was not perfected to a point where the thing could be held absolutely stationary.

Then a rifle smacked. Others followed. A machine gun made rapid stuttering sounds.

From within the compound, they were shooting at the ball, striving to drive it away. The gunfire became a continuous volley.

Suddenly, a round spot of light appeared on the undersurface of the ball. A port had been opened.

Below the ball, dropping swiftly, came something small and black. It fell lazily. In size, it was like a beer keg. Another of the articles appeared, then a third—a fourth—a fifth. All five of them were in the air—when the first hit the ground.

The world turned blasting white as the nitroglycerine struck, and the earth heaved and tumbled and trees fell over. Bushes lost their leaves. The wind of the explosion, reaching as far as where Doc and his party stood, upset them, and the ground, shaking, tossed them about as if in an earthquake.

From the compound, there was no screaming. Possibly no man lived to scream after the blasts. Flame and debris were in the sky, and the ball, fantastic thing that it was, had backed up into dark nothingness until it was now invisible.

Debris falling back made a great roar; it added more fuel to the flaming compound, and slavering copious quantities of black smoke kited upward.

"The gasoline tank!" Lanca Jaxon said hoarsely.

After that, no one said anything.

The balls in the compound had been shattered. They could not see them. The smoke spread, mushrooming, and the light of the flames jumped above it and played like scarlet goblins on a black toadstool.

Doc said, "We had better see if we can do something."

But before they could move there came a sobbing noise from above, as of a gigantic bat in swift passage, and the ball of Moore and Randweil was suddenly above them.

"They're gonna attack us!" Monk shouted.

THEY were standing in an open space, plainly lighted by the flames. They had been seen. Doc sent out an arm and started them for the cover of the nearest tree. The girl was past running swiftly, and he carried her.

As soon as they were under the foliage, such of it as still stuck to the trees, the bronze man urged them sharply to the left. Fallen limbs were thick on the ground.

"Get down under this stuff and crawl," Doc directed.

They did that. A minute passed. Two. Then the earth heaved under them, a fabulous crash set their eardrums ringing, and there was white fire in the air, as if lightning had struck. Debris fell all about, making sounds like fast running animals.

"Nitro!" Renny howled. "They're trying to finish us!"

The branches under which they lay had shifted a little, and Doc Savage, looking up, could see the ball, the open hatch like a round, evil red eye. It bobbed toward them, something hideous and incredible in its movement. They could hear the noise of machinery inside.

A man had head and shoulders over the hatch opening. He was a plump, rounded man—Quince Randweil, no doubt, and he was looking down. They could see him waving an arm behind his back. He had seen them, was directing Leases Moore, at the controls, to bring the ball directly over them.

Then Quince Randweil drew back for a moment, and when he showed himself again, he was gripping a container of nitro as large as a beer keg. He had some difficulty holding it, and, leaning down, made ready to drop it.

Monk said in a dry, shrill voice, "Ham, if we're gonna die now, I want to apologize for riding you.'"

Ham mumbled, "You big ape—"

Doc Savage rapped, "Renny! That revolver you are—"

A revolver went *bang!* beside them. There was a louder report overhead, so infinitely much louder that it beggared description.

Doc Savage, who was looking directly at the ball and Randweil, knew the nitro Randweil held had exploded. One instant the ball was there; the next it was not—and the bronze man's eyes held only pain, and knowledge of terrible danger from exploding parts of the aerial vehicle.

He did not know how long afterward it was that someone spoke. It was Renny's voice.

"I didn't intend to do that," Renny said.

He was shifting his revolver from one hand to another, as if it were hot. He looked at Doc.

"What else could I do?" he mumbled.

"Nothing," Doc told him.

"I didn't intend to hit the nitro," Renny groaned. "Honest, I didn't. I figured on shooting past that Randweil bird and scaring him into dropping the stuff before he reached us. But no man can shoot straight in this light."

"You didn't do bad," said Monk, who was inclined to be the bloodthirsty member of Doc's crowd.

"No man can shoot straight in light like this," Renny grumbled again. "I should've let Doc do it. You were asking for the gun just as I shot, weren't you, Doc?"

"Yes," said the bronze man. "Come on. Let us see what we can do at the compound."

THEY could do nothing. That was evident when they came close. The blast of the nitro had been terrific, and had shattered not only the four balls, but the workshop and the tank as well.

One missile must have landed directly on the workshop—possibly more; for hardly a trace of the place remained other than twisted steel and blasted woodwork. Even the compound walls had been broken into surprisingly small pieces.

Doc Savage gave particular attention to where the safe had been. Hope that it had survived faded, for he distinguished one side and back standing where the flames were hottest. The floor of the workshop had been low, and the ruptured gasoline tank had poured it contents into the depression.

There was no hope that the "hearts" of the weird aerial balls, the mechanism which was the secret of their amazing performance, had survived.

"Holy cow!" Renny said gloomily. "It looks like nobody is ever gonna know how them things worked."

Doc Savage nodded slowly. He would investigate, of course, but it was doubtful if the secret could be solved. Some new theory must have been stumbled upon, by accident. But he would work on it, work hard for the next few months, he resolved.

Monk took his eyes from the flames and looked pained, as if something had just stung him.

"We should have thought of it before!" he exploded.

"What?" Renny boomed.

"Lanca Jaxon, here, knocked out the mastermind, the bird who invented these balls," Monk explained. "She said she left him unconscious. Maybe he's around somewhere. If so, we can grab him and make him tell—"

"No use," Lanca Jaxon said, hoarsely.

"Why?" Monk eyed her, puzzled.

"I left him close to the compound wall," she said. "He was killed with the rest. I am sure of it."

Monk returned to gloomy depths, but almost at once started again, seized by another thought.

"Who did you knock senseless?" he asked.

"Stunted," said the girl. "That runty fellow—Stunted."

Renny made some comment that had to do with the way things had come out. His voice was a throaty roaring as Doc Savage listened to it.

That roaring! It might have been a forewarning of what the future held, an omen of the terror and mystery and awful destruction that was to come; an advance echo, as it were, of the fantastic, eerie thing that was to give Doc Savage and his aides some of their most grisly minutes. *The Roar Devil!*

The Roar Devil—they heard it first in the mountains of New York State. Sound of it defied those terror-stricken souls who tried to describe it. And the earth trembled, heaving as from tread of a solar colossus, and dams burst, and men died.

The Roar Devil. They heard it. They felt it. But it was never seen. Or was it? Hideous, inexplicable things had happened to certain men in a position to discover this fantastic horror.

But Renny, not having been gifted with the ability to fathom what the future held, went on with his roaring-voiced conversation.

THE END

INTERMISSION by Will Murray

One of Doc Savage's specialties was investigating weird phenomena that baffled the authorities. This volume focuses on that aspect of Doc's career.

At the end of *The Spook Legion,* Dent blurbed our lead novel this way:

> There was, also, the matter of *The Sky Corsair,* which was to be the next menace that confronted Doc Savage and his aides. *The Sky Corsair* was something different, something difficult for men to comprehend, and because men, since time immemorial, have feared what they cannot understand, it brought terror.
>
> A man was seized in San Francisco at noon. His dead body was found in New York City exactly three hours later. That was *The Sky Corsair*'s doing. And because the dead man was a friend, Doc Savage took a hand—and found himself in the most concentrated melee of terror, death and mystery which he had ever confronted.

Dent's outline bore no title, but ultimately he decided to call the story *The Secret in the Sky.* It's a yarn which evokes for modern readers reports of Unidentified Flying Objects—a phenomenon which did not begin until 1947—a dozen years in the future of this 1935 adventure.

Lester Dent wasn't being as prescient in offering the concepts behind *The Secret in the Sky* as he was in other Doc adventures. The science fiction pulp magazines like *Amazing Stories* and Street & Smith's own *Astounding Science-Fiction* were exploring similar ideas in their own pages.

For his own part, Dent seems to have been inspired by rival pulpster Erle Stanley Gardner's 1929 *Argosy* serial *The Sky's the Limit!* Dent and Gardner were rivals in the word-production pulp race of the 1930s. Gardner's hero, newspaperman Click Kendall, faced very similar sky phenomena in that story—although the Gardner tale went in extraterrestrial directions Doc Savage never explored. No doubt Dent remembered this story. *Argosy* was his favorite pulp magazine, and Lester read it religiously every Wednesday evening.

Although Gardner entered the fiction field some years before Dent, they shared several eerie parallels in their respective careers. Both studied law and became expert sailors. Both wrote some of their earliest pulp stories for Street & Smith's *Top-Notch Magazine.* Self-styled fiction factories, both owed their unbelievable production to their skill composing stories via dictaphone and assisted by a secretary. That very prolificity required them to sometimes resort to pen names. And amazingly their most famous creations were born in the same month.

A little-known morsel of popular culture trivia is the parallel development of both characters. Dent began writing Doc Savage on December 10, 1932, finishing just before Christmas.

On December 9, Gardner wrote his new publisher concerning a novel he was revising, then titled "Reasonable Doubt." It starred a combative young attorney Gardner was having trouble naming.

On that date, Gardner explained:

> I am making him into a new character, and since your editors apparently disapprove of both Stark and Keene as names, I am calling him Perry Mason, and the character I am trying to create for him is that of a fighter who is possessed of infinite patience. He tries to jockey his enemies into a position where he can deliver one good knockout punch.

Dent himself once observed, "…a mason is a builder, and the word parry means to fend off; which is the way the character works—fending off numerous enemies while building his case."

Doc Savage was similarly named. Both the nickname "Doc" and his given name of "Clark" suggested the character's superior intelligence, while "Savage" symbolized great physical prowess.

Like Dent, Gardner raced to deliver his novel by Christmas. It seems strange to reflect that during those short weeks two pulp speed demons were

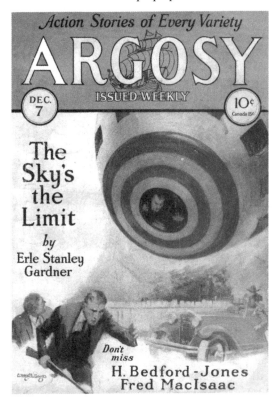

Erle Stanley Gardner dictates a story.

simultaneously spewing out words that would endure longer than either dreamed.

Doc Savage and Perry Mason debuted within weeks of one another. *Doc Savage Magazine* hit newsstands on February 17, 1933. The first of the many Perry Mason novels was slated to be issued by William Morrow on the 15th. *The Case of the Velvet Claws* was delayed to March 1st, however. Like the first Doc Savage novel, the last chapter promised another adventure very soon. The second installment of each series was written in January 1933.

Both characters went on to become immensely successful well beyond the lives of their creators. No doubt Perry Mason and Ham Brooks are two of the most famous fictional barristers ever created.

Which brings us to one of the secrets behind *Secret in the Sky.*

Although the storyline ranges from New York to California, much of the action takes place in Tulsa, Oklahoma where Dent was toiling as a telegraph operator and teletype repairman for the Associated Press when he first broke into print in 1929. The A.P. office was on the fourth floor of the Tulsa World Building on South Boulder Avenue.

As Lester so often told the story, he arrived early for the night shift, only to find a fellow telegrapher industriously pounding away at the office typewriter. When he discovered his coworker was writing a fiction story, Dent

thought it was a big joke. He changed his mind when the other coolly turned over a check for $450.00—about $10,000 in today's buying power.

"I was out to spend any and all $450 checks I could get my hands on: that's all I thought about," Dent later asserted.

The identity of that writer has never been established. But we do know thei names of Dent's coworkers, which were Leonard F. Presse, Lynn L. Morris, George Dickens and J. L. Shoemaker. Although Dent's main Doc Savage ghost writer, Harold A. Davis, oversaw the telegraph desk, Davis is not known to have written professional fiction prior to 1932. And while Davis is surely high on the list of suspects, astonishingly, the Tulsa *World* was hotbed of writers.

Dent once mentioned a Tulsa *World* night editor-who was also a pulpster. Probably this was Davis' assistant, George Ketchum. And there was J. Nelson Taylor, who in 1929 was a police reporter, and wrote for contemporary detective magazines. Consolidated Press telegrapher Lawrence A. Foster was another who dabbled in fiction on the side. City editor Manton L. Marrs was assisted by Edward Burks, brother of one of the most prolific pulp writers in the business, Arthur J Burks, although it's unknown if Ed Burks ever tried fiction. He was a rewrite man. Some of these moonlighting pulpeteers may have been inspired by Dent breaking into the field, as he once explained:

Nobody takes the other guy's ambitions to write seriously. When I first started, I got hoorawed from all sides. I got it at home, when the frau picked love scenes out of the yarns to laugh at, and I got it at the office, where I was 'S. S. Van Dine' or whoever happened to be the popular writer at the moment. Okay. That's human nature, and I never did like human nature much. But one day Uncle Sam brought us a check, and it was human nature to pass it around. That was the metamorphosis. Maybe the hoorawing did not change, but for me, it did. No longer did it have that essence of vitriol. Then the erstwhile jokesters began bringing me, in dead seriousness, stories to criticize, and that was the pay-off. Boy, was their yarns lousy!

In Chapter 7 of *The Secret in the Sky,* Doc Savage consults a feature writer for the Tulsa *Graphic* whom he describes as "a dresser whose sartorial perfection rivaled that of Ham."

This glancing mention assumes greater significance when you understand that Dent had originally called that paper the *World.* Editor John L. Nanovic changed it. And the nameless reporter Dent alluded to was yet another writing crony.

Walter F. Biscup (1904-1981) joined the *World*

Lester Dent

staff in 1926. Early on, he was their courtroom reporter. A 1929 *World* article lauded him this way:

> One of the outstanding feats for The *World* by Biscup was a midnight interview with a desperado who, armed with revolvers and a machine gun, had battled his way out of the county jail. Biscup gained an exclusive story for The *World* that was reprinted in scores of cities. He also had worked on fully a dozen murder mysteries, and in some instances printed facts that enabled criminals to be brought to justice.

Biscup led a colorful career that stretched over five decades. He also moonlighted for publications as diverse as *The Underworld* and *Esquire.* He and Dent were fast friends. There is no doubt that Dent had Biscup in mind when writing that brief scene.

Those were the days of the infamous Oklahoma bank robber Charles Arthur "Pretty Boy" Floyd. By some strange synchronicity, Biscup bore a startling resemblance to Floyd. It was so remarkable that Floyd's own son once mistook the reporter for his much-wanted father. On another occasion, Biscup was eating lunch in a downtown Tulsa restaurant when a police officer walked in and stuck a submachine muzzle into his back, thinking he had captured Oklahoma's feared Public Enemy No. 1.

After Floyd killed retired Checotah police chief Ervin A. Kelley on April 9, 1932, Biscup interviewed Floyd's wife, Ruby, who told him, "Well, that son of a bitch won't trail him any longer, will he?" Her reaction to Biscup's uncanny resemblance to her husband went unrecorded.

The inevitable finally caught up with Pretty Boy Floyd. He was killed in October 1934. After that, Walter Biscup no doubt breathed—and dined—easier.

Former Tulsa *World* managing editor Gene Curtis recalled Biscup as "a dapper dresser who always wore a shirt with French cuffs and cuff links. Every day, he would come in, take off his jacket, remove his cuff links, roll his sleeves up exactly one roll, and start writing. Walter Biscup had a computer-like mind. He remembered very tiny details about everything he ever covered. You could ask him about a murder case from 15 or 20 years before, and he'd still know everything about it."

Biscup rose to the position of chief editorial pages writer, a position he held until his death in September, 1981.

Was Walter Biscup the writer who inspired Lester Dent? Probably not. For Biscup was a crime reporter, not a telegraph operator. But Dent's

Walter Biscup

Courtesy of the Tulsa World

description of his unnamed writer's sartorial flair begs this question: did Biscup inspire Dent's portrayal of dapper Ham Brooks? Seems likely.

During his three years on the Associated Press wire, Lester developed into an inveterate and somewhat screwball practical joker. The story is told that while working at the *World,* Dent set a trap for his boss. Rigging a thin electrified wire to a coin, he lowered it from an upper-story window to the sidewalk and waited for his victim to arrive for work. However, it happened that no less than the publisher of the *World* spied the trick coin first and, picking it up, received a painful but harmless shock. When the publisher tried to fire Dent, he found to his disgust that Lester was an Associated Press employee and therefore beyond his power to fire. Dent kept his job.

Another time, Lester wired a door so that anyone who touched it would be trapped by the charge until released. Probably this pranking was an escape from the boring routine of handling the routine daily telegraph traffic of his profession. Lester simply went to more imaginative extremes than the average office jokester.

One associate, Virgil D. Curry of the Tulsa *Tribune,* recalled Dent warmly. "Much of Dent's work was on the night shift, and I met him usually when he was going off duty and I was coming on. I knew him only casually, but favorably, as an affable, jovial fellow, always in for some fun. He encountered many slack periods on the 'graveyard' and used this time constructively by dabbling at fiction. His efforts were so successful that he left Tulsa eventually for more advantageous climes in the East."

The Secret in the Sky has the distinction of having been written aboard the *Albatross* late in 1934. Dent was taking the boat to Miami for the first time. The manuscript was mailed from the Francis Marion Hotel in Charleston, South Carolina, where Dent had put in to have the schooner overhauled.

As reported in the February 15th, 1935 issue of *The American Fiction Guild Bulletin:*

> Stewart Sterling, writer of more radio programs than most of us would know what to do with, went southward in his 72-foot yacht awhile back and stopped for dinner at a Charleston, S.C., hotel. He had just started on the oysters when he heard a hail off the starboard bow and there was Lester (Doc Savage) Dent and wife, also dinner-

bound at the moment. Dent's schooner and Sterling's yacht rubbed sides all the way south.

Sterling—in real life Prentice Winchell—was a top pulp writer familar to readers of *Black Mask,* and scripted so me early *Shadow* radio dramas. They knew one another through mutual friends in the pulp writing community, Norvell Page and Theodore Tinsley. Winchell was also headed south to Miami on his yacht, the *Scotty II.* Such was the life of the top-selling pulp writers. Florida was a favorite winter getaway state for New York pulpeteers. When the ships reached Miami, both the *Albatross* and the *Scotty II* docked at the City Yacht basin.

Sometimes Dent followed his outlines to the letter and Street & Smith copyedited the story lightly. This was one such time. By this period, Dent was writing very lean stories, no longer dwelling on Doc's wartime past, his Mayan gold reserves, or his main purpose in life.

Doc Savage would return to Tulsa many times in the future, and Lester Dent would later claim that Monk Mayfair was a Tulsa boy. You wouldn't know it to read *The Secret in the Sky.* Monk doesn't at all act like he's back home.

We leap ahead to 1939 for *The Giggling Ghosts,* a fun romp which once again finds the Man of Bronze investigating baffling phenomena.

The opening of the Lincoln Tunnel connecting Manhattan to New Jersey in December 1937, appears to be the trigger for this premise. At this time, America was beginning to stir from the doldrums of the Great Depression. Begun in 1934 and costing 43 million dollars, the Lincoln Tunnel was built by WPA workers. The Works Progress Association was only one of President Franklin D. Roosevelt's New Deal relief programs that helped put America back to work in the 1930s.

One of the signal events pointing to a better future was the opening of the New York World's Fair in 1939. Although not yet open at the time of publication, the Fair—considered the most iconic of the 20th century—was taking shape in the Flushing Meadows. Dominated by the massive Trylon and Perisphere, the fantastic fairgrounds proved irresistible to Lester Dent. Doc and his men experience a brief but exciting brush with the World of Tomorrow—which sets the stage for one of the novels we'll be reprinting in our next volume, *World's Fair Goblin.*

One of the world's top pulp fiction historians, Will Murray is the author of over fifty novels, including eight posthumous Doc Savage collaborations with Lester Dent under the "Kenneth Robeson" byline, and forty in the long-running Destroyer series.

Prentice Winchell, aka Stewart Sterling

Ghosts and giggles; mystery and menace—and a smashing climax that makes Doc Savage risk everything for

The Giggling Ghosts

By KENNETH ROBESON

Complete Book-length Novel

Chapter I
GIGGLING GIRL

THE dictionary says:

GIGGLE: To laugh with short catches of the breath and voice; to laugh in an affected or a silly manner or with an attempt at repression.

That is the definition of a giggle as given in the dictionary.

There is nothing extraordinary about giggling. Most persons giggle a little at one time or another. The psychologists claim that it is a form of laughter, and therefore good for you.

But when ghosts giggle, it is different.

The giggling these ghosts did was not good for anybody, it developed.

Like many unpleasant and momentous events, the existence of the giggling ghosts began as rumors. There was nothing very definite. Just stories.

A small boy came tearing home one night and told his mother he'd heard a ghost giggling in a brush patch. Now most ghosts are seen by small boys, and so the story was pleasantly smiled upon.

No one thought anything about it. Naturally it didn't get in the newspapers.

A New Jersey politician—the giggling ghosts seemed to haunt only New Jersey—was the next man to see a ghost. His constituents had long ago stopped believing anything the politician said about lowering taxes, so they treated his story dubiously.

He'd been taking an evening walk in a Jersey City park, and he'd heard a giggling ghost, and caught a glimpse of it. This little item got in the newspapers, and quite a number of people humorously remarked that more politicians should be haunted.

Two or three other giggling ghost stories got around, and at this point a bad mistake was made: too many people thought the stories were being imagined. This was the Twentieth Century, the age of realism in thought and action. There were no such thing as ghosts.

Particularly, there could be no such thing as giggling ghosts.

A girl was the first one to make the awful discovery that the ghosts' giggling was catching.

"MIAMI" DAVIS was the girl's name. She had been standing with her head shoved through a hole where a pane had been broken out of a window of an old storehouse just across the Hudson River from New York City.

She had heard a giggling ghost. She was trying to see it.

She had been trying to see the ghost for about three minutes when she caught the giggling.

The giggling of girls is usually pleasant enough to listen to. Girls will giggle if you tickle their necks, and when you tell them nice little lies.

The giggling of Miami Davis was not pleasant to listen to. Not in the least. It was terrible.

Her sounds were made with short catches of the breath; there was certainly an attempt at repression; she did not want to make the noises. She was giggling, according to the literal word of the dictionary definition.

The girl grabbed her mouth with her right hand, her nose with her left, and tried to stop the sounds coming out. She had no luck. Then she tried to gag herself with a mouthful of her own coat collar. That failed.

She ended up by fleeing wildly from the storehouse.

The storehouse was made of brick, had a tin roof. It looked as if the Bureau of Public Safety should have ordered it torn down about ten years ago. The storehouse was full of steam shovels, dump trucks, excavators and other construction equipment.

At one end of the storehouse was the Hudson River. Past the other end ran a typical waterfront street: rutted, dirty, haunted by smells.

The sky was a dome of gloom in the late dusk, crowded with clouds, promising rain. It had showered about an hour ago, just enough so that the marks were visible where rain drops had splattered the dust on the pavement.

The girl got in the middle of the street and ran. Ran as if something were after her. She covered about a block and reached a car—a small convertible coupé, new and neat—and pitched into it.

The girl was frightened. She jabbed at the rearview mirror, knocking it around until she could see herself in it. She saw a pert, dynamic small girl with an unusual quantity of copper-colored hair, large blue eyes, inviting lips, and a face that was distinctly fascinating in a bright way.

Suddenly she giggled. Convulsively. She couldn't help it. And complete terror came on her own face.

She started the car motor and drove away speedily.

FIFTEEN minutes later, some policemen listened to the girl—and smiled. She was an easy girl to smile at. Also, her story was ridiculous, and that encouraged them to smile.

"How did you happen to be looking into a storehouse for a giggling ghost?" a cop asked skeptically.

Miami Davis giggled hysterically.

"I followed the ghost there," she said.

"Oh, you followed it. Well, well!"

"I was working late," the girl said. "When I left the office—it's in a factory not far from this storehouse—I saw a shadowy figure. It was a ghostly figure." She looked at them, giggled, then screamed wildly, *"A ghost figure, you hear? I followed it. It giggled!* That's why I followed it. I had been hearing those stories about giggling ghosts."

"Was it a male or a female ghost?" a cop inquired.

The girl giggled angrily.

"You don't believe me!" she said, between giggles.

"There have been some yarns about giggling ghosts floating around," one policeman admitted.

The captain of police came in then, and heard the story. He did not believe it. Not a word of it.

"Go home; go to bed and call a doctor," he ordered.

The girl stamped an irate foot, giggled wrathfully at him, and flounced out.

A cop followed her, and stopped her when she reached her coupé.

"Look," the cop said, "why not go to Doc Savage?"

This apparently failed to mean much to the girl.

"Doc—who?" she asked.

"Doc Savage."

The girl frowned, trying to remember, then said, "There was a story in the newspapers a while back about a man named Doc Savage who had discovered something new about atoms or molecules or some such thing. But why should—or do you mean he treats—crazy people? Well, I'm not crazy!"

The cop waited until she stopped giggling.

"You've got me wrong," the officer said. "This guy's a scientist, but that ain't his main racket. He puts in most of his time going around helping people out of trouble. And the more unusual the trouble they're in, the better he likes it."

"I don't understand," the girl said.

"It's his hobby, or something. Helping people. I know it sounds crazy, but this Doc Savage is a good man to see about this giggling ghost business."

The girl giggled while she thought that over.

"It won't be much trouble," the girl said, "to see this Doc Savage."

"No," the cop said, "it won't be much trouble."

They were both wrong.

THE girl drove across the George Washington Bridge into New York City, guided her car to the uptown business district, and parked her car near a very tall building.

The elevator starter in the big building said, "So you want to see Doc Savage?"

The girl nodded, and she was ushered to an express elevator.

A man hurried and got in the elevator with her.

The man was tall, thick-bodied, and wore an expensive gray hat with a snap brim, fuzzy gray sports oxfords, and gray gloves of high quality. He also wore a yellow slicker.

Miami Davis—she was not giggling as much now—noticed what the man wore. She did not see the man's face, because he kept it averted.

The elevator climbed up its shaft.

Suddenly the man in the slicker yelled, "Operator! *The girl is gonna hit you—*"

Then the man himself hit the operator. He knocked the fellow senseless with a blow from behind, a skull blow with a blackjack which he had whipped from a pocket. The operator could not have seen who had hit him.

Because of what the man had yelled, the operator would think that the girl had struck him.

The man who had slugged the operator showed cigarette-stained teeth in a vicious grin.

"He'll think you slugged 'im," he told the girl. "That won't do you any good."

He bent over, lifted one of his trousers legs, and removed a double-barreled derringer from a clip holster fastened, garterlike, below his knee. He pointed the derringer at the girl.

"This wouldn't do you any good, either!" he said.

Chapter II
CHANGED MINDS

THE girl stared at the derringer.

The gun was not much longer than the middle finger of the man who held it, and the barrels were one above the other so that looking into their maws was like looking at a fat black colon. She could have inserted her little fingers in either barrel without much difficulty. She could see the bullets, like lead-colored bald heads.

"This thing"—the man moved the derringer—"will do as much damage as any other gun."

The girl moved, pressed herself into a corner of the elevator, and went through swallowing motions several times.

The man said, "When we get back to the lobby, we say the elevator operator fainted, see? Then you walk out with me." He gestured again with the gun. "Make any cracks, sis, and they'll be your epitaph!"

The girl tried to swallow again.

The man folded his newspaper carefully and tucked it in a pocket so it wouldn't be left lying around for fingerprints. He stepped to the elevator controls. When the operator had dropped after being slugged, he had instinctively shifted the control lever to the center, so that the cage had come to a stop.

The man set the control at "Down." He seemed confident. He leaned against the side of the cage, cocking an eye on the girl, whistling idly as he waited. Abruptly his confidence got a puncture.

"What the devil?" he gulped.

The elevator was not going down. It was going up. *Up!* The man doubled over, stared at the controls. The handle was on "Down." But the cage was going up.

The man yanked at the handle, thinking control markings might be reversed—but the cage kept going up. The controls now seemed to have absolutely no effect on the elevator.

The man's mind leaped instantly to the conclusion that he was in a fantastic trap. He made snarling noises, even fired his derringer at the elevator controls, but accomplished nothing except to deafen himself and the girl.

His eyes, searching for escape, found the safety escape hatch in the top of the cage. He jumped at that until he got it open. With a great deal of grunting, kicking and snarling, he managed to pull himself through the hatch at the top of the slowly rising cage.

The girl let him go.

The man crouched on top of the cage; there was no stable footing. He clutched at a cable to steady himself, but the cable was moving, and he cursed.

The elevator was rising very slowly, although it was an express lift, and expresses in this building normally traveled at high speed. Obviously there was some kind of emergency mechanism in operation.

The skyscraper was served by a battery of elevators, all operating side by side. There was no division between the shafts—only the vertical steel tracks on which the cages operated.

The man peered upward, saw another cage descending in the adjacent shaft. He made a lightning decision to take a long chance; he jumped for the top of the other cage as it passed. And he made it!

THE elevator in which Miami Davis was left alone with the senseless operator continued its snail-like progress upward.

The girl stood with her back against the cage, palms pressing against the side panels. When the elevator stopped, the girl took hold of her lower lip with her teeth and giggled a little.

"Miami" Davis

For a moment there was silence.

Then, outside, a voice spoke. An unusual voice. It was a calm voice, with a remarkable tonal inflection, a quality of repressed power.

"The door will be opened in a moment," the unusual voice said. "The best thing you can do is to come out peacefully."

A moment later, the elevator door did open, and Miami Davis saw a giant bronze man.

The bronze man was so remarkable that she knew instinctively that his was the voice which had spoken a moment before. It had been a striking voice, and this bronze giant was striking.

There was a symmetry about his physical development which took away from his apparent size, until he was viewed at close range. He seemed normally built at a distance. His features were regular, his skin was an unusual bronze hue, and he had eyes that were like pools of flake gold being stirred by tiny winds.

The bronze man stood not more than a pace in front of the elevator door—where, Miami Davis thought suddenly, he could have been shot down by any gunman inside the elevator.

The bronze man was so close that he saw the elevator was empty, except for Miami Davis and the unconscious operator.

"You slug the operator?" the bronze man demanded.

Miami Davis shook her head and giggled. "No, I—"

"There has been trouble before in elevators that lead up here," the bronze man said. "We installed a mechanical device, that, if the operator doesn't hold the control in a certain fashion, causes the cage to rise slowly to this floor. Also, an alarm bell rings. Now what happened?"

Miami Davis heard an electric bell buzzing steadily somewhere. Probably that was the alarm which the bronze man had said rang when something went wrong in the elevators.

"There was a man in here." She pointed at the roof of the cage. "He climbed out. I think he jumped to a cage in another shaft."

From below came shot sounds: two reports; a pause about long enough for the man to have reloaded the derringer followed; then came two more reports.

A man screeched. The screech was faint, with an eerie quality lent by the great distance it traveled up through the elevator shaft.

"You see!" the girl gasped. "He's down below! Shooting!"

Miami Davis then stepped out of the elevator, advanced—brought up with a gasp. She had walked into something she couldn't see! She explored with her hands. Bulletproof glass, she decided. It must be that.

She fumbled for a way around. The panel was like a fence in front of the elevator door. No wonder the bronze man had felt so safe!

The bronze giant moved to a second elevator, entered, and sent the cage down. This was a private lift, and it sank with almost the same speed with which it would have fallen free, then brought up at the first floor with enough force to cause the bronze man to brace himself. He got out.

People were running around in the lobby, and the proprietor of the cigar stand was under the counter for safety. Out on the street, a cop was blowing his whistle furiously.

"Anyone hurt?" the bronze man asked.

"Something queer just happened, Mr. Savage. A man rode down on top of one of the cages. We started to ask him questions. He fought his way out."

"He shoot anybody?"

"No, Mr. Savage. He had a derringer, and you can't hit much with one of them things."

The bronze man went out to the street.

A cop said, "He got away, Mr. Savage. A guy in a car picked him up."

WHEN Doc Savage returned to the eighty-sixth floor, Miami Davis had given up trying to get past the bulletproof glass around the elevator door.

She had discovered the panel did not quite

reach to the ceiling, and that accounted for her having been able to speak to the bronze man. She didn't feel like trying to climb over the top.

Doc Savage went to a wall panel in the corridor, opened it, and disclosed a recess containing small levers. He moved a lever and an electric motor whirred and the glass panel sank into the floor, its edge then forming part of the modernistic design of the floor. Miami Davis looked at the bronze man.

"What I read about you in the newspapers must've been straight stuff," she said.

"What do you mean?"

"I read you were a remarkable guy with a lot of scientific gimmicks."

"Oh."

"And I was told that your business is helping people out of trouble. Is that right?"

"It isn't far from the truth," the bronze man admitted.

"I've got trouble. That's why I am here." Miami Davis made a grim mouth. "More trouble than I thought, it begins to seem."

Doc Savage led the way into a reception room which was furnished with a huge safe, an exquisitely inlaid table, a deep rug and comfortable chairs.

The window afforded a startling view of Manhattan spires, and an open door gave a glimpse of another room—a great paneled room, where all available floor space was occupied by bookcases.

"Have a chair, please."

The girl sat down weakly.

"Now, suppose you give me some idea about this trouble of yours," Doc Savage suggested.

"That man on the elevator tried to stop me from coming here—"

"Go back to the beginning."

"Oh—well—" Miami Davis took a moment to assemble her information. "It began this afternoon when I saw the ghost sneaking into a waterfront storehouse and I followed it."

"Ghost?"

"Well—I thought so."

The girl giggled a little, helplessly.

"You were curious and followed a ghost into a storehouse," Doc Savage said. "So far, it's—well, unusual. But go on."

"Then I began to giggle," the girl said. She shuddered.

"You what?"

"Giggled."

"I see."

Miami Davis knotted and unknotted her hands. "It sounds silly, doesn't it?"

"Well, at least extraordinary," the bronze man admitted.

"It was horrible! Something just—just came over me. I seemed to go all to pieces. It frightened me. So I fled from the storehouse."

"And after you fled from the storehouse, then what?"

Miami Davis did not look at Doc Savage. "A policeman told me about you. It just occurred to him you might be interested. So I came here."

Doc Savage's metallic features gave no indication of what he might be thinking.

"Let us hope," he said unexpectedly, "that you are telling the whole story."

"Oh, but I am."

Chapter III
THE MAN WHO OWNED A STOREHOUSE

WITHOUT speaking, the bronze man took the young woman by the elbow, guided her into a vast room which contained a great deal of laboratory equipment, seated her in a modernistic metal chair and did several things: first, he had her inhale and exhale several times through a tube which led to a complicated-looking contraption; then he examined the young woman, giving particular attention to her eyes. When he finished, he seemed slightly puzzled.

"You're not intoxicated, apparently," he said.

"I like that!" the girl gasped.

"Your eyes indicate that you are not a drug addict, and you seem earnest, although excited."

"Maybe I'm crazy," Miami Davis said dryly.

"We might have a look," Doc Savage said, "at the storehouse where you trailed the giggling ghost."

"Please," the girl said earnestly. "Let's do that."

"Just a moment."

Doc Savage went into the library, picked up the telephone, and spoke for some minutes. The telephone was fitted into a boxlike device which, when pressed against the face, made it possible to use the instrument without being overheard by anyone in the room; the girl did not catch anything that the bronze man said. Doc put down the telephone.

"All right," he said. "We'll go now."

Rain had started to leak out of a sky that was grimy-looking, when Doc Savage, driving one of his cars, headed into the street. The rain came in drops as fine as fog, so it would probably continue for some time. It was rain that obscured vision, and most cars had their headlights turned on.

Doc Savage's car was a coupé, long, heavy, of expensive make, but with a subdued paint job that did not attract attention. There was little outward indication that the machine was armor-plated and equipped with bulletproof glass. Doc used his car in preference to that of the girl's, which he placed in his garage that lay under the towering skyscraper.

Finally the bronze man said, "This seems to be it," and pulled up before the old brick storehouse with the tin roof.

"You still think I'm a phony?" Miami Davis demanded.

"I still think it is unusual for a woman to follow a ghost."

"Well, I—" The girl giggled, although she tried not to do so.

Doc asked, "What did it look like—this ghost?"

"I—it was just a shadowy figure."

"Did it make a noise walking?"

"I didn't hear any noise."

"If you would tell the truth—"

The girl put up her chin indignantly. "I told you everything that happened!"

Without commenting on that, the bronze man wheeled his car over the curb and up to the side door of the storehouse.

When the bronze man went to the storehouse door, he carried a piece of apparatus which he had taken from a compartment in the car.

This device had three principal parts: the first part, which he fastened to the storehouse door with suction cups, was small, and insulated wires ran from this to an electrical amplifier; and from the amplifier other wires ran to a telephonic headset which the bronze man donned. He switched on the contrivance and listened.

The device was a high-powered sonic amplifier which took the smallest sound and increased its volume several hundred thousand times.

Somewhere in the storehouse a rat ran and squealed, and in the amplifier headset it sounded as if an elephant had galloped over a wooden bridge and trumpeted. The girl came close and listened, too.

They had not listened long before they heard the giggling.

THE giggling was inside the storehouse. Three or four gigglings, all going at once, judging from the sounds.

It was fantastic. No other sound—just a concert of giggling inside the storehouse.

"Now," the girl said, "what did I tell you?"

"You think that is your giggling ghost?"

"It sounds like more than one."

Doc Savage took the listening device back to the car and replaced it in its compartment.

The bronze man returned to the storehouse carrying a small cylindrical metal container holding anaesthetic gas under pressure. The container was equipped with a nozzle and valve. He inserted the nozzle in a crack at the bottom of the storehouse door and turned the valve.

With a hiss, gas rushed out of the container into the storehouse. Doc waited, depending on the sound of rain on the tin storehouse roof to keep the "ghosts" inside from hearing the gas. Evidently the rain on the roof was the reason they had not heard his car coming.

The girl pointed at the cylinder. "I don't get this."

"Gas. Anaesthetic. Practically no odor or color. There are men inside the storehouse, and the gas will make them unconscious without doing them any lasting harm."

"Oh."

Eventually the bronze man tried the storehouse door. It wasn't fastened; it came open at his shove. Inside, there was a cavern of gloom inhabited by the strange crouching shadow monsters that were the machinery. The place was full of the sound of the rain on the roof.

Doc Savage waited until the gas lost its potency—it underwent a chemical reaction with the oxygen of the air and became impotent usually in about a minute—then went into the storehouse. The flashlight which he used—he had taken it from a door pocket—threw a beam that was like one long white finger.

There were four unconscious men in the storehouse.

One man was very long, with a body which gave the impression of being a tube filled with round things. He had an Adam's apple like a golf ball, a large melon for a stomach, but not much of anything for a chest. His eyes were closed in senselessness, but it was evident that they must be very large. His nose, his mouth, his ears, were also large. His face had a benevolent expression.

The other three men were policemen in blue uniforms.

All three policemen were slumped in the cab of the steam shovel. The long-looking loose-limbed man was lying beside the caterpillar tread of the shovel.

Doc Savage went out and got the girl and took her in to look at the men.

"You recognize any of these?" he asked.

Miami Davis shook her head while examining the policemen, but frowned when she came to the loose-jointed man. She seemed a bit doubtful about him.

"This one"—she pointed at the long-looking man vaguely—"sure needs some exercise."

"You know him?"

"I thought for a minute I had seen him somewhere. I guess I was wrong."

DOC SAVAGE was a scientific product. He had undergone specialized training from childhood to fit him for the unusual work which he was doing. Surgery had been his first training and his most specialized; but through patient effort he had managed to acquire an amazing amount of knowledge concerning geology, chemistry, electricity and other sciences.

This anaesthetic gas was a product of the bronze man's chemical skill. He had managed to keep the composition of the stuff a secret. Victims of the gas, however, could be revived by the administration of a proper stimulant made up in the form of tablets, pills that were large and a deep-blue color.

After Doc Savage administered stimulant pills to the men he had made unconscious—the tablets came from his carryall vest he wore—it took about fifteen minutes for the victims to revive.

The cops came out of it first, and squirmed around, got their eyes open, then sat up, one at a time, acting like men who had been in a sound sleep.

Doc Savage and the girl were both keeping out of sight behind the steam shovel. Doc wanted to listen.

The cops looked at each other for several moments before they spoke. Finally one giggled, then asked, "What the blazes happened?"

The trio scratched their heads, rubbed jaws, and giggled.

"It seemed," one said, "like we got the giggles, then went to sleep."

"That's crazy!"

The other pointed at the loose-jointed man, who was snoring softly.

"Birmingham Lawn looks like he is asleep, don't he?" he demanded by way of proof.

The first policeman scrambled over to the long-looking man.

"I hope he's all right," the cop said. "He's a swell old guy. Funny-looking, but swell. Always whistling."

"Whistling?"

"Sure. Whistles all the time."

"You're sure he ain't a giggling ghost, then?"

"Ghosts—hell! Don't let's start believing such lop-eared stuff. I've known Birmingham Lawn for years. I bought my little home through the real estate firm he runs." The officer went over and shook the long-looking, loose-limbed man. "Wake up, Lawn! Wake up, dang it!"

Birmingham Lawn opened one eye, then closed it. He licked his large lips, then opened both eyes, and worked his face around in puzzled shapes. He sat up and felt of himself, then started giggling a little.

Apparently in an effort to stop giggling, he whistled, pursed his lips and whistled a bar or two from a popular song.

"You feel all right, Mister Lawn?" asked the policeman who knew him.

"I do not feel," Birmingham Lawn said, "in the least like giggling. And yet I cannot help giggling."

Doc Savage came from behind the steam shovel and asked, "Did you gentlemen follow a giggling ghost here, too?"

The cops stared at the bronze man; then they gave him a brisk salute. They had recognized him and remembered that he held a high honorary commission on both the New York and New Jersey police forces.

Birmingham Lawn stared, looking puzzled, then amazed, then delighted. He giggled.

"Look here!" he exploded. *"Aren't you Doc Savage?"*

Doc admitted it, and Birmingham Lawn became as excited as a movie fan meeting a picture star. He bounced up, rubbed his hands together and glowed.

"Marvelous!" Lawn exclaimed. "I am delighted! I have read about you and I have heard about you. I have certainly wanted to meet you. This"—he was very earnest—"is a high point in my life."

Doc Savage looked uncomfortable. Being the focus of admiration was something he found embarrassing, which was one of the reasons he kept out of the public eye as much as possible.

IN a calm voice, Doc began telling the policeman and Birmingham Lawn what had happened.

"I thought from the giggling I overheard," Doc explained, "that the—er—ghost the girl followed was still here."

"That checks exactly!" Lawn ejaculated.

"Checks with what?" Doc asked.

"I own this storehouse," Lawn said. "This is my construction equipment here. I heard about the girl having caught the giggles when she followed a ghost to the storehouse, so I got these policemen and came to investigate. We were here only a few minutes when we—well, we got the giggles, too."

Doc Savage asked the policemen, "You searched the place?"

The cops said they had, and that they had found nothing. They added that they didn't believe in ghosts, giggling or otherwise.

"Mind if I look around?" Doc asked.

They didn't mind.

The bronze man moved around, pointing his flashlight at different objects. After a while, he went to the car, came back with his fingerprint paraphernalia. Birmingham Lawn trailed Doc closely, watching every move the bronze man made with hero-worshipping earnestness. Judging from his expression, Lawn expected to see a procession of miracles performed. Doc was busy trying to find prints.

At last Lawn looked disappointed when nothing startling occurred. He began to poke around for himself, ambled about aimlessly. He was drawing near the girl, Miami Davis, when he doubled over abruptly, then straightened.

"Huh!" he grunted. "Here's something!"

Miami Davis came over and looked at it.

She emitted a strangled gasp. "Oh!" she choked. "I—dropped that!"

"But—"

"It's mine!" The girl snatched the object.

Lawn shrugged, looked puzzled. He walked back and devoted his energies to watching Doc Savage.

Miami Davis went to the bronze man. She had a pale, desperate expression.

"I'm sorry," she said, "but I lied to you."

Doc looked at her.

"You what?" he asked.

"I lied to you," the girl said. "I wasn't even in this storehouse. I didn't have any giggling fit. It's all a lie. A big lie."

Chapter IV
WAR OVER A WATCH

THE men gathered around the girl and stared at her in astonishment. The cops frowned, Birmingham Lawn looked amazed, and Doc Savage's metallic features remained composed.

The girl looked at them wildly.

"Don't you understand?" she gasped. "I didn't tell you the truth! Nothing that I told you was the truth!"

A cop shook his head skeptically.

"Then how come you went to Doc Savage with the yarn?" he asked.

The girl laughed; she seemed to get the laugh out with the greatest difficulty.

"Why wouldn't I want to see Doc Savage?" she demanded. "He's famous. I've read about him. I just—well, I wanted to see him. That's all."

The cop began, "Now, look—"

The girl whirled and raced wildly to the storehouse door and flung through the drizzling rain, not looking back, flight her only object.

As the girl fled, she held, clenched in her right hand, the object which she had taken from Birmingham Lawn.

The policemen started to chase the girl.

"Let her go!" Doc Savage said.

"But—"

"Let her go," the bronze man repeated, but didn't elaborate his instructions.

The cops stared at Doc, apparently wondering what his object might be.

The bronze man turned to Birmingham Lawn. "You gave the girl something?" he asked Lawn.

"You—you saw it?" Lawn seemed startled.

"Yes."

"I—it was a small article I found," Lawn explained.

"What was it?"

"It was a girl's wrist watch. I picked it up off the floor."

"Woman's watch?"

Lawn nodded. "It was back there in the corner where someone must have dropped it."

"And it excited the young woman?" Doc demanded.

"It did seem to," Lawn admitted.

"What do you make of it?" Doc asked him.

"Me? I—I—why—why should I make anything of it?"

The bronze man did not comment, and this seemed to confuse Birmingham Lawn.

A policeman jammed his clenched fists on his hips angrily. "That girl was lyin'!" the cop said. "She was lyin' like nobody's business!"

"Obviously," Doc agreed.

"Somebody tried to stop her gettin' to you, remember? When she changed her story, she forgot that!"

Doc Savage went out to his car, got in and switched on the radio. It was not an ordinary radio; it was a shortwave transceiver. He picked up the microphone.

"Monk!" he said into the mike.

A small, squeaky voice answered. "Yes, Doc?" it said.

"You are following the girl who just fled from the storehouse?" the bronze man asked.

"We sure are," said the squeaky voice. "Me and Ham both."

"Keep on her trail," Doc Savage directed. "Let me know where she goes."

"What's up, Doc?" the squeaky voice asked.

"We're not sure yet, Monk," Doc explained. "But it is something strange. This girl was frightened into flight by the fact that a woman's wrist watch was found in the storehouse."

That ended the radio conversation.

"MONK," known as Lieutenant Colonel Andrew Blodgett Mayfair, and Brigadier General Theodore Marley "Ham" Brooks were two gentlemen so remarkable that people frequently followed them on the streets to stare at them.

The two were alike in only one way: both were associates of Doc Savage, assistants to the bronze man. They differed in every other particular.

Monk Mayfair came near being as wide as he was tall, had arms longer than his legs, and he was covered with a prodigious quantity of rusty-looking hair; he resembled, in fact, an ape. But despite his looks, Monk was one of the world's leading chemists. People did not follow Monk down the street to admire his erudition; they followed him because he was as funny-looking as a baboon.

Ham Brooks, on the other hand, was lean and dapper, and when people gaped at him, it was because Ham was living up to his reputation of being one of the world's best-dressed men. Ham changed his clothes at least three times daily, always carried a slim black sword cane, and was admitted to be one of the most astute lawyers Harvard had ever turned out.

Monk and Ham were riding in a large limousine, with Monk driving. Ahead of them was a taxicab which the girl, Miami Davis, had hailed.

While they trailed the girl, Monk and Ham diverted themselves by quarreling. They could quarrel on any subject. Now they were squabbling about marriage, both of them having barely escaped getting married in the course of a recent adventure.*

Monk leaned back, gullied his homely face with a big grin, and announced, "The only reason

---

The Submarine Mystery in *Doc Savage* Volume #5.

Miami Davis whirled and raced wildly to the storehouse door and flung through the drizzling rain, not looking back, flight her only object.

I ain't never got married is because I don't believe in likes marryin' likes. Now, if I could find a girl the exact opposite of me, I'd marry her in a minute."

Ham said, "Surely you could find an honest, beautiful girl of high character?"

Monk said, "No, I don't—" Then he got the dirty dig and glared at Ham. "Hey, that was a crack!" he squealed.

"Merely a statement of fact, you hairy oaf!" Ham said.

Monk looked indignant.

"You—you seed!" he bellowed. "I could eat you alive, you overdressed runt—and you'd probably taste like a scallion!"

Ham snorted.

"In that case you'd have more brains in your belly than you'll ever have in your head!"

While Doc's aides drove along in the wake of the girl's cab, the two continued this type of discussion, doing so with a loudness and violence that was deceptive; for it seemed that they were continually on the point of stopping the car and trying to murder each other, whereas they were actually the best of friends. There had been a time or two when each had actually risked his life to save the other.

In the back seat of the car, a minor edition of the Monk-and-Ham bickering flared up occasionally between their two pets. Two pets named Habeas Corpus and Chemistry. Habeas Corpus was a remarkable-looking pig. The pig had long legs, winglike ears, a snout built for inquiring into holes. Chemistry was a freak edition of an ape. Chemistry looked rather remarkably like the homely Monk.

Habeas Corpus, the pig, belonged to Monk.

Chemistry, the ape, belonged to Ham.

The car made very little noise. The *swick-swack* of the windshield wiper was louder than the motor or the rain. Occasionally they crossed low places in the pavement, and the wheels sent water sheeting outward. It was beginning to get dark.

Monk stopped squabbling to remark, "The girl seems to know where she's goin'."

"Apparently she's going toward Sheepshead Bay," Ham admitted.

"Yep, as much as I hate to admit you're right about anything," Monk grumbled.

Later, the girl's taxicab swerved over to the curb and stopped.

Monk promptly turned off the street to get out of sight. They were a block behind the girl. Their car jumped over the curb and stopped behind a rattletrap building bearing a sign which said:

FRESH BAIT

Monk squinted at the sign.

"I hope that ain't an omen," he muttered.

Ham pointed suddenly. "Hey! Who's that?"

Monk squinted in the direction Ham was pointing and saw nothing but some old rain-drenched buildings and growing gloom.

"Who's what?" he asked.

Ham explained, "I thought I saw a man start toward us, then jump back out of sight after he got a better look at us."

"Maybe we'd better go see about that," suggested Monk.

Monk was happiest when he was in trouble.

HAM had actually seen a man. The man had come out of a long, narrow, discouraged-looking building of planks. He had fled back into the same building. This structure had no windows, and one whole end was open. The building was a place where small boats had once been built, and what was left of a marine railway sloped from the open end down to the bay water.

The mysterious man was the same individual who had attacked Miami Davis in Doc's headquarters.

The man watched Monk and Ham through a crack in the planks. He wore his yellow slicker, gray hat, gray gloves, gray suit and gray sport shoes, all rather soggy with the rain.

When he saw Monk and Ham coming toward the building—the pets had been left in the car—he gave a disgusted grunt and plucked his silk handkerchief from a pocket and held it ready to hide his face if necessary.

The man then ran to the open end of the building and made a quick survey of the marine railway. It was obvious that he could get on all fours, crawl down the bed of the abandoned railway, and get to the edge of the water. So he did this.

There was a retaining wall of piling and timbers along the shore, and many ramshackle wharves. The man found cracks which gave purchase for his toes and hands, and worked along until he reached a dock to which several fishing boats were moored. He crept out under the dock, clambering from one stringer to another, until he reached a fishing boat.

This fishing boat differed very little from several others. It was a party boat of the kind which, for a dollar and a half, took you out to sea a few miles, furnished your dinner and a hook and line, and you could fish over the side.

The man crept down a companionway into the lighted cabin of the fishing boat.

Three men in the boat cabin looked relieved when they recognized him, but when they saw the grimness on his face, they grew uneasy again.

"Somethin' wrong, Batavia?" one asked.

Batavia nodded.

"The girl showed up, like we figured she would," he said. "She's probably on Hart's boat now."

"That's hunky-dory, then."

"It's a hunk of trouble!" Batavia growled.

"Huh?"

"Two guys named Monk and Ham showed up right behind the girl," Batavia said.

The other man scratched his head. "Who're they?"

Batavia looked disgusted. "Two of Doc Savage's men; that's who they are!" he snapped.

"I don't see anythin' to get in a sweat about." The other man shrugged. "I think you and the boss, and everybody else, are gettin' steamed up too much about this Doc Savage."

Batavia put his fists on his hips and looked utterly disgusted.

"Those have been the last words of more than one smart cluck," he growled. "This Savage is worse than lightnin'; you can generally tell by lookin' at the sky when there's any chance of lightnin' strikin'."

The other subsided.

Batavia said, "We gotta get the girl!"

"What about this Monk and Ham?"

"We'll tie a rock to 'em, and drop 'em in the bay!" Batavia said.

While the other men got guns and flashlights, Batavia pulled up his left trousers leg and examined a skinned area on his shin. The damage had been done when he had leaped from one elevator to another in the skyscraper which housed Doc Savage's headquarters.

MONK and Ham had poked around in the ramshackle boathouse and found nothing.

So they stood for a few moments and abused each other.

"You and your imagination!" Monk piped disgustedly. "Saw a man, did you?"

"You dish-faced ape," Ham said, "I did see someone!"

They went back to their car, and peered around the corner of the building which bore the sign "Live Bait."

The girl's taxicab was driving away.

Miami Davis went down a rickety dock and stopped beside a small schooner which was held alongside the dock by springlines. She picked up an oar and whacked the deck of the schooner.

"Hey, on board!" she called.

The schooner was about fifty feet long, two-masted, a pleasure type of craft. It was gaff-rigged. Also, it was elderly, but well kept. There were patched canvas covers over the furled sails to keep out the rain, and a cockpit awning that was also patched.

The girl gave the deck another whack.

"Hart!" she cried. "Are you aboard?"

Miami Davis got on the schooner. She was evidently accustomed to boats, because she used care that her high heels did not cut the deck. She went to the cabin hatch, opened it and entered. The cabin of the schooner was neat, and arranged in a way which showed the boat-owner was no landlubber.

The girl searched the boat. She looked in a little stateroom aft, in the galley, the forecastle; then she came back and slumped down on a transom seat in the cabin.

There was no one aboard the boat.

Miami Davis had turned on the electric lights in the craft. She let these burn.

MONK and Ham had followed the girl to the boat by now. Also, they had been able to tell, from the way lights had gone on in the boat, that the girl had searched the craft.

Standing on the dock, they could see her crouched tensely on the transom seat. The two aides retired to the shore end of the dock for a conference.

"This is a goofy business!" Monk complained.

"How do you mean?" Ham asked.

"It don't make sense. Ghosts that giggle. Is that sense?"

"We haven't dug into it yet, stupid!"

Monk said, "One of us better report to Doc. He said he wanted to know where the girl went."

"Go ahead, dunce," Ham directed. "It will be a pleasure to get you out of sight."

Monk walked away, rather resembling an ambling wart in the murk. He grinned as he moved along; he was always happy when involved in some kind of mysterious excitement. To be sure, Monk didn't know what they were mixed up in. That bothered him.

When Monk reached the car, he switched on the radio receiver with which the car was equipped.

"Doc!" he said into the microphone.

"Yes, Monk?" Doc's voice answered almost at once.

Monk advised the whereabouts of the spot to which they had trailed the girl.

"Look, Doc," the homely chemist added, "what's this all about?"

"There is no way of telling, just yet," the bronze man explained.

Monk was not entirely satisfied. He rubbed his jaw, scratched his nubbin of a head, and smoothed the bristling hair down on his nape.

"What do you want us to do?" he asked.

"Keep an eye on the girl," Doc Savage said. "And eavesdrop."

"Eavesdrop?"

"Try to find out why the fact that she found a wrist watch made her take flight," Doc explained. "In case you can't learn anything by eavesdropping, you might grab the girl."

Monk grinned.

"Grabbin' that girl would be a pleasure!" he chuckled. "She's a looker, what I mean!"

That ended the radio conference.

Chapter V
THE JAMEROO

MONK closed the car doors, locked them, and went back to the dock where the schooner was tied up. He walked out on the wharf confidently, came to a patch of gloom behind a piling, about where he had left Ham, and stopped.

"Ham," he said, "Doc says—"

The bunch of shadow that the chemist had thought was Ham straightened. Monk suddenly found a gun jammed into his middle. A gun snout that made a rasping noise as it hit his belt buckle.

"Pipe down!" said a strange voice.

Monk peered, trying to make out the features of the speaker. He got a slap in the face for his pains.

"Where's Ham?" Monk gulped.

Considering that during the last hour he had stated at least a dozen times that he intended to tear Ham limb from limb, Monk's anxiety was inconsistent.

"Shut up!" said the man with the gun.

Men appeared on the schooner. They had been hiding behind the deckhouse and dinghy. The men climbed onto the dock.

"Search this clunk!" ordered Monk's captor.

"Sure, Batavia," one man said.

Monk swelled indignantly as he was searched, but there seemed to be nothing he could do about it.

"Now," Batavia told Monk, "you get on the boat."

Monk climbed down on the boat and entered the cabin.

"Ham!" the homely chemist yelled.

Ham was lying on a bunk, motionless. Monk leaped to him, clutched the dapper lawyer's wrist, and was relieved to discover pulse. Ham was alive! More than that, he was in the act of regaining consciousness, it appeared, for he squirmed, blinked open his eyes and focused them on Monk. As soon as he had organized himself, Ham began to scowl.

"What's the idea," he snarled, "sneaking up behind and banging me on the head?"

"Listen, Blackstone," Monk said, "I didn't bang you—"

Batavia came over, gouged Monk with the gun muzzle and said, "Sit down and shut up!"

Monk sat down on the transom seat near the girl.

Miami Davis was tied hand and foot. She was trembling, but she made no sound because of the adhesive tape which crisscrossed her lips.

Batavia moved toward the companionway, his slicker rustling.

"I'll see if I can get hold of the chief," he said to his men. "Gotta find out what to do with these three."

Batavia climbed the companionway and went out.

Monk said, "What I want to know is about them ghosts—"

A man came over and showed Monk another gun. "Listen, you gimlet-eyed baboon, you're on the spot! Keep that ugly trap shut!"

Monk subsided.

Rain washed the cabin roof, sluiced along the decks, and the wind slapped the halliards against the mast. Little waves gurgled like running water along the hull.

BATAVIA came back a little while later. He was scowling.

"We croak 'em later," he said. "I couldn't get hold of the chief."

Monk frowned at the girl, Miami Davis.

"When you talked to Doc," he accused, "you left out some stuff."

The young woman nodded. Her mouth seemed to be too tight with strain to let words come out.

Monk said, "That was a mistake. Now we're in a jameroo."

Batavia took a fid out of a rack. The fid was a steel rod a foot long, half an inch in diameter at one end and tapering to a needle point. The fid was used to separate the strands of rope while splicing.

Batavia waved the fid under Monk's nose. "Another blat out of you, and I'll peg your tongue down with this fid!"

"Why don'tcha let us loose?" Monk asked hopefully.

"Brother," Batavia said, "you've been unlucky. You got messin' around with somethin' too big for you."

"Too big?"

Batavia poked Monk in the chest with the sharp end of the fid.

"You're just a beetle," he said, "that got in front of the wrong steamroller."

Batavia then gave a number of orders.

"We'll get rid of their car first thing," he said.

A man muttered, "Ain't Doc Savage liable to trace these two guys?"

"We're going to make some preparation for Doc Savage!" Batavia said.

Batavia had a craggy face. All angles of his face were sharp; the nose was also, and so was his jaw; his eyes had a piercing intentness, and his ears were pointed. He was either darkly tanned, or of Latin extraction. Beside his fondness for grays in dress, he had one other principal character tag: this other was his cigars.

Batavia's cigars were thin, hardly half ordinary thickness, and about two inches longer than the usual cigar. The ends were equipped with cork tips.

Batavia removed the Cellophane wrapping from one of his cigars, put it in his mouth and tried to light it with one of the modern flameless type of lighters designed for lighting cigarettes alone. The lighter didn't fire the cigar immediately.

"Damn this gadget!" Batavia complained.

He finally got his cigar going. Then he took a five-yard roll of one-inch adhesive tape out of his slicker pocket. Strips of this tape he crisscrossed over the mouths of Monk and Ham.

"Adenoids!" Monk croaked wildly just before the tape was slapped on his lips.

Bad adenoid cases will suffocate to death if gagged.

Monk then pretended to be unable to breathe through his nostrils. He faked suffocation. He flounced around, made whistling noises through his nose, blew out his cheeks, did his best to make his face go purple.

Batavia got behind Monk and slugged him with the heavy end of the fid. Monk fell his length on the floorboards, momentarily dazed, and began to breathe in a normal fashion.

"That homely ape," Batavia complained, "is full of tricks. What d'you think of that—tryin' to get out of bein' gagged?"

The prisoners were prodded out of the hatch, goaded onto the dock, and led to the street.

Batavia said, "We better get rid of their car."

BATAVIA went to the limousine which Monk and Ham had used. A couple of men went with him. He opened the door, started to get in, and was greeted by a belligerent grunt and an angry chattering noise. Batavia turned a flashlight beam into the rear seat. He was curious.

The pig, Habeas, and the ape, Chemistry, batted their eyes in the flashlight glare.

"A regular zoo!" Batavia grumbled. He got into the car. When the pets tried to escape, he slammed the door and kept them in the automobile.

Batavia drove the car out on a dock, headed the machine toward the wharf end, and jumped out and slammed the door. The car ran to the end of the dock, nosed over, and entered the water with a *whoosh!* of a splash.

"You left that pig an' the ape in there!" a man muttered.

Batavia stood at the dock edge and listened to big bubbles make *glub!* noises. He dashed his flashlight beam down briefly. The water was slick with oil, and bubbles kept bounding out of the water like frightened white animals.

"You left that pig an' ape in the car!" the man muttered again.

Batavia said, "I didn't like the way the danged things looked at me."

Batavia threw his cork-tipped cigar in the water, took a fresh cigar out of his clothing, removed the Cellophane band, threw it at the bubbles and put the cigar in his mouth. Then they led the prisoners to two cars parked in nearby side streets. The captives and half of Batavia's men loaded in one machine.

"You fellows take the prisoners to the boss' place."

"What are *you* gonna do?" a man demanded.

Batavia took his cork-tipped cigar out of his mouth and laughed grimly.

"I'm gonna rig somethin' for Doc Savage," he said.

The car pulled away with the captives. Batavia vanished in the darkness, headed back toward the little schooner. Half of his men followed him.

Chapter VI
HUNT FOR A WATCH

DOC SAVAGE had completed a thorough examination of the old bleak storehouse with the tin roof. But to all outward appearance, the search netted nothing.

Birmingham Lawn seemed disappointed. The golf-ball protuberance that served Lawn as an Adam's apple went up and down as he swallowed. He had whistled something from a tune, and the rest of the time he had giggled, or just watched.

"I was hoping," he said, "that you would solve the mystery."

Doc Savage did not comment.

The policemen by now had tired of the mystery, and in addition, they held a suspicion that the whole business would not look so good in the newspapers.

"The public will think the Jersey police are a lot of jackasses," a cop muttered, "once the newspapers get hold of this."

"Then why notify the newspapers?" Doc asked. The bronze man didn't like newspaper publicity.

The policemen thought that was a swell idea.

One cop said, "Furthermore, maybe there ain't nothin' to it. The girl admitted her whole story was a lie. She just made the thing up so she could meet Doc Savage."

Doc Savage neglected to remind the cops that an attempt with violence had been made to prevent the girl reaching him.

Finally the cops took their departure.

Doc Savage began loading his fingerprint paraphernalia in his car. Birmingham Lawn trailed the bronze man around.

"Matters seem to have become quiet for the time being," Doc Savage told Lawn. He extended a hand. "It's pleasant to have met you, Mr. Lawn, and let us hope that your property is not molested again."

Birmingham Lawn made a big grin.

"Could I make a request?" he asked.

"Request?"

"I haven't the slightest doubt but that you are molested a great deal by pests," Lawn said. His melon of a stomach shook as he chuckled. "But I should like very much to go along with you, providing you have any intention of continuing to investigate this—ah—mystery."

"Why do you wish to go along?"

"Well, I've read a great deal about you." Lawn squirmed and looked embarrassed. "Matter of fact, I'm a great admirer of yours. I'd give a lot to watch you work for a while." He smiled fatuously. "I suppose it's a form of hero worship, and I'm fully aware that you probably consider me a silly pest."

Doc Savage said, "It may be a little dangerous."

"In that case," Lawn said, "you can depend on me to run. I am not a brave man."

Doc Savage got into his car.

"My aides, Monk and Ham, are trailing that girl," he explained.

TAKING for granted that he had permission to accompany the bronze man, Birmingham Lawn planted his long-limbed, loose-jointed frame on the car cushions and settled back, looking eager, and also nervous, like a man who has started out rabbit hunting with a shotgun and just remembered he is in bear country.

Doc Savage worked with the radio.

"Monk! Ham!" he said into the microphone.

He said that several times, then remarked, "Probably they are away from the other transceiver."

Doc Savage drove away from the storehouse, turned right, and drove toward the spot from which Monk and Ham had last reported.

Rain came down steadily, the drops swirling like snowflakes in the glare of the headlights. Several times Birmingham Lawn opened his mouth, as if he wanted to say something, but was unable to think of anything to fit the occasion.

"You have no idea," he told Doc finally, "what a reputation you have." He fell to whistling bars from a popular tune.

When Doc Savage brought his car to a stop near the ramshackle boat house, Monk and Ham's car was nowhere in sight.

Doc Savage listened to his radio. The transmitter in the other car was switched on; the transceivers were always kept ready for instant communication while Doc and his men were investigating.

The carrier wave of the other transmitter sounded very close, which meant the car was not many yards away. But where was it? It wasn't in sight.

Doc Savage swung out and examined the car tracks. It was dark enough now so that he had to use a flashlight. In the mud, he found car tracks with distinctive tread design used on the machine driven by Monk and Ham.

It was obvious that Monk and Ham's car had backed out into the street; but there, the rain had washed away any traces that might have been visible to the unaided eye.

Doc Savage went back to his machine. From a compartment—all the spare room in the car was occupied by compartments—he got a device which resembled nothing so much as an old-fashioned magic lantern. This contrivance, however, had a lens which was almost jet-black.

"What's that?" Birmingham Lawn wanted to know.

"Self-contained ultrviolet ray projector," the bronze man explained.

"Ultraviolet ray?"

Doc Savage pointed the lantern lens at the tracks left by Monk and Ham's car, switched the device on and, although it emitted no light visible to the eye, tiny flecklike spots glowed with greenish luminance on the pavement where the tires of Monk and Ham's car had rolled.

Birmingham Lawn proved to have enough scientific knowledge to solve this phenomenon. He said, "There are chemical substances which glow, or phosphoresce, when subjected to ultraviolet light. Some such chemical must have been incorporated as an ingredient in the tires of the car your two associates were driving. Am I right?"

"That," Doc Savage admitted, "is correct."

THE bronze man followed the trail of Monk and Ham's machine down the street, and out to the end of the dock; a splintered patch, where the bumper had dragged as the car went over, told him instantly what had happened.

The bronze man shucked off his coat and dived off the dock edge. The water was cold and intensely black.

The submerged car lay on its side with the doors closed and the thick bulletproof windows intact. Ordinarily, with the windows closed, the machine was airtight, this feature having been incorporated in its construction as a defense against gas. Like most of the cars used by Doc Savage and his men, this one was a rolling fortress.

Doc wrenched, got the car door open. An air bubble a yard across leaped past him, and rushing water sucked him into the machine.

Later, when he swam to the top, Doc had the two pets, Habeas Corpus and Chemistry. After handing the animals up to Birmingham Lawn, Doc climbed to the dock.

"I don't understand this!" Lawn gasped.

Lawn sounded frightened, confused.

Doc Savage took Lawn's elbow and led him off the dock and to the car, Lawn all the while stuttering demands to know what it was all about. Doc put Lawn in the back seat of his car, placing Habeas Corpus and Chemistry in with him. The bronze man then slammed the car door shut, twisting the handle in a certain way that automatically closed all the other doors. Lawn tried the car handles, then beat on one of the bulletproof windows.

"Hey!" he complained. "You locked me in here."

"Where you'll be safe," Doc Savage explained.

"I've got enough of this!" Lawn howled. "I don't like it. I want to go home. Let me out!"

The Bronze man shucked off his coat and dived off the deck edge.

Doc Savage moved away. Lawn would be as safe in the machine as anywhere, and out of the way—if there was going to be trouble.

Doc used his ultraviolet lantern. His aides, when operating alone, were under instructions to blaze their trail frequently, using a special chalk which each carried.

This chalk resembled the styptic pencils used to heal small cuts, and were made of a chemical composition and left a mark which was invisible to the naked eye, but which fluoresced when subjected to ultraviolet light. Doc found marks on a dock dolphin. Ham had printed:

GIRL ON THIS SCHOONER

An arrow indicated the schooner.

The bronze man went to the boat. There was a light in the cabin. Doc craned his neck, saw no one, then swung quietly on to the schooner and put an ear to the cabin top.

There was no sound to indicate life aboard the boat, and he moved toward the companionway.

Blinding glare from a flashlight jumped over him.

"Just keep the peace, friend!" a voice advised coolly.

THERE was a man standing in a dinghy under the dock, holding a flashlight. The man shoved a gun out into the light, a gun that was a single-action six-shooter, looking big enough for elephants.

"Lie down on the deck!" the man ordered.

Doc lay down on the deck.

The man pulled the dinghy to the rail and swung aboard the schooner. In the glow from his flashlight he was a large young man who seemed to be composed mostly of shoulders. He had black curly hair. His black slacks and dark polo shirt were drenched, the wet shirt sticking to his torso closely enough to show some unusual muscles.

This burly fellow jabbed Doc with the gun and said, "Get down in the cabin!"

They entered the cabin. The young man had blue eyes, a grim mouth.

He growled, "There's somethin' familiar about you."

Doc Savage said, "Is there?"

"I dunno what this is all about, but I'm gonna find out." The young man cocked his single-action six-shooter. "I find my hooker has been searched. Then I see you monkeyin' around. Now spill it! What's the idea?"

"Where is the girl?" Doc asked.

"Eh?"

"The girl who was aboard this schooner."

"I live on this hooker alone. There's no woman around. I like boats. I don't like women."

Doc Savage said, "Would you know anything about two men named Monk and Ham?"

"No. Never heard of 'em." The brawny young man squinted one eye thoughtfully. "I still think I've seen you somewhere before."

"What is your name?"

"William Henry Hart," the young man growled. "I ain't ashamed of it."

"And your profession?"

"Is none of your damn business!" the young man grunted. "However, I'm an inventor."

"Inventor?"

"We won't go into that," the other growled. "I manufacture things, too. I'm not such a small-timer!" He waggled a thumb around at the boat. "Just because I live on this hooker, it don't mean I can't afford a penthouse." He beetled his brows and added, "I don't like women."

Doc Savage explained, "I'm looking for two friends of mine who were led here when they trailed a young woman who claimed she caught a strange giggling fit from a ghost."

"That sounds crackpot!" The young man shoved out his jaw and his gun. "Come across with a story that makes sense—or I'm gonna get tough!"

He took a step forward, hooked his thumb over the hammer of his gun, so the gun would not discharge, used the big six-shooter as a club to strike at Doc Savage's head.

Several blurred things then happened. The gun clubbed the spot where Doc's head should have been, but the bronze man had moved. The young man went off balance. Doc grasped his gun wrist.

The young man started struggling—struggling confidently—but his confidence went out of him like air out of a split balloon. For the gun was yanked out of the young man's hand; he was slapped down on the floor, held there, searched, and although all the while he struggled—he was a very strong young man—his muscles might have been as soft and unmanageable as a sack of mice.

He peered dazedly at the bronze man.

"Now I know why you seemed familiar!" he muttered. *"You're Doc Savage!"*

Doc Savage did not answer that. He was examining an interesting object yielded by the young man's pockets: a woman's wrist watch.

Chapter VII
ROAD TO DEATH

EARLIER that evening in the storehouse, Doc Savage had seen the wrist watch that Birmingham Lawn had handed to Miami Davis. Lawn had also described the watch in detail: small purple jewel in the stem, the two small diamonds, one at either end of the dial.

This was undoubtedly the watch which had scared the girl into flight.

William Henry Hart

And now it had been in William Henry Hart's pocket.

Doc Savage tossed the burly young man's big six-shooter overboard. Then he took a yachting book off a shelf and glanced at the flyleaf; the book was marked:

PROPERTY OF WILLIAM HENRY HART

"Do you know a girl named Miami Davis?" Doc asked.

Effect of this on the brawny Hart was pronounced. He slapped both hands against his chest and gaped, his mouth very wide.

"Who?" he exploded.

"Her name," Doc Savage said, "is Miami Davis. This is her watch, supposedly?"

"I—uh—wuh—" The young man hauled himself up and sprawled on the transom seat. "She's my secretary," he said.

Doc Savage pointed at the watch. "How did this watch get in your pocket?"

"I found it lyin' on the chart table when I came back," Hart said.

"That all you know about it?"

"I gave the watch to Miss Davis as a Christmas bonus," Hart said. "A couple of days ago, she said it had stopped runnin'. I told her I would get it fixed. She gave it to me, and I guess I put it on top of the chart table and forgot all about it." He scowled. "Now what about it?"

"For one thing," Doc said promptly, "someone might have taken the watch and made her think you lost it in that storehouse."

"What storehouse?" The young man with the large shoulders looked puzzled.

"Again, *you* might have lost it in the storehouse," Doc said.

The other glared. "What's this storehouse talk?"

"Is she in love with you?" Doc asked.

"Love—who?"

"Miami Davis—with you."

"How the hell would I know?" Hart yelled.

Doc Savage opened a galley locker, took out a can of coffee and poured it on a galley table. He reached for the salt.

"What in blazes you doin'?" Hart yelled.

"Going to give your boat a thorough search," Doc explained.

"Over my dead body, you will!" the burly young man howled.

The search proceeded over his bound and gagged body; during the incidental fighting and kicking, a locker door was caved in, the table kicked loose from its fastenings, and some dishes broken.

The note had been jammed hastily into the mouth of a brass chart case.

It was a plain white envelope with Hart's name on the outside. Its content was a single sheet of white paper. Printed on this:

Hart:
    The two Doc Savage men and the girl have been taken out to Beach Road.

Doc Savage held the note in front of Hart's eyes. Doc removed Hart's gag.

"What do you say to this?" the bronze man demanded.

"I've been framed!" Hart yelled.

"That is hardly original," Doc said.

BIRMINGHAM LAWN was beating on the car window, trying to break them, when Doc Savage returned to the machine. Doc unlocked the doors.

"This is no way to treat an innocent bystander," Lawn said indignantly. "Locking me in the car!" Lawn pointed at Hart. "Who's this fellow?"

"Ever see him before?" Doc asked.

"No—never."

Doc Savage explained. "Monk, Ham and Miami Davis have been seized and carried off. I intend hunting for them."

"You can take me home," Lawn said sourly. "I've got enough of this mess!"

Doc Savage's patience was about exhausted, but his words, rather than his tone, betrayed the fact.

"There is no time to chauffeur you home," he said. "Either you walk, or you go with me."

Birmingham Lawn peered around at the drizzling darkness long enough to lose his taste for a walk in the rain. He licked his lips, changed feet, then whistled a bar.

"If your car is as hard to get into as it is to get out of," he muttered, "I'll probably be safe."

He got into the rear seat with Hart, whose ankles and wrists Doc had bound.

Doc put the car in motion.

"Where we going?" Lawn wanted to know.

"A note said they had taken the prisoners out Beach Road," Doc explained.

Beach Road was the name applied to a rough, winding thoroughfare along the shore of New Jersey. The shore was a marshy district, with many shoal bays and inlets. The road passed through dune sections, where sand had drifted like dirty snow across the rutted blacktop pavement. Bridges were frequent.

Doc's car traveled fast, bucking in ruts, sloughing when it hit sand. The rain washed down steadily, and there was fog.

They had covered all of a dozen miles down the Jersey coast when Birmingham Lawn screamed.

LAWN'S yell was strangled, agonized. Simultaneously, the rear door of the car flew open—Doc hadn't locked the doors this time—and Hart's burly form shot out of the speeding machine.

Doc stamped the brakes; the car skidded, went broadside, straightened, turned broadside the other way, then stopped. Lawn was making barking noises of fear on the back seat.

"You hurt?" Doc rapped.

"He kicked me!" Lawn howled. Lawn held his melon of a stomach. His squawling could have been heard a mile away. A man badly hurt could not yell like that, so Doc left him.

Doc Savage ran to the spot where Hart had jumped, flashlight in hand. Rain beat against the bronze man's face; his feet knocked up water. Hart wasn't where he had landed.

Doc dashed the flashlight beam about searchingly. He saw wet, disturbed sand where Hart had landed, but no tracks led into the dunes which shoved up drably on either side of the road; so the escaping prisoner must have gone down the road.

Doc turned the flashlight beam down the road, and it picked up nothing. The bronze man ran down the road, using the flash continually, and still found no footprints.

He was hunting when the rifle report smashed out.

The bullet cut the air close to Doc's head, its sound like a big fiddle string breaking. Possibly it missed the bronze man only because he was holding the flashlight so as to give a wrong impression of where his body was—a habitual bit of caution. Doc extinguished the light. He doubled down, whipped to one side.

The rifle began slamming again; it was an automatic gun, and put out a dozen bullets in the time it would take a man to swallow. Then somebody cursed somebody else for shooting too quick. Feet retreated. There were evidently two men with the rifle.

Doc set out after the fleeing gunmen. He did not catch the retreating riflemen because they had a motorcycle hidden in the dunes. The cycle engine started, as noisy as an angry bulldog; its headlight jumped whitely; the cycle wallowed in the sand.

The two gunners, straddling it, kept it upright with their legs. The motorcycle reached the road and went away like a scared rocket.

Doc Savage reached the spot where the motorcycle had been, and found a greasy canvas cover which had been over the machine to keep off the rain. Doc examined the cover and the sand around about. The cover was just dirty canvas, and the sand was too sloppy to retain footprints.

But he found two soggy cigar stubs, cork-tipped cigars, discarded on the sand.

The bronze man stood, listening, and the rain reached through his clothing with cold fingers. Then suddenly he spun and raced back to the car and whipped behind the wheel.

"Hang on!" he ordered.

An utter silence in the back seat caused Doc to look around. Now Birmingham Lawn was gone.

Birmingham Lawn must have been frightened—he had said he was a very timid man—so it was logical to think of him leaving the car and fleeing into the sand dunes, frightened by the rifle fire.

Doc splashed flashlight glow on the sand beside the road. Yes; there was a man's tracks, leading into the dunes.

There was no time to follow Lawn.

Doc started the car motor, maneuvered the machine around, and set out after the riflemen on the motorcycle. Fifty miles an hour was as high as he dared send the car over this crooked, rutted, sand-drifted, rain-flogged road.

When Doc had covered four miles, he knew that the motorcycle had turned off somewhere, and that the riflemen stood a good chance of escaping.

THE two riflemen on the motorcycle were reaching the same conclusion; they thought they were going to escape, too. They had turned off about two miles back, and had ridden to an abandoned summer bungalow. Paint was scabbing off the sides of the bungalow, and the roof was leaking strings of water into the rooms.

One of the riflemen was Batavia. Batavia stood shaking sand off his trousers with one hand—the front wheel of the motorcycle had plastered him with the wet stuff—and with his other hand, he held a telephone receiver.

He kept saying, "Hello, dammit!" into the telephone. Finally he got an answer.

"Look," Batavia said, "did you get Monk, Ham, and the girl hidden?"

"Did you get Doc Savage?" the telephone voice wanted to know.

"I asked you," Batavia yelled, "if you got the prisoners hidden!"

"Yes, yes—keep your shirt on! Did you get Doc Savage?"

"Not yet," Batavia explained. "Savage hasn't crossed the bridge yet. Hart escaped from Savage's car just this side of the bridge; we knew from Lawn's yell that Hart had got away. Then Doc Savage came huntin' Hart, and we cut loose with a rifle. We figured if we didn't get Savage, we'd at least give Hart a chance to vamoose."

"Did Hart get away?"

"I don't know yet."

"You sound excited," the other said.

"Excited—hell!" Batavia barked. "If you had been ridin' a damn motorcycle with Doc Savage after you, you'd be excited, too!"

"How you gonna know if Hart got away?"

"Some of my boys are waitin' at the bridge with a speedboat," Batavia explained. "They'll pick up Hart."

"And Savage will—"

"He'll probably go on across that bridge," Batavia said. "When he does, we're rid of him."

This terminated the telephone conversation. Batavia went outdoors to stand in the rain and listen for some sign of Doc Savage. Then he took the motorcycle around to the back, where there was a small wharf; he wheeled the cycle out on the wharf, and toppled it into the water.

"No use leavin' evidence around," he muttered.

The man who had been with Batavia was a squat fellow who wore the coat half of a suit of oilskins. He was stamping his feet and grunting, trying to get a grain of sand out of his eye.

Suddenly there was noise of a boat, and a light out on the water. The bungalow stood beside one of the sea-water tidal creeks which indented the shore of New Jersey.

The boat came to the dock off which Batavia had toppled the motorcycle.

"That you, Batavia?" a voice asked.

"Did you find Hart?" Batavia demanded.

"Yep." The fellow jerked a thumb at Hart, who stared angrily from his seat in the boat.

Batavia said, "We gotta blow from here in a hurry." He dropped down into the boat. Batavia's companion on the motorcycle ride also got in the boat.

Batavia exclaimed aloud, pointed at a strange figure in the boat. "Who's this?" he barked.

Birmingham Lawn, who sat with a gun jammed into his back, said peevishly, "I am Birmingham Lawn, and an innocent bystander in this whole disagreeable matter."

"He's the lunk who owned that storehouse," a man said. "How he got messed up in this, I don't know."

"I am an absolutely innocent bystander," Lawn insisted.

Batavia dropped on a seat in the speedboat.

"Pull her ears down!" he said.

The man running the craft pulled the gas lever down and the speedboat went away from there at a great speed.

A FEW minutes later, Batavia ordered the boat stopped, directed that the bow searchlight be extinguished. The boat then floated silently on black water with rain slopping down. A man bailed occasionally with a tomato can.

Doc splashed flashlight glow on the sand beside the road, saw a man's tracks leading into the dune.

From this spot, they could watch the location of both the bungalow and bridge—a bridge where the road spanned the tidal creek. It was too dark to actually see much more than their hands before their faces. The bungalow was in the distance. The bridge was closer at hand.

Suddenly a light appeared at the bungalow. It went off and on repeatedly, and disappeared inside the house, came out, then progressed out on the dock.

"That'll be Doc Savage," Batavia muttered. "He's lookin' around. Fat lot of good it'll do him!"

Doc's distant light vanished and the bronze man's car headlights retreated in the direction of the road.

Batavia laughed shortly.

"The next ten minutes makes or breaks the whole thing!" he said grimly. "If Savage crosses that bridge—"

The speedboat got broadside to the waves and began rocking violently, and Batavia growled an order to the man in the bow to put out a small anchor. Raindrops made a steady sobbing on the water.

William Henry Hart sat very still, scowled, did not say anything at all.

Birmingham Lawn squirmed and tried to say again that he was an innocent bystander, but someone got hold of his ear, twisted it, and snarled an order, and Lawn fell into silence.

"Hey!" Batavia hissed. "Stand by to signal!"

A car was approaching the bridge, headlights pushing a great fog of luminance ahead of it. The bridge was of wood with plank banisters, and it appeared ancient. The car rolled out on the bridge.

"Put a light on the bridge!" Batavia barked.

The speedboat searchlight beam sprang at the bridge in a blinding white streak which landed on a car. Batavia strained his eyes.

"It's Doc Savage's machine!" he yelled.

He whipped out a gun and fired twice at the water—the signal.

The bridge came apart under the car. Came apart with blue-white flash, ear-splitting roar. Parts of the bridge climbed up—up—fragments that swirled around the car.

The car, armor-plate though it was, split; opened like a tin can. Water under the bridge rushed back to leave a great hole. Scores of yards in all directions, concussion knocked trees flat.

The glare of the explosion went away and left blackness, and for moments there was the sound of heavy things falling back and splashing and crashing.

"Whew!" a man in the launch muttered. "We danged near blew this neck of the woods off the map!"

"Pick up the man who fired the charge," Batavia ordered.

The launch angled over to a bank of the creek, where a man stood, the man pumping his ears with the palms of his hands to get rid of the effects of the explosion. At the man's feet lay a generator of the type used to detonate explosive.

The man got in the launch.

"That," he said, "was what I call blowin' your troubles away!"

Chapter VIII
THE EARTHQUAKE-MAKERS

THE most placid hours of the day in New York City are probably those from three o'clock in the morning until dawn. The city does not quiet down much before three o'clock in the morning, even on rainy nights.

It was after three o'clock in the morning and very dark when Batavia rolled a large sedan to the curb, near an array of imposing stone buildings in uptown New York. The buildings were very large. A name was chiseled on the facade of one of them. The name:

METROPOLITAN UNIVERSITY

Batavia got out of the car, and three men followed him. All of them wore dark suits, dark-blue shirts, black hats and dark gloves.

Batavia said, "Don't waste any time!"

The men went directly to one of the larger buildings; they stopped at the steps leading up to the front door. One of the men lay down on the walk. A second man crouched beside him.

Batavia went up the steps, grabbed the door handle, began to shake the door and shout.

"Help!" he yelled. "Help!"

The remaining member of the party had eased back into the darkness, where he wasn't likely to be noticed.

Batavia continued to shake the door and shout until the watchman appeared, unlocked the door, and came out. The watchman splashed light on Batavia's face. Batavia then looked as scared as he could.

"He's had a heart attack, or something!" Batavia pointed at the man lying at the foot of the steps.

The watchman ran down the steps and stared at the prone man.

"I'll telephone for a doctor!" the watchman exclaimed.

"I'm a doctor," said the man kneeling beside the prone one.

"What do you want me to do?" the watchman asked wildly.

"Just wait a minute," said the man who claimed

to be a doctor. "I'll see if we can bring this poor fellow out of it."

During the excitement, the fourth member of the party had left his concealment in the shadows, and had entered the building through the door which the watchman had unlocked and left open.

The man who entered the building seemed to have a very definite idea of where he was going, what he wanted to do. He galloped through the massive halls—his rubber-soled shoes made little noise—until he came to a room which housed the scientific instruments.

This was the science hall of the university.

The man stopped before a seismograph, the complicated and highly sensitive device which registered, by recording microscopic earth convulsions, the occurrence of earthquakes.

The marauder put a flashlight on the seismograph recording apparatus. He removed the cover with skill and speed which showed he knew a great deal about seismographs, then studied the inked record. With infinite care, he reached into the seismograph.

He made the seismograph show an earthquake which had not occurred.

The prowler then replaced the cover, satisfied himself there was nothing to show the seismograph had been tampered with, and eased back to the door.

The watchman was standing, staring at the man lying at the foot of the stairs. He did not see the prowler quit the building. A few minutes later, when the man who had been lying on the sidewalk got up and vouchsafed, with a proper amount of shakiness, that he felt able to navigate, all the men went away.

The watchman returned to his duties, having no suspicion that anyone had gained entrance to the building by the use of an elaborate trick.

BATAVIA and his men got in their car and Batavia drove grimly, holding his mouth tight. Several times he grumbled about the long trip from the New Jersey bridge, where they had dynamited Doc Savage's car, to the city.

"The length of that trip delayed us," Batavia growled. "It made us get started at this business too late in the night!" He was full of complaints. Then he turned to the man who had entered into the science hall. "You sure you fixed that seismograph?" he snarled.

"I know my business," said the man who had tampered with the seismograph.

"Them things show the direction of an earthquake, don't they?"

"Leave that part to me!" the other said ill-temperedly. "I know more about seismographs and earthquakes than you ever read. You do your part

as well as I do mine, and we won't have any more hitches!"

"Who's caused hitches?" Batavia snarled.

"You have!" said the seismograph expert. "You tried to stop the girl from getting to Doc Savage in the first place, and got scared out of your wits!"

"For a little," Batavia grated, "I'd stop this car and knock that sass out of you!"

Batavia speeded the car up, made a left turn, traveled a few blocks, took a right turn, and pulled up on the obscure side of the block of buildings on Central Park which housed the American Museum of Natural History.

"This one may be a little tougher," Batavia said.

"If we get one seismograph, we've got to get them all," the seismograph expert said.

"Oh, shut up!" Batavia growled.

There was no elaborate trickery about their method of gaining admission to the museum; their ruse was simplicity itself.

A man opened the door for them and greeted them impatiently; he was one of Batavia's men, and he had hidden himself in the museum before the closing hour. He had made sure no watchman was in that portion of the museum.

"You guys been taking in night clubs?" the man demanded. "You were due three hours ago!"

"Pipe down!" Batavia ordered. "We been busy."

They went to the room which contained the seismograph, and the others took up positions of lookout while the expert went to work on the instrument. When he had caused the university seismograph to record a fake earthquake, the expert had noted the time to the split part of a second—he wore a jeweled wrist watch with a large second hand for this purpose.

The expert then made a fake earthquake register on the Museum of Natural History's seismograph, made it show at the precise instant that he had recorded the one at the university.

"That fixes it," he said finally.

THEY left the museum the way they had come. The man who had hidden in the place to let them in, left with them. Batavia consulted his watch as he got into the car.

"We may make it," he admitted grudgingly.

They drove to the nearest hotel, and found a telephone booth. Batavia scowled at the seismograph expert.

"You call Washington," Batavia ordered.

The expert was in the booth several minutes, part of which time he spent ringing the bell with quarters, to pay the toll on his Washington call. When he came out, he looked pleased.

"Bub will call me back," he said.

"How long will it take?" Batavia demanded.

"An hour maybe."

"We'll wait."

They settled in the hotel lobby chairs, where it was murky and quiet. Street cars went clanging past occasionally, and now and then the exhaust of a bus made noise.

Batavia growled, "You sure the mug in Washington knows his business?"

"He's no mug. He's my brother," the seismograph expert scowled.

Batavia subsided. The hour dragged past, and still there was no call from Washington. Suddenly thunder gave a great whopping gobble outside, and it began to rain again. Finally the telephone rang; it was Washington.

The man who knew all about seismographs talked to his brother in Washington and laughed several times. He came out of the booth chuckling.

"Perfect!" he said.

"He have any trouble getting to the Washington seismograph?" Batavia demanded.

"Nope. He had keys to the place." The expert chuckled again. "He made the Washington instrument show a quake at the same place and time that we faked one on the two machines here. You know, I'm beginnin' to enjoy this gag."

"You're sure," Batavia asked, "that these seismographs are the only ones in this part of the United States?"

"The only ones in operation," the expert said.

"Then we got us an earthquake all fixed up," Batavia declared.

Chapter IX
THE GIGGLING PEOPLE

THE next instance of a giggling ghost came to the public notice about nine o'clock the next night. The newspapers did not print the story of this giggling ghost that night; that came later.

No giggling ghost actually appeared this time.

A man just caught the giggles.

He was not a very happy man, which made his giggling all the more startling; startling at first, that was, before it began to be realized that being happy or sad had very little to do with the giggling.

This first victim was a grocer; he ran a store, which he kept open evenings. The store was close enough to his residence that he could go home for dinner, and he habitually took a short-cut across a vacant lot which was thickly overgrown with weeds.

On this night he took his usual short-cut. He was rather a bug on health, and he always walked with his chest out and head back, taking deep breaths.

He did not see a ghost.

He began to giggle shortly after he had crossed the weed-grown lot. He started with small snickers. When he got home, he sat down on his front porch and tittered. He snickered until he had to hold his sides, but strangely enough, there was no joy on his face. Rather, there was growing terror.

The grocer's wife came out on the porch. His wife was a large woman with affirmative ways, and after she had asked him several times what he thought was so funny, and her husband only snickered at her, she lost her temper and gave him a kick in the ribs.

Her husband toppled over and continued to shake with his giggles.

"Gug—gug—get a doctor!" he giggled.

His wife did not believe in doctors. She hauled him in the house, and tried doctoring him herself with good old-fashioned remedies such as castor oil, ice packs, smelling salts, and a hot foot bath. But by midnight the grocer was so much worse that his wife grew really scared, and called an ambulance.

The ambulance attendants looked puzzled as they carried the grocer, quaking and giggling, out to the white vehicle. The ambulance moaned through the streets to the hospital.

In the hospital, all the doctors looked puzzled.

The giggling merchant went into the diagnosis room, where he was X-rayed, had his reflexes tested, his metabolism measured. Most doctors joined the conference.

Then all the doctors stood around and shook their heads. The giggling merchant had them stumped.

When five other giggling people landed in the hospital the following day, it was a much bigger mystery. The newspapers got hold of it. The giggling ghosts became an incredible story.

IT had been a quiet day for the newspapers; the international situation was calm, the stock market was stationary, and there had been no interesting murders. True, there had been a mysterious bridge explosion on a remote New Jersey road two nights before.

Residents of the thinly populated district had heard this detonation, but no one had been found who had witnessed it. This mystery of a destroyed bridge was played up in the early newspaper editions, but lost prominence after an anonymous note reached the sheriff of the New Jersey county, a note stating that some unruly boys had been experimenting with a homemade bomb.

This note caused the authorities to start looking for unruly boys; it kept them from dragging the deep water under and around the bridge, something they had been considering doing; so the note succeeded—Batavia had sent it—in its purpose: a ruse to keep Doc Savage's submerged car from being found.

There also appeared in the newspapers a small item to the effect that William Harper "Johnny" Littlejohn, the eminent archaeologist and geologist, had stated that Doc Savage had disappeared.

Johnny Littlejohn was another one of Doc Savage's five assistants.

The fact that Doc Savage had disappeared would have received a burst of newspaper publicity, except that William Harper Littlejohn declared there was no justification for any belief that the bronze man might have met with foul play. Johnny made this tempering statement because he knew of Doc Savage's dislike for publicity.

The bridge explosion, the missing Doc Savage, were wiped off all the front pages by the giggling people.

By six o'clock five gigglers had turned up in hospitals, in addition to the merchant.

Some of these insisted they must have caught the giggles from the giggling ghost, or ghosts.

Automobiles loaded with doctors kept rushing from one hospital to another, trying to diagnose the epidemic. As might be expected, there was disagreement among the specialists, some contending one thing, and some another.

Gradually, however, they all agreed that the giggling was caused by spasms of the respiratory muscular system, undoubtedly was the result of something drastically wrong with the respiratory nervous centers.

By ten o'clock that night, over twenty gigglers were in Jersey hospitals. The gigglers were all in Jersey: there were none in Manhattan, the Bronx, or Staten Island.

Each victim of the giggling malady became steadily worse.

The police investigated, of course. The police at once noticed that all gigglers were being found in Jersey—in a certain area of Jersey, to be exact. The sector was confined to a district on the riverfront, near the mouth of a vehicular tunnel which had been recently constructed under the Hudson River.

It was a region of low-priced homes, not a particularly fashionable neighborhood. By dawn the following morning, it was absolutely certain that every giggling victim had come from this sector. So had the stories of the giggling ghosts.

Also by morning, it had been ascertained that each of the gigglers had one thing in common: they each had taken a walk that day, or that evening. In every case, the victim had walked through the streets in the riverfront district.

At nine o'clock the next morning, A. King Christophe put in an appearance.

A. KING CHRISTOPHE was a very fat man, with round eyes, not much of a nose, a puffy face and very black hair. When A. King Christophe blew out his cheeks and glared, which he had the habit of doing on the slightest provocation, he looked very fierce. He was a geologist. Newspaper investigators later in the day learned that A. King Christophe was a rather well-known geologist.

Geologist A. King Christophe got a load of newspaper publicity that day, for it was he who came forth with a discovery of the source of the giggling malady.

A. King Christophe arrived in a taxicab. When he alighted from the cab, he carried a suitcase, large and much worn. He immediately had a quarrel with the taxi driver over the fare, and blew out his cheeks and looked so fierce that he bluffed the driver.

When A. King Christophe's worn suitcase was opened, it proved to contain litmus papers and other scientific aides for analyzing the composition of earth and air. For two hours he prowled over the region, using the devices. Then he went to the police.

"See!" he said. "I have idea."

"Go away," the cops said. "Everybody seems to have ideas around here today. Ghosts with the contagious giggles! All kinds of ideas!"

A. King Christophe blew out his cheeks, glared and intimidated the officer into listening.

"She are gas that make all this giggle!" Christophe declared. "She are gas, and she come from ground!"

"What kind of gas?" the cop wanted to know.

"Give me time, give me time!" said A. King Christophe indignantly.

The policeman called other policemen, and they called chemical experts; and A. King Christophe demonstrated to the satisfaction of everyone that the earth in certain parts of the Jersey gas area was undoubtedly saturated with a mysterious vapor.

The newspapers broke out their biggest type.

MYSTERIOUS EARTH GAS, NOT GHOSTS, CAUSING GIGGLE DEATHS!

Two giggling victims had died by now. The poor grocery merchant went first, and the other victim was a truck driver.

A. King Christophe was hailed as a hero; he had accomplished nothing, but he was hailed anyway. He had learned there was gas.

But what kind of gas was it? That was the question.

"Have chemists make analysis," suggested A. King Christophe. "They might learn."

Why did the gas happen to be coming from the ground? That was another question. A. King Christophe pondered that.

"I have theory." Christophe blew his cheeks out. "Suppose this gas are deep in earth for long time. Suppose she not get out because of strata of rock over it, like a lid. Suppose earthquake crack the stone lid."

"Earthquake?"

"I say it may be."

It appeared, however, that no one had felt any earthquakes around New Jersey recently. The giggling ghost story seemed as sensible.

"Many earthquakes no one are notice!" A. King Christophe said angrily. "To find earthquake, look at instrument made to record them—instrument called seismograph!"

They consulted the seismographs at the university, the museum in Washington; so they found evidence of a subterranean earthquake in the vicinity of Jersey.

A score of people then popped up to declare they had felt the earthquake at the precise time the seismograph records said it had occurred. These people even described how pictures danced on the walls and glasses had jumped off tables; such is human nature.

Now it was generally concluded that a mystery gas had been imprisoned under the earth's crust for centuries, that an earthquake had cracked the crust, and that the gas was coming out and making people giggle themselves to death.

Ghosts—nothing!

Then William Harper Littlejohn put in an appearance, and the affair began to get complicated.

AS a geologist, William Harper "Johnny" Littlejohn had a reputation considerably exceeding that of A. King Christophe. Johnny was just about tops in the geology business.

Johnny Littlejohn was also probably the longest and the thinnest man who had ever been in that part of Jersey; newspapermen liked to label Johnny as being two men tall and half a man thick, and he came near being that. Johnny's clothing never fitted him, for no tailor could quite manage to cope with such a broomstick physique.

Johnny appeared in the gas disaster district to conduct an investigation of his own. Johnny's scientific instruments were more complicated than those used by A. King Christophe. Because Johnny had a geological reputation, a number of newspapermen followed him around, awaiting his conclusions.

When Johnny voiced his findings the first time, nobody understood him.

"I'll be superamalgamated!" Johnny exclaimed. He had a habit of never using a small word when he could think of a big one.

"An ultraconsummate mumpsimus!" he added.

The reporters copied Johnny's big words down; the tongue-knotters always made good color in a news story.

"Now, just what do you mean?" the reporters asked. "Ghosts?"

Reluctantly, Johnny fell back on little words.

"There is gas," he said. "There is no doubt that the gas is causing the giggling, because it seems to be some nature of pulmonic—"

"Whoa!" a reporter interrupted. "Little words—if you don't mind."

"A pulmonic," Johnny explained, "is an agent affecting the lungs. In this case, it is causing spasmodic behavior, and eventual disintegration of the affected nervous area."

"So that's what you said," a reporter grunted. "That's what you meant by ultra-ultracon—"

"No, it isn't," Johnny corrected.

"Huh?"

"What I said," Johnny explained, "is that there has been a tremendous mistake."

"Mistake about what? *You don't mean there is a ghost?*"

"The earthquake."

"Meaning?"

"There wasn't any earthquake," Johnny said.

WORD of this remarkable statement reached A. King Christophe who, after sneering several times, blew out his cheeks.

"Who is this William Harper Littlejohn?" he jeered.

"He's got a bigger reputation than you have," he was told, but more impolitely.

"Poof!" A. King Christophe let the air out of his cheeks. "He has reputation as Doc Savage hanger-on! I not consider him authority."

The reporters, on the lookout for the dramatic, made an inquiry. "Would you like to tell Johnny Littlejohn that to his face?" they asked.

"Yes," said A. King Christophe.

The two geologists met and surveyed each other like two strange roosters. Physically, they both came rather close to being freaks, and the news cameramen got busy taking pictures.

"I'll be superamalgamated!" Johnny said grimly.

A. King Christophe looked startled.

"Which?"

William Harper Littlejohn said, "In Doc Savage's headquarters there is a seismograph."

"But—"

"And this seismograph of Doc's did not register an earthquake," Johnny said.

"But three other seismographs did register one!" A. King Christophe shouted.

"I don't care what registered which!" Johnny yelled. "There wasn't any earthquake! I stake my opinion on Doc's machine!"

A. King Christophe stamped away making remarks about long, lean walking dictionaries.

Chapter X
FAKE QUAKE

WILLIAM HARPER LITTLEJOHN did not care for reporters, because of the joy the scribes took in exaggerating the long, lean geologist's characteristics.

As soon as Johnny had given the press his opinion about there having been no earthquake, he retired to the midtown Manhattan skyscraper where Doc Savage made his headquarters.

Johnny was worried about Doc. The bronze man had been missing two days. Johnny had learned of the excitement here in the building two days ago, when someone had tried to prevent a young woman from reaching Doc Savage.

This was the effort Batavia had made to stop Miami Davis, but Johnny had no means of knowing that; he just knew there had been some trouble, following which Doc had disappeared.

Johnny had been at headquarters about an hour when there was a knock on the door. The gaunt geologist and archaeologist hurried over, hoping it was Doc, and opened the door.

"Oh!" he said.

The visitor was a stranger, a tall young man with great shoulders and a body that was impressively muscular. The visitor scowled at Johnny.

"I'm William Henry Hart, an inventor and manufacturer," he said.

Johnny frowned at Hart, whom he had never seen before. "Is replication exigent?" he asked.

"Huh?" said Hart.

Johnny translated, "What do I say to that?"

"You mean I'm William Henry Hart—and so what?"

"Equiparably correct," Johnny said.

William Henry Hart looked puzzled. He put out his jaw. "Look here," he growled, "use little words, if you don't mind."

"What do you want?"

"I've got important bad news," Hart said. "Ah—Doc Savage is missin', isn't he?"

"Doc seems to have disappeared," Johnny admitted.

"He's dead," Hart said.

Johnny took a step back, sank in the chair. His face blanched. His fingers tightened until they bit into the chair arm. His jaw sagged.

BECAUSE Doc Savage led a life of constant danger, Johnny had always feared of disaster befalling the bronze man. As a matter of fact, all Doc's men were in enough danger constantly to make them concerned about each other's safety.

It was several moments before Johnny could speak.

"Who—what—" He still couldn't frame a coherent sentence.

Hart hooked a long leg over the desk corner.

"I could've broke it easier," he said. "But I figured bad news was bad news."

Johnny's hands shook. The shock was tremendous. He could not believe that the bronze man was—was—

He said, "What happened?" hoarsely.

William Henry Hart got off the desk, clasped his muscular fingers behind his back and tramped the length of the office, then back again.

"I don't like women!" he said.

Johnny looked up. "What?"

"Well, a girl was the cause of this. A girl named Miami Davis. She's the one who got me and Doc Savage mixed up in it."

Johnny said, "Please tell a coherent story."

"O. K.," Hart said. "Here it is—plenty coherent. Miami Davis followed a—a gigglin' ghost to a storehouse, or so she said. In the storehouse, she got a gigglin' fit. Then she came to Doc Savage. A man tried to stop her, but failed. The girl took Doc to this storehouse. Then she found her wrist watch; she'd given me the watch to have fixed. The watch was lyin' in the storehouse.

"The girl then came rushin' to the boat where I live. Why, I don't know. Some men grabbed her at the boat. At the same time, the men grabbed Monk and Ham, who were trailin' the girl."

Hart explained how Doc Savage had arrived at the boat, and found the note saying Monk, Ham and Miami Davis had been taken out to Beach Road.

Hart then described the incident on the way.

"This Birmingham Lawn," he said, "kept tightening the knots of the ropes which bound me. He must have pulled the wrong rope end or something, because the ropes got looser all of a sudden. So I got loose and jumped out of the car."

"Strange thing for you to do," Johnny said grimly.

Hart put out his jaw and glared.

"Look!" he snapped. "Any time a guy barges in on me and ties me up with a rope, I'm gonna do somethin' about it! I don't care if the guy is Doc Savage!"

"You jumped out of the car," Johnny prompted. "Then what?"

"I went tearin' across the sand dunes," Hart

explained. "I hit the beach, and about that time a bunch of mugs popped out and shoved guns into my ribs. They put me in a speedboat."

Then Hart described in blunt detail the blasting of the bridge when Doc Savage's car appeared upon it.

"They killed Doc Savage right there," he finished.

JOHNNY sat and contemplated his own feet with blank intentness, and no muscle in his long body seemed to stir, his eyes did not blink, his breathing was imperceptible, and the throbbing of a vein in his forehead was the only sign of life about him.

"Why did you come to me?" he asked hollowly.

The burly young man said, "Well, hell, what else could I do?"

"They turned you loose?"

"They did."

"Can you give any clues?"

"You mean clues to who those men were—or where you can find them? Or clues to—well, this giggling ghost stuff?"

"Any of that."

"Not a clue," Hart said. "They blindfolded me in the boat, after the explosion. They kept me blindfolded until they kicked me out of a car. They kicked me out on a New Jersey road."

Johnny growled, "You say this Birmingham Lawn was also taken a prisoner?"

Hart scowled.

"Yes," he said. "And I ain't plumb satisfied about that mug, either."

"What do you mean?"

"Lawn seemed too damn innocent to me!" Hart growled.

William Harper Littlejohn got up and shuffled to the window. He seemed to have become as stiff as an old man. An oppressing shroud of fog lay over the dark, smoky towers of Manhattan.

"When did Miami Davis have her giggling fit?" Johnny demanded.

Hart gave the time.

"Then the girl was a victim before the time this earthquake is supposed to have happened! That is important!"

Hart was puzzled. "Before the earthquake—"

"It proves," Johnny said grimly, "that an earthquake had nothing to do with the gas!" Johnny turned away from the window. His face looked so sunken that it seemed composed of nothing but bone. "What about Monk and Ham?" he asked.

"I think they were goin' to kill them," Hart said.

Johnny winced. His mouth worked.

Hart got up, straightened his coat on his wide shoulders, and jammed his large fists in his pockets.

"I thought I'd tell you this," he said. "Them guys promised to croak me if I opened my mouth to anybody, but"—he stuck out his jaw—"let 'em hop to it! And if they harm that girl"—his voice lifted to an angry yell—"I'll tear the heads off every last one of 'em!"

Hart went over and clasped Johnny's arm. "Look here," he continued, "I'm worried about that girl. The snip! If they dare hurt her—"

"You are in love with Miami Davis?" Johnny asked.

Hart swallowed.

"I don't know," he growled. "But I'm worried as hell about her."

Johnny said, "I am going to call on you if you can be of any assistance."

"Do that," Hart said grimly. "I got a rushin' little manufacturing business to look out for, but it's gonna be neglected until I find that girl is safe."

Hart then stamped out of the office, holding his jaw out belligerently.

Johnny flung to a telephone.

"Long Tom!" he said into the instrument.

"Yes!" a voice responded.

"A man is leaving the office"—Johnny described Hart—"and I want you to follow him."

"Right!" "Long Tom" said. "Who is he?"

Johnny said, "Man named Hart. He says Doc is dead. I think it's queer he came to me with the story, instead of going to the police."

The other man, Long Tom, made a horrified noise over the telephone. "Doc—you say—but it can't—"

"Follow Hart, Long Tom."

"I'll follow him. Renny is with me. We'll both follow Hart."

The man called "Long Tom" was Major Thomas J. Roberts—specialty electricity; avocation that of Doc Savage assistant.

"Renny" was Colonel John Renwick, a great engineer, also a great hand to prove he could knock panels out of wooden doors with his huge fists. He, too, was an aide to Doc Savage.

These three men—Johnny, Long Tom, and Renny—with the missing Monk and Ham, comprised Doc Savage's staff of five associates.

Chapter XI
NO MEDDLERS

BY now there were almost fifty giggling victims in the hospitals. Each one of these had come from one small section of Jersey. Only this area was affected. Police had roped off streets leading to the district, and were keeping back the spectators. Some of the curious were idiots enough to want to venture into the affected zone and take chances with the gas, solely to see what was going on, or look for giggling ghosts, if there really were any.

Evacuation was commencing. Just as river bottoms menaced by flood waters are cleared of inhabitants, so was the gas area to be cleared. Huge moving vans, piloted by policemen wearing gas masks, moved in and out, carrying household goods.

The evacuation was a pitiful spectacle. The section was one of small homes. The homes were unpretentious, often shabby, but nevertheless homes in the real sense, because the homes were owned by those who lived in them.

These people were stubborn. They did not understand. They could not see the gas, not actually see it, and many of them were inclined to be suspicious of the attempt to get them out of their homes.

The fact that the gas did not completely blanket the district made the exodus more difficult to arrange. The gas appeared only in spots; whole blocks were not affected.

A company of national guardsmen were sent to the scene to assist.

Meanwhile, geologists and scientists went around, wearing gas masks, trying to figure out some way of blocking off the gas. Many possibilities were suggested; one possibility was that deep wells might be drilled, the gas drawn off through these, and piped out to sea.

Army engineers came to investigate the chances of compressing the gas and storing it in containers, to use in the next war.

THAT night, in the vicinity of all this confusion, a sinister meeting was held.

It was held in a very large, very old house. This house stood alone in the center of a vast lot that was jungled with shrubbery. The house was made of concrete blocks, and it had four entrances, one on each side.

Batavia was first to arrive at the house, and he bustled around, unlocking all the doors, making ready for the meeting. Tonight Batavia wore a different assortment of gray clothes, and he chewed a cork-tipped cigar.

He did not seem happy.

Men who arrived for the conference came furtively. They entered the house by different doors, coat collars turned up, hats yanked down, handkerchiefs held to their faces. Two or three, apparently not caring, made no effort to conceal their visages; one of the latter was the man who had fired the blast under the bridge as Doc Savage's car was crossing.

The interior of the house was kept dark. Each man had to give a password. Beyond that, little talking was done, and this was confined to grunts.

Several times, however, there were outbursts of giggling.

When more than a dozen men were present, Batavia called order by clearing his throat loudly. Then he turned a flashlight on his own face and let all the men see him.

"I am Batavia," he explained. "Some of you already know me."

His audience was silent, except for one man, who couldn't help giggling.

"I am the man who hired all of you," Batavia said. "Your orders came through me."

He paused to let that sink in.

"There is another over me," he said. "I am not the real leader."

This got two or three surprise grunts from the assemblage. The men squirmed uneasily, for the spooky atmosphere in the old house had their nerves on edge.

Batavia said, "Progress has been satisfactory. The public is being fooled into believing gas from the earth is causing the giggling. No one now believes there were any giggling ghosts."

Batavia threw his cigar on the floor and put a fresh one in his mouth.

"It's a good thing for us," he said, "that we got that ghost story stopped."

He added, "Doc Savage was disposed of. That was good work, too."

Someone in the audience started giggling, and Batavia waited until the man could control himself.

"Some more trouble has developed," Batavia said. "One of Doc Savage's aides, a man named Johnny Littlejohn, is causing the trouble. This Littlejohn is going around claiming there wasn't any earthquake. We can't have that!"

Batavia now called out four numbers; evidently the men in the organization answered to numbers rather than names.

"I want you four men," Batavia said, "to go with me, tonight. We're going to get rid of this Johnny Littlejohn as fast as we got rid of Doc Savage!"

A man in the background muttered, "What about this guy named Birmingham Lawn?"

Batavia laughed harshly. "Don't worry about Lawn!"

"And that geologist, A. King Christophe?"

"Christophe is harmless," Batavia said. "Forget him."

Batavia extinguished the flashlight which had been glowing on his features.

Then he did something dramatic.

"Gentlemen," he announced, "I have a surprise."

Tense silence dropped over the room.

Batavia said, "I told you a moment ago that another man was the real leader of this. That man is here now. He wants you to see his face, wants you to know him, so that, when he gives you an order, you will know who he is."

Batavia pointed his flashlight at an open door.

The light struck full on the face of a man standing there.

At least one of the group knew the face by sight, because this individual emitted an exclamation.

"William Henry Hart!" he ejaculated. "The inventor!"

Batavia laughed.

"Yes," he said. "The boss is William Henry Hart."

GEOLOGIST WILLIAM HARPER LITTLE-JOHN habitually drove an old goblin of a car that appeared as incapable of efficiency as its owner, but which was just as deceptive in appearance. Johnny had been known to go at top speed for an astonishing length of time without sleep or food, and his old car had like qualities, except that it never fasted; it drank prodigious amounts of gas.

It was midnight—an hour after the meeting in the old cement block house—when Johnny, driving his ancient chariot, drew up beside the waterfront curb.

A man came out of the darkness and got in the car.

The new arrival, besides being big, was distinctive for two features: he had a long going-to-a-funeral face, and his fists were nearly the size of quart pails. This man was Colonel John "Renny" Renwick, engineer, fist-smasher of door panels, and a Doc Savage aide.

"Holy cow!" Renny said, trying to find a soft place in the car cushions. "That Hart sure led us a chase."

Renny had a voice reminiscent of a lion roaring in a cave.

"Has Hart done anything suspicious?" Johnny asked.

"Heck—no! He just bounces around like the Irishman's flea. I never saw a guy do more work than he's done."

"You haven't lost sight of Hart at any time?"

"Long Tom and I have watched him every minute," Renny said.

"Where is Hart now?"

"In the Digester Company plant just around the corner. You might as well walk."

Johnny got out of his traffic hazard. Alongside Renny, Johnny looked incredibly thin. They walked about two blocks, and were confronted by a new brick factory building which, while not extremely large, was neat and modern. A sign across the front of the factory said:

HART DIGESTER COMPANY

"What's a *digester?*" Johnny asked.

"It's a contraption they put on smokestacks," Renny explained. "It takes the soot and smell out of smoke. This patent digester of Hart's is something a little extraordinary. It purifies the air. If it could be generally adopted, they claim it would be a boon to cities."

"How does a smoke digester purify the air?"

"I'm no chemist!" Renny grunted. "But it takes the impurities out of the air, and puts back oxygen, or something. Works with chemicals."

"Works with chemicals? That seems significant."

"We thought so, too," Renny said grimly.

"If Hart invented the purifier, he's a chemist."

"Hart is a chemist, all right."

"It would take a chemist to develop a gas that makes people giggle themselves to death."

"Still," Renny said, "I wonder if that business about giggling ghosts ain't more important than we figure."

Looking thoughtfully over their conclusions, the two men entered a vacant lot located directly across the street from the factory. The lot was surrounded by a tall board fence.

Long Tom was posted at a knothole in the fence, using a pair of binoculars.

It was a fact that undertakers always brightened when they saw Long Tom Roberts, because he appeared to be an immediate prospect for a funeral.

Long Tom had been a weakly baby, and a feeble-appearing youth, and all through his manhood he had looked as if he ought to be in a hospital. This appearance of being an invalid was misleading; Long Tom could lick nine out of ten of the average run of men on any street.

"Hart is still working," Long Tom explained disgustedly and pointed. Johnny put his eye to the knothole.

HART was seated at a desk in his factory. Hart had his jaw shoved out, and he was doing things to papers with a pencil. He was plainly visible because the entire wall of the room was windows.

"That all he's been doing?" Johnny asked.

"Yep," said Long Tom.

"You sure?"

"Listen!" Long Tom said belligerently. "We ain't taken an eye off him since he left Doc Savage's headquarters!"

"I'll be superamalgamated!" Johnny complained. "I hoped he'd lead us to Monk and Ham."

They stood there gloomily, thinking of Doc Savage and Monk and Ham, and the fate that had befallen them.

"Well, Hart hasn't made a guilty move," Long Tom said finally.

Johnny sighed. "We might as well get him and

take him with us. He said he was willing to help. As long as he's with us, we can watch him."

"Take him with us where?" Renny demanded.

"We're going," Johnny said, "to interview a man named Birmingham Lawn."

When Johnny, Long Tom and Renny walked in, William Henry Hart flung one hand on a handkerchief lying on his desk. Hart glared at them, a burly and belligerent young man.

He pointed at Renny and Long Tom. "Who are these guys?"

Johnny explained that Renny and Long Tom were more Doc Savage associates.

Hart then took his hand off the handkerchief, picked the handkerchief up, and disclosed a large automatic pistol under it.

"I ain't takin' chances," he explained. "I've had enough funny business to do me for a while."

Johnny said, "We hope you will join us."

"I got work to do!" Hart said.

Johnny said, "We will look for Miami Davis among other things. We thought you—"

This had an immediate effect on Hart. He put down his pencil, kicked his chair back, and picked up his gun and tucked it in the waistband of his trousers.

"Let's go hunt bear," he said.

They left the smoke-digester-air-purifier manufacturing plant.

"We'll start our hunt," Johnny said, "with Birmingham Lawn."

"He's one of our bears, if you ask me," Hart said.

They reached Johnny's old car and got in.

When the engine started, it shook the whole elderly vehicle, and when the conveyance got in motion, there was a suspicion that one or more of the wheels were square.

William Henry Hart took his gun out of his belt, and began unloading it.

"What's the idea of that?" Johnny asked.

"I'm afraid this car will jar it off!" Hart explained unkindly.

Chapter XII
THE RESCUED

LAWN might not have had the largest house in the country, but it was unlikely there were many houses with more dignity. Lawn's house was as dignified as an art gallery; it also looked rather like an art gallery, being made of light-colored stone, and it was the shape of a long cube, with no ornate gimcracks or decorations. Everything was so simple and reserved.

The house sat alone on a grassy knoll, and there were a few trees. A white gravel driveway wound

from the house to a gate in a bleak stone wall. It all looked a little like Mount Vernon, Washington's home, except that the house was more severe.

There was a gatehouse at the gate, and a gate-keeper.

Johnny pulled up before the gatehouse, stopping his rattletrap by some combination of which he alone was the master.

"An abode of attitudinarianism," Johnny remarked.

Hart looked at Johnny. "Huh?"

"He means a showplace," Long Tom translated.

"It would be easier for him to say so," Hart muttered.

A gatekeeper came out of the gatehouse to frown disapprovingly at the old car.

"We wish to see Birmingham Lawn," Johnny said.

The gatekeeper went back into the gatehouse and, judging from the sounds, he telephoned an inquiry about whether or not he should admit the visitors, because he put his head out the door to demand their names.

"Mr. Lawn will be glad to see you," he announced then.

Johnny drove through the gate, along the winding gravel walk.

Johnny looked at Hart. "I thought you said the gang had Lawn prisoner."

"They must've turned him loose," Hart said.

"Humph!"

Hart made a growling noise and shoved his face almost against Johnny's.

"You wouldn't," he grated, "be insinuating that I'm a liar!"

"You said Lawn was a prisoner. But he isn't."

Hart yelled, "I'll take the hide off anybody who calls me a liar!"

Renny blocked out his two huge fists and shoved them under Hart's nose.

"You see these?" Renny demanded.

Hart ogled the fists.

"Water buckets!" he muttered.

"They're the buckets to pour water on that temper you've got!" Renny said.

THERE were no more verbal pyrotechnics. The car arrived before the impressive entrance of Lawn's house, and stood shaking itself until Johnny turned off the motor. A butler in a resplendent uniform told them that Birmingham Lawn would see them in the library.

Lawn did not seem very enthusiastic about the visit. Lawn stood behind a large library table in a softly lighted study where there were many bookcases. "Good evening, gentlemen," he said.

Hart walked around the table and looked Lawn up and down.

"Last time I saw you," Hart said, "you were tied up with ropes."

Lawn looked uncomfortable and swallowed two or three times. He whistled a bar from a popular song.

"They turned me loose," he explained.

"You saw Doc Savage—killed?" Johnny asked with an effort.

Lawn looked at the floor.

"I—yes, I saw it happen."

"Why didn't you tell the police?" Johnny grated.

Lawn paled and sank into a chair. "I—well—"

Johnny came over, said, *Why didn't you?"* savagely.

Lawn seemed to shrink. "I—well, I was afraid. They said they would kill me!"

Hart sniffed. "They told me the same thing."

"I'm not a brave man," Lawn said plaintively.

Johnny said, "Lawn, we want every particle of information you have."

Lawn sat and frowned at the desk top. He chewed his lower lip. He whistled for a moment, then stopped.

"I know nothing," he said.

The floor then literally jumped under everybody's feet.

A PART of the ceiling also came down on their heads, the part of it that was plaster. Big cracks appeared in the floor; dust flew up out of these. The dust fogged the room.

When the commotion subsided, it was evident one wall had received the brunt of the blast. The wall was out of shape.

"A bomb!" Long Tom gulped.

"Anybody hurt?" Renny howled.

Apparently no one had been seriously hurt.

The bomb, obviously, had exploded outdoors.

There was a window, covered on the outside with huge ornamental iron bars. The bars were still in place. But the bars had been loosened by the blast.

Renny clamped his huge fists to the bars, set himself, began yanking. The bars gave slowly.

"Listen!" Long Tom exploded.

From outside came sounds; blows, angry gasps and threshing of shrubbery. There was a fight going on in the darkness outside.

"Fight out there!" Renny ejaculated.

He got the bars loose. Then Renny and Johnny leaped outdoors, used their emergency flashlights they carried in their rear pockets. The air was so full of dust it was hard to distinguish details. They did manage to distinguish a shaking in a clump of shrubbery.

Long Tom suddenly whirled from the window.

He discovered Lawn in the act of opening a desk drawer. Long Tom leaped over and knocked the drawer shut.

Lawn pointed at the drawer. "A gun in there, if you want it," he said.

Long Tom said, "We don't use guns."

William Henry Hart growled something and started toward the window.

"Stay here!" Long Tom ordered.

Hart ignored Long Tom, so the feeble-looking electrical wizard ran over, stuck a foot out and tripped Hart. Hart got up, snarled. He swung a roundhouse right at Long Tom.

Long Tom caught the arm, went through a convulsion, and Hart sailed up in the air, turned over, hit the floor flat on his back, knocking up a cloud of plaster dust. He didn't have breath enough to get up.

Outdoors, Renny and Johnny were floundering around in the bushes where the mysterious fight was going on. Their flashlights picked up three figures.

The air reeked of burnt cordite. Apparently the bomb had been lying on the ground when it let loose, for shrubbery had been torn out of the earth.

Two of the figures lay on the ground, apparently just knocked senseless. The third man stood.

"Holy cow!" Renny boomed.

He tried to say more, but was incoherent.

Johnny went rigid.

Long Tom put his head out the shattered window and yelled, "What's goin' on out there?"

Then he saw the standing man.

"Doc!" Long Tom whooped.

Doc Savage pointed at the two senseless men at his feet.

"These two," Doc said, "threw that bomb at me when they found out I was following them."

Chapter XIII
ACCIDENT

BY the time Doc Savage had carried the two senseless bombers into Lawn's house, Renny, Johnny and Long Tom had tamed down with their delight. They had stamped gleeful circles in the lawn, yelled, whooped.

The entire party now gathered in another room of Lawn's house.

William Henry Hart stood in glaring silence.

The prisoners—two heavily constructed, unpleasant-looking men—sat on chairs. They wore dark clothing, gloves, and both had expressions of deep gloom. They had been gagged.

"Did they follow us here?" Renny demanded.

"No," Doc said. "They came later. I am the one who followed you."

"You followed us?"

"Exactly."

"But why?"

"Because it was logical to think someone might make an effort to get rid of you."

"Oh, then these men with the bomb were—"

"Were probably sent to kill you."

At this point, William Henry Hart came over and poked a puzzled finger at Doc Savage.

"I don't get this," he said. "I saw 'em blow you and your car higher'n a kite, along with your traveling zoo!"

Doc Savage's metallic features remained inscrutable. Right now the pets were safely hidden away in a vacant house that Doc had taken them to after the explosion. He had then followed his aides with a coupé he'd taken from his hangar. But Doc didn't elaborate on all this.

"You saw them blow up the car—just the car," he said to Hart

"You weren't in it?"

"I got out just before the machine rolled onto the bridge."

"How in the devil did you know enough to do that?"

"I was suspicious of the bridge in the first place. Bridges have been blown up before. So I stopped down the road, left the car, and investigated the bridge. It wasn't difficult to find the explosives."

"But it was dark."

Long Tom, the electrical wizard, said, "Doc has an infra-ray device to see in the dark."

Birmingham Lawn and William Henry Hart stared at Doc Savage, bewildered. Renny, Johnny and Long Tom did not look as surprised, being familiar with the bronze man's strange working methods.

"You let us think you were dead!" Lawn muttered. "I don't see the reason for that!"

Doc said, "As long as the men think I am dead, they will not try to interfere with me."

DOC SAVAGE removed from his coat pocket three small metallic disks. These appeared to be made of stainless steel and were the size of English pennies—about twice as large as American one-cent pieces. Each disk bore an address.

Doc Savage indicated these medallions.

"These," he said, "are keys."

He gave one of the metal disks to William Henry Hart, and another one to Birmingham Lawn.

Doc put the third disk back in his pocket.

Lawn and Hart eyed their disks, puzzled.

"Keys?" Hart muttered.

"On each disk," Doc Savage said, "there is an address."

Hart eyed his disk. "A street name, a house number, and a room number," he said.

"Exactly," Doc Savage agreed. "Go there if you wish to get in touch with me."

"Where does the key part come in?"

"On the door will be a small black spot," Doc said. "Press your disk against this spot, and the door will open. It's a magnetic lock. Those disks are magnetized."

"Then this address is where you're hiding out?" Hart demanded.

Doc Savage nodded.

The bronze man then picked up the two prisoners, handling them both without apparent difficulty, and prepared to leave.

"Wait, Doc!" Johnny gasped. "I've got questions! A lot of questions! What's this all about?"

"What do you think?" Doc Savage countered.

"Well," Johnny said, "I—we—you see—well—"

"It's got us superamalgamated!" Long Tom said.

"It would superamalgamate anybody," Doc told him.

Doc Savage went out carrying the prisoners.

"I'll get in touch with you," he said.

DOC SAVAGE kept under cover of one of the hedges and carried his prisoners to the road, then down the road some distance to a spot where an inconspicuous coupé was parked. Doc put the captives in a rear compartment of the coupé and locked the lid. Then he got behind the coupé wheel and drove.

Reaching the nearest boulevard, the bronze man turned toward the city. In a short time he was passing through the new vehicular tunnel under the Hudson River, the coupé running quietly, and the gleaming white sides of the tunnel flashing past. Despite the length of this new tunnel, the air was clean and pure. This was the tunnel that had recently been completed, with its New Jersey mouth near the sector affected by the gas.

Doc Savage ignored the skyscraper which housed his headquarters, and drove to the Hudson River water front; he came to a stop before a huge, somber brick building. This structure had a weather-beaten sign which said:

HIDALGO TRADING COMPANY

This was Doc Savage's waterfront hangar and boathouse. The doors opened automatically as his coupé approached, a matter accomplished by a radio device, an apparatus similar to the type which anyone interested in gadgets can buy on the market. Doc drove into the great vault of gloom that was the warehouse interior.

He removed the prisoners from the rear compartment. They glared at him, buzzed around their

Renny's and Johnny's flashlights picked up three figures. Two of the figures lay on the ground. The third man stood.

gags; he had also tied their wrists and ankles.

The warehouse hangar had for a long time been a secret establishment, but now the bronze man suspected that quite a number of persons knew of its existence.

Doc Savage looked at the prisoners. "I have to hide you here," he said. "And still your friends may know about the place."

They glared at him.

Doc Savage dragged the pair to the other end of

the building. Here, among a mass of paraphernalia stood a diving bell—a type of contrivance sometimes called a bathosphere, and used for diving to great depths.

The bell was of thick steel; there was a ring in the top for a cable, also a hatch for entrance and exit.

"You can avoid trouble," Doc advised the prisoners, "by telling all you know. Begin with the rumors about the giggling ghosts."

He removed their gags.

"Blazes with you!" one man snarled.

The other man was more detailed about where the bronze man could go.

Two or three times, Doc tried to get information out of them, but with no success.

"Unfortunately," Doc said, "there is no time to go through a process of extracting information."

Doc then put the men inside the diving bell. They fought as best they could, being bound. Doc closed the diving bell lid on the pair.

IN order to prevent the lid being opened from the inside, Doc wired the patent dogs with which the lid was secured. Inside the bell the men kicked angrily and screamed. Then, with a jerk, the prisoners felt the bell rise off the floor.

They gave each other terrified looks. They felt the bell swing slowly. There was clanking, as a hydraulic lift lowered them. There was a gurgle as water closed about the bell. Finally the bell settled on the bottom with a thump.

The men squirmed around, managed to roll together, worked on each other's knots. They got free. They threw the ropes aside.

One man kicked the interior of the diving bell angrily.

"Sank us in the water!" he snarled.

The other growled agreement.

"Maybe we can get out, though."

They worked with the hatch fastenings until their fingers began leaving crimson smears. Having failed to budge the lid, they looked at each other uneasily.

"Not a chance," one croaked, "of gettin' out."

The men sat there, swearing until they ran out of breath. Then they noticed something else—

something that horrified them. It was a buzzing sound, a tiny buzzing sound such as water makes coming through a small hole.

"A leak!" one yelled.

They sprang up wildly and tried to find the leak. They succeeded. The leak was under the floor grille, and when they tried to wrench up the grille, they could not, for the grille was riveted down.

One got down on his knees, shoved his fingers as far as he could through the grille. He jerked the fingers out as if they had been bitten.

"Water!" he gasped. "I feel the water!"

It was intensely dark, and the men fumbled through their clothing for matches, finally found one, and struck it, then crouched close to the grille, popping their eyes at the water which they could see coming in a thin needle stream, bubbling and buzzing.

The match went out; the man dropped it, and the end sizzled in the water under the floor grille.

Horror held the men speechless. Then, suddenly, as if both had the same mad hope at the same instant, they began to scream.

They squalled, "Help!" and, "We're drowning!" until the lining almost came out of their throats. After that, they lay panting and speechless, listening for an answer that did not come.

Chapter XIV
NO QUAKES

DOC SAVAGE stood at the far end of the warehouse, where there was no possibility of hearing sounds that might be made by the two men in the diving bell.

Doc was disguising himself. He pulled a wig over his head, rubbed bleaching compound on his bronze skin, fitted faintly colored glass cups over his eyeballs to change his eye color.

He began chewing a chemical substance which would stain his teeth, and give them a poorly tended look. Lastly, he put on a rather loud suit and began carrying a cane.

Doc Savage got in the coupé, left the warehouse, and drove to a neighborhood drugstore. From a telephone booth inside this store, he got in touch with a newspaper which, he happened to know, employed a reporter named Bill Sykes. Doc got the city editor on the wire.

"Bill Sykes," he said, using Bill Sykes' tones as nearly as he recalled them. "What's the address of this geologist named A. King Christophe?"

"The Twentieth Avenue Hotel," the editor said. "Say—what the hell? Here's Bill Sykes sitting at his desk!"

Doc hung up and drove to the Twentieth Avenue Hotel, which proved to be a hostelry located on upper Broadway above the theatrical district. It was an imposing edifice, as far as size, but not too high in quality.

It had, for instance, a doorman who needed his shoes shined and his brass buttons polished; and the lobby floor could have stood a scrubbing. The clerk behind the desk also had no business smoking a cigar while on duty. It was that kind of hotel.

Doc Savage said, "A. King Christophe—what room?"

"He's not in his room," the clerk said. "He's over in Jersey, where they're havin' that giggling ghost trouble."

"Exactly where?"

The clerk gave the address.

DOC SAVAGE left the hotel, drove to Jersey, to the address the hotel clerk had given him. He put on a gas mask, which he took from the car.

A. King Christophe was crouching on a vacant lot, working with some apparatus. He wore a gas mask, one of a type which, like the one Doc was using, permitted the wearer to talk. A telephone headset was clamped to his ears.

"I'm very busy," he said impatiently. "Go away!"

Doc Savage saw that the contraption with which Christophe was working was a sonic device for exploring the subterranean strata of the earth. Geologists use similar devices to locate formations favorable to oil.

Doc Savage bent close to Christophe's ear.

"Keep this a secret," the bronze man whispered, so no one else could hear. "I am Doc Savage."

A. King Christophe made a gulping noise inside his gas mask and sprang to his feet.

He said, "I—what—who—Doc Savage?"

Then, because Doc wore a disguise, the stubby geologist concluded there was a mistake. A hoax. He puffed out his cheeks fiercely.

"You are not look like Doc Savage!" he snapped.

"Disguise," Doc explained.

"But why—"

"I'm supposed to be dead," Doc warned. "Do not tell anyone differently."

"What do you want with me?" Christophe demanded.

"There is a question of an earthquake," Doc reminded him, "between yourself and an associate of mine, William Harper Littlejohn."

A. King Christophe blew out his cheeks to the fullest.

"Littlejohn—that skinny bluffer!" he exclaimed. "He try to claim that are no earthquake. *Pah!* All seismographs are show one. Still he claim there are no earthquake! *Pah!*"

The stubby little man said, *"Pah!"* several times, and ended with an expressive, *"Phooey!"*

Doc Savage pointed at the sonic apparatus for exploring the depths of the earth by the use of sound waves.

"What are you doing with that?"

"I try to locate fissure that gas come through."

"I see," Doc said. "Will you be kind enough to give me any information you may secure?"

A. King Christophe beamed as much as a man could beam behind a gas mask.

"I should be delight!" he said.

Doc Savage took out the third disk of metal which looked like steel. He gave the disk to A. King Christophe.

"I would be very pleased if you brought the information to the address on that disk." Doc said. "I am—oh—hiding out at that address."

He explained how the coinlike piece functioned as a key.

"I do that," A. King Christophe said. "I tell you what I are learn. That Littlejohn—*pah."*

Doc Savage asked, "Have you found any trace of ghosts that giggle?"

"Ghosts—*pah!"*

Doc Savage went back to his car, consulted his wrist watch as if he had an appointment. Apparently he decided he had plenty of time, because he drove at a leisurely pace through the district which was affected by the gas.

For the sake of safety, he rolled up the car windows. This coupé, like all of his closed cars, could be shut up until it was completely gasproof.

THE bronze man was taking advantage of his first opportunity to survey the district haunted by the giggling ghosts. His previous knowledge was secondhand, gained from the newspapers, and newspaper accounts were often overdramatized.

The picture he saw now was grim, as heart-rending as an evacuation in the path of a war. Most houses were now empty, but a few moving vans were backing up to doors or rumbling along the streets. The district already looked dead, despite the fact that the gas had first appeared only a few days ago. Newspapers littered the sidewalks; shrubbery looked ragged.

Real signs of the giggling gas terror were few. A few dead birds and pigeons lay in the streets. At one place lay a peddler's horse, dead from the gas, which the Department of Sanitation had not yet removed.

Doc Savage got out a gas mask, put it on, then opened the car windows. He opened a cardboard box which contained empty bottles having airtight rubber corks.

The bronze man got air samples throughout the gas zone in these bottles.

Doc Savage then drove back to his warehouse-hangar on the Hudson River waterfront. The big hangar doors opened with the radio device; he rolled the car into the vaulted gloom.

Doc showed no immediate interest in the bell or the two prisoners inside it; he made, in fact, no effort to see how they were getting along.

In the warehouse-hangar was stored quantities of equipment: mechanical devices the bronze man had used in the past, others he'd prepared for future emergency. Most of the regular equipment was kept here, for this was the point from which Doc and his aides started expeditions by plane or boat.

One item was Monk's portable chemical laboratory. Monk usually took this on expeditions. The laboratory contained, among other things, a device for spectroscopic analysis—a contrivance for ascertaining the chemical makeup of anygiven substance by examining a burned vapor spectrum.

Doc Savage used the analyzer to examine the air samples from the gas district. These were not the first gas samples he had analyzed; he had taken others from the storehouse, at the beginning of all this strange mystery. But examination of these had not been especially helpful; they had contained such microscopic quantities of the gas.

When Doc Savage finished analyzing the gas samples, he stood frowning thoughtfully. Now he knew the composition of the gas. Knew it exactly. It was not exactly a pioneer discovery. The police chemists had already managed to ascertain the general nature of the gas.

The stuff affected the human respiratory centers and associated nervous system, eventually producing complications which resulted in death. But that was already known.

Where was it actually coming from? That was what Doc was trying to learn. Had he secured any clue? The sample bottles were numbered, and he'd made a mental note of where each sample had been selected. He knew, now, exactly where the gas was thickest.

The bronze man stood contemplating the results of his efforts.

Then, almost imperceptibly, there came into existence in the huge warehouse a tiny, trilling note, a low, strange, exotic sound which rose and fell. A sound with a strangely human quality, this trilling; and yet it was eerie, as fantastic as the call of some rare jungle bird, or a chill wind in an Arctic waste.

It had a quality of ventriloquism; although the sound was perfectly real, it would have been almost impossible to locate the exact source. It was the sound of Doc Savage. The sound he made without conscious effort.

The sound invariably presaged, or accompanied, a state of intense mental activity or a discovery.

Doc Savage went back to the place where he had sunk the captives in the diving bell.

THE two men in the diving bell had lived longer than they had expected; had lived too long. Too long by ages, as time in terror is measured.

They were pale. They trembled. They had spent so much of themselves in fear, that they had hardly vitality to move. The water was rising. Rising, rising, and rising; it should have filled the diving bell long ago. Strangely it had not.

At times, hope had come to the two, only to leave. Maybe air pressure would keep out the water! Maybe the bell would fill only so high, no higher! But when they got one of these frenzied hopes, they would see the water had crept above another seam. Above another bolt or another rivet head.

The pair stood now with only their chins out of the water. Their eyes, wide and mad, were fixed in the darkness.

"We haven't—haven't—"

"Not a chance!"

One man took hold of his own throat; the water was up high enough that part of the hand was underwater.

Earlier, the men had cursed profanely. They had raved, beat and kicked the walls of the diving bell. But now that ugly fire was gone, and they were limp. They were men who were looking at death with plenty of time for doing it.

"If we—we—"

"If we'd talked, you mean?" the other croaked.

"We—could have told him Monk and Ham are alive. And the girl."

"We should've done it!" the other said wildly. "We should've told him the prisoners were at Hart's penthouse!"

"Yeah!" the other croaked. "And then Hart would've fixed us!"

They were trying to keep up their spirits. They did not have deep minds, so their talk was not spiritual, not philosophical. It was talk of realities. But even that did not keep up their courage.

One man suddenly began to scream. To his mad mind came somehow the idea that his partner was responsible for his predicament. He struck out at the other, clawing, digging, biting. They went under water.

Later, half drowned, they had to stop fighting. They came to the top separately, stood choking, panting like animals.

They did not realize the diving bell was being lifted out of the water. Then the hatch opened. The hatch! A hole through which they could crawl back to life!

The men fought to be first through the hatch; once through it, they jumped around, yelled, swore. They were mad with delirious pleasure.

But the joy took a drop when Doc Savage fell upon them. Doc tied their wrists and ankles.

"What—what—" The men glared at him.

"You could've drowned us!" one snarled.

"Hardly," Doc Savage said quietly. "Didn't it seem strange you were able to breath the whole time? Normally, the oxygen would have been used in a short while. You would have suffocated."

"But—"

Doc said, "Oxygen was being supplied to the bell automatically. Too, the water level was not allowed to get over your heads."

They gaped at him, puzzled.

One said, "But why—"

"This is why," Doc said.

The bronze man went to a device in a portable cabinet, a mechanism for recording sounds picked up by a microphone.

Doc said, "The microphone of this recorder was in the top of the diving bell."

He set the recording device to play back. The "playback" functioned through a loudspeaker. For some moments there was clatter, thumping, grunts and curses—the noises as Doc Savage first put the prisoners in the bell.

Every word, every curse, every whisper in the diving bell had been recorded.

The prisoners stared at each other.

"So Monk, Ham, and the girl are being held in a penthouse owned by Hart," Doc said.

DOC SAVAGE contemplated the prisoners gravely. "What is behind this giggling ghost business?"

They glared at him, for they had recovered courage.

"Devil with you!" one gritted.

"It's too big for you to stop, anyway!" the other snarled.

Doc's face was grim. He picked the two up, popped them into the diving bell.

"There will be no oxygen this time," he said. "No control of water level."

Then the men yelled. Horror faced them; their nerves broke.

Doc Savage hauled them out and they talked.

The men knew little, really. Only that a man named Batavia had hired them. At Batavia's orders, they had helped with the bridge trap for Doc Savage.

Tonight, Batavia had ordered them to follow Long Tom, and Johnny and Renny; to kill them if possible. But principally, about the giggling ghosts, they knew nothing.

"You are sure," Doc asked, "that you do not know the reason for the gas? *And you don't know what the giggling ghosts are?*"

They knew nothing about the gas, or the reason for it.

Doc Savage got a hypodermic needle, administered to each prisoner a drug which would cause them to remain unconscious for some time. Doc then sent the captives away to his upstate criminal-curing institution—the "college", as they called the institution.

A weird place, that "college," its existence unknown to the world. At the "college," criminals underwent delicate brain operations that wiped out memory of the past, after which they received vocational training to fit them as honest citizens.

They were turned into assets to society.

Chapter XV
HIGH TROUBLE

WHEN Doc Savage walked into the skyscraper headquarters, William Harper Littlejohn was frowningly contemplating an inked seismograph recording. The record was off Doc's seismograph the night there was supposed to have been an earthquake.

Johnny glanced at Doc Savage and frowned. He did not recognize the bronze man; Doc still wore a disguise.

"I'll be superamalgamated!" Johnny complained. "Can just anybody walk into this place—"

"Make anything out of that record?" Doc asked.

"Oh!" Johnny recognized Doc's voice.

Johnny got over being surprised, pointed at the seismograph record. "There wasn't any earthquake!" he said.

Doc asked, "Did you compare that record with the recording of the seismographs at the university, the museum, and in Washington?"

Johnny nodded. "I did. Funny, too. The other records are exactly like this one except for this single earthquake. Our seismograph doesn't show the earthquake. The others do."

Doc Savage said, "Monk and Ham are still alive. We have a line on their whereabouts."

Johnny sprang up from the table; he looked as delighted as a man who had won a sweepstakes.

"Renny!" he howled. "Long Tom! Come here!"

The other two came running out of the laboratory.

"Doc's got a line on Monk and Ham!" Johnny shouted.

"Where are they?" Renny roared.

Doc gave them what information he had secured from the two prisoners.

"The two didn't know what is behind this devilish gas business?" Renny demanded.

"They did not know," Doc said. "They did not know the truth about the ghosts, either."

"There's an infernal mystery behind the gas," Renny grumbled. "That giggling ghost business is the most puzzling of all."

Doc Savage consulted a telephone directory. He found William Henry Hart listed in an apartment on Riverside Drive.

"Holy cow! Reckon Hart don't live on his boat all the time," Renny rumbled.

Because they might need more than one car before they were through, Doc and his aides took two machines for the short trip to Riverside Drive. Doc drove his coupé; the others rode in a sedan.

When the bronze man pulled to the curb in a side street near Riverside Drive, the other car drew up behind him, and Renny, Long Tom and Johnny came to Doc's coupé.

"How we gonna work this?" Long Tom wanted to know.

"You wait here," Doc said.

The bronze man walked around the corner, found the number listed as William Henry Hart's address.

It was a tall brick building, one of the most impressive on the Drive, where there were quite a few impressive buildings.

The sign said:

APARTMENT HOTEL

Doc Savage entered the building, went to the rental agent. Doc had little fear of being recognized, for he had not discarded his disguise.

"Penthouses?" the agent murmured.

"Yes. I'm interested in one," Doc said.

"I'm sorry. We have only one. It is rented."

"Is there any possibility of it being vacated soon?" Doc asked.

"I—ah—can't say."

"If you will show me a floor plan of the penthouse," Doc said, "I might be interested in the future."

Any hotel, apartment or otherwise, likes to keep one hundred per cent rented. The proposal appealed to the rental agent.

"I have a floor plan!" he said quickly.

"Who is the present renter?" Doc asked.

"A man named William Henry Hart, a young inventor and manufacturer," the agent explained. "Here is the plan."

DOC SAVAGE took the penthouse layout and went back to his men. They got in the larger car to hold a consultation and examine the penthouse plan.

"This is gonna help," Long Tom grunted.

They saw the penthouse contained almost a

dozen rooms, was actually on the roof of the hotel, with a terrace taking in all the rest of the rooftop.

"As a battlefield," Renny rumbled, "there's plenty of room!"

Long Tom said, "How'd they manage to get Monk, Ham and the girl up there secretly?"

Doc Savage pointed out the probable method. "Notice the private elevator. It does not open into the hotel lobby, but into a private hallway, with a side door, on the ground floor."

"They probably got lookouts all over the place!" Renny boomed.

"We will see."

Doc went to the side door which admitted to the private penthouse elevator hallway. He walked in nonchalantly, immediately stopped, and looked as confused and surprised as he could.

"Er—doesn't this door lead to the hotel?" he said uncertainly.

"Naw!" said the man. "It don't."

The man was built for guard duty. He had big hands, thick arms, sloping shoulders, and a scowl-ridden face. Also a natural look of suspicion.

From the ceiling, a flexible wire ran down to the man's right fist; he was evidently holding a push button on the end of the wire. He must have to hold it all the time he was standing there.

"This door is private!" he growled.

"I'm sorry," Doc said.

The bronze man then backed out, and went back to his men.

"They have a guard," he said.

Long Tom growled, "I'll get a messenger boy's uniform. I'll take him a telegram—and bop him on the head."

"It will not work," Doc said.

"No?"

"The guard is holding a push button in his fist," Doc explained. "The moment he releases it, an alarm will probably start ringing."

"Holy cow!" Renny rumbled. "Then we can't gas the guy, or rush him, or nothin'!"

That was about the situation.

Doc Savage said, "Wait here."

"But—"

"The fireworks will start in about twenty minutes," Doc said. "When it does, you fellows use your own judgment."

DOC SAVAGE got in the coupé, took the express highway south, making as much speed as possible without menacing other traffic. Later he pulled up before his waterfront warehouse-hangar.

The hangar portion of the building housed a number of planes, ranging from a huge speed ship—three-motored, capable of making a jump half

around the world on one fueling—down to a small gyro, or "windmill", which could descend vertically.

Doc took the gyro. He ran fuel into the craft, started the motor, and while it was warming, opened the great doors in the river end of the hangar. The plane was equipped with both pontoons and retractable wheels, so it could operate from land or water.

The bronze man loaded equipment he needed for the immediate project. He guided the craft out on the river, and took to the air.

It was late afternoon. Sidewalks of Manhattan spread below, crowds hurrying from work. Down the bay, two liners were leaving, one behind the other, headed out to the Atlantic Ocean. The sea stretched away in gray-blue flatness until it was lost in the haze. Few clouds. The clouds were very white.

Doc flew north, the gyro nose pointed upstairs, gaining altitude. When he was high over the lower end of Riverside Drive, he cut the motor. The craft began to settle. The windmill craft did not glide forward after the fashion of an ordinary plane, but settled straight downward.

From time to time, Doc gave the craft enough headway for maneuverability, so he could keep descending directly above the roof of the tall apartment hotel on Riverside Drive.

The sole sounds the gyro made were about the sounds that a big bird would make flying.

Doc hung his jaw over the cockpit edge, watched. He studied the penthouse, judged possibilities. It did not look so good.

This building, unlike many structures on Manhattan, did not have a water tank tower on the roof. The roof was flat and unobstructed, except for some wires which appeared to be a radio aerial. So far, good.

But the penthouse itself was a wide building of Spanish architecture, with a sloping tile roof and a patio in the center. In the patio there was a swimming pool.

All the rooftop surrounding the penthouse had been planted in grass and shrubbery. That was the bad part. It would be like landing in a backyard rock garden.

There was no doubt that the plane could get down safely. Whether it could take off again was doubtful.

Two hundred feet over the roof, Doc dropped two large grenades overside. They were not explosive grenades. These contained anaesthetic gas. Being fish-shaped and stream-lined, the grenades fell faster than the craft, and hit the roof ahead of it.

Doc had time to put on an abbreviated gas mask.

First, the gyro hit a radio aerial. It tilted. It slid sideways, landed with a crash. Undercarriage snapped, the ship tipped over, two of the rotor blades smashed into the shrubbery and lost shape.

Doc was out of the craft instantly; he seemed to bounce out. He went headlong for shelter of bushes. The shrubs grew in sunken boxes of earth.

Doc made concealment, waited and listened.

SCREEN doors banged and men came tearing out of the penthouse to see what had happened.

"A plane hit the roof!"

"Hell's bells!"

A strangled sound; the noise of a body falling. At least one man had inhaled the gas.

"Hey! What's happened to Joe?"

"It's gas!"

The screen doors all banged again as the men ran back inside. Next, there was shouting in the penthouse. Rushing around. Excited bawling of orders.

Someone began to pump bullets through a window into the plane. The gunman fired methodically, emptying clip after clip, five shots to the clip, into the craft.

A louder voice now shouted angrily that they would have to leave, that the uproar would bring the police.

"Get the prisoners into the elevator!" this voice ordered.

Doc Savage worked through the shrubbery to a window. He tried it. The sash was open. He shoved it up, dived through into a room which had a bare tile floor and furniture of Spanish type and a gaudy blanket hanging on one wall.

Doc whipped across this room to a door, had almost reached it, when a man came through holding a gun. The gun holder asked no questions. He fired.

Doc Savage, twisting, bent down to let the bullet pass over his head. There was a rug on the floor; Doc yanked it. The other man tilted over, firing again, his bullet gouging plaster out of the ceiling.

Doc got hold of the gun arm, and the arm went out of joint and the man began screaming, one shriek after another, in agony.

There was now shouting through the penthouse, enough to indicate men were running to see what had happened. Doc tossed a smoke bomb through the door. It was a small bomb, but it made big smoke. A pall of sepia spouted, grew; smoke that was as black to the eye as drawing ink from a bottle. The charging men got in the smoke and swore and shot off guns.

DOC SAVAGE left the room through the window by which he had entered. Looking for another way in, he came to a window covered with steel shutters.

The window shutters were shaking; someone was pounding on them from the inside. The one doing the pounding was also yelling in a squeaky voice that could be recognized anywhere.

Monk! It was Monk!

A bar fastened the shutters from the outside. Doc wrenched the bar loose, got the shutters open.

Monk peered at Doc. "Who—who the blazes are you!"

"Isn't it Doc Savage?" Miami Davis demanded.

"It don't look like him!" Ham said.

Which was a tribute to the bronze man's disguise as an old man.

"Out!" Doc said.

He could talk through his gas mask.

The girl came through the window, then Ham. Monk, coming last, all but got wedged.

Ham peered at Doc's size.

"It's Doc all right," he said. "But—but they told us they blew up—"

"How do we get out of here?" Doc demanded.

Ham said, "There's only one way out; that's the elevator."

Inside the room the prisoners had just vacated, there were yells. The escape was discovered.

"Away from here!" Doc said.

They dived through the shrubbery, turned right, were in a kind of flower garden. The flowers, fortunately, were tall; there were entwining vines on trellises overhead. Good concealment.

Bedlam was all through the penthouse. Batavia's men seemed convinced the roof was bathed with poison gas. Evidently they had no masks, for none came out to investigate.

They did not hesitate, however, to shoot through the windows at every object that might conceal an attacker. The bullets, all from high-powered rifles, were not pleasant things.

Doc Savage crawled to the roof edge. Here, there was a blind spot, one point which could not be covered by gunfire from any of the penthouse windows.

Doc took from his clothing a thin silk cord that was long, and to one end of the cord was affixed a light, collapsible grapple. This cord was little larger than twine.

"Let me tie this around your waist," Doc told the girl.

She stared at the thin cord.

"What—"

"We'll lower you to a window," Doc said. "You break the window, then climb in."

The thinness of the cord horrified the girl.

"On that—" She stabbed a finger at the cord. *"We're twenty floors up!"*

Then the girl closed her eyes and dropped, completely slack, to the rooftop.

Ham said, "She fainted—"

Then he, too, fell over.

"Blazes!" Monk said. "Ham fainted, too—"

And then Monk went down.

The gas which had been in the aerial bombs was not exactly like that used in the little pocket grenades that the bronze man carried. This gas did not lose its strength so soon after it became mixed with the air. Doc had broken a couple in one hand and held his breath.

MIAMI DAVIS would have been really frightened if she could have seen what happened next, if she had seen Doc Savage gather the three of them together—Monk, Ham and herself—and lash them all in a cluster on the end of the silk cord. Then he lowered them over the roof edge.

There was not enough cord to reach twenty floors, of course. Doc lowered the burden to the first window, then tied the line to a steel pipe, part of the trellis supporting the vines.

The silken cord was equipped with knots—bulky knots for climbing purposes—and the bronze man went down after the captives, apparently unaffected by twenty floors of space below.

He had overguessed the distance to the window a little; that was not as bad as an underguess. He broke the window with a quick kick, driving the glass inward.

Reaching in, Doc turned the lock, after which he raised the sash. A step in through the window, a little more trouble hauling the gassed victims inside, and it was all over.

They were now in an apartment, modernistically furnished, with bright-colored walls, gaudy rugs, furniture all straight lines. Apparently no one was home.

Doc went out into the hallway and began trying to cut off electric current to the elevator that ran to the penthouse. Without power, the elevator could not move; flight from the penthouse would be cut off.

But he was too late. The elevator had already been used in flight.

There was a crash of shots, a slamming volley of them like buckshot on a tin roof, in the street. Doc caught the regular passenger elevator downstairs.

He was in time to see two policemen come flying in the door, one of them reeling, holding an arm which was leaking blood. Both cops had been tear-gassed.

Doc Savage made for the door, but stopped when tear-gas fumes bit his eyes. He retreated, got his own mask back on. Then he went out into the street.

The street was full of tear gas and excitement. Came an explosion, sudden, terrific, jarring the earth. Doc's big armor-plated limousine—the car which Johnny, Long Tom and Renny should have been occupying—turned half a flipflop, lit on its back. A high-explosive grenade had gone off under the machine.

At the far end of the street were two cars, going fast. They rocketed around the corner, and were out of sight.

"RENNY!" Doc called.

No answer.

"Long Tom! Johnny!" Doc shouted.

The bronze man's voice was a great anxious crash in the street.

There was no trace of Doc's three aides.

Doc Savage whipped back to the front of the hotel. A police squad car stood there, motor running. Doc dived into the machine.

"Around the corner!" he said. "We've got to chase! Quick!"

The cop driving the machine looked at him.

"Who—who the blazes are you?"

"Doc Savage," Doc explained.

The cop snorted, "Listen, I know what Savage looks like and you're not kiddin'—"

Doc lost time explaining there was such a thing as a disguise. By the time they set out in pursuit of the fleeing cars, none of the machines were in sight. There was nothing, no trace, to show where they had gone.

The private elevator from the penthouse was down and empty. There was no sign of the guard, no trace of anyone in the elevator. Doc rode up to the penthouse, accompanied by policemen. There was not a soul to be found.

"They got away with Renny, Long Tom and Johnny," Doc decided grimly.

Chapter XVI
THE GOOD MAN

THE excitement at the penthouse on Riverside Drive got considerable publicity in the newspapers.

Doc Savage, however, managed to keep his connection with the affair unknown, and as a result, most newspapers attributed the fracas to a dispute of gangland. It was a good story because of the unusual fact that a gyro had been used.

The giggling ghosts still monopolized the newspapers, however.

The giggling mystery received a new impetus. A fresh angle entered the situation. The fresh angle was the S.R.G.V.

The S.R.G.V. was the abbreviation the newspapers used. The letters stood for "The Society for the Relief of Gas Victims."

There is almost always a mushroom growth of relief and aid agencies after a disaster, most of them well-intentioned. These new chicks rarely get much attention, the old agencies such as the Red Cross being the ones depended upon.

The S.R.G.V. was different. It hit the public prints with a bang, and for a sound reason. The S.R.G.V. was going to do a great good; it was going to buy up the homes of the giggling victims. It was going to see that no one was impoverished by the disaster.

That is, if its money held out the S.R.G.V. was going to do all that. It was rumored a group of wealthy philanthropists was behind the S.R.G.V., men who didn't want their names to be known.

The S.R.G.V. began to buy homes, paying, it was explained, all that it was possible to pay. Payment, in a great many instances, was not nearly what owners thought they should get. But the S.R.G.V. said it didn't have all the money in the world to spend, that the whole thing was philanthropic, and that it was impossible to pay pre-disaster prices. No one, the society added, was being forced to sell.

The gas scare got fresh impetus when sonic devices for exploring the subterranean strata of the earth indicated the presence of faults. This bore out the theory that gas came from some pocket deep in the earth, where it had lain unsuspected for no telling how many centuries.

Apparently it did not occur to anyone that the faults might have been in the strata for ages, too, and might have nothing whatever to do with gas.

However, there was one rumor that ghosts with the giggling disease might have come out of the cracks. It was laughed down, of course.

It began to be suspected that people could never again live in the area. In view of that, it was considered kind of the S.R.G.V. to take property off people's hands.

As Lieutenant Colonel Andrew Blodgett "Monk" Mayfair said, "Human nature is sure a great thing."

"What's great about it?" Ham asked him.

"Well, you overdressed shyster, you take this S.R.G.V.," Monk pointed out. "Look how they're helpin' out them poor gas victims. That's wonderful, that is."

MONK and Ham had recovered from the effects of Doc's anaesthetic gas. So had the young woman, Miami Davis. The three of them were now at Doc Savage's skyscraper headquarters, in the great library.

Doc hadn't explained why he'd used the anaesthetic gas on them, but Monk and Ham suspected he'd done so in order that he could work alone to find a way out and attempt to capture some prisoners. Later on, after the disappearance of Long Tom, Johnny and Renny, Doc had returned and brought them to headquarters, where he had revived them.

Doc Savage was in the reception room now, seeing some policemen.

Later, when Doc Savage rejoined them, the bronze man seemed pleased.

"The police," Doc explained, "are going to keep the newspapers from learning that we had anything to do with the fight at the penthouse."

The homely Monk frowned. "As I understand it, Doc, you are still supposed to be dead. Is that right?"

"That's it," Doc told him. "That is, if we can fool anybody into thinking so."

"But why? What's the idea?"

"No one hunts buffalo any more."

"Huh?"

"Because everyone knows there are no buffaloes to hunt."

"Oh. I see."

"For the first time since the penthouse business, we have time to talk. What did you learn while you were prisoners?"

"They just kept us tied up," Monk said.

Ham nodded.

"Can you add anything to that? Surely you learned something."

"How long did they hold us?" Monk countered.

"About three days," Doc told him.

"Well," Monk said, "I never learned less during three days in my life!"

"It would help," Doc said, "if you got some idea about the reason behind this whole grim mess."

Monk said, "We didn't get a smear of an idea."

"I hate to agree with hairy ignatz"—Ham jerked a thumb at Monk—"but he's right. We didn't learn a thing."

"Not even about who their leader is?"

"The leader," Monk said, "seems to be a guy named William Henry Hart. But you musta knowed that. You found us in his penthouse."

"This Hart is an inventor," Ham said. "He has a factory manufacturing a smoke-digester."

"How did you find out that?" Doc asked.

"Oh, we heard our captors talking," Monk explained. "I guess they figured we'd be unable to repeat what we heard."

"What I don't understand," Ham said, "is why they kept us alive."

Monk peered at the bronze man. "Doc, can you explain why they didn't kill us?"

Doc said, "Perhaps because they wanted someone around to overhear what they had to say."

"Huh?"

Doc tossed a smoke bomb. A pall of sepia spouted, grew; The charging men got in the

"What do you mean, Doc?" Ham barked.

"Let us drop that point until we have more information," Doc said.

Doc got up, went into the laboratory, and came back with the two animals, Habeas, the pig, and Chemistry, the questionable ape. Monk and Ham greeted the two animals with enthusiasm.

"Miss Davis," Doc said, "maybe you can help us."

MIAMI DAVIS had been silent. She sat on a large chair—a pert, dynamic girl, with copper-colored hair in a tangle, a haunted look in her large blue eyes.

Her breathing was irregular, and often she was bothered by a convulsive affliction of her respiratory nerve centers which made it seem she was giggling—the aftereffects of the slight gassing she had received in the warehouse, at the beginning

smoke that was as black as drawing ink from a bottle.
smoke and swore and shot off guns.

of the mystery. The dose she'd received hadn't been enough to kill her like the other unfortunate victims.

Doc Savage went to her. "How do you feel?"

"Not so good," the girl admitted.

Doc asked, "What did you mean by inferring that perhaps you can help us?"

The girl bit her lips.

"I hate to say anything," Miami Davis said, "because I—well, I'm in love with him."

"That was why you ran away from the storehouse that night, wasn't it?" Doc asked.

She nodded.

"You decided he had been in the storehouse, didn't you?"

"Yes." Miami Davis nodded again. "He had been there, too. It was my watch. I had given it to him to have fixed, and he had lost it there in the storehouse."

Monk said, "I take it you're talkin' about Hart." The girl winced, bit her lips, looked down.

"Yes," she said.

"He's the guy behind this," Monk insisted.

Doc Savage did not comment. Miami Davis apparently did not want to speak either, because she kept silent for a long time; then, finally, she doubled over in her chair and put her face in her hands, sobbing.

"Do you know the reason for this giggling mystery business?" Doc asked her.

The girl got out several wrenching sobs before she could answer. "No," she said. "No, I don't know a thing about any ghosts."

Doc Savage showed no inclination to question her further. He got up, went out into the reception room, and worked the combination of his huge safe, leaving Monk and Ham and Miami Davis behind in the library.

Now Monk and Ham made two or three stumbling attempts to strike up a conversation with Miami Davis. They wanted to get her mind off William Henry Hart. They failed. She was so miserable that she even depressed Monk and Ham, so they fled into the reception room, where Doc had gone.

Doc Savage was before the huge safe, fingering through government bonds and gilt-edged securities.

He carried the securities over to the inlaid table and put them down.

"Ham," he said.

Ham—he was dapper again, his first act of freedom having been to change his clothes—came over and eyed the securities. Ham now wore immaculate evening dress, and carried one of his innocent-looking black sword canes, a supply of which he kept on hand.

Doc said, "Your legal training makes you the man to take charge of our next move."

"Charge of what?" Ham was puzzled.

"We are going into competition," Doc Savage explained, "with the S.R.G.V."

"With the what?"

"The S.R.G.V.—the Society for the Relief of Gas Victims."

Ham frowned. "Competition! But it strikes me that society is doing good work."

"Have you noticed prices they are paying for property?"

"No."

"If you had, it might change your ideas about the philanthropy of the S.R.G.V."

Ham frowned, rubbed his jaw thoughtfully and suddenly looked blank. The blankness was followed by an I-begin-to-see-through-this expression.

"Say!" he exploded. "Could it be that—"

"We had best not jump at conclusions," Doc Savage said. "But we will go into this ghost district and pay full value for any property that any victim wants to sell. Buy anything and everything offered. Do not let anybody rob you, but pay full prices."

"Right," Ham nodded.

"Also," Doc Savage added, "tell everyone who sells you property that he can buy it back for the same price at any time."

"Righto."

HAM went to work on the project at once. He sat down with a pencil and paper, composed handbills and newspaper advertisements and dispatched these; then, although it was late at night, he routed out a landlord near the gas area and rented a suite of offices.

Ham got painters at work putting a sign on the front of the building; by electric light, it read:

DOC SAVAGE RELIEF AGENCY

That was the name of the new organization. Ordinarily, Doc Savage did not permit his name to be used in connection with any public benevolencies, but this was different. It was believed that Doc's name would draw, create confidence.

Ham maintained a law firm of his own that was so expertly staffed that it could run itself for months while Ham was off adventuring.

Ham supplied the new organization with employees from the law firm, and by ten o'clock the next morning, handbills were being scattered; newspapers carried half-page advertisements saying the "Doc Savage Relief Agency" would pay full price for all property in the ghost zone.

Ham's venture into real estate began to do a rushing business.

Ham did a landoffice trade all that day, and most of the night. His appraisers went around, wearing gas masks, and estimated the value of property being offered for sale.

Such was the reputation of Doc Savage—as the wrong fellow to try to pull any crookedness on— there were few attempts to get half a dozen prices for property. In fact, such was the bronze man's name for fairness, the appraisers were often permitted to set a price, which was at once accepted.

All sellers were promised that they could buy the property back any time they wished, for the same price.

It was mid-afternoon on the second day after the establishment of the Doc Savage Relief Agency, when Birmingham Lawn put in an appearance.

Birmingham Lawn came into Ham's office jauntily, his round melon of a stomach jumping up and down as he walked. He was whistling something.

"Hello, Mr. Lawn," Ham said.

"You know me?" Lawn exclaimed.

"I've heard you described," Ham told him. "What can we do for you?"

Birmingham Lawn seemed to have something very pleasant on his mind. He perched on a chair, folded his hands over his tummy, and changed his tune.

"Look," he said. "I have a remarkable idea!"

"Yes?" Ham was interested.

"The newspapers," Birmingham Lawn pointed out, "are full of this great work you are now doing, buying up this property."

Ham did not comment, but it was a fact that the newspapers were giving Doc Savage's relief agency considerable space.

Lawn continued, "I have become very interested in this project, and I want to help." He repeated the last for emphasis. "I want to help!"

"Help—how?"

"I want to put my own money into your project. I am quite wealthy, you know."

"You mean," Ham demanded, "that you want to help us see that the gas victims don't lose anything?"

"Exactly."

Ham was amazed. He was accustomed to gestures of grand philanthropy on the part of Doc Savage, but it was rare enough elsewhere and Ham was inclined to be bowled over.

Birmingham Lawn became, for such a lugubrious-looking man, extremely businesslike. "I will place unlimited cash at your disposal," he said, "and I will also put part of my own real estate office force to helping you. Will you accept?"

Ham considered the proposition. He called Doc Savage on the telephone, explained Birmingham Lawn's proposal, and asked advice.

"Take him up," Doc said.

So Ham accepted Birmingham Lawn's offer to join the Doc Savage Relief Agency.

THAT evening, fireworks began. A tabloid newspaper, which had never been particularly friendly to Doc Savage, was first to make insinuations.

The story was played up under frontpage headlines, and evidently the newspaper's phalanx of lawyers had gone into a huddle over the item, because it was cleverly worded. It said everything it was intended to say, but left no cracks through which the spear of a libel suit could be rammed.

The yarn took the form of several questions:

WHERE IS DOC SAVAGE?

WHAT COULD DOC SAVAGE TELL ABOUT THE MYSTERIOUS GIGGLING GHOST IN NEW JERSEY?

WHY IS DOC SAVAGE BUYING UP PROPERTY IN THE GAS DISTRICT?

SAVAGE IS REPORTED TO BE A HUMAN BENEFACTOR, BUT WHY DOES HE SURROUND HIMSELF WITH MYSTERY?

These thinly veiled insinuations created a stir and comment, favorable and unfavorable.

Monk became extremely angry. The homely chemist called up the newspaper and went into detail about what he thought of the sheet. They were not impressed.

"We smell a rat in this property buying," the editor said.

"You smell yourself!" Monk snarled at him.

The homely chemist went looking for Doc Savage.

Doc Savage had been dividing his efforts. Part of the time he sought some trace of Renny, Long Tom and Johnny, and the rest of the time he devoted to the gas victims.

The bronze man's skill in surgery and medicine was probably the greatest training he possessed; it had been his first application, his most intensive. Although he was skilled in many items, it was in surgery and medicine that he excelled.

AT odd times, Doc Savage made furtive expeditions on which he did some things that seemed senseless. For instance: the sole object of the secret trips seemed to be to climb on top of factory buildings and apartment houses and look at smokestacks. Not only did he look at smokestacks, but he wore a gas mask while he was doing so; and sometimes he spent as much as an hour around each smokestack, making chemical tests.

He did not seem to be interested in any smokestacks except those in the gas zone.

Doc told no one of these trips; but the results must have satisfied him, because on a number of occasions he made the strange, low, exotic, trilling sound which was his characteristic sound in moments of excitement, mental stress, or satisfaction.

Monk found Doc in a Jersey hospital, where the bronze man was working as a volunteer surgeon. Doc had managed somehow to keep his identity unknown.

Monk explained about the tabloid newspaper insinuation.

"I saw it," Doc Savage admitted. "It is one of those things."

"But they're insinuatin' there's somethin' dirty about your relief agency!" Monk yelled.

"Do not let it bother you," Doc said.

Monk sighed disgustedly. When anybody stepped on the homely chemist's toes, his impulse was to kick shins and knock heads together.

"O. K.," he grumbled. He changed the subject. "You doing any good helping these giggling victims?"

"Some," Doc said. "At least, we do not think there will be any more deaths. And in time, we will undoubtedly get a cure."

"I call that accomplishin' a lot!"

Monk got up, took two or three turns around the room, stamping, gnawing his lip. "But about Renny, Long Tom and Johnny," he growled. "I—we—well, we haven't accomplished a thing toward helping them. And Hart—what about him? Hart is the guy behind this, you know."

"Hart is innocent," Doc said.

"What?"

Doc nodded.

"In fact," the bronze man said, "we had better pick Hart up and keep him out of sight for his own protection."

DOC and Monk drove to William Henry Hart's little boat, tied up to the wharf at Sheepshead Bay, where he lived.

He was not aboard.

"He's probably at his factory," Monk said.

They drove to the factory. The moment they turned into the street before the little manufacturing structure, they knew something was wrong. The crowd! Half the crowd was police. There were two ambulances, white-clad internes, and stretchers on which men lay.

Doc Savage swerved to the curb and he and Monk sprang out.

"Kidnapping," a cop explained grimly.

"Kidnapping?"

"They got William Henry Hart a few minutes ago," the cop said. "We don't know who it was. They were a tough-looking bunch of mugs. There was shooting. The plant foreman tried to stop them, and he got shot, and a workman got shot, then Hart was carried off."

Doc Savage asked, "Any description of the raiders?"

There was description enough to identify one of the snatchers as a tall man who wore grays. Later, Doc found, discarded on the scene, the stub of a cigar which had a cork tip.

"Batavia!" Monk exclaimed.

"Yes," Doc agreed. "Batavia undoubtedly seized Hart."

Chapter XVII
GUILT

INVESTIGATION convinced Doc Savage there was no way of tracing William Henry Hart and his kidnappers. The bronze man got in the car, with Monk, and they drove away.

"Maybe the snatch was a fake anyway," Monk said. "Maybe he staged this kidnapping to make himself look innocent."

Monk had expected Doc Savage to drive back to the high headquarters building, but the bronze man did not do this. Instead he headed toward the East Side of Manhattan, and stopped in a section of brownstone fronts, second-rate rooming houses.

"What's this?" Monk demanded.

Doc Savage said, "You remember those metal medallions?"

"Metal—"

"The three metal disks about the size of an English penny," Doc Savage said. "On each was an address."

"Oh, I remember," Monk said. "You told me about that. You gave one disk to William Henry Hart, one to Birmingham Lawn, and one to A. King Christophe."

Monk looked startled. "I been wondering why you did that."

"There was a very good reason," Doc told him.

The bronze man got out of the car, went up the steps of the old brownstone house and examined the door. At the top of the panel, where it would not have been noticed, there was a seal which looked exactly like a spider web—a seal Doc had placed there to show whether the door had been opened.

From his pocket, Doc Savage took out a small device which resembled a diminutive box camera, except that it had a dark-blue lens. In reality, it was a tiny projector of ultraviolet light.

Making an impromptu dark room with his coat, Doc turned the device on, focused the rays on the seal. The seal glowed blue.

"First blank," Doc said.

"I don't get this!" Monk complained.

They got in the car again and Doc Savage drove to another address, this one on the West Side. It was an old building, a walk-up apartment. They went in, climbed steps, and once more the bronze man examined a door and found the seal unbroken, found it glowed blue under the ultra-violet light.

"Second blank," he said.

By now Monk was bewildered. He planted himself in Doc Savage's path. "Explain this chasin' around, Doc!" he grumbled.

"We have a number of suspects in the gas mystery, Monk."

"One suspect as far as I'm concerned—and it's Hart."

"Each of the medallions had a different address," Doc explained.

"But I don't see—"

Instead of going into explanations, Doc Savage visited the third address. This one was a private house, across the river in New Jersey. A house that stood alone, windows bolted, rear door planked

MONK

shut. The only ready entrance was through the front door, which Doc examined.

THE seal this time was a piece of chewing gum, and it was apparently intact. But when Doc Savage put the ultraviolet light rays upon it, this one glowed distinctly yellowish—not blue.

"This is it!" the bronze man said.

"It?" Monk said, puzzled.

"The door is not sealed with the gum I used. My gum would fluoresce blue."

"Oh! Then somebody's been here!" Monk grew excited. "Who had the key with this address?"

Doc Savage apparently did not hear the question; the bronze man had a habit of appearing not to hear a query when he did not wish to answer. Monk was accustomed to this trait, but he looked disappointed.

"We going in?" the homely chemist demanded.

"Not through the front door," Doc said.

The bronze man went around to the rear, where there was a dilapidated coal shed. He got on the shed, then to the roof of the house. He tore off a patch of shingles, wrenched up sheathing, and made a hole large enough to pass his bronze frame. It was fortunate Doc entered the house in that fashion.

The house was mined. There was almost five hundred pounds of high explosive in the basement. The TNT was wired to windows and doors, so that it would explode the instant anyone tried to gain admission by that route.

Doc Savage rendered the gigantic bomb harmless.

Then he went out, got Monk, and showed him what was in the house.

"Blazes!" Monk showed an immediate desire to leave.

"The person who had the disk with this address," Doc Savage said, "planted this death trap."

Monk shuddered.

"Who was it?"

"Birmingham Lawn," Doc said.

DOC SAVAGE was grim as they drove back, as grim as he ever became, although he rarely showed emotion.

The car pulled up before the Doc Savage Relief Agency office. Ham sat at a large desk—he had a liking for big desks—contemplating the bareness of the office. The place was practically empty of customers.

"It's been that way all afternoon," Ham complained. "Say, did you read that tabloid newspaper story? A bunch of dirty insinuations, and thinly veiled hints that we're crooks stealing this land."

Doc Savage asked, "Where's Birmingham Lawn?"

Ham brightened. "Now, there's a swell guy! Letting him help us out was a good idea. He brought his real estate men, who are trained in this line."

"Where is he?" Doc repeated.

Ham pointed, "In the back room."

Monk scowled at Ham. "Your swell guy is just the devil behind this giggling business!"

"What?" Ham gasped.

"You heard me!" Monk gritted.

"But—but—"

"Lawn's medallion," Doc Savage explained, "was used to open a bungalow where we found a death trap set for me."

Ham made croaking noises, looked bewildered.

"But Lawn has been helping us; he put his own money into this thing of buying property—" Ham stopped stuttering and pondered. "Ah-h-h—I get it. The man is going to falsify our records! He is going to change the deeds so he can take over the property we buy!"

"After he gets rid of us!" Monk agreed.

The homely chemist appeared angry enough to bite heads off spikes.

"Wipe that man-eating look off your face," Doc told Monk.

"Why not just go in and bat 'im one?" Monk snarled.

"We can use further proof," Doc said. "So far, the only thing we have against him is that disk that we connected with the death trap."

Monk subsided reluctantly; Monk was seldom

in favor of cautious tactics. He preferred slap-bang drag-out. When the homely chemist had his face straightened, he and Doc entered the rear room.

Monk's utter homeliness gave him one advantage: it was impossible to tell, from looking at him, what emotion he was experiencing.

Birmingham Lawn greeted them. Doc returned his handshake cordially. Lawn shook hands with Monk. Monk, however, could not make his own hairy paw seem like anything but a dead fish.

Birmingham Lawn seemed worried. He motioned, indicating he desired they should all get in a corner of the room where they could be alone. And when they were all in the corner, Lawn stood staring at them, and abstractedly whistled a few bars from something that sounded like a funeral march.

"I have had a strange thing happen to me!" he said hollowly.

MONK barely refrained from saying that a lot of things were going to happen to Lawn.

"What do you mean, Lawn?" Doc asked.

"That metal coin you gave me," Lawn explained.

"What about your disk?" Doc asked.

"A man came to me," Lawn said, "and offered me five thousand dollars to trade disks with me."

"Five thousand!" Monk exploded. "Offered you—"

Lawn swallowed, making his golf ball Adam's apple go up and down in his neck.

"It happened last night," he said. "I—well, I didn't know what to do. Five thousand dollars is a lot of money. The only condition of the bargain was that I should never tell you about the trade."

"You made the trade?" Doc asked.

"I did," Lawn said. "I traded. The man gave me five thousand dollars and his medallion, and I gave him my medallion."

Monk looked blank.

Lawn continued. "This morning, I turned the five thousand dollars in as a voluntary gift to help reimburse the poor inhabitants of the gas district for their loss. You will see the five thousand on our books. In the meantime, I began trying to get in touch with you to tell you that I had traded."

"Just why," Monk demanded, "did you trade?"

"Five thousand dollars," Birmingham Lawn said, "can do a lot of good in this poor world."

"Then why break your word?" Monk barked. "You promised not to tell us about the trade."

"I am not an honest man," Lawn said, "when I think I am dealing with a crook."

Doc moved to one side. Monk followed the bronze man; they stood together close to the door, while Lawn was still at the desk in the corner, out of earshot.

"Doc," Monk breathed, "it looks like somebody got Lawn's disk to throw suspicion on him!"

Doc Savage studied the homely chemist. "But a few moments ago—"

"I know; I thought Lawn was the guy with the horns and tail!" Monk scowled. "I jump at conclusions too quick."

"Who, in your opinion, is the one who set the explosive trap?" Doc asked.

"Whoever traded medallions with Lawn," Monk said.

They went back to Lawn. Doc Savage put a question.

"Who traded disks with you, Lawn?"

"The man named A. King Christophe," Lawn said.

MONK, Ham and Birmingham Lawn got on telephones, began calling different places in an effort to locate Christophe. In order not to arouse the suspicion of the cheek-blowing, eye-popping geologist, they let the impression go over the telephones that they were newspaper reporters who wanted to interview the man.

Christophe had been interviewed so often recently—he was getting a reputation as the man who had first discovered the gas came from subterranean fissures—that he should not think it strange the press wanted another session.

While the telephoning was going on, Miami Davis approached Doc Savage. The young woman had been helping Ham with the activities of the Doc Savage Relief Agency.

Miami Davis looked worried, and appeared to have been recently in tears.

"Ham was telling me about William Henry—about Hart," she said in a low voice.

"You mean about his disappearance?"

"About that—yes."

"I wouldn't worry too much about it yet," Doc told her.

Miami Davis bit her lips and blurted, "But they may have killed him!"

"There is reason to think he is alive now," the bronze man said.

The young woman tightened. She got something from the remark that horrified her. She began to tremble. Suddenly she grabbed the bronze man's arm.

"You think he's the leader of this! You—you're wrong!" she screamed.

Her trembling increased and she began to lose color. She was close to a breakdown.

"Stop that!" Doc Savage said. There was such a quality of power and command in the bronze man's voice that it quieted the young woman although Doc himself was a little surprised that he got results; he could never tell about women.

Monk, Ham and Birmingham Lawn rushed into the room, looking as if they had accomplished something.

"We got A. King Christophe located!" Monk yelled.

"He's got a headquarters!" Ham rapped. "A house on the edge of the gas zone! We've got the address!"

They raced outside to their car. Lawn galloped after them. Lawn, it developed, wanted to go along in his own car. Monk volunteered to ride with Lawn.

Doc and Ham were getting into the other car when Miami Davis came running up. She was excited, also determined.

"I'm going with you!" she cried.

"But——" the bronze man began.

"You may find some trace of Hart!" she gasped; "I'm going along! You can't stop me! I may be able to help!"

Rather than face a prolonged argument, Doc Savage gave in, and told the young woman to ride with himself and Ham. Their car was an armored machine, and she would be safe enough.

It did not take long to drive to the spot where they hoped to find A. King Christophe.

It was early night, and darkness was unusually black.

It was a very large and elderly house which stood alone, like a gray wart, in the center of a huge lot. The house was made of concrete blocks, had doors on four sides, and the lot which surrounded it was a jungle of shrubbery.

When Lawn peered at the old structure, he gave a start of surprise.

"Why," Lawn ejaculated, "I handled the renting of that place!"

The other stared at him. "You rented it?" Monk gulped.

"I'm a real estate man, you know," Lawn said. "My firm rents property here and there—business buildings, apartments and residences."

"Who did you rent this house to?" Monk asked. "To A. King Christophe?"

"No."

"Who, then?"

"To William Henry Hart," Lawn said.

EFFECT of this on Miami Davis was stark. She recoiled—recoiled with such a jerk that Ham, who was sitting beside her, jumped also. The girl put her fingers over her lips.

"Hart—rented—" The words choked up in her throat.

"Hart rented the place all right," Lawn said grimly.

"In that case," Monk muttered, "maybe he's hiding out in there. I want to see that guy Hart. There's too much evidence against him!"

The girl screamed, "But he was kidnapped—"

Ham gripped her arm, said warningly, "Not so loud, miss!" The dapper lawyer added, "Hart could have faked the kidnapping. We were hot on his trail, and that kidnapping happened mighty conveniently."

The girl lost control. She lunged forward, slapped Ham, crying something incoherent. Ham dodged. Monk grabbed the girl and held her.

"You got no right to accuse Hart!" the young woman screeched. "He's—he's—I love him!" She began to sob.

Monk said, "You may love 'im, but it don't make 'im as pure as driven snow."

"You better lay off that line, homely face," Ham told him. "She'll scratch out them little gimlet eyes of yours."

Monk subsided. They waited for the girl to get control of herself, and in a few minutes, she managed to do that.

"I'm all right," she said, brokenly, wiping at her eyes.

There were four gates in the wall around the old house, and four sidewalks that led through the shrubbery to the four doors in the scabby-looking cement-block house.

Doc's party went through one of the gates, immediately got off the sidewalk into the shrubbery.

It was extremely dark now, with clouds packed in the night sky. They had stopped the cars where the headlights could not be seen from the house, so that it was hardly likely that their arrival had been discovered.

"I hope we ain't expected!" Monk muttered.

Doc Savage said, "We will go closer to the house. Then you will wait. Lawn and I will look around."

They did that, the bronze man going in the lead, opening a silent path through tangled brush. Later, they stood about twenty yards from the house, in a tiny open space that was walled around with shrubbery.

Doc said, "Lawn, you and I will look the house over."

Lawn gulped, "But why me?"

"Your real estate firm rented the place," Doc explained. "You have been in it. You can be of help. You know the layout of the rooms, and things like that."

"All right," Lawn agreed reluctantly. "But remember, I am not a courageous man."

Doc and Lawn went on. Their going was ghostly in its silence.

The others waited—a minute—two—five—saying nothing and doing nothing, except to hold their breath a great deal of the time. They could feel suspense.

Then unexpected disaster hit them. Miami Davis had been standing tense, much too tense, and Ham had been holding her arm. Now, so suddenly that the surprise made her successful, she wrenched away from the lawyer.

Simultaneously, she snatched a flashlight which he was carrying in his hand, but not using. The girl jumped away. The next instant, she thumbed on the flashlight, impaled them all in its white glare.

"Get your hands up!" Miami Davis said grimly.

Her hand—the hand that was not holding the flashlight—appeared in the luminance. It gripped a flat automatic pistol, not large, but plenty dangerous.

"I've been afraid I would have to do this!" Miami Davis gritted.

The next development was about the most unexpected thing that could have happened.

THE giggling ghosts appeared.

There was more than one ghost. From the very first, there had been a question about the number of ghosts. No one knew whether there was one, or more. But now Monk and Ham knew the truth. There was more than one.

Also, from the very first, there had been doubt about whether giggling ghosts really existed at all. They had been more rumor than actuality. They had never been seen distinctly at any time. No one had observed them at close range.

But then, few ghosts are ever seen at close range.

This was Monk and Ham's first experience with ghosts.

They heard the giggling. It was low, stifled. But it was very close. So near that they whirled wildly. They knew with terrible certainty that the giggling ghosts were literally upon them.

The girl made a gasping sound. Her fingers must have slipped off the flashlight button, because the beam extinguished.

Monk and Ham were a long time forgetting what happened next.

They tried to fight. Ham began jabbing with his sword cane, in the hope that the chemical-coated tip would put a ghost or two to sleep. Oddly enough, his sword cane seemed to pass through air. Suddenly, something grabbed his sword cane, and Ham was forced to use his fists. Next to him Monk roared, as he always did in battle.

Monk and Ham always insisted they put forth their best resistance. But there was no time, and it was all so weird, so impossible, so utterly—well,

it was ghostly business—that they really accomplished nothing at all.

Doc's aides were rendered unconscious. It happened violently. The insides of their skulls seemed to explode. Shock, crash, colored pain-lights, described what happened to their heads.

There were forms there, darksome ghostly forms that floated out of the shrubbery. Monk and Ham could tell that, an instant before the explosions occurred.

Then everything was still and black.

Chapter XVIII
THE MESOZOIC AGE

PSYCHOLOGISTS claim one of the strongest traits in mankind is the impulse for self-preservation.

There is some argument about whether self-preservation is man's strongest impulse. In the case of animals, there is evidence indicating the impulse of self-preservation may be subjugated by the emotion of rage.

Small dogs, for instance, will attack much larger dogs, even when there is every certainty that they will meet defeat, maybe death. Men, on the other hand, seem to be motivated more by the desire to preserve their lives.

Monk awakened with this impulse for self-preservation. Monk, who had the stamina of an oak post, was first to revive. However, he lay still, batting his small eyes and running his tongue around his lips, and deciding his mouth felt as if it had been recently inhabited by a cat. Because he saw no sense in advertising the fact that he was conscious, he made no sound. He thought of the giggling ghosts, and fell to shivering.

Where was he? How long had he been unconscious? At first, he believed he was blindfolded; then he decided he was lying in a dense darkness, and there must be a roof overhead because there were no stars. He began feeling around. Ham! What had they done to Ham? Was he here?

Ham was there, close at hand. Ham must have been bordering on regaining consciousness, must have been in the state in which sleepers find themselves when they involuntarily give big spasmodic jumps. As soon as Monk's hand touched him, Ham gave a great jump.

"Sh-h-h!" Monk quickly admonished. "Quiet!"

Ham went, "Huh?" and "Wuh!" confusedly. To stop that, Monk took a handful of Ham's mouth and nose and held it. He kept that muffler on the dapper lawyer until Ham had assembled his wits, then released him.

Ham snarled, "Choking a man is no way to wake him up!"

"Pipe down!" Monk said. "It's the way I'd love to wake you up!"

"Where are we?" Ham wanted to know. "Where are the ghosts?"

Monk took another look around. Getting no better idea of where they were than before, he decided to let Ham draw his own conclusions, and said nothing.

Monk arose, took two or three steps, with his hands out in front, exploring. A yank at his ankle toppled him on his face.

"What's the matter?" Ham demanded.

"Sh-h-h!" Monk hissed.

He added some things that he had not learned in Sunday school.

"There's a chain around my ankle," he explained.

"Mine, too," Ham said.

They investigated the chains and found them large enough to qualify as log chains. The chains were padlocked to their ankles; the other ends of the chains seemed to be locked around thick iron bars.

"Blazes, I hope we ain't turned into ghosts ourselves," Monk croaked, "with chains an' everything!"

THE bars interested Monk and Ham. They investigated and found a bar about every six inches, each one more than an inch thick.

"Cage!" Ham gulped. His hand moved toward a pocket for his matches. A moment later, he swore. "Got a match, Monk? I've lost mine."

Monk fumbled through his clothing until he found a match, then debated whether to strike the match. He listened; when he heard no sounds, he rasped the match along the steel bars, and made a reflector for it with his palms.

"Whew!" Ham said, relieved. "We look too solid to be ghosts. So do the bars."

"It's a cage, all right," Monk said.

"We're outside it," Ham added. "Thank our stars for that!"

In the fitful, dancing glow of the match, Doc's aides saw that there was a concrete sidewalk inside the cage. A sidewalk about a dozen feet wide with another set of bars on the other side. They looked to see how long the sidewalk was and it dawned on them then that the sidewalk was a long tunnel of steel bars. How long they could not tell.

"A sidewalk protected by steel bars!" Monk muttered. "That's a queer one."

All around where they stood was jungle! Such jungle! The growth was grotesque. Monk stared, his small eyes popping, at a leaf beside him—a leaf so large that he could hardly have spanned it with his long arms. There were fernlike plants, closely resembling the ferns in window boxes, except that these must be more than thirty feet tall; the match light revealed they extended up at least thirty feet, and they were even higher.

But all this jungle growth was not Gargantuan in size. Some of the leaves were delicate, tiny. There were vines as thick as Monk's barrel chest, but there were also creepers as fine as silk thread.

The match burned Monk's finger, and he yipped, dropped it. Darkness clenched around them, as black as a squid's juice.

"Some place!" Monk breathed.

"Strike another match," Ham ordered.

Monk went through his pockets. "I haven't got one."

They stood silent and puzzled, wondering what kind of place they were in.

"Blazes!" Monk said hollowly. "Blazes!"

"What do you make of it?" Ham asked.

"Never saw nothin' like it before." The homely chemist sat down and felt of the padlock which held the chain to his ankle.

"But there ain't nothing mysterious about this lock," he said. "It's ordinary."

"They didn't take our clothes," Ham said meaningly.

Monk said, "O. K. Let's get these locks off."

MONK was—this was generally admitted—a chemical wizard. Working with Doc Savage, Monk had developed innumerable chemicals useful in the strange career which the little group followed. For Doc and his men fought with such trick weapons.

Monk had worked out ingenious methods of carrying chemicals. Men's suits, for instance, had a stiffening fabric around the shoulders and collars. Monk had impregnated this fabric with a stiffening agent that was really a thermite compound—a concoction which burned with metal-melting heat.

Doc's aides got to work on the locks. They tore the fabric out of their collars, wrapped it around the locks, and lighted it by grinding a vest button against it. The button was a firing agent for the thermite.

There was a fizzling, a bright glare that blinded them completely. But they managed, in the middle of it, to kick their chains off.

After the thermite burned out, it was several moments before they got over being blinded.

"What do we do next?" Ham asked.

"Let's just strike out," Monk growled. "We dunno where we are, anyway."

They crept away from the spot where they had been chained, feeling ahead in the intense darkness with their hands. The jungle growth felt amazingly coarse. Leaves were as thick as planks, and as hard. They skinned themselves on bark; they got into thickets of thorns that were like needles.

Monk got involved with a vine, a thin spider web of a thing, and it was strong as wire and he came near not escaping from the tangle.

"Blazes!" the homely chemist muttered.

They came to what felt like a cliff of stone. They had no way of telling how high this was. They had no light. They could not reach the top of the cliff and it was too slick to climb.

"Let's follow along the base of the thing," Ham said.

Monk gulped suddenly; he had something on his mind that he wanted to get off, something he had to say.

"Ham," Monk said, "I—well, that girl must have been working with—er—the giggling ghosts, from the first."

"Why did you wait this long to say so?" Ham demanded.

"Er—she fooled me."

"Hah!"

"And why didn't you mention it earlier, either?" Monk demanded.

"Er—she fooled me, too," Ham confessed.

"I feel like a sucker."

"Here, too," Ham said.

It was a rare occasion when these two admitted accord about anything; it was practically a record.

"I WONDER where Doc is?" Monk mumbled.

"And Hart, Lawn, and Christophe," Ham added. "Not to mention Renny, Long Tom, and Johnny."

They stood and worried about that, temporarily forgetting their own predicament.

"The ghosts didn't catch Doc when they got us, did they?" Monk asked.

"I don't think so."

"Maybe they caught him after they got us."

They were worried about Doc. They were embarrassed over the way the girl had fooled them. Ham always went through an unconscious gesture when he was embarrassed: he hooked a thumb in his waistcoat pocket. He did this now. And immediately he was aware that one thumb had touched something. He dug the object out of the pocket.

"Matches!" he exclaimed.

"Matches!" Monk muttered. "I thought you looked in your pockets before."

"Er—I always carry my matches in a certain pocket. When they weren't there, I thought I had none."

"You nickelwits!" Monk gritted.

Discovery of the matches took their minds off the fate of Doc and the perfidy of the girl. They continued their efforts to escape by creeping along the stone wall or cliff, or whatever it was.

"Ugh!" Monk said suddenly. He stopped.

Ham breathed. "What—"

"Sh-h-h!" Monk said. "Come over here! Feel this!"

Ham moved to Monk's side, passed his hands over the shape that had aroused Monk's startled wonder.

"What d'you think it is?" Monk wanted to know.

"Like nothing I could describe!" Ham said. "I'm going to strike one of my matches."

Ham's matches were in a little book and he tore one out, closed the cover, and rasped the match head on the striker composition. Light jumped over the object about which they were so curious.

The item was about fifteen feet tall, and thirty or forty feet long—they could not tell how wide. It had the hide of an elephant, but it had warts, also. Warts as big as knots in a pine board. It had four legs. The two front legs short and small, small in proportion, that was, for they only had claws a foot long. The monster was half sitting up, and looking down between its paws at them.

The monster's mouth had four rows of sharp teeth, the size and shape of dirty candles, and the mouth was large enough to take a bite of approximately half a horse.

"Yeo-o-ow!" Monk squalled.

WITHOUT any thought of why, wherefore, or anything else, Monk took off from that spot. He crashed into Ham. They went down. They got up. They ran. They tripped, smashed into things, all but beheaded themselves on tough vines.

Because they ran blindly, they fell into the fissure.

Monk and Ham fell headlong into the crack, sprawling. For one horrible flash, they thought they were going to their deaths, but the fissure wasn't that deep. Only a dozen feet or so deep. They hit the hard bottom.

Monk had started yelling, a hair-splitting squall, and when he hit, the yell ended in a sound like a bad note out of a trumpet.

Almost instantly a weird greenish light appeared and suffused the crevice in which they lay. The light increased, and they began to see their surroundings.

Ham stared upward. His eyes got round with horror.

"Monk!" he croaked hoarsely. "It's—look—"

The monster—if not the one they had seen, but one very like it—was looking down into the crevice, and it appeared that the thing could easily reach them with its jaws.

Chapter XIX
THE BLOW-BACK

ONE of mankind's strong traits is also his impulse to show off; be an exhibitionist.

All through history men have shown off. The Romans had triumphal parades; kings have always had pomp and pageantry, and the circus is popular the world over; and so are the exhibitions commonly called world's fairs.

New York City's latest world's fair was being advertised as an exposition to top all expositions, a mammoth undertaking; a phantasmagoria beside which the recent international show in Paris or the Century of Progress in Chicago, would be rather ordinary.

For more than two years, work on the exposition grounds, buildings, and exhibits had been in progress. The fair would not open for some months, but many of the exhibits were already complete.

Doc Savage was driving his car into the exposition grounds. The bronze man pulled to the side of a street, stopped the car, and worked with the dials of a portable radio direction-finder.

Doc Savage's face was grim. Back at the old house of cement blocks, his men had been whisked away before he could do anything to stop it. Doc had been inside the old cement house with Lawn. There had been no enemies inside the house. They were all outside, seizing Monk and Ham and Miami Davis.

Doc had been unable to follow the men who had seized Monk and Ham. Unable to follow them at once. The reason was very simple.

Doc's car had been stolen. So had Lawn's machine. Batavia and his men had taken both machines.

Now Doc was taking up the chase, almost an hour late. He had been forced to go to the basement of his skyscraper headquarters and get another car.

Lawn stared at Doc. Lawn was puzzled. For Doc Savage seemed to be trailing the prisoners. Trailing them—but how? Lawn was wondering.

He got it.

"Oh!" Lawn pointed at the direction finder. "That is a radio direction finder! But what is it locating? Where is the other transmitter?"

"In my car," Doc said.

"You mean the car they took when they grabbed Monk and Ham?"

"Exactly."

"I see. But why haven't they noticed the transmitter?"

"It is concealed in the body of the car," Doc explained. "Unless they knew it was there, they would not find it. It is just another of the gadgets we keep in operation, to help us get out of trouble."

Doc Savage put his car in motion again. They passed huge trucks loaded with strange items—whole trees, a small airplane, a Venetian gondola, a meteorite as large as a room. Construction in the fair grounds was proceeding on a day-and-night basis.

Lights blazed everywhere, and truck drivers yelled; hoist engines clattered, and welding torches sent lightninglike glare over the confused scene. The unfinished buildings were fantastic shapes.

When Doc Savage stopped, it was beside a huge structure, a building that was like a gigantic half a muskmelon. It was about the color of a muskmelon. Inside, it must be as large as Madison Square Garden.

Birmingham Lawn doubled over his stomach to look at the vast dome. "Goodness! What a huge thing!"

"The dinosaur exhibit," Doc said.

"Dinosaur?"

"A name designating prehistoric monsters," Doc said. "This building contains an exhibit constructed for the fair. It is supposed to be remarkable."

"I see," Lawn said vaguely.

"The prisoners are in there, apparently," Doc said.

THE bronze man seemed in no hurry to leave his car. Instead, he leaned back, and there was a trace of a frown on his metallic features. "I think," he said, "that we're very near the end of this thing."

Lawn looked startled. "I—why—I hope so," he gulped.

"For the sake of clarity," Doc said, "we might gather factors together and array them. There has been some confusion. It should be straightened out."

"I—yes," Lawn said. "Straighten out the confusion. Yes indeed."

"Several months ago," Doc Savage said, "a new vehicular tunnel was completed, from Manhattan under the Hudson River to that part of New Jersey directly opposite thickly populated New York City. For the first time in years, a particular section of Jersey then became easily accessible. At a stroke, as it were, part of Jersey was placed at the front door of Manhattan."

"What has that to do with this?" Lawn asked.

"That part of Jersey near the tunnel became suitable for residential apartments," Doc said. "If anyone could get a large block of the section, it could be turned into a profitable apartment development."

"Why—that is true," Lawn admitted.

"But it was hard to buy land in the section. The people did not want to sell their homes cheaply. So someone thought up a hideous scheme of forcing the land on the market, and buying it up for almost nothing."

Lawn stared at Doc blankly, said nothing.

Doc said, "The giggling ghosts rumor was an accident. It was not intentional."

"Ghosts—accident?" Lawn said foolishly.

"The giggling ghosts," Doc said, "were men who were preparing to perpetrate the gas hoax. Some of those men, in handling the gas, got dosed with the stuff. Not seriously. But enough to give them the giggles occasionally. We know that the gas takes effect to varying degrees. These men moved about furtively as they got ready to perpetrate the gas hoax.

"These men who perpetrated the gas hoax," Doc continued, "were seen moving about furtively, and their giggling was heard, hence the stories about giggling ghosts."

"Hoax?" Lawn said stupidly. "The giggling horror was a hoax? And the giggling ghosts were men who whiffed a little of the gas while planting it?"

DOC SAVAGE nodded. "All a hoax," the bronze man agreed. "Seismograph records were faked to make it seem cracks had opened through which the gas might come. The ground in that part of New Jersey was impregnated with chemicals. Then the gas was distributed by means of smoke-digester-air-purifiers which William Henry Hart had manufactured."

Lawn grew suddenly excited.

"Hart! Then the gas came from Hart's smoke-digesters! William Henry Hart is guilty—"

"Hart is the goat," Doc said. "All along, Hart has been framed. Many of the hired thugs were led to actually think a man named Hart employed them. Hart was to be the victim. Probably they were going to conveniently 'discover' that the gas really came from smoke-digesters." The bronze man paused. "Of course, once it was learned gas was *not* coming from the earth, the land would become valuable again," Doc added.

"I—I—" Lawn swallowed. "Incredible!"

"A. King Christophe, the geologist, is a crook hired by the crooks to pose as the real Christophe, who, at present, is away on a trip for his health," Doc went on. "They may have gotten the fake Christophe out of the way, because we were getting hot on his trail. They also kidnapped Hart, because we were too close to learning that Hart was innocent. And they grabbed my men, of course, because we were fighting them."

Lawn gulped, "What about the S.R.G.V.—the Society for the Relief of Gas Victims?"

"That," Doc Savage said, "is the medium through which Jersey land was to be bought cheaply."

Lawn said, "But the girl—"

"The girl was only a bystander—in love with Hart. That is all. She saw some strange-acting men watching Hart, and followed them. It was Batavia and his gang. They went to a storehouse, when they saw the girl following, and tried out the gas on her, before they released it on the Jersey district. She got scared and came to me."

Lawn mumbled, "You—er—have you found out—"

"Yes," Doc Savage said, "we have a good idea who is behind the whole thing."

"You know the leader?"

"His identity should come out in a few minutes," Doc said.

Lawn said, *"It will come out before that!"*

Lawn then took a gun out of his coat pocket, jammed the muzzle against the bronze man's chest.

Lawn said, "Now you know I'm the man behind the gun—all the way."

DOC SAVAGE sat very still and watched Lawn back away an inch at a time, until he sat at the far side of the seat.

"Make one move," Lawn said, "and I'll kill you!"

Batavia

The bronze man's face remained fixed.

Lawn said, "Drive up to the main door of the dinosaur exhibit! Honk your horn. Honk it three times long, twice short!"

Doc Savage did that. He was careful to make no quick moves, for Lawn's gun hand was nervous. There was a wait after the bronze man honked the signal in front of the door.

Doc said, "It was difficult to understand why the prisoners should be brought here. It seems strange. The reason must be that the chemists you hired to concoct the giggling gas must be working on this exhibit."

"Shut up!" Hart said.

Doc, apparently not hearing, said, "The dinosaur exhibit is supposed to be a scientifically exact reproduction of the world as it was millions of years ago. Strange vapors and volcanic gases rise from fissures in the earth in lifelike fashion. The chemists called in to create the vapors must have made your gas, too."

"You sure figured it out!" Lawn said.

"We—"

"Shut up!" Lawn meant it this time.

The dinosaur exhibit door opened a crack. It did not open wider for some moments, evidently while the men inside were making sure that it was safe. Then the big panels rolled ajar.

"Drive in!" Lawn told Doc.

Doc drove in. The car rolled across a concrete floor, stopped on the fringe of modern man's idea of a prehistoric jungle.

Lawn ordered Doc Savage out, and the bronze man left the car. Lawn followed him, holding the gun ready. Men gathered around. The men seemed to be excited.

"What is wrong?" Lawn demanded.

"That damn Monk and Ham!" Batavia explained. "They picked the lock and got away. That is, they got to wanderin' around in the exhibit."

"Where are they now?" Lawn snarled.

"We got 'em cornered. I think the boys have grabbed 'em."

This proved to be true, because shortly a group of men approached, dragging a crestfallen Monk and Ham. Monk and Ham exchanged uncomplimentary remarks, each accusing the other of not having sense enough to know that the monsters they had seen were not real ones.

They fell gloomily silent when they saw Doc Savage.

One of the captors doubled over with laughter.

"Haw, haw!" he whooped. "Oh, golly! Haw, haw!"

Monk glared at him.

"Funniest thing I ever saw!" the tickled man chortled. "These two gooks"—he indicated Monk

and Ham—"thought them was real monsters. They was scared green."

Monk and Ham said nothing. Privately, they suspected it would be a long time before they lived this down, providing they had an opportunity to live it down.

LAWN asked, "Have we got all of them?"

"The girl and Hart are over here." The man pointed. "The other three—Johnny, Long Tom and Renny—are with them."

"Then we'll finish this up right now!" Lawn said.

Some of the men apparently had never seen Lawn before, and wondered how he came to be giving orders.

"Who's this big mouth?" A man jerked his thumb at Lawn.

"Shut up!" Batavia told the man. "That's Lawn—the chief!"

"But I thought the boss was a guy named Hart—"

"Hart is the goat, you fool!" Batavia snapped. "Hart is one of the prisoners we've got here!"

"But that Hart ain't the one you showed us in the old cement block house that night—"

"That was just a guy who pretended he was Hart," Batavia said. "We had it fixed so everybody would think Hart was the guy running this."

Lawn said, "Get the prisoners all together. We'll knock 'em in the head, then throw them in one of the volcanic cones and run in that cement you are going to use for fake lava."

A. King Christophe arrived, shoving out his jaw and looking important. He saluted Lawn airily.

"What about the Jersey land, chief?" he asked.

"My S.R.G.V. bought up a lot of it," Lawn said. "And I've got my people in the Doc Savage Relief Agency office. We'll grab what land Savage bought, too."

Several men went away, came back dragging Long Tom, Renny, Johnny, Miami Davis and William Henry Hart.

The girl, Miami Davis, stared at Monk and Ham, and bit her lips.

"I'm—sorry—sorry—I pointed that gun at you," she said jerkily. "I thought—I was afraid—you were going to grab Hart."

Monk peered at her. "You didn't know Lawn's men were around that old cement block house?"

The girl shook her head. "No."

"Cut that out!" Batavia ordered.

"Take 'em to the volcanic cone," Lawn commanded.

"Just a minute," Doc Savage said.

The bronze man had been standing motionless, watching Birmingham Lawn's gun. The muzzle of Lawn's weapon had not moved for an instant from Doc's chest, and the bronze man had waited, seeming to do only one thing: his lips had moved at intervals. Moved as if he was calculating the passage of a certain interval of time.

The men stared at Doc Savage.

"Damn you!" Lawn snarled. "If you pull—"

"It has already been pulled," Doc said.

"Huh?"

"In the car." The bronze man moved his head slightly. "A bomb! Under the car frame, wired to a clockwork device. The clockwork starts when a little switch is thrown under the dash. I threw the switch."

Lawn yelled at Batavia. "Go see—"

The command was never executed. There was a slamming explosion—not so much a detonation as a great *whoosh!*

Whoosh! It came from under the car, out in all directions. With the noise, there leaped black smoke. Intensely black smoke that shot a score of yards in every direction in the bat of an eye.

DOC SAVAGE was already moving. He went into the smoke, eyes shut, holding his breath. The containers under the car were loaded with smoke-bomb chemical impregnated with tear gas.

Doc reached the car, flung inside, got a pocket-knife out of a door compartment. There were also airtight goggles, a breath filter, and he put those on.

There was yelling now, and shooting. Men slugging at each other. Monk, Ham and the others were tied with ropes, and Doc sought them, holding the knife ready to free them.

A man staggered against him. Doc grabbed the fellow, tried to learn if he was one of the prisoners by feeling whether the man's hands were tied. While Doc was doing that, another man stumbled into him from behind. The newcomer slugged, asking no question.

They fell down, Doc and the two men. Neither man was a Doc aide. They flopped around, and Doc lost his knife. Then he got an arm around the neck of each man, and brought their heads together, not with skull-crushing force, but hard enough, and they collapsed. Doc got down on all fours and lost time seeking the knife.

Someone fell over him and said, "Holy cow!"

"Renny, here!" Doc cut the big-fisted engineer loose.

Lawn was screaming in agony.

"Somebody shot me!" he bawled.

Batavia barked, "Don't use those guns, you fools! We'll kill each other!"

After that, shooting stopped.

Doc yelled, "Get in the car!" He yelled it in ancient Mayan, a practically unknown tongue which he and his men spoke fluently, and used when they did not want to be understood by outsiders.

"Take Hart!" Doc called in Mayan. "And the girl, too!"

A phantom in the black smoke, the bronze man whipped in search of the other prisoners; he found Monk and Ham, cut Monk loose, and ordered the chemist in Mayan to carry Ham to the car.

Renny bellowed in Mayan that he had found William Henry Hart and was taking him to the car.

Doc located Johnny. Johnny and Long Tom were working on each other's rope, trying to get free. Doc slashed Johnny loose, and Johnny carried Long Tom toward the machine.

"Miss Davis!" Doc barked in English.

"Here!" cried the girl's voice.

Doc lunged, got her, swept her away, just as two men charged for her voice. Doc carried her to the car, and heaved her unceremoniously into the back seat, which seemed to be full of squirming forms.

Doc then got in the front seat.

"All in?"

"Think so," Monk gurgled.

Doc tried to slam the doors, and got all of them shut but one; there was somebody's leg hanging out of that one, and whoever it belonged to was too excited to move it. Doc started the car motor, meshed gears, backed blindly, feeding the machine gas.

The car got headway. It was heavy, tons heavy, and when it hit the door, which had been closed, there was an earthquake crash and a rending ripping, and the door caved. The car went out.

Doc kept on backing. Wind whipped in the open door, made the black smoke vapor boil around and leave the car. Then the bronze man could see a little.

He drove down the street a short distance, stopped the car.

Police were running toward them.

In the back seat Monk suddenly yelled, "That danged Lawn got in here by accident!"

"Hold 'im!" Renny rumbled. "I'll pop 'im!"

There was a long moment of quiet, then Monk made a muttering noise.

"You wouldn't want to hit a corpse!" the homely chemist mumbled.

THE verdict of the coroner's jury: in the case of Birmingham Lawn, death came about accidentally as the result of a bullet fired by a malefactor employed by the deceased.

"That's a long-winded way of sayin'," Monk explained, "that he got in front of one of them bullets the gang was throwin' around so free."

Said the police chief: "We are satisfied,

gentlemen of the press, that with the aid of Doc Savage, we have every crook in this case in custody."

"He means all Lawn's gang are in the calaboose," Monk explained.

Said a tabloid newspaper:

DOC SAVAGE EXPOSES GIGGLING
GHOSTS AS HORRIBLE HOAX

"And that means," Monk explained, "that we'll have to hide out to keep newspaper guys from runnin' us ragged, wantin' to know details."

Monk was wrong about that, though. This time Doc Savage did not run from the glare of newspaper publicity. He did not exactly seek it, but he did not disappear. Doc stuck it out so he could work in the hospitals.

Every day the bronze man made rounds of hospitals where gas victims were confined, helping with the treatments, studying them. Largely as a result of Doc Savage's tremendous medical knowledge, the victims eventually recovered.

The families of those who had died sued the estate of Birmingham Lawn, and got enormous cash settlements. Ham, the lawyer, saw to that.

Ham and Doc Savage also saw that the land bought up by the S.R.G.V. was returned to the former owners. The land bought by the Doc Savage Relief Agency was also returned. Too, heirs of Birmingham Lawn were persuaded to turn over Lawn's estate to recompense gas victims, and it was to be suspected that Ham had a good deal to do with that, also.

"It begins to look," Monk explained, "like everything ain't gonna be so bad."

Monk also had a complaint to make. A disgusted one.

"When we get this giggling ghost mess straightened up," he grumbled, "I guess we gotta go to a wedding."

He meant the wedding of William Henry Hart and Miami Davis.

THE END

THE MAN BEHIND DOC SAVAGE

Lester Dent (1904-1959) could be called the father of the super-hero. Writing under the house name "Kenneth Robeson," Dent was the principal writer of *Doc Savage,* producing more than 150 of the Man of Bronze's pulp adventures.

A lonely childhood as a rancher's son paved the way for his future success as a professional storyteller. "I had no playmates," Dent recalled. "I lived a completely distorted youth. My only playmate was my imagination, and that period of intense imaginative creation which kids generally get over at the age of five or six, I carried till I was twelve or thirteen. My imaginary voyages and accomplishments were extremely real."

Dent began his professional writing career while working as an Associated Press telegrapher in Tulsa, Oklahoma. Learning that one of his coworkers had sold a story to the pulps, Dent decided to try his hand at similarly lucrative moonlighting. He pounded out thirteen unsold stories during the slow night shift before making his first sale to Street & Smith's *Top-Notch* in 1929. The following year, he received a telegram from the Dell Publishing Company offering him moving expenses and a $500-a-month drawing account if he'd relocate to New York and write exclusively for the publishing house.

Dent soon left Dell to pursue a freelance career, and in 1932 won the contract to write the lead novels in Street & Smith's new *Doc Savage Magazine.* From 1933-1949, Dent produced Doc Savage thrillers while continuing his busy freelance writing career and eventually adding an aerial photography business.

Dent was also a significant contributor to the legendary *Black Mask* during its golden age, for which he created Miami waterfront detective Oscar Sail. A real-life adventurer, world traveler and member of the Explorers Club, Dent wrote in a variety of genres for magazines ranging from pulps like *Argosy, Adventure* and *Ten Detective Aces* to prestigious slick magazines including *The Saturday Evening Post* and *Collier's.* His mystery novels include *Dead at the Take-off* and *Lady Afraid.* In the pioneering days of radio drama, Dent scripted *Scotland Yard* and the 1934 *Doc Savage* series.

DOC'S AIDES by Will Murray

According to *Doc Savage* editor John L. Nanovic, the entire cast of characters that comprised the bronze man's iron crew were based on real people whom Doc co-creator Henry W. Ralston knew, beginning with Doc himself, who was modeled after the remarkable Colonel Richard Henry Savage, a soldier of fortune who died a year before Lester Dent was born.

Nanovic always maintained that the heroic sextet was hammered out with Ralston over a series of 1932 lunches at Halloran's, a restaurant on New York's 6th Avenue.

"The only notes I had was the names of the characters and their descriptions," he later recalled. "Now the description of the characters was pretty much Ralston. He had lived with these guys. He knew them all, including their fingernails. He based that on his knowledge of guys."

It may be impossible, 75 years after the fact, to trace the true roots of these memorable characters, but some are definitely known, and it's easy to speculate on others.

According to Dent, Doc and his men first met during the Great War, as World War I was then known. Dent never described the circumstances, but it's clear from Nanovic's comments that Ralston was not harkening back to his own wartime buddies.

For example, Ralston seems to have come into contact with Richard Henry Savage through their mutual association with the Street & Smith publishing company. S&S published a hardcover collection of Savage's short stories in 1898.

Nanovic recalled that Ham Brooks was named after Hamilton "Ham" Peck, a writer of true crime stories known to Ralston, who later edited true-detective magazines.

But inspiration may run deeper than any one man—or any one creator. Take Monk Mayfair. Nanovic recalled that Ralston named and described the apelike chemist in an early character-planning conference long before Lester Dent was brought in.

Yet from the beginning of his pulp fiction career, Dent had populated his stories with villains by that name, in other cases delineating characters who matched Monk Mayfair's description. The crooked scientist, Monk Cullin, who appeared in one of Dent's stories the year Ralston first conceived Doc and his crew, is a striking example of this. Apish, tough and slangy, he looks and talks exactly as Monk Mayfair would only a year later. The story in which Monk Cullin debuted was *The Sinister Ray,* the first of Dent's series about a scientific detective named Lynn Lash. Cover-featured in the March, 1932 *Detective-Dragnet, The Sinister Ray* may be the story that first brought Dent to the attention of Henry Ralston.

The explanation for this is simple: both men may have taken their inspiration from the notorious turn-of-the-century New York thug, Monk Eastman. Born Edward Osterman, Monk Eastman dominated Manhattan's East Side gangster scene in his day. A half-comical brawler who wore a too-small Derby atop his bullet head, he was fond of animals, particularly cats and canaries, whom he kept. He also liked to brain his foes with a club he carried for that purpose. Every time the bull-necked, broken-nosed pug-ugly bashed in a skull, some contemporary accounts claim, he cut a notch in his club. Eastman racked up over fifty notches.

Monk Eastman

"Paul Kelly" Vaccarelli

Eastman's main rival was "Paul Kelly," a dapper and sophisticated bantamweight boxer-turned-criminal with whom he had a long-running feud. Born Paolo Antonio Vaccarelli, Kelly was the leader of the notorious Five Points Gang, out of which came the first generation of Mafia chieftains like Al Capone and Lucky Luciano. Although criminals, Eastman and Kelly were exact opposites.

After a ruinous brawl between the combative pair in 1904, a truce was brokered and Monk and Paul made peace. But war soon broke out anew over control of the Bowery, and it was decided the two gang leaders would settle their differences in a public fistfight. It ranged on for two bloody hours, with neither man giving an inch of ground. A draw was declared. The war resumed. Eastman soon went to prison for attempted robbery. The Eastman Gang broke up, ceding control of Manhattan's rackets to Kelly, who flourished into the 1920s. As Paul Vaccarelli, Kelly became vice president of the International Longshoremen's Association, and was based in New York's Chelsea area, where Street & Smith was headquartered. He died in 1936 of natural causes.

Monk Eastman had served in World War I, distinguishing himself in action. Observing his many battle scars during his induction physical, the doctor asked Monk which prior wars he had served in, to which Eastman famously replied, "Oh! A lot of little wars around New York." Eastman fought in France with the 106th Infantry Regiment of the U.S. 27th Division, better known as "O'Ryan's Roughnecks." He was shot to death in 1920.

Lester Dent's specific characterization of the Monk Mayfair-Ham Brooks feud stems from a popular literary source. Dating back to the same war, the portrayal of Sergeant Quirt and Captain Flagg as bickering wartime enemies in the 1924 play *What Price Glory?* was the stylistic model for Monk and Ham's peremmial squabbling. Maxwell Anderson and Laurence Stallings' stage play proved so successful that it was made into a silent film two years later, and remade in 1952.

The suspected influence of Tulsa *World* reporter Walter Biscup on Lester Dent's depiction of Ham Brooks is covered in the "Intermission" elsewhere in this volume. One might surmise that the dapper lawyer's last name was borrowed from the fashionable men's clothier, Brooks Brothers. Marley no doubt derives from Charles Dickens' *A Christmas Carol,* and the infamous firm of Scrooge & Marley. Ham's affected Harvard accent was no doubt taken from that of President Franklin D. Roosevelt.

It's perhaps too easy to wonder if electrical wizard Thomas J. Roberts earned his first name from the inventor of the light bulb and other wonders, Thomas Edison, known as the Wizard of Menlo Park. But there's more to it than the obvious. Lester Dent explained that Long Tom got his nickname from a wartime misadventure with a "long tom" cannon of pirate vintage.

Yet Long Tom was originally the nickname of our third president, Thomas Jefferson of Virginia. Add that to the fact that in his *Doc Savage* radio scripts, Dent directed that Long Tom speak in a Southern accent, then it's likely that his full name was actually Thomas Jefferson Roberts.

The connection—if any—between Long Tom's last name and the original version of the Doc Savage house name of "Kenneth Roberts" is unknown.

John Nanovic once recalled that "I think Renny was added in the fourth meeting." Here again, the name can be traced back to both Ralston and Dent. Renwick was the surname of a famous family of mechanical engineers associated with Columbia University during the 19th century, beginning with James Renwick, whose sons, Henry Brevoort and Edward Sabin Renwick, were renowned in that field. A third son, James Renwick Jr., forsook engineering to become an architect, and went on to build some of New York's most magnificent buildings of the pre-skyscraper era, including Saint Patrick's Cathedral. A gallery of the Smithsonian Museum is named in his honor.

Significantly, Dent had penned a 1931 radio script in which one character was called Dr. Renny. But the physical model for the character—a sad-faced hulking giant of a man with fists the size of gallon (or quart) pails goes back to a Dent pulp hero named "Bellow" Brill from 1930. Dent's Oklahoma detective Curt Flagg also shares these unique characteristics. Flagg appeared in *Scotland Yard* magazine, also in 1931. Dr. Renny was featured in an episode of the *Scotland Yard* radio program.

Like many writers, Dent drew from his own father for inspiration. Bernard Dent was a dour-faced giant of a man with tremendous hands and feet, and strength to match. The story goes that once Bern Dent confronted a vending machine that refused to surrender a handful of Chiclets after he put in his penny. Bern brought down one mallet of a fist to give the machine a jar—and it came crashing off the wall—literally torn off its bolted mounting. In his own notebooks, Dent described Renny Renwick as a proficient pugilist with the habit of snatching flies out of the air with his tremendously fast fists. These two characteristics were properties of legendary prizefighter Jack Johnson, the "Galveston Giant" who flourished early in the 20th century, and was the first black man to became World Champion in that sport. For some reason, Dent did not include these ideas in any of his novels.

The most dramatic true-life inspiration for any Doc Savage aide goes to William Harper Littlejohn. The character's name seems to be a combination of that of *Adventure* writer William Harper and the name of one of Robin Hood's Merry Men, Little John—who like Johnny Littlejohn was reputedly six feet tall. His habit of manufacturing big words of his own invention stemmed from a habit of Dent's own.

But during the era of Doc Savage one of the most prominent archeologists was an Englishman, John Devitt Stringfellow Pendlebury, who by a strange coincidence was born the same day as Lester Dent, October 12, 1904.

Where Dent described Johnny Littlejohn as a long thin man with the endurance of a marathon runner, John Pendlebury was himself an athlete and a marathon runner. Blind in one eye as a result of a

John Pendlebury

childhood accident, the glass-eyed Pendlebury seems to have inspired Johnny Littlejohn's similar affliction. He also carried a sword-stick, not unlike Ham Brook's elegant sword cane. But no monocle magnifying glass. That device was something Lester borrowed from a pulp detective named Duke Ayers, who appeared in the pages of *Detective-Dragnet* in 1932, while Dent was writing that magazine's lead stories.

An Egyptologist, Pendlebury was also interested in Crete. From 1930 to 1936, he was Director of Excavations at Tell el-arna in Egypt, and served as Curator at Knossos, Crete between 1929-34. Beginning in 1936, he oversaw archeological excavations on Mount Dikti in eastern Crete.

Foreseeing Nazi Germany's long-term plans for conquest, the swashbuckling Pendlebury returned to his native England and received military training. In May of 1940, he was back in Crete, outwardly functioning as British Vice Consul. After Crete was invaded in April of 1941, Pendlebury helped organize partisan anti-Nazi resistance. Wounded in a Stuka attack, he was captured. Found without any identification, Pendlebury was stood up against a wall and executed as a spy on May 21, 1941. His last words were said to be a familiar Anglo-Saxon epithet not known to be in the rich polysyllabic vocabulary of his *doppelganger,* Johnny Littlejohn.

As a group, Doc Savage's colorful collection of assistants might also derive from Frank Merriwell's in the Street & Smith dime novels of a prior generation. But there's no question that they emerged from the joint imaginations of business manager Henry W. Ralston and Lester Dent.

After those lunches at Halloran's, Ralston and Nanovic sat down with Lester Dent late in 1932 to brainstorm the Doc Savage cast of characters. It was at that point that both the Dent and Ralston versions of Doc and his men merged. Nanovic was then tasked to coalesce their ideas into a blueprint he called "Doc Savage, Supreme Adventurer."

As Nanovic once remarked, "If you read that 15,000 word outline, all the characters are just figures. Lester Dent breathed life into them and made them interesting. The popularity of Doc Savage is 90% Lester Dent and only 10% for Bill Ralston and myself for discussion of plot." •

Bernard and Allie Dent